TEMARRIAN BOUND

TEMARRIAN BOUND

A novel by

Jenn Tolman Allen

www.ideacreationspress.com

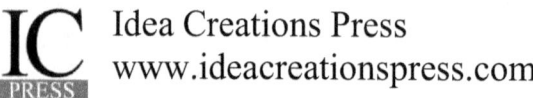

Idea Creations Press
www.ideacreationspress.com

978-1948804165

Publisher's Catalog-In-Publishing Data

Allen, Jenn Tolman, author
Temarrian Bound / Jenn Tolman Allen,
First trade paperback original edition. | Salt Lake City: Idea Creations Press, 2019.
ISBN 978-1948804165 | LCCN 2019954142
Science Fiction | Fantasy. | BISAC: FICTION / Science Fiction / Action & Adventure

For my sisters, who give me wings to fly...

Chapter One

Alena had the sickening feeling that she was being watched. Of course, she was always being observed, every single day, due to her regrettable situation in this nightmare of an intergalactic science center that was nothing more than a glorified space zoo. But this time was different, she wasn't being scrutinized from behind the glass of the observatory by her alien captors, she was being watched from somewhere inside her biome enclosure. The hairs on the back of her neck bristled as she turned and found herself facing a pair of intense, amber-orange eyes that wore the expression of both anger and yearning, like a wild, caged beast of prey. The man glared unashamed, almost predatorily at her through the glass.

He was definitely human but by far the most otherworldly-looking of the menagerie of humanoids that she had seen inhabiting the primate section of this despicable underwater zoo. Alena stared boldly back at him while hurriedly taking in his physique, his features, and his demeanor. He looked powerfully muscled with skin the color of bronze. His burning orange eyes, unkempt shoulder length hair, and grim set mouth made him look all the more wild and discomforting. Alena shuddered and turned away, searching for a place to conceal herself from his unwanted attention, wondering aloud if her situation could be any more miserable.

She headed for her sleeping place, a sort of hammock that was slung between two of the trees that reached to the ceiling of the biome. They weren't real trees, of course, just modeled replicas that looked eerily close to the ones on Earth. Sighing once more, Alena climbed up through the branches of the closest "tree" to the highest hammock, her hammock. Alena's arms and legs had grown quite strong and muscled in the last several years in the biome. If she had been home on Earth, Alena would have been quite pleased at the great shape that she found herself in. But here in this enclosure it was crucial to be fit and strong to escape from the horrors that continued to surround her each and every day.

Alena shared her current enclosure with Jenna, who had once been her Chief Navigator, and Jenna's two-year-old daughter Emmy. Fortunately, they also shared the enclosure with Kelly, who had formerly been her overly-energetic medical specialist, and her 6-month-old daughter Olivia. Alena listened to the sound of Jenna playing with Emmy and Kelly rocking Olivia as she lay back in her precarious hammock and stared at the ceiling of the biome. She reflected on how her awful Cephalopod captors had placed her here in this particular enclosure 5 months ago, probably in the hopes that being with the babies would make her desire one for herself. But Alena knew she could never bring a child into this environment, not if she could help it. She found herself swinging back and forth in anger and frustration, fuming at the life that she now endured. For three years Alena had been able to outwit the heartless, depraved Cephalopods and the lecherous traitor, Anthony, but for how much longer? What would become of her, and what would become of her biomates? There were several of her crewmates that had simply disappeared after being subjected to Cephalopod atrocities. Were their lives to be spent being bred to each other in this cosmic, underwater zoo?

There was a small round window at the very center of the ceiling of the biome that let in the natural light from the surface of the planet. Sometimes Alena would get a glimpse of the odd jagged clouds or the blue-colored sun that cast an eerie, pale cerulean light over the biome in the morning. Once she had even seen a strange pterodactyl type creature fly directly over it. Today there was nothing but an abnormal whiteness about the sky. It made her shiver. She turned over onto her stomach. She would never get used to this dreadful place.

Her thoughts returned to the amber-orange eyed creature that was now in the adjoining biome. Where had he come from? It definitely wasn't Earth, not with his bronze skin and orange eyes. Was he as wild and uncivilized as he looked? Why had her alien captors put him in the next biome instead of Ian, who used to occupy the enclosure? Alena knew it must have something to do with trying to impregnate her. Reproduction seemed to be the Cephalopod's main reason for almost everything the members of her crew had to experience. Her thoughts turned to poor Ian. Where had they taken him?

Ian had been her Chief Technology Officer aboard the Horizon. He was painfully shy, and not very good with people, but he was brilliant—the smartest person she had ever known. She had watched him in the last several months withering away. The filmy, large-headed Cephalopods had taken away his soul when they had cut him off from learning. Ian was the only person Alena had ever known that still read books—honest to goodness books made from paper and leather, rather than learning exclusively from the AEIO—the Advanced Educational Interplanetary Organization database that was linked to everyone through their personal comps. At least that was how it had been before this whole mess happened. The squid-like Cephalopods had ruined him by trying to make him copulate with various members of Alena's crew and a whole other spectrum of humanoid females that came from who knows where. The sea-monsters would have made it easier on him if they had torn him limb from limb and watched him disintegrate before their huge knowing eyes. Ian had a good heart and would never have hurt even the tiniest insect. There was no way his brain could conceive of the atrocities these tentacled Cephalopods had subjected him to.

The last few weeks Ian had been in a daze, hardly moving, refusing to eat, and even soiling on himself. Alena had tried to get his attention, pounding on the glass, encouraging him to keep going, but Ian had looked her way only once. It was a look that Alena had seen several times before; the expression was one that she had learned to dread. Alena knew it was the look of being finished—the look of not being able to choose how to live, so choosing to die instead. "Stop!" she wanted to scream at him, "Don't let the monsters win! Keep going!" But she wasn't sure herself anymore whether it was better to live or die. She'd placed her hand up to the glass and mouthed "I'm sorry, Ian. I'm so, so very sorry."

Ian's biome had been empty for a week. The sentient, water-breathing monsters had been gradually changing the environment of the biome, she now realized, to accommodate the orange-eyed wild man. Whether Ian still breathed, she would probably never know. They had taken him the day after he had given up. At least in her small way she had been able to tell him goodbye.

Alena rocked back and forth in her hammock. Emmy was giggling. Jenna tickled and chased her, laughing. It was a happy sound, a hopeful sound but a sad sound too. Through the glass on the north side of the enclosure below her, Alena could see the Cephalopods observing them. Always they were watching and passing by, bringing their jellyfish-like children to see. Always they would be watching, every hour of every day. Alena glanced over her shoulder to the west. She wondered if the wild man was still there. Was he watching too? But Alena could see nothing moving in his jungle-like enclosure.

Emmy giggled again and shrieked, enjoying the game with her mother. Alena was grateful that neither of the babies looked like their father who was a wicked excuse for a human. Anthony was far worse than the slimy, long-armed sea monsters that had captured them; Anthony had betrayed them all with his inhuman behavior.

Human nature was an interesting thing, and had Alena been a psychologist, surely this whole experience would have been truly fascinating. Anthony had been her 2nd in command. Although he was several years younger than she was, he had always been self-important and arrogant. He had attempted to usurp her authority and make her feel inept at her command.

They had been contemporaries at their prestigious flight school, competing for the same positions and advancements. Even though Anthony was probably innately smarter than she was, he was not nearly as disciplined. He had spent all his days living the high life, relying totally on his natural ability and celebrity good looks. Alena had outpaced him by sheer determination, careful study, and many grueling hours of practice. He had detested the fact that she had received her command before he did, but what he had hated even worse was that she seemed unaffected by his male prowess and unwavering attempts at seduction.

Several years later when he had been assigned under her command for the Tau Ceti mission she had pleaded with the Head of the Interplanetary Commission for a replacement only to discover that Anthony's father, who was a decorated General, had requested this specific mission for his son. Ironically, Anthony came from a family that had a long tradition of service in the Intergalactic Space Program. His father was well-respected; although Anthony's constant indiscretions were beginning to tarnish that reputation. General Pauleni wanted his son sent as far as possible into the reaches of space, hoping that the unspecified time away would help his son to, in effect, "grow up."

Alena had been given the unpleasant task of "babysitting" the General's overly-indulgent spawn. She regretted the ill-fated day that Anthony Pauleni had entered the Horizon acting the part of 2nd in command, when his title should have been Chief Womanizer or Chief Malingerer instead.

Their mission was supposed to have lasted only five years, taking in mineral samples from a group of planets in the Tau Ceti System. It was an important mission in a previously unexplored region of the galaxy. Her small crew of 18 had taken two years to arrive at their destination and a year to study the topography and geology. They had taken a vast quantity of samples from each of the five rocky planets in the system, as well as several of the moons. The discovery of an abundance of terinthium crystals on one of the planets had made the Tau Ceti mission successful beyond measure. Unfortunately for all of them, however, their voyage home had gone dreadfully wrong thanks to their chance encounter with the Cephalopod-like beings.

They had been 11 weeks and two days into their return journey when tragedy struck. The Horizon had suddenly lost her forward thrust. A check of the systems told them that all was in order, and yet, the craft would not respond. They soon found that they were unable to maneuver the Horizon at all. It was as if they were locked in a stationary position. It was not until the menacing shadow of the gigantic ship had passed over the hull of the Horizon that they had understood. The monstrosity hadn't even shown up on their radar. They had journeyed and explored for over three years and had never come across another sentient being. How could it be that just weeks into their triumphant journey home they would be captured by a horrifying race that they had never known existed?

Her crew had fought courageously, but they had few weapons that were effective against the Cephalopods. Three fine young men on Alena's security team had died in the initial takeover. Two more members of her crew had drowned when they were taken aboard the massive ship. Alena remembered thinking how odd it was to drown in space, but their captors were sea creatures of magnificent intelligence, and they lived and traveled in an atmosphere of water. Alena and her crew had been forced into a rounded holding cell that had been transfused with air. It was like being in a fishbowl, except the water was on the outside.

Alena and her twelve remaining crew members had huddled together in a state of shock. Jenna had wept hysterically while Miriam had tried to quiet her constant sobbing. Miriam was the oldest member of the crew at forty-seven and a brilliant scientist. She had been a kind of a mother figure to all of them for the duration of the mission as well as in the immediate days following their capture. She had bravely stood between Anthony and the other female members of the crew. Unfortunately for all of them, Miriam had gone completely insane in the last two years. She endlessly wandered the perimeter of her biome muttering incoherently to herself. Alena had observed Miriam's obvious deterioration while she had shared an enclosure with her and sweet, shy Elizabeth. That was before she had been transferred to her current biome.

Alena wondered how young Elizabeth was fairing being left with Mad Miriam. Alena hoped that one of the more solid female members of her crew like Janet or Gwen, had been moved into the enclosure, otherwise Elizabeth would be sure to follow in Miriam's footsteps. Alena let out a big exasperated sigh. Insanity would probably take them all eventually, anyway. Alena simply could not imagine the rest of her days as a sane person cooped up in this watery hell.

Alena wished that she could blame Anthony's behavior on insanity. Perhaps then everything wouldn't be quite so horrific. Alena knew, however, that Anthony had always wanted to dominate and feel power over women. He had always acted as though they were nothing more than an object of pleasure for him and yet, secretly he hated women. Alena could see it in his face when he… when he… she cringed and closed her eyes. She just couldn't stand to think about it. She listened to Emmy giggling and let the sound of her laughter drown out the ghastly memories.

Chapter Two

The monsters, which Alena and her crew had named Cephalopods based on their similarity to the squid and octopi from their own planet, were dispensing the evening meal. Alena hated this part of the day worse than any other. "Feeding time" meant more visitors and more of those sickening filmy creatures with gigantic foreheads watching—their pinkened children shrieking that horrible high-pitched sound from their elongated beaks with utter delight; as if watching a human eat was the most exciting thing they had ever seen. It didn't help that Alena was housed with Jenna and Kelly and their offspring. Human babies seemed to be the main attraction for all Cephalopods, although any baby of any species seemed to bring the Cephalopod monsters in droves to watch.

Alena frowned. She was only aware of one other human baby besides Emmy and Olivia that had been born here at the intergalactic science center and that was baby James. He had been the first of the human babies and had lived for only seventeen days. The sea creatures had taken the baby from his mother, Helen, so often in the first few weeks that he had grown sickly and died. It had all been in the name of science she was sure, but the Cephalopods had been stupid, irresponsible, and ridiculously heartless. Alena had never seen Helen from that moment on without her cheeks stained with tears and her eyes red and swollen. Helen and the babies' father, Steven, had been shipped off a few weeks later to another "zoo" along with Alena's lifetime friend and confidant, Raisann. She and Raisann had been so excited to have the good fortune to be assigned to the same mission. It hardly seemed at all fortunate now. Alena was sure she would never see any of them again. Helen and Raisann were far better off with Steven than they would have been with Anthony, however. At least Steven had a soul.

Due to Alena's current sullen mood, she chose to keep to herself this evening. She waited until Kelly and Jenna and little Emmy got their fill of supper before climbing down. At six months of age baby Olivia was still nursing and didn't show any interest in receiving nutrition from any other source besides her mother. Even at the age of two, little Emmy had only just become completely weaned herself. Alena examined what was left of the evening meal. There was the usual mixture of greens, a square flavorless cube that contained something akin to vitamins, the bland protein substance that her biomates always referred to as gunk, and nothing more. The meal was typical. Only occasionally was there something of interest added to their supper. It was usually the same day in and day out. Although it wasn't the most palatable sustenance, it was fortunately packed with nutrition.

Alena knotted her hair behind her to keep it out of the way. Her thick dark hair was well past her shoulders now, longer than she had ever worn it. For several years she had worn nothing more than a short crop of hair. Soon after she and her crew had been captured, all their heads had been shaved, and they had been stripped of their raiment. The crew had been left quarantined for several months and placed in solitary enclosures. The tortures that they had been subjected to, in order to make sure they were free of disease and who knew what else, had been utterly horrifying. Alena had felt lower than an animal and far more like she was the subject of some strange science experiment than anything else. After that ordeal, they had been sent to the science center. They all had been given mesh-like porous garments to wear—clothing that looked like it had come straight out of the sea. It was far less elaborate and less colorful than what the Cephalopods adorned their filmy bodies with, but at least it was something. It was bad enough having to live as they did, but at least Alena didn't have to feel like she was living in a nudist colony. Having clothing was a small tender mercy.

Alena picked up an olive-green kelp blade and started to munch on it, much to the amusement of the Cephalopods who were at that moment peering in. The monsters had placed their food in the location that was optimal for up-close and personal viewing. Their big whirling eyes still gave Alena the creeps. She hid her face from them. An excited Cephalopod child banged on the side of the enclosure with her tentacled sets of hands to get Alena's attention. The sound echoed back and forth like she was living in the heart of a giant bell. *Bong! Bong! BONG!* Alena suppressed the urge to cover her ears. Experience told her that doing so would only make the little monster more likely to continue. She was relieved when the child finally swam away with the rest of its group.

Alena turned her back as another group came up to observe her. She scooped up some of the reddish-brown protein gunk on a big wide leaf, swallowed the vitamin cube, grabbed a few more kelp blades, and started to move toward the center of the biome, which was far more protected from unwanted examination. Alena hadn't gone far before she felt a sudden spine-chilling prickle travel up the length of her back. She shivered, turning toward the source of her discomfiture and found herself locked in the gaze once again of those disquieting, amber-orange eyes. His hateful, yet yearning expression startled her, and she dropped the kelp blades.

The bronze-skinned, wild man only stared brazenly at her, watching her every move. Alena bent down to gather the blades, hoping that he would somehow disappear, but when she straightened herself, he was still glaring at her unabashed. She began walking the length of the enclosure. He followed her along the length of his biome like a tiger hunting his prey. She turned her back on him and sauntered away. What was his problem, anyway? Why was he so intense? She prayed that she wouldn't need to add stalker to her list of troubles. She had thought that nobody could be worse than Anthony, but maybe she was wrong.

Alena found a comfortable spot in the center of the biome amidst all the artificial foliage and settled down to finally eat in peace. Eating wasn't something that brought her any pleasure, anymore. It was just something to do to fill up the empty spaces. The protein gunk was pretty tasteless but was far more filling than the greens. She alternated bites of gunk with the salty kelp blades so that the food actually had some flavor. When the chore was finally done, she went to wash up in the tiny stream that ran through the system of biomes.

It was a synthetic stream, just a brook really, of fresh water that was piped in and out of each enclosure. Alena was glad for the constant steady flow of cool water; although every time she drank from it, she felt as if she were drinking out of the gutter. Kneeling on the stony bank, she cupped the water into her hands and splashed it into her face. The water was a little warmer today, so she decided to give her hair a wash too. She dunked her head under the water and scrubbed at her scalp. There was no soap to speak of, and so she was careful to do a thorough job. When she brought her head up, she heard a horrible high-pitched squeal coming from one of the Cephalopod children. Alena sighed. She was great entertainment for this monster child, who had obviously never seen a human put her head underwater.

Alena twisted her hair to squeeze all the water out. She would have done just about anything for a fluffy towel right now. Getting her hair to dry was a most unpleasant task due to the air temperature. Their biome stayed at a constant temperature of about 68 degrees. That felt awfully cold if your hair was wet. Alena would have preferred the temperature to be at least five degrees warmer. She shook her head briskly and ruffled up her hair with her hands. She felt like a dog shaking off water. Alena always did her heavy-duty bathing at night when the lights were dimmed and there were no Cephalopods shuffling around, even though it felt even cooler then. Several of her crewmates no longer cared too much about their personal modesty, but Alena clung to hers. It was something that she had been able to choose for herself.

Alena could feel the amber-orange eyes studying her again. He watched her for more than 30 minutes while she finger-combed her hair until it was dry. She then took a little bundle of short sticks which she had bound into a makeshift comb and combed her hair until it was soft and glossy. Alena was drawing quite an audience with her primping. Dozens of Cephalopods, along with her orange-eyed neighbor, watched in fascination as she wound her hair into a rope-like braid and fastened the end with a bit of seaweed. Even the nervous, ghostly people in the enclosure on the other side watched her, although they did so only now and then out of the corners of their eyes.

Her albinal neighbors in the eastern enclosure were an interesting lot. There were five of them in that biome: one adult male, two adult females, and two very young children that Alena wasn't able to determine the gender of. They were a taller race of humanoids—more long, slender, and willowy. The male was probably seven and a half feet tall and the females were at least seven. They weren't really "albinal" either, for they had these amazing silver eyes. But their skin was ghostly white like a strange apparition and so that is how they had gained the unfortunate nickname, "the ghost people." They were an extremely nervous and shy race that kept themselves in close proximity to each other. Perhaps that is why the male was allowed to stay with them, making up one bashful little family.

Anthony was housed alone. There was no way that Anthony could have been housed with any number of them being the awful brute that he was. In the beginning, their captors had tried, but Anthony was no match for three fuming females that were out for blood. That had been particularly true early on when Alena and Miriam were together, especially when they were trying to protect young Elizabeth. Anthony might have done better facing a trio of enraged mama bears. The memory gave Alena something to smile about, but it was not long before her expression changed to one of malevolence. Anthony had been no match for them in groups, but he had been a merciless tyrant one on one.

Alena suddenly filled with dread. How many days had it been? She began counting… six… seven… eight… nine… She started over again and came to the same conclusion. It had been nine days since the beginning of her last cycle. That meant that either tomorrow or the next day she would be at her most fertile, and she would be subjected to… Alena winced. She would have to be prepared. Anthony had almost succeeded the last time.

The Cephalopods had resorted to medicating her the last few months to get her "safely" into the private enclosure. Luckily the drugs only lasted a very short time; otherwise, Alena was sure that the drugs would put an end to her months of outwitting both Anthony and the monsters. She wondered how long it would be before the Cephalopods got smart and left her medicated. There was no doubt that they would succeed in impregnating her then. Perhaps they were worried about how the drugs would affect her ability to conceive? Alena could think of no other reason why they had not already done so.

Anthony's last attempt had left him unconscious on the cold stone floor. After quite a chase around the small "captive breeding room," which was attached to both the northwest section of her biome and the southeast corner of the adjoining biome, Alena had leapt onto his back and managed to get an arm around his neck, cutting off the air to his windpipe. He had beaten her and tried to wrench her free, but she had hung on like a crazed wildcat until he had passed out on the floor. She thought she had killed him at first and was weeping with gratitude at his demise, when she felt a shallow breath on her arm. Enraged, she pulled his head up by the hair and slammed it back onto the stone before she did a desperate little dance of terror on his chest like she was trying to trample a mouse. By then, the enormous-headed Cephalopods had arrived to rescue their battle-scarred sperm donor.

She was sure that the headache Anthony experienced later was significant but only an infinitesimal fraction of what he deserved. Alena's own bruises had finally just healed with the exception of the tender bruise on her forearm. It was about the size of small stone and had turned a sickly yellow. She was happy to see that it had faded more around the edges. Alena placed her head in her hands and sat with her back against one of the simulated tree trunks. She hoped that she would be faring just as well in the next day or two, but she knew better. She dreaded what was to come. It wasn't that she didn't want to have children. She just didn't want to have them this way... not ever.

The others had learned to disconnect emotionally from the horrible act but not Alena. She still had most of her fight left, and she was certainly going to do everything in her power to keep it from happening to her. She glanced around. If only she had some kind of weapon. Her eyes wafted to the artificial branches above her in the tree. Perhaps she could dislodge one of them. She climbed high into the branches to work on a branch that was slightly bigger around than a pencil. It was a tedious task but after bending it back and forth dozens of times it finally snapped.

The branch was made of harder stuff than a natural tree, much to Alena's satisfaction. She worked to break off the tiny smaller branches until it was nothing more than a stick that was about eight inches long. Dropping from the tree, Alena found a rough batch of stone. She spent a good hour sharpening the stick into a fine needle-sharp point. Emmy toddled over a few times to see what she was doing. She would always throw her arms around Alena's neck and say, "Lena!" and then laugh at her own private joke. Alena glanced up as Emmy ran back to her mother. She found Jenna studying her. Alena didn't particularly like the expression on Jenna's perfectly oval face. With some hesitation, Jenna came and stood over her with her hands on her hips, watching her work for a long time.

"It's no use, Alena," she finally spoke, "at some point you are going to just have to come to terms with reality. Pregnancy is going to happen to you sooner or later, so you might as well just get it over with. It's not worth fighting against. You can't save yourself any more than you can save the rest of us."

Alena stopped sharpening the stick for a moment. How could she explain to someone that had already given in that, while she still breathed, she never intended to stop fighting? For just a moment, a look of hatred passed over Jenna's face. That look was all Alena needed to understand that Jenna utterly resented her for being able to hold out for so long.

"Quit trying to be such a heroine! You're going to bring more trouble down on all of us. This is our life now, Alena. Can't you see that?" Jenna waited for Alena to answer, but Alena didn't give her the satisfaction. She just continued sharpening instead. Jenna picked up Emmy and sauntered away to express her concerns about Alena to Kelly.

Alena continued sharpening, but her eyes brimmed for the moment. It was becoming harder and harder to deal with the uneasy isolation that Alena had been feeling for some time. She and Jenna had been close, once—the best of friends until their capture. Alena missed their old camaraderie, when they had whispered and teased about Anthony's antics aboard the Horizon. But Alena was entirely different from both of her cellmates, now. She didn't share their common bond by having a child of her own, and she didn't have any desire to just accept their current circumstances. She wiped her eyes and examined the sharpened stick, hoping with all the inner strength that she could muster that the stick would be enough to save her.

Alena turned to find the amber-orange eyed man watching her. She didn't know how long he had been there. His serious expression was one of genuine interest. She held up the pointed stick so that he could appreciate it, in order to warn him that she was someone that he should never take lightly. It was then that she noticed that he held up a stick of his own in one of his large masculine hands. She stared at those hard, rough hands and was grateful it was Anthony she would have to face and not this one. She watched in dismay as he bent down and began sharpening his own stick on the rough stone floor.

Chapter Three

The sound of the ocean current made the biome ring with hollowness. Sometimes when the weather was especially turbulent Alena could feel the disquieting current against the enclosure. The hammocks would sway in the treetops, and she would have to climb down and sleep on the hard floor to avoid being tossed from her bed. She hoped that the weather wouldn't be so tumultuous tonight. It was hard enough trying to sleep with all the regular problems she had to worry about. It would be even harder if she had to try to do it on the stone-cold floor. Alena listened to the sound of the current against the south wall of her biome. She felt uneasy sometimes about being so far under the ocean and was glad that at least the top of the biome was above water to let in a bit of natural light. There would be no moonlight tonight, however, with the storm rolling in. The cold darkness of the planet washed over her, and she shivered. Sometimes Alena longed for more warmth, not just warmer temperatures but warmer colors as well. Everything on this planet appeared to be a muted shade of blue or gray, or contrasting shades of black and white. Alena yearned for a fiery sunset, a field of wild flowers, or anything colorful at all.

It was then that she remembered the amber-orange eyes of her wild neighbor. How odd to think of those eyes at a time like this, but they were the only thing she could think of that she had seen in the last three years, aside from the occasional brown, that resembled anything warm in color. Those untamed predatory eyes flamed like two miniature burning suns. They intrigued her. She seemed unable to get them out of her mind. Always they seemed to be watching. Even now, as she tried to sleep, she could imagine them blazing in the darkness.

She rolled over, forgetting for a moment the sharpened stick that she had discretely hidden under her clothing. Alena almost stabbed herself and swore as she hurriedly changed her position once more. She would have to be more careful or the stick would bring about her own demise. Olivia whimpered in the darkness below. Alena would have to be quiet or none of them would sleep at all tonight.

There had been many nights when Alena had lain awake, listening to Jenna and Kelly trying to quiet their babies. Often one of them would finally drift off to sleep only to be reawakened by the cry of the other. Those nights were nightmarishly long and made their time in the biome exceedingly mind-numbing. Alena rocked herself back and forth, listening to the sound of the ocean currents once more. She let the ebb and flow of the water finally lull her into a dreamless sleep.

When Alena awoke, she couldn't make sense of where she was. Her body ached like she had been bruised in a good fall, and her mind felt numb like she had been drugged recently. The realization of her present circumstances came flooding into her consciousness in a panicked rush as she hurriedly tried to sit up, but she found that she couldn't since her wrists and ankles had been bound. Her hands had been tied above her head on either side of her and her feet had been tied much the same way but wider apart.

So, the Cephalopods had resorted to tying her up. Alena screamed in defiance. They were not going to get her this easily. She pulled against her bound wrists savagely and found that there was some give to whatever they had tied her with. She was able to work her right hand free and then her left, although it left both wrists raw and bleeding. Alena pushed herself up on the sterile table-like surface, ignoring the jab of the sharpened stick still hidden in her clothing, and began working frantically on her right foot. But she was too late. A shadow passed by just outside the room, and she felt the steady vibration as the door slid slowly open.

Anthony's mouth curved into a sickening smile as he observed Alena's predicament. His stone-gray eyes flashed with both wicked anticipation and cold hatred as he approached her.

"For years I have endured your proud face and your defiant self-importance," he slapped her across the face with the palm of his hand, "but not anymore. Now you will feel what it's like to be put in your place." He hit her again until she cried out. "I will show you who is your master now, Alena, and you will be on your knees begging before me—begging!"

He leapt upon the table and pinned her arms to her sides. Pushing her down, he placed the weight of his whole body upon her while he fumbled with her clothing. She struggled, but he pinned her tighter until she could hardly breathe. For a moment Alena was frozen with terror, sickened by his hot breath on her face. But there was also a part of her that refused to give in. It suddenly registered in her mind that her biceps were pinned against her, but her forearms and hands were free, and she had a weapon, if only she could get to it.

At first, she couldn't find it in the folds of her clothing, but after a good deal of fumbling, she was finally able to locate it. Her hand closed eagerly around the slender stick. With one determined and abrupt motion of her wrist, she stabbed the dreadful, sharp object into Anthony's gut. She felt his body jerk with pain and surprise as he released her. Anthony stumbled backwards in alarm with the stick lodged deeply into the left side of his abdomen. Already the blood had begun to flow profusely. Anthony screamed with rage.

"You stone-hearted witch! I'll make you regret this!" He clutched his stomach in terror and staggered towards the door. The Cephalopods were already there in their water suits that sloshed as they moved. Without ceremony, they hurried Anthony away, leaving Alena alone, her clothing in tatters and covered in blood. Alena wept and tried to extricate herself from the bonds that still held her feet, but it was hard to see through her hysterical tears. After weeping for a long time, she forced herself to stop. Choking down one last sob, she wiped her tears and worked at liberating herself.

When she was finally free of the chords that bound her feet, she swung her feet over the side of the metallic table and straightened herself. Bruised and sore, she found herself face to face with the amber-orange eyed man who stood staring back at her on the other side of the glass. The man's bronze face was tight and flushed with anger. They regarded each other for a long moment, and then he turned and disappeared into his enclosure. Alena wondered how long he had been there watching her. It made her feel completely creepy all over. She shivered, hating that this awful room was also connected to the bronze man's biome.

Alena didn't wait for the filmy Cephalopods to come for her. She had learned from experience how to work the doors. They were a system of doors really. Only one could be opened at a time. As one door closed it released the lock on the other. She could choose to return to her biome or walk down a long catwalk of sorts past the other biomes, but that lead to nowhere except a dead end or into the amber-orange eyed man's biome, she supposed. The other biomes had always been inaccessible to her when she had tried them.

As Alena returned to her biome, short energetic Kelly was there waiting for her. Being the ship's medical doctor, she was still always eager to do what she could to help in such circumstances. She examined Alena's wounds in the early morning light. Alena's face was already starting to swell, and her wrists looked awful.

"Come here, Alena. We need to wash out those abrasions and get some cool water on that poor face of yours. Anthony is such a brute, but I think he got the worst of it this time. We'll see how those Cephalopods deal with his injury."

Jenna, who was holding baby Olivia, gave Alena a harsh, disapproving look as she and Kelly passed by. Alena fought back tears. So, Kelly and Jenna had both been watching her horrible drama with Anthony unfold. Alena could not be sure, but she thought she saw a look of profound disappointment on Jenna's critical face.

Kelly helped Alena wash her wounds thoroughly. For the moment Alena appreciated Kelly's calm, nurturing presence. Kelly encouraged her to splash her face with cool water while she went for some clean clothes. Mercifully, clean clothes were supplied daily so that they didn't have to live in filth or, in her case, Anthony's blood.

Kelly stood between Alena and the western enclosure while Alena washed and changed her things. Oh, how grateful Alena was for Kelly for giving her a bit of privacy from those amber-orange eyes that were still watching. When she had finished dressing, Kelly put an arm around her. Alena shuddered. She was trying so hard to keep it together.

"Captain, you're going to be alright. I want you to climb up into your bed and sleep awhile, doctor's orders!" Alena nodded but didn't say anything. Her chin trembled. She was close to tears. It had been a long time since anyone had called her captain. Kelly might not agree with Alena's methods and probably disapproved of her just as Jenna did, but Kelly could not have given Alena a more precious gift than her simple acts of humanity and words of respect.

It was a struggle to arrive at her hammock. Alena was dizzy and exhausted in every way. She tried to sleep, but her dreams turned to nightmares, and she had to will herself awake again. So, she rocked herself back and forth and stared up at the cerulean sky. Ominous clouds swept by the window above her, warning of another impending storm. Already the wind howled in anger outside the biome, making the biome shudder. Alena sighed. It was going to be a very long day, much longer than the usual very long day that she had experienced every day for over a thousand days.

Alena propped herself up on one elbow and stared down into the enclosure below. The morning meal had finally come, but she was not hungry. She was too queasy from her episode with Anthony. She watched Emmy munching delightedly on a kelp leaf. She was biting it with ferocity and grinning like sunshine. It was good to be around children, she decided. They were so easily pleased and so happy to face each day. Still, what kind of life would Emmy have? Would life in this underwater zoo be enough for her in spite of the fact that she had never known anything different? Would she continue to be happy as she grew into maturity? Alena wasn't sure. She hoped so, but she doubted it. At least Emmy had her mother and a couple of "aunts" to help her along the way.

Alena shifted her attention to the walkway that ran along the biome and sat up with a shock, almost dumping herself from her hammock. Jim? She couldn't believe what her eyes were telling her, but there he was, as angry as ever, being led or rather pulled and prodded down the walkway toward what Alena guessed must be a new enclosure. His face turned briefly in her direction and even from this distance she could still see the rage in his mad expression. The huge headed Cephalopods were having a time of it too, trying to get Jim to go where they wanted him, but he wasn't going to make it easy for them and he never had.

Jim had been the only one of her security team to survive. He had blamed himself for the deaths of his comrades and the ship's unfortunate capture. Jim suffered more from his own self-torture than at the tentacled hands of the Cephalopods. He had been a good man, a trustworthy man, aside from his hot temper. And now, even now, he channeled that temper into one of rage against his captors. For months Alena had wondered what had become of him; Jim had not been seen by anyone for at least two years. She watched, dumbstruck, as he knocked two of the eight iridescent Cephalopods off balance and lunged at them with fury. They were still afraid of him even after all this time.

The giant headed Cephalopods had been unable to handle Jim from the very beginning. He was a danger to them and a danger to himself. For many months, before he had disappeared, they had kept him in solitary confinement stripped of anything but his person. Both the Cephalopods and every humanoid creature in the biome had been afraid of his violent outbursts. Even Alena's own crew had shrunk from him and abandoned him to his internal demons. Alena pitied him, even now, as she watched his struggle unfold before her. How lonely he must be. Alena wondered, however, if the violence had not worked for Jim—for the Cephalopods had been unable to break him, at least not completely. She and Jim were alike in that way. They seemed to be the only two left who were still fighting.

Jim now had the attention of Kelly and Jenna and Emmy who ran to her mother with an expression of fear. They stared at him open mouthed. Alena could see through the spaces in the trees that Jim also had the attention of the amber-orange eyed man in the enclosure next door. Where had Jim been all this time? Probably on another facility, she supposed, like Steven, Helen, and Raisann. Perhaps he had been too much trouble for them, and they had shipped him back? Alena climbed down and joined Kelly and Jenna just in time to come face to face with Jim. His steel blue eyes locked with hers, and his horrible expression changed ever so briefly. She could read somehow in that brief soul-searching look that he had found what he was looking for. Satisfied, his expression turned once again to rage as he continued to torment his captors. Alarmed, Alena turned away. What had he seen in her face, she wondered?

Ultimately, the Cephalopods had to tranquilize Jim to subdue him. Alena watched with shame as he slumped over helpless, and they dragged him far down the walkway to the biome they had prepared for him. They weren't at all gentle, and Alena didn't envy how bruised Jim would feel when he awakened. She rubbed her own bruises and chafed wrists in sympathy.

"Honestly, I don't know why he has to thrash about so much," Jenna said with disgust. "He just makes it harder on himself and everyone. What good has it done for him to fight? It's awful to have to see them drag a man down the walkway like that when he could have so easily walked himself. Just look at him!"

Jenna's comments infuriated Alena. She turned to Jenna with ferocity, eyes blazing.

"Frankly, Jenna, I find Jim's approach much more constructive than your whiny defeated attitude. There are some of us that haven't chosen to give up just yet."

Jenna gave her a look of snooty exasperation. "You think you are so much better than the rest of us, Alena. Someday soon Anthony is going to give you what's coming to you, and I won't be a bit sorry." She pulled Emmy behind her and faced Alena defiantly. Alena, who always prided herself on remaining so composed in these types of situations, felt her face flush and her heart pound treacherously in her ears. Angrily, she lunged toward Jenna, ready to tear Jenna's hair from her self-important head. Kelly's face drained of color as she leaped between the two of them and placed a steadying hand on Alena's arm. She was petite compared to Jenna and Alena, but right now she was a formidable boundary between the two of them. Emmy started to whimper and Olivia, who Kelly carried in a sling, began to positively howl. Olivia's wails helped Alena check herself from rattling the insides out of Jenna's hypercritical mind. She pulled her arm crossly away from Kelly and stood there fuming—the tension of the biome was thick with resentment that dripped like rain from their edgy faces.

Olivia's howling cries were deafening. They all shifted uncomfortably and regarded each other with contempt. Finally, Kelly, the wisest and the most composed at that moment, said simply, "Alena, do you mind taking Olivia for me for a little while, I would really like to change my clothes and freshen up a bit. She needs a nap just now, and I think that you would do well to get some sleep yourself."

Without waiting for an answer, she handed baby Olivia to Alena, who instantly quieted herself and yawned as her mother walked to the other side of the biome. Emmy playfully peaked out at her from behind Jenna's legs, and Alena, sighing with resignation, turned her back on them both and returned with Olivia to her own hammock. As she did so, Alena was keenly aware that many eyes followed her ascent, including those belonging to the amber-orange eyed male that was housed in the next biome. Would he ever stop watching her? She tried not to think of him and yet her thoughts kept drifting back to the mystery of her wild-looking neighbor until she grew balmy with the warmth of Olivia sleeping, and she also slept.

It was the hollow ringing and shuddering of the biome that awoke her a few hours later. Alena hated these types of storms and this one was shaping up to be the biggest one yet, judging by the motion of the biome. They occurred frequently during what Alena thought must be the summer months on this waterlogged planet.

She noticed the Cephalopods that ran the "zoo" anxiously moving about, making sure everything seemed secure. There were no "visitors" just now which was odd for an afternoon. Kelly and Jenna were talking quietly below. Alena strained her ears to hear what they were saying, but she couldn't make out any words; the sound of the storm and Olivia's deep, rhythmic breathing drowned out any chance of that. The biome shuddered violently and sent the hammock pitching wildly. Alena clutched the hammock and Olivia precariously. After waiting for the hammock to stop its dangerous swinging, she slid hurriedly out of it and shimmied down the tree.

The biome shook again as the waves crashed about them with violence. Olivia was awake now and eyeing Alena with bewilderment. She handed Olivia to her mother, purposely avoiding both Kelly and Jenna's eyes and went toward the eating place. Alena didn't feel like eating in the least, but her stomach complained loudly, and she felt dizzy from lack of nourishment. Methodically, she picked up a few of the kelp leaves that were now wilted and laboriously managed to down a few of them. She felt wretched. Her jaw hurt and when she tried to drink from the stream her wrists stung from the moisture. She winced, bracing herself against the pain as the wind howled above, and the waves from the outside continued to make the biome shudder.

"What a horrific day!" she said out loud to no one. She wondered if her own personal loneliness would have felt better somehow if she had been imprisoned alone. Bruised and seemingly friendless, she found a secluded spot away from the others and spent the afternoon musing about her own predicament.

Alena was unnervingly aware, throughout the course of the day, that the amber-orange eyes still watched her. After a time, the discomfort those eyes caused her became more than she could bear. Eventually, she could do nothing but challenge him. Defiantly, she met his gaze and stared boldly back at him. She watched his bronze colored skin deepen slightly in color from her unexpected attention. She pondered what he was thinking at that moment as she watched his expression change to one of unease. Wildly, he paced his enclosure never once taking his eyes from her. She watched his discomfiture grow until finally in anger he forced himself to turn away, leaving her once again musing to herself.

Why was he giving her all this unwanted attention? He didn't spend more than a fraction of his time "watching" the others and no time at all "watching" whatever was in the other enclosure next to his. Alena shook her head and closed her eyes, trying to burn his image out of her brain, but it did her no good; all she could see was his angry, yearning eyes. What was it about her that made him so incredibly angry, anyway? She was grateful that he watched her no more that afternoon. She wanted no more of those dreadful, colorful eyes upon her.

Chapter Four

They were fed their evening meal earlier than usual, and there was actually fresh fruit tonight. The storm made night appear to come prematurely. It was going to be a rough evening with the biome shuddering as it was. There was no way that any of them would be sleeping in their hammocks, which meant that Olivia and Emmy wouldn't be doing much sleeping. Alena sighed, finishing the sticky-sweet sea fruit that she found easier to chew than the kelp blades. After washing up, she went off to find a place to bed down for the night. It was difficult enough for Alena to sleep on the hard, cold surface let alone, Kelly and Jenna and their offspring.

Alena lay awake in the darkness for hours listening to Olivia and Emmy's tired uncomfortable whining amid the thrashing of the storm. Even though it was a long time before they slept, sleep still eluded Alena far into the night. Exhausted beyond reason, she tossed and turned on the cold, stone floor, unable to find a comfortable position. The sound of the others breathing deeply in slumber only further annoyed her. Finally convinced that she would never sleep, she arose in the utter darkness and wandered the enclosure.

It wasn't long before she lost all sense of direction and found herself unable to make sense of her surroundings, shrouded as they were by the deep blackness of the tempestuous night. She was glad when her outstretched hand felt the cool smoothness of the side of the biome enclosure. She walked along it for a while, her mind numb to any thoughts except rest. At last with her back against the wall, she slunk down to the floor. The glass seemed warmer near the bottom, and snuggling her back into it, she felt strangely secure and content. Her mind didn't try to process the oddity of it; she only gratefully embraced the sleep that finally came.

Morning dawned late for all of them. Alena's dreams were interrupted by the sound of the morning meal being dispensed. Lazily, she opened her eyes and stretched. She was warm and content and would have gone straight back to sleep if she hadn't noticed a look of amused alarm on Jenna's face a short distance away. Emmy was pointing at Alena and babbling something unintelligible to her mother who nodded and sat up with a mocking smile.

"Aren't we just cozy this morning," Jenna snickered.

Confused and not quite awake, Alena gave her a spiteful look and turned herself away only to realize with a shock that she lay next to the amber-orange eyed man in the next enclosure. The glass separated them of course, but that didn't keep Alena from jumping hysterically to her feet and leaping away from him. Had she spent the whole of the night sleeping next to him, sharing body heat with that creature through the glass?

The alarm that was apparent on his face didn't help matters. He went into a sort of rage and screamed at her. Of course, she could hear nothing of his ranting, but Alena shrunk from him as he pounded on the side of the biome. Jenna practically shrieked with laughter, and Alena would have pounded her if she hadn't been so upset. She turned and ran, climbed faster than ever before, and hid herself in her hammock.

It was a long time before Alena came back down. Alena didn't like feeling humiliated, so she spent a considerable amount of time nursing her pride before she was able to face them. As hard as it was to face Jenna, the thought of facing that man again was unthinkable. Gratefully, he must have felt the same because it was at least a week before he finally dared to even look at her. Jenna on the other hand was a different matter, and Alena knew she would never hear the end of Jenna's mean-spirited mocking. Things had been tense between them at best during the week, and it had become extremely difficult to steer clear of another confrontation with Jenna, behaving as she was. Alena had resorted to simply avoiding Jenna, but how do you avoid someone that lives and breathes the same air that you do every day? Alena had done her best, but it had been far too thorny. Kelly tried to make amends between them, but even she had washed her hands of it in time.

Emmy didn't seem to understand the rift that had grown between her mother and Alena. Today she was as earnest as ever, pulling on Alena's hand with a lightning grip.

"Come play, Lena!"

Alena shook her head, slowly.

"Lena, come play!" Emmy demanded, her bright eyes shining with determination.

Emmy wasn't taking no for an answer, and her mother seemed to be ignoring them both at the moment. Alena really liked inventing games for Emmy. She was a bright, precocious child. It was a waste for her to be locked up in a place like this.

"Okay, but just for a little while, Emmy."

Emmy smiled and pulled on Alena's arm until she came along with her.

"Play hawscotch."

Hawscotch is how Emmy said Hopscotch. Alena had introduced her to the game about a month ago. She had managed to scrape out the pattern and numbers by rubbing some of the kelp on the hard, stone floor. Emmy was far too young to play the game. She jumped more on the lines than not, but it was fun for them both to bounce around. Alena knew Emmy just liked hopping around anyway and throwing a dried piece of sea fruit in place of a rock or a hoppy taw. Hopscotch was a game that Alena's aunt, who was a brilliant sociologist, had taught her as a child. It was an old Earth game that the children had played before the technological era.

Alena and Emmy bounced around on the hopscotch until they were both laughing and breathless. It was only then that Alena noticed a scowling Jenna standing nearby. Her eyes narrowed as she lashed out at Alena.

"You think you're so clever trying to take my daughter away from me!"

"I'm not doing anything of the sort…" Alena began to say before Jenna cut her off.

"I know you. You're so calm and so calculating… You still delude yourself into thinking that you can control everyone. Well, you are not the captain anymore, and you are not to come near my daughter."

Jenna grabbed Emmy's hand and pulled her away from their game. Emmy yowled in complaint as Jenna hurried them away.

Bewildered, Alena started to go after them, but stopped with a sudden realization. She turned towards Kelly who had listened to the exchange. She could see from the look on Kelly's face that what Alena suspected, Kelly suspected also. Paranoia had begun to set in. Why hadn't she seen it before? Alena could blame only her own stupid pride. Looking back on some of the exchanges she and Jenna had had in the past month, the paranoia Jenna was experiencing became apparent.

Alena watched, with uneasy dismay, as that paranoia became more obvious over the next few weeks. She often found Jenna looking at her with calculating contempt or stalking her every move with her eyes. When they crossed paths, Jenna always had a mouthful of condemnation to rain down upon her. Alena's concern for Jenna's sanity and the safety of little Emmy had tempered these insults that were so maliciously given. Alena had even been able to rebuff Jenna's attempts at drawing her into a confrontation at least until this fateful morning.

The day dawned yawningly just like countless others. Alena slipped from her hammock when the morning meal came. Her effortless munching was interrupted by Jenna launching herself upon Alena in a fit of rage.

"What have you done with her?" Jenna screamed, clawing at Alena's face and hair.

Alena tried to protect her face, while attempting to free herself from her attacker, who had now tackled her to the ground.

"Jenna, I don't know what you are talking about."

"Of course, you do. This is your doing! I know it is…" Jenna was in hysterics and would probably have pulled all of Alena's hair out of her head if Kelly hadn't come to her rescue. Kelly had quite a time hauling Jenna off her, but she was strong despite being smaller in stature than both of them.

"She's taken Emmy from me!" Jenna shrieked, breaking down into frantic sobs.

"Calm down, Jenna, Alena wouldn't take your daughter from you." Kelly tried to quiet her in her most reassuring doctor voice.

"Then where is sheeeeeee?" Jenna wailed disconsolately.

Alena and Kelly looked at each other with worry. Where was Emmy, anyway?

"I'll bet the Cephalopods have just taken her for a check-up, that's all." Kelly comforted Jenna. "She'll be back before you know it." Kelly put an arm around Jenna and guided her towards her hammock. "Why don't you rest for a bit, and we'll let you know just as soon as Emmy is back." Jenna only nodded in dazed resignation.

It became apparent, however, as the hours stretched on that Emmy was not going to be returned that day or the next. Alena watched Jenna pacing the perimeter of the biome day and night. She did this for three days until she crumpled from exhaustion. Kelly clung tighter to Olivia and an uneasy quiet settled over the biome. After a week, they all knew that Emmy was probably never coming back.

The silence was broken one morning by an unnatural wailing that emanated from a desperate mother. Alena had never heard such a sound of suffering and loss. The sound did nothing but magnify her own suffering and grief, for Alena had loved Emmy too and deeply. Alena couldn't help but wonder what the monsters had done with poor little Emmy. She tried not to think about it, but that was next to impossible. Where had they taken her? Was she okay? How would she get along without her mother? Were these creatures so heartless as to divide a mother and child? Surely, they knew that Emmy couldn't care for herself?

None of them had much of an appetite. Their eyes and faces were red and swollen and they were all numb with misery. After two weeks Jenna curled up in a corner and rarely moved. She would accept food and water from Kelly on occasion but never from Alena, even though Alena went to great lengths to befriend her again. No matter what Alena did, there was still a level of malevolence that she recognized in Jenna's expression whenever she happened to glance her way. The grief at Emmy's disappearance and Jenna's understandable breakdown made Alena forget to keep track of the days and weeks, so she was completely unprepared when she found herself waking up once more in "the captive breeding room."

He was standing over her as she awakened, his amber-orange eyes glowing with intensity. Startled by his proximity, Alena tried to sit up, but found herself bound once more. Angrily she strained against her bonds, but there was no saving herself this time. She screamed. She kicked. She contorted her body against the bonds, but they held her fast. She struggled until her skin was raw and bleeding. Fuming, she turned and faced her unusual adversary; at least it wouldn't be Anthony who finally triumphed over her. Alena was stunned by the piercing hatred she discovered exposed in those warm, glowing eyes. They practically burned with venom. She tried to conceal a shudder as he inched closer and closer to her. She waited, locked in his dangerous expression. The air between them seemed hot and suffocating. She could feel the searing heat of his breath on her face and smell his musky masculinity. He studied her carefully with an obvious loathing and a bitter, hungry desire until she knew he could stand it no longer.

Alena's intake of breath was sharp and biting as she realized with sudden clarity that this man did not intend to molest her, but to end her miserable life. She found herself wondering why he wanted so passionately to murder her as he raised his sharpened stick above her pounding heart. Alena closed her eyes and waited for the welcome pain of her final demise. Gratefully, his well-muscled arm would bring a swift and masterful death.

She was ready and unafraid. Her breathing was careful and shallow as she waited patiently for him to be done with it.

When death didn't immediately come, she began counting to herself, counting each inhale and exhale. After what seemed an eternity, she finally opened her eyes and was surprised to find herself entirely alone. She lifted her head up slowly and cautiously looked around. Where had he gone? Confused momentarily by the change of events, she was at a loss at just what to do. She lay back down, seething with rage and uncertainty. Why hadn't the bronze man just taken her life? It would have been far easier that way, wouldn't it? That was what she had wanted, wasn't it?

"No," Alena finally told herself. She didn't want the Cephalopods to win. She could not let that happen. They had not defeated her, at least not yet. She wanted to go down fighting the Cephalopods, not the bronze man in the next biome. Anger washed over her then like an ocean and then the tears came. Why did the amber-orange eyed man hate her with such intensity? She couldn't begin to make sense of his actions, but nothing made sense in the biome.

Eventually, after a good cry, Alena worked herself free from her bonds and straightened herself up, her head still numb and in a quandary. The amber-orange man had thankfully left her undefiled, which meant she could still face Jenna and Kelly. Now all that remained for her to do was to return to her own wretched existence in her biome prison.

Chapter Five

The bronze man's treatment of her in the "captive breeding room" had an unexpected effect upon Alena. His actions only seemed to fuel Alena's curiosity about her neighbor biome-mate. She found herself studying him, frequently, watching his every move. It was as if they had somehow switched places for he seemed to no longer have any interest in her whatsoever. Whenever she did manage to find him looking in her direction, he always wore the same venomous expression that he had worn at their last meeting—one of hate and repugnance toward her. Alena often wondered why he despised her so much. Was it because of that fateful night when they had slept in such close proximity to each other? Had she broken some horrible moral code or law that made her detestable to him?

Alena was grateful to Kelly. At least she attempted to be sociable. The amber-orange eyed man and Jenna's palpable objection to Alena's very existence were really starting to get to her. Her honest efforts at trying to befriend Jenna in her deep mourning had gone miserably. Jenna continued to waste away into just a little wisp of her former self. She was almost violent with Alena when she tried to bring her food, so she left that job completely to Kelly. The Cephalopods had become alarmed at Jenna's health as well and had taken her away a few times to transfuse her with nutrients.

In the aftermath of the loss of Emmy, they all had some readjusting to do. Kelly, although as compassionate and nurturing as ever, hadn't been quite the same since Emmy, Olivia's half-sister, had been taken away. She was quiet and elusive. Alena guessed she was having an enormous difficulty dealing with the fact that, someday, she too would have to be parted from Olivia. It was rare now for Kelly to give Olivia to Alena for safekeeping. It was only when she had to take care of her own personal necessities that she reluctantly let Alena take her. Otherwise, she clung like a desperate mother to her child. Kelly had made the mistake, just once, of letting Jenna take Olivia. Jenna had refused to give her back for two whole days, despite Kelly's anxious urging. Jenna had regressed into believing that Olivia was Emmy, a much younger Emmy but Emmy nonetheless. Kelly and Alena had managed finally to trick her into relinquishing Olivia, and yet the fallout afterwards had been terrible until Jenna had made herself right in the mind once more. Jenna had wept and railed at Alena and Kelly, calling them all sorts of nasty names. She'd tried to attack them whenever she found the opportunity and even upset their hammocks at night sending them hurtling to the ground below.

It took many weeks from the time the Cephalopods took Emmy before Jenna began to recover physically, although emotionally she became more silent and withdrawn. At least she moved about the biome a bit now. The Cephalopods, with their enormous heads, continued monitoring Jenna's health rigorously and seemed pleased at her progress. The only good thing that had come from Emmy's disappearance was that the "visitors" to the science center spent a lot less time gathered about their biome. With Kelly keeping Olivia hidden most of the time in her sling and the rest of them quiet and remote, there wasn't a whole lot for the Cephalopod onlookers, with their huge whirling eyes, to see. The attention had shifted instead to the biome next to the amber-orange eyed man. Even he was giving that biome all his attention these days. Alena guessed that there must be a "new arrival" in that enclosure based on the interest of the Cephalopod children. If anything about the Cephalopods was completely clear, it was that they were obsessed with babies.

Days stretched into weeks and just about the time Alena and her companions had all adjusted somewhat to the new "norm", the Cephalopods had come in the wee hours of the morning for Jenna. Evidently, they were keen on providing Jenna with another child. They didn't bother binding her like they did Alena, for they considered Jenna a more willing subject. Still how could they be so cruel and attempt this so soon after they had taken Emmy? The horror of it washed over Alena like an ocean. It was enough to drive every one of them insane. Alena had a clear view of the "breeding room" from her hammock. Once Alena caught sight of Anthony, however, she couldn't bear to watch. Alena turned away, fuming with hatred for the filmy, tentacled Cephalopods and fuming with something worse than hatred for loathsome Anthony. This was beyond monstrous. Alena's eyes swarmed with tears, and she buried her face in her hammock.

When Alena saw Jenna again, her cheeks were hallowed and her eyes sunken. But what concerned Alena more was Jenna's absent expression. Jenna did nothing when Kelly put an arm around her and tried to help her. She faced forward looking neither to the right nor the left as if in some sort of trance. Alena couldn't help but get the impression that Jenna was no longer there. It was Jenna's body, but Jenna wasn't present anymore. Jenna behaved as if Alena and Kelly weren't there either. Both Alena and Kelly watched as Jenna made the automatic climb to her hammock where she stayed without uttering a single sound for the rest of the day and well into the night.

It was Kelly who discovered Jenna dangling by her neck in the early morning. Her sobering shout of alarm made Alena instantly awake. Alena and Kelly worked desperately through hysterical tears to get Jenna down, clawing at the strings of shredded hammock that closed about her windpipe, but it was too late. The Cephalopods were alerted by this time and the biome was filled with too many of them. Alena lost sight of Kelly through the mass of huge-headed, sucker studded Cephalopods. Panic-stricken to be among so many, Alena backed away still crying uncontrollably. She had to get out of here, she had to get away from this horrendous nightmare, so she ran—far away from the image of her lifeless hanging companion and the monsters who had killed her.

Alena was confused to find the biome door open in her tear-blinded hysteria. She somehow found herself standing in the walkway that connected the biomes. The Cephalopods must have left the biome doors open in their rush to save Jenna. Frantically, Alena ran down the walkway but turned herself about again away from the filmy Cephalopods who were approaching and ran the other way. She soon discovered there were Cephalopods coming from the other direction as well. Alena realized with horror that she would be trapped between them. In her desperation, she searched for an escape and finding none, tried the nearest enclosure door. To her tearful amazement, the door slid open, and she closed it behind her. Alena sank down onto the floor sobbing, only vaguely aware that the biome she had entered was warmer than her own and felt subtropical. She could only curl up in a ball and cry her heart out.

It wasn't until the amber-orange eyed man came near and stood over her that Alena realized where she was. In her flight, one direction and then the other, she had made little ground and ended up in the next biome. Through blurred tears, she glanced at him as he angrily glowered over her, but Alena didn't care in the least. She just kept right on weeping. Nothing mattered now. She half hoped he would take hold of her and tear her apart. She just couldn't live in this madness any longer.

After some time, much to her chagrin, he did take hold of her. Effortlessly, he picked her up in his arms and climbed with her over one shoulder into the trees of his biome. The shock of it made the tears stop momentarily as Alena tried to maintain her precarious balance as he pulled her with him into his hammock. She didn't dare look at him. She didn't want to, but he held her carefully next to him. Warily, she lay beside him, resting her head on his chest. Still the tears came in a quiet flood, although she felt a strange sense of relief. He stroked her dark hair until the tears were nothing more than sniffles, and then he just held her; he held her for a long time.

They lay like this for hours, while neither of them dared to move. Alena was keenly aware of everything about him: his strong arms, his musky smell, his bronze-golden skin, the steady beat of his heart, and the rhythm of his breathing. She wondered at his kindness to her. It seemed well out of character for him to be behaving this way, considering what she had learned from observing him these last couple of months. After all, her last incident with him seemed the polar opposite to this one. It wasn't until she finally looked at him, hours later, that she saw how pained he was by this experience. Outwardly, he was calm, gentle, and concerned. Inwardly, he was a wild and caged beast of fury. His eyes were amazing and colorful, but they hid nothing.

Alena could see the battle that waged there. For the past few hours, she had felt safe, but one look into those heated eyes and that security was swept away.

"I'm sorry....," she started to say, but her voice made him jump, and they almost toppled out of the hammock. She gripped onto him tightly as the hammock swayed. To be touching and now face to face was something neither of them seemed ready to deal with. Alena turned away and tried to sit up. She couldn't stay with this creature if she was tormenting him. Carefully she positioned herself to climb down, but the man caught her arm. With an aggrieved yet tender expression, he motioned for her to stay with him. Alena took his hand, squeezing it briefly but shook her head. She couldn't possibly stay now, not when she could see his repulsion to her so clearly. A grateful, "Thank you," was all she could muster. She watched his face soften a little, and he seemed to understand at least that she was appreciative. He placed her hand on his chest and motioned to himself.

"Tiernan," he said, and it was Alena's turn to jump with astonishment. His voice was exceedingly deep and had a rich musical quality, like rolling thunder. It fit with his wild looking exterior and muscular build. Alena decided she rather liked it.

He motioned to himself once more and repeated the word, "Tiernan," and then motioned to Alena. It took her a moment to catch on to the fact that he was introducing himself.

"Alena," she answered as she slid from the hammock and climbed down.

"Alena..." she heard him repeat under his breath as she moved away.

Alena was surprised to find the large headed Cephalopods waiting for her as she reached the stony ground. She had not considered what their reaction might be to her rendezvous up in the hammock with…Tiernan. She had not considered it at all. The Cephalopods had been studying them with great interest, she decided. It was not every day that one of their science experiments escaped into the next enclosure. They were all a buzz with excitement, clacking at each other in their strange language of clicks and whistles. Alena couldn't stand to have their enormous whirling eyes upon her. She moved cautiously away from them toward the door. They all watched expectantly for her next move. Without a glance behind, she slid through the door and made her way back to her own enclosure.

All the evidence of the nightmarish morning had been removed from the biome. It felt strangely empty and quiet without Jenna, even though she had been hardly more than a shadow the last several weeks. Alena went and sat near Kelly who was discreetly nursing Olivia. Kelly gave her the tiniest whisper of a smile of greeting before she returned to grieving. Alena knew that Jenna's death was going to be incredibly difficult for Kelly. Kelly and Jenna had been close. They had been together for almost their entire captivity.

"I'm sorry I ran out on you."

"That's all right; I actually really needed the solitude." Kelly sniffled and raised an eyebrow. "I have to say that I was a bit worried when I saw where you had gone to."

"I was a little out of my head. I didn't know where I had gone until I arrived there, actually."

"I kind of figured that. I don't think you would have purposely drawn that much of the Cephalopod's attention to yourself. Anyway, I'm glad to have you back now. It feels kind of creepy in here alone after a while."

Their voices made Olivia stop nursing. She wanted to socialize instead. She babbled and smiled at Alena while reaching for her. Kelly let go of her reluctantly. But Olivia only came to Alena for a short visit anyway, before wanting to return to her mother. She had grown a lot in the last month and was now sitting up by herself. Kelly looked panicked suddenly and voiced her fears to Alena.

"It's been hard enough losing, Emmy and Jenna...," she trailed off. "Alena, I just can't go on if they take Olivia from me."

Alena studied Kelly's weary face. The desperation that she saw there was sobering, even after all they had been through that day. Alena squared her shoulders, feeling determined. "That's not going to happen," she answered resolutely. "We have suffered, enough. While I live and breathe, I won't let them take Olivia from you."

Kelly looked at her hopelessly. "What can you possibly do, Alena? You know like I do that it will happen eventually. They treat us just like animals, really. Someday they will come and take my Olivia away, and there will be nothing that you or I can do about it." She cried openly while Alena put an arm around her, and Olivia looked wide-eyed at the both of them.

Alena waited patiently for Kelly to cry herself out before she spoke again. "The way I see it, Kelly, we have some time on our side. They didn't take Emmy from Jenna until after she had weaned herself at two. Surely, we can come up with something in the next fifteen months to avoid this whole experience. I'm sure their failure with Jenna will make them think a little harder about separating the two of you."

"You really believe that?"

"Of course, Kelly, it broke my heart when they took Emmy. I won't let it happen again. I swear to you."

Alena could tell that Kelly didn't quite believe her. How could she? Did they really have any control over what happened in their lives? Alena was determined to change that even if they had to escape.

"We're going to be fine," she said out loud. "We have to be," she told herself in a whisper.

Neither Alena nor Kelly ate the evening meal when it came, although they both took a long drink from the stream before going to bed for the night. Alena noticed that Tiernan hadn't eaten either. She wondered briefly at it, wandering closer to the glass barrier that divided their adjoining biomes. Tiernan came closer as well, watching her every movement. His amber-orange eyes were still heated and piercing, but he seemed to want to at least take notice of her again. She placed a shaking hand upon the glass, as a sort of half wave of friendship before retiring for the night and was stunned when he placed his own hand opposite hers on the other side of the glass. She gave him a little smile, but his expression did not change. Alena realized then that she had never seen him smile, not even once. She withdrew her hand slowly and watched him do the same. He regarded her for a moment and then walked away.

They repeated this ritual every night for the next several days. It was a simple acknowledgment really that they shared something difficult, that they had a common enemy, and that they both suffered under their circumstances. She always smiled. He never did. She came to look forward to this ritual, and he was always there waiting for her with a crazy, pained look in his amber-orange eyes.

Chapter Six

Young, shy Elizabeth was moved into Alena and Kelly's enclosure about ten days after Jenna's death. Alena hadn't seen her since she had been moved away from her and Mad Miriam many months before. Both Kelly and Alena kept quiet about what had happened to Jenna and Emmy, because poor Elizabeth was about six or seven months with child. They both knew that the knowledge of what had happened to Jenna and Emmy would make pregnancy and delivery too much for her. Alena was pretty sure the baby was Anthony's, although none of them ever talked about it. She was angry, however, to learn just how soon that this had happened to Elizabeth after Alena had been transferred. It could not have been more than a few short weeks.

Elizabeth was only a fifteen-year-old student when she had come aboard the Horizon. She was bright and efficient and painfully shy. She had been given the opportunity to join their mission as part of the Study in Space Program. Alena had been irritated at first when she had been assigned a Study in Space student; after all, she already had her hands too full with her immature first officer to look out for, but Elizabeth had proven to be a wonderful member of the team. She had an amazing gift for identifying mineral deposits and had played a key part in the discovery of the terinthium crystals. Elizabeth still looked like a teenager, although she had to be a least twenty-one now, for they had been three years into their mission when they were captured, and they had spent another three here in this zoo.

Elizabeth brought news of Mad Miriam, Janet, and Gwen. She related to Alena and Kelly that Miriam was even more insane than before. Miriam still endlessly wandered the perimeter of her enclosure, but now she wailed incessantly while doing so. Elizabeth related to them that this had driven level-headed Janet so crazy that she had tried to harm Miriam on a number of occasions. Finally, the Cephalopods had transferred Janet out because of her frequent attempts to quiet Miriam.

"Where did they take her?" Kelly couldn't help wondering aloud.

Elizabeth couldn't say, but she suspected that Janet had been sent to another facility.

Elizabeth then spoke of how Gwen had been with her and Miriam for the last several months. Gwen for some reason had been unable to conceive and so was subjected to endless examinations and experiments with other male humanoids. As a result, Gwen had become just a small whisper of her former self.

"Gwen is living in constant state of terror." Elizabeth tried to explain. "She alternates between being fearful and withdrawn to screaming mournfully in a violent fit of rage. Living with the two of them was like living in an insane sanctuary."

Alena grieved greatly for Gwen. Out of all the members of her crew, Gwen had shown the most promise. She was the most talented engineer that Alena had ever known. The Tau Ceti Mission was to have been Gwen's final mission, giving her the credentials she needed to join the elite group of engineers, who designed all the most advanced systems. How terrible it was to have her locked up in a place like this.

It seemed that Gwen, because of her difficulties in conceiving, was faring far worse than the rest of them. Alena would lay awake at night thinking about it. She felt responsible for all of them, hated what they had become, and wished that there was something—anything she could do to change their situation. As the days dragged on, Alena felt more and more subdued. She was their captain and she had failed them, plain and simple. At least six of her crew members were now dead, five were unaccounted for including Janet and Ian. Gwen, Miriam, and Jim were mentally ill; Anthony could be considered a fourth mental patient, but he had always been the way he was. Alena, Kelly, and Elizabeth were all that remained of a once promising crew, and they balanced precariously on the edge of insanity themselves, not to mention that there were now several children to be concerned about, of which Emmy was also unaccounted for. Thinking about all of this made Alena feel wretched.

Alena wandered the biome at night when she couldn't sleep. This seemed to happen more and more frequently lately. Once, on her nightly journey, she caught a glimpse of Tiernan wandering about in his enclosure also. He would have been hard to detect if his murderous eyes hadn't glowed a fiery orange in the dark. She found herself wondering if Tiernan could see well in the black of the night. After all, Tiernan's eyes were more like a tiger's than human. This made her feel suddenly uncomfortable. Had he been watching her at night all this time? And what was he able to see? There were many private things that Alena and her companions did only in the cover of darkness. The thought made her only want to run for the safety of her hammock.

That night Alena dreamt that she was being handled by the Cephalopods. She was screaming violently and trying to escape from their tentacled grasp, but she was held firm and felt a searing pain in her upper arms. They called her by name in a voice like thunder, "Alena… Alena… Alena!" It took her some time to realize, as she forced herself awake, that it wasn't the sickening Cephalopods that had hold of her but Tiernan. He was calling her name and trying to shake her into awareness. She was embarrassed to find herself in Tiernan's enclosure. How had she arrived here? Had she walked in her sleep somehow in the night? As she set herself upright, she knew, however, that she had been delivered here by the Cephalopods. She could still feel the effects of the drugs they had used to tranquilize her. Her head swam, and she lay back down, trying to gain some sense of equilibrium.

Her compulsion to lie back down didn't seem to go over very well with Tiernan, however. He took hold of her and lifted her to her feet, pushing her towards the door. Alena took a few wobbly steps, but found the ground coming up to catch her. She crawled toward the door instead, eager to do what Tiernan obviously wanted by leaving the premises. When she arrived at the door, she found it unfortunately impassible. The wicked Cephalopods had locked her in. She was not going anywhere. She shrank against the door and tried with more effort to clear her woozy head.

Tiernan was not happy. In fact, he was outraged. He strode over to the door, roughly moved her out of the way, and tried to tear open the door himself. When he didn't achieve success, he paced the perimeter of his biome like some crazed animal. Alena warily watched him go round and round the enclosure as she waited for her own world to stop spinning. She decided after a few moments that watching Tiernan was counterproductive; Tiernan and her world seemed to spin in the same direction.

What was wrong with him, anyway? What did he think she was going to do? Surely, he knew that she had no interest in any type of... Her thoughts trailed off as Alena remembered how murderous Tiernan had been the month before in the "captive breeding room." His demeanor had been much like it was right now. Perhaps there was something about her person that was driving him mad... What if his sense of smell was as keen as his eyesight seemed to be? Perhaps he was extra sensitive to her pheromones when she was fertile. Oh boy, those fat-headed Cephalopods were really something, locking her up with this creature that she wasn't sure was more civilized or more instinctual. And the fact that they were using her to torment him made Alena incensed. She pounded on the door and yelled in defiance at the Cephalopods, who she was sure observed them, even now, with interest. Her sudden outburst practically made Tiernan jump out of his skin. Alena had never seen his eyes look more wild and ferocious. She sank down once again with her back to the door, trying to decide what to do. Should she ignore Tiernan until the Cephalopods came for her, or should she try to reason with him?

Tiernan had stopped pacing and was watching her with a pained homicidal expression. Alena decided on the more civil approach to their immediate problem and motioned for Tiernan to seat himself, which he did, gratefully, a good distance away from her. She proceeded to try to communicate with him using hand motions and simple words. After a few attempts at apologizing for their predicament he seemed to at least get the point of what she was trying to say and relaxed a little, although his eyes remained lethal. They spent the next several hours attempting to learn something of the others language, although Tiernan seemed much more adept at it than she was. His guttural language was just too hard for her to pronounce, let alone remember. Soon, after a bit of frustration on her part and a heated exchange between them, they resorted to Tiernan just trying to learn simple words of communication in English. It was the beginning of an unlikely friendship in which Alena could never decide whether Tiernan accepted her or wanted to shred her to pieces.

She watched him tremble at the sound of her voice at times and watched the veins stand out on his arms as he clenched his fists in an effort to maintain control of himself. Often, he would look away from her and close his eyes while speaking in an effort to shut her out. She knew that whatever his trouble was concerning her that this whole experience was nothing short of agonizing for him. She pitied him much more than she pitied herself.

Something in the enclosure east of them caught Tiernan's attention, and Alena turned to see what it was. She was amazed to see one of Tiernan's own kind observing them from the other side of the glass. The woman was paler in color to Tiernan, but she still had the same amazing amber-orange eyes and golden hair that hung to her waist. She was beautiful, even by Earth standards. She looked at the two of them disapprovingly, a hand on one hip and the other cradling a tiny baby.

"Sceria," Tiernan spoke to Alena crossly, motioning to the woman in the next biome. Alena found herself suddenly wondering if Sceria were one of the reasons for Tiernan's discomfiture towards her. Was this Tiernan's family? She felt a tiny pang of jealousy and wondered about it. Peering closer at the newborn she looked for any features that would identify Tiernan as the child's father. Seeing nothing conclusive, she turned back with relief to Tiernan who had been watching her closely.

"They are beautiful!" She finally told him and spent the next half of an hour trying to help this deadly tormented man understand the word beautiful.

Alena was glad that the creepy Cephalopods came for her before nightfall. The thought of spending the night in there with Tiernan was frightening on many levels. Alena feared the unknown more than she feared Tiernan, who immediately took on a more content and relaxed expression immediately following her departure. He still approached the glass for their nighttime ritual, placing his hand opposite hers as he always did, which made Alena feel suddenly as if she had a whole stomach full of butterflies. The man had spent the day as far away from her as he could get, and yet the minute they were back in their own enclosures he was content enough to be inches away from her.

"Pheromones," Alena muttered to herself, as she made the climb into her hammock. She felt Kelly and Elizabeth's eyes following her. She knew that she owed them some sort of explanation for going off to bed without first discussing her day in Tiernan's biome with them, but she just couldn't talk to them right now. She was disturbed at that moment by her feelings of envy towards Sceria. What they amounted to, she wasn't sure, but they bothered her enormously, and she was certainly too irritable to talk to anyone just now. Besides, whatever her feelings were towards this poor tormented man—they were dangerous—far too dangerous to entertain.

Much to Alena's chagrin, she dreamed of Tiernan in the night. Even in her dreams, she couldn't get away from his murderous longing eyes. In the dream she was running from him, running desperately for her life through a forest of haunting trees. She knew she could not be caught, for the results would be disastrous, and everything she had fought for would be lost! At some point in her flight, Tiernan turned into the despicable Anthony, and she was running from him instead; his stone-gray eyes were full of evil and planned treachery. She raced down a crooked path, stumbling over loose stones, breathing hard now. He was too near! His shadow overtook her, and she could feel his hot breath on her hair. With a frightened cry she plunged ahead. She could see a solid figure waiting for her in the distance… a male figure…Tiernan. if only she could reach him in time. Alena shook herself awake. Even in her dream state she didn't like what it could mean. Tossing and turning, she forced herself to return to a restless sleep, dreaming of vermillion cliffs, and a wide, open sky.

When Alena first felt his amber-orange eyes on her the next morning, she blushed furiously, which only made her more annoyed. She turned away, certain that he could not have missed her reddened skin. Kelly was also watching her. She motioned for Alena to come and join her for breakfast. Elizabeth was still sleeping. She slept late most mornings because her pregnancy made her toss and turn in the night.

"The Cephalopods are really pulling a number on you and our bronze neighbor," was all Kelly said when Alena sat down next to her.

Alena nodded, munching on some sea fruit and the usual kelp leaves. She didn't have to wait long before Kelly spoke again, "I hope that they know what they are doing. Certainly, they could not have put two more different species together, I can't imagine how strange your children will turn out to be."

Alarmed, Alena glanced up at Kelly. It took her a moment to determine that Kelly was just teasing her. When Kelly saw the severity of Alena's expression, she couldn't keep a straight face and burst out laughing. Alena threw a piece of kelp at her which caught her right between the eyes. Kelly groaned, rubbing the spot, but she was still smiling.

"Seriously," she said, "is he even human? He looks as if he would like to devour you most of the time, and he is always watching you, Alena, like a tiger hunting its prey. Surely you can't help but notice?"

"How can I not notice?" Alena mumbled miserably. "He is always watching. I am pretty certain he studies me at night too, for those piercing eyes even seem to penetrate the darkness." Alena sighed before continuing.

"I don't know if he is human. At times he seems all animal; for he is wild, tortured, and full of rage, and yet he also shows a certain amount of compassion and intelligence. He doesn't seem human," she added, while deep in thought. But her own words disturbed her. Wasn't Tiernan far more human than Anthony had ever been? And hadn't Jim acted in a way that was far more heated and tormented than Tiernan? Alena didn't know what to make of it. Who could say anymore what was human and what was not?

"Yesterday, before you awakened in his enclosure, I thought that you were done for Alena…"

"Done for… but why?"

"He had hold of you—he was shaking you like you were a piece of cloth, trying to awaken you or murder you, but then he stopped suddenly and held you for a long moment. You should have seen his face, Alena. I have never seen any man look at a woman that way. But when you started to stir, he went back to shaking you again. I think that the creature both loves and despises you."

Alena felt chills going up and down her back. It made her feel creepy to think of Tiernan holding her with longing and then wanting to harm her in the next instant. So, Kelly saw it too—this peculiar love, hate sentiment that Tiernan seemed to have for her. Alena didn't know what to think, and she did not know how to feel about the whole thing either.

"The creature has a name," she announced finally. "His name is Tiernan." Alena told Kelly about trying to communicate with Tiernan and also about the woman and babe of his kind in the next enclosure.

Kelly listened with obvious interest, before saying, "Be careful. From what you have told me, Tiernan is dangerous to you, even more dangerous than Anthony!"

Alena bristled at the mention of Anthony's name. "How could he be more dangerous than Anthony?" she asked aloud, thinking once more of Tiernan's more humane treatment of her.

"Anthony can steal your virtue, but Tiernan can steal your heart."

"Nonsense, Kelly, how could I begin to give such a man my heart? He gives me the creeps, and he's not even one of our kind. Really, how can you entertain such an idea?"

Kelly gave her a knowing look. "Just be careful, Alena. The way I see it, if the Cephalopods keep putting the two of you together, that man will either have you, heart and soul, or he will kill you with his own bare hands."

Alena didn't want to believe it, but she knew deep down that Kelly was probably at least right about the fact that it was dangerous for the Cephalopods to keep putting them together. She vowed from that moment on to ignore Tiernan as much as she possibly could. That proved harder than it seemed, however, for the more she tried to avoid Tiernan, the more she found herself thinking of him and observing him, especially when he reciprocated her obvious avoidance of him with some straightforward avoidance of her in return. Alena found that she was bothered quite painfully by his lack of any observable regard for her. She vowed then and there to get a hold of herself. She was behaving like some slighted school girl the way she was moping about, gawking at him secretly through the trees, hoping he would glance in her direction but not while she was observing him, of course. The way she was acting and feeling was simply ridiculous for a woman of her years. She had to be done with it—done with the silly adventure. Whatever feelings she had begun to feel for this wild creature, she was over and done with them too. At least that is what she told herself over and over every time she found herself looking in his direction.

Alena chided herself for allowing the fat headed Cephalopods to tempt her to lower herself to entertain their intentions. She was not going to let 3 years in a "space zoo" turn her into nothing more than an animal to be bred at will. She forced herself to turn her mind to more important subjects like the upcoming birth of Elizabeth's baby and searching for any possible means of escape from their tragedy of a life. She was still the captain of those that remained, whether they chose to follow her or not, and it was her responsibility above everything else to see what she could do for them.

Chapter Seven

Elizabeth was growing rounder by the minute. Alena hadn't been with Jenna or Kelly before the births of their children to make any comparison, but Elizabeth seemed larger than she should be. Alena could see from Kelly's face that she seemed concerned too. Day after day Alena watched that concern grow larger as Elizabeth's belly expanded at an alarming rate. Elizabeth was forced to move about slowly—if she moved at all. Both Alena and Kelly could see that she was enormously uncomfortable, but Elizabeth didn't complain. She seemed kind of dreamy about the whole affair and content to let her baby take over her body.

Kelly climbed up into Alena's hammock early one morning, which surprised Alena so much that she nearly tossed herself out of it.

"Sorry to disturb you, Alena, but I wanted to talk to you in private about Elizabeth. I don't want to worry you, but I know that something isn't right and well…"

"I've noticed that she does seem excessively large," Alena whispered.

"Yes, it's normal in the last trimester for a baby to have significant growth, but frankly the growth has been alarming, either she is expecting more than one child, or she is carrying a child that is not human!"

"What? Not human?"

"That's what I'm afraid of. And Alena that's not the worst of it. Whether she is expecting multiples or a baby of another race, I don't think that she can survive the birth."

"Why not?"

"Well, whatever it is, it's too big for her. She is so slender through the hips and barely more than a teenager."

"You're petite, Kelly, far more petite than Elizabeth, and you managed just fine."

"You don't understand, Alena, I delivered a normal sized baby. Elizabeth is not done growing yet. According to Elizabeth's estimates, she is no more than seven months along."

"What?"

"Yes, it's true. She won't give me any details, but she knows for a certainty the day of conception, and it was only seven months ago."

"Well, surely the Cephalopods will help her through?" Alena choked in a high-pitched whisper.

Kelly shook her head. "Both Jenna and I delivered on our own, with only the help of each other…"

"But you're a doctor!"

"I don't have the equipment to safely deliver a baby of this size."

"So, what do we do?" Alena asked in alarm.

"In the old days before the dawn of the space age, they used to deliver babies Cesarean section or C-section," Kelly explained, making an imaginary cross-section across her stomach.

"You're not serious? That's barbaric!"

"It may be the only way to save her."

"Does she know?" Alena asked with apprehension.

Kelly sighed, "I don't think she could handle the stress of it."

"But we have no tools…no anesthesia?"

"That's why I need your help."

"My help…How can I help?"

"Well, you're good at making sharp instruments, and you can get us the anesthesia if you are very careful, but you'll have to be very alert. We have only one chance, maybe two."

"What do you mean?"

"Well, the way I see it, in a couple of weeks you'll be fertile again, right?"

"Right?"

"When the Cephalopods come for you, they generally shoot you with a dart that drugs you and puts you out for a few hours. If you stay alert, Alena, you can pull the dart right as it is shot into you, most of the drug will then be left in the dart and we can use it for Elizabeth. Better yet, you will be more prepared for our wild neighbor when they dump you into his enclosure."

"The horrible Cephalopods always seem to catch me unawares, Kelly. That's like asking me to stay awake for three entire nights."

"Why not sleep as much as you can during the day? I can keep watch for you then. We'll just tell Elizabeth that you're not feeling well."

"If we can do this, when do you intend to tell Elizabeth?"

"Not until we have to. Maybe not until it's over. There is still a chance that she can do this on her own, especially if there are multiples in there, but I want to be prepared for the worst just in case. I don't want to lose anyone else on my watch."

Alena could certainly understand Kelly's feelings about not wanting to lose another person that she was responsible for. She wondered if there were others that remained of her crew that felt this way as well. Alena was going to do her best to see that Elizabeth came through this okay.

"Okay, what tools do you need?" Alena asked with genuine determination.

"Something like a knife...at least something with a sharp edge that will cut like a scalpel and a needle—an extremely sharp needle at the very least."

"Alright, Kelly, I'll see what I can do."

Alena went to work immediately that morning, trying to pull small branches from the "trees." It took some doing, but eventually she was able to dislodge a few of them. She then went to work making the smallest ones into sharp points. She was able to hide what she was doing from the view of the whirling eyes of the Cephalopods, but not from Tiernan. She could hide from either one or the other, but not both. She felt Tiernan's burning eyes on her at last. She glanced at him once and saw his face twisted with fury. What was he so upset about, she wondered? But Alena continued with her task. She made the needles first, because they were the hardest, especially the eyes through the center that she had to scrape through with the sharpened points with the tips of the instruments and then sharpen them once again when the eyes were completed. It took her the entire day just to make three needles.

Kelly was delighted with her success and congratulated her on her skills. "Great," Alena thought sarcastically to herself, "all my years of training have certainly been useful. I can make sewing needles." She went to join Elizabeth for dinner. Alena couldn't help but notice Tiernan a little while later, as she finished up her supper, working on something of his own. He didn't hide the sharp and deadly object as she walked by on her way to her hammock. In fact, he made of point of letting her see it. Alena sighed. Tiernan probably thought that she was making plans to damage him at their next meeting. "Well, how wonderful," she thought with cynicism. In a few short weeks she would be turned loose in that enclosure with the fervent, fuming Tiernan and his cache of lethal weapons.

It only took Alena another day to form a couple of thin razor-sharp scalpels. She then helped Kelly carefully unravel one of the pieces of clothing that they were issued every day. It was made of strong stuff almost like fishing wire, but not so heavy. Alena wound the strings of strong thread around and around until they formed a ball the size of a small piece of sea fruit.

Alena noticed that Tiernan was itching with curiosity at their latest task. His frown deepened, and Alena could see that he was trying his best to come up with a purpose for their wanton destruction of the clothing. Elizabeth, on the other hand, was not interested in their activities in the least. Alena guessed that she was just trying to merely survive her trial as a human incubator now that her size was such an encumbrance to her. She and Kelly had slung Elizabeth's hammock nearer to the ground, as it was impossible for Elizabeth to climb without mountainous effort. Alena often heard her moaning in the night, attempting without success to discover a comfortable position to sleep in. She felt bad for Elizabeth and worried for her survival and the survival of whatever it was that she carried.

Alena lay awake that night and stared up in fascination at the round window at the top of the biome. Tonight, there was a rare sliver of an immense moon directly above the window that cast in its cerulean light. It illuminated the edges of the window in an eerie ghostly fashion. Alena didn't know whether it was the moon directly overhead or her position at that moment in the hammock, but she noticed something different about the window that she had never noticed before. The window was not perfectly symmetrical, and a tiny piece of the framework cast a small shadow onto the portion of the window that was farthest from her. What was it that was creating the shadow, she wondered? She climbed higher into the tree to get a closer look at it. Was it a sort of latch? She couldn't quite tell. The window was still a good four feet from her head. But there was definitely something there. She wondered if it were possible to escape through the ceiling of the biome; if only it were possible to get closer to the window, somehow?

A cloud suddenly covered the moon, and the biome was bathed once more in darkness. Alena shivered for she was precariously balanced; one misstep and she would go hurtling to her death. She couldn't hope to make the descent to her hammock in the dark. She clung to the top of the tree helplessly and waited for the cloud to pass, but in the meantime, she contemplated her discovery. How could she get to that window? There had to be a way.

At the first bit of moonlight, she carefully made her way back down into her hammock. Sleep eluded her. Her mind was too alive, wondering if there was a chance at escape and wondering most of all what lay just beyond that window. She lay awake for a long while, watching the blessed moon until it wandered slowly out of sight.

Alena slept late into the next day. Even Elizabeth was up hours before she was. Elizabeth was sitting upright in her hammock humming to herself and to her swollen belly. Alena questioned whether Elizabeth was entirely sane, or if it was normal for mothers to sing to their unborn children?

After some wilted breakfast, a quick "bath", and a change of clothes, Alena climbed high into the tree again to see what she could make of the window in the cerulean light of the late morning. She could see Tiernan, Elizabeth, Kelly, and the ghost people all craning their necks to watch her. It was like being center stage in a trapeze act. Well, she wouldn't disappoint. She climbed until the tree lurched dangerously, and she swung back and forth. Alena soon noticed that her actions caused the huge headed Cephalopods great consternation. Were they afraid she would fall? Or were they afraid that she would escape?

Alena examined the window above her trying to work out the mechanics of the latch. If only she could reach it and touch it with her hands, it would be so much easier to figure out. If only there was some way to span the distance between the tree and the window. It was then that Alena happened to glance into the top of Tiernan's biome. She had never paid much attention to the top of his biome, but from her point of view the trees in Ternan's biome were much taller than the tree she was perched precariously upon. Alena vowed that the first thing she would do if she were ever dumped into Tiernan's enclosure again would be to go on a little fact-finding mission to the top of Tiernan's trees.

It took her a long time to shimmy down. Everyone watched her careful descent. It hadn't seemed this hard in the dark? Perhaps it was because she couldn't see the floor and how far she would fall if she had a misstep. Alena was relieved when she finally reached her hammock, and she rested there a while, mostly because she couldn't stand to have everyone's eyes on her any longer, especially the amber-orange ones.

She heard Kelly yelling up at her. "Alena, what are you doing? Are you trying to break your neck?" Alena only ignored her and contemplated a possible escape. She wasn't going to tell anyone about the window right now. She didn't want anyone to get their hopes up. She spent many hours during the next several days in the top of the tree trying to figure out ways to get to the window and how to unlatch it—if she ever did succeed. But soon even the novelty of the window wore off when she found that it was impossible to get to.

Chapter Eight

The last week had crawled by slowly. Alena had been awake for two nights now and had been sleeping during the day. She had even pitched in to take care of Olivia at night. This enabled Kelly to be more alert during the day so that they would be prepared when the suckered Cephalopods came for her.

Olivia was crawling all over now. They had to constantly watch her, so she wouldn't crawl into the stream, or the refuse pile, or anything else dangerous. She was also trying to climb a bit. Kelly had found it necessary to lower her hammock, just to make sure Olivia didn't wake up and tumble to the ground in the night. Alena was glad that Olivia was sleeping well tonight. Olivia had become such a handful—a sweet handful but a handful, nonetheless.

Alena had been more tired than usual tonight. Her body was having trouble adjusting to this nocturnal schedule. It didn't help that she had been lying around for several days now. Her muscles were cramped from being in the hammock so long. She was starting to think that the Cephalopods had forgotten about her, but then she heard the unmistakable slosh of the water suits, and she knew that they had finally come.

Alena should have been more prepared for the pain when it hit her, but she had always been asleep when it had happened before. The dart stung like a vicious bee, and hastily Alena ripped it out of her thigh, accidentally dropping it in the process. The Cephalopods must have noticed because Alena was unprepared for the second dart that came and then a third, which she managed to rip from her body in succession. Enough of the poison eventually numbed her senses, however, because by the time she felt the sting of the fourth dart, everything went dark and she felt herself falling... falling... falling...

Alena was sick and bruised when she awoke, and it took her a moment to figure out that she was being searched, not by the awful Cephalopods, as she had feverishly first supposed, but by Tiernan. She abhorred the roughness of his hands on her body. She struck out at him in flailing desperation. He only pinned her hands to her sides and continued searching. What in the world was he searching for? Did the idiot think she carried a weapon? Did he think that she could possibly defend herself from him? The thought made her laugh out loud. Her laughter made Tiernan stop cold. He regarded her with indignation, his amber-orange eyes seething. She stared back at him boldly, laughing again, challenging him to make his next move. This only made him more enraged, and he brought something sharp to her neck and held her fast.

Alena thought she was done for. She couldn't move. He brought his face close to hers. His murderous amber-orange eyes flashed with rage and something else that Alena couldn't read. Time slowed to a standstill for Alena as her life precariously hung in the balance. Her eyes were locked with his, so drawn by the power in them that she couldn't look away. She tried not to flinch as Tiernan pressed the weapon against her skin, while he debated within himself.

Alena grew conscious of the scent of him and the heat of his skin as his eyes bored into her, but she was shocked when instead of taking her life, he kissed her savagely instead. She was unprepared for the ferocity of it. "Stop," she tried to scream, but she couldn't breathe. She kicked at him as she struggled for air, but he wouldn't release her. She remembered thinking, before her world went black, how ironic it was that she wouldn't die by his hand but by his suffocating kiss of death.

When she came to, he was kneeling next to her looking perplexed. But now it was Alena's turn to be angry. She slugged him in the jaw as hard as she could, which was enough to throw him off balance, but not much more. He rubbed his jaw with something like remorse, until he caught sight of her fuming face and clenched fist. He regarded her with amused fascination and grinned broadly. It was the first time she had seen him smile and the expression was so beautiful that it almost made her heart leap out of her chest. Kelly was right, she was probably done for, but she wasn't going down without a fight. Alena backed away from him until she was far enough away to jump to her feet and run.

Alena was completely exhausted and angry and confused at his odd treatment of her. She felt the tears stinging her face before she knew she was crying. It didn't take Alena long to register that there was no place to run to, so she climbed up into the canopy of Tiernan's undersized jungle instead. There was no place to sit that wasn't dangerous except for Tiernan's hammock, so eventually she headed there. She was relieved when Tiernan didn't follow her. She definitely needed space right now to figure out her topsy-turvy, upside-down world. She tried to shut out her surroundings and the fact that she was in Tiernan's enclosure, but that was impossible since the enclosure was so much warmer and more humid, not to mention that Tiernan's hammock bore the enthralling scent of him.

She observed Tiernan seated on the ground almost directly twelve feet below. He was sober and deep in thought. Alena didn't understand the creature, especially not his love/hate behavior towards her all the time. She felt ill and abused. She didn't know how much of that resulted from the tentacled Cephalopod's treatment of her or Tiernan's. She lay down in the hammock and tried to rest, rocking back and forth and closing her eyes. She was surprised, a little while later, to find Tiernan peering over her. She scooted over to the part of the hammock that was farthest from him and wagged a finger at him. He seemed to understand and sat on the opposite side.

He seemed strangely calm, calmer than he had ever been in close proximity to her, but his amazing eyes were still far too intense for her. The expression she read there was different than she had ever seen before: serious, noble, repentant, and way too involved. She jumped as he pulled out that sharpened weapon of his and handed it to her. What did he expect her to do with it? Defend herself? Hurt him? Hurt herself? He watched her carefully and waited.

"You're certainly a hard brute to figure out!" Alena finally said aloud. "I'm really angry at you right now, you big dork! What was that all about before?" She unconsciously touched her bruised lips.

She didn't think he understood a word she spoke, but he seemed to understand her anger.

"Yeah, I'm angry," she repeated, "ANGRY!"

"ANGRY!" He repeated in that awesome voice of his. He sounded far more frightening than she did.

"Well you had better not do it again, Tiernan. You should be SORRY! Yes, I think I want to hear you say it! SORRY!"

"SORRY!" He repeated back to her. And the amazing thing was that he seemed to understand what he was conveying to her.

"Sorry!" he repeated, reaching out to her in a remorseful manner. Veins stood out on his hand and arm. She felt him tremble just a bit as he touched her hand. Alena met his gaze and could see clearly the pain that this man was feeling. The rage had dissipated, but the pain was raw. Alena hoped she would be able to understand this poor tortured creature someday.

"Sorry." he said again almost in a whisper and touched her lips with his fingertips.

Alena wanted to leap out of the hammock and run away. His gentle touch was far more shocking than his roughness had been. Her expression must have conveyed her feelings because he moved away from her again, sliding further away from her than he had in the beginning. They stared at each other with thoughtful expressions. Alena couldn't help noticing that Tiernan was more comfortable at this distance and wondered why he had bothered to make the effort in the first place. Did he really care what she felt? She decided that on some level he must, for she knew that it was agony for him to be so close to her. And yet he remained with her, waiting for her to make the next move.

Alena became uncomfortable beneath his quiet piercing expression. She tore herself from his gaze and examined the weapon he had handed to her. It was far more intricate and detailed than she had expected. Tiernan had carved leaves and animals and birds into the handle. It had been a long time since she had seen anything so artistic.

"This is beautiful, Tiernan…. Beautiful!"

"Thank you."

Thank you? How did he know to say thank you? Tiernan was far brighter than he seemed. She looked back at him stunned, trying to remember the words she had taught him during their last encounter. Well, there was no time like the present to try to teach him some more. He seemed to pick it up so easily.

"You're welcome," she answered. "Would you like to learn some more of my language?" But that was a bit much for him to understand. And so, she decided to begin by naming body parts… arm… leg… head… teeth… hair… Before long she could point to something and he would tell her what it was all on his own. She moved on to other objects in the biome and it only took a short time before he could name every object in the enclosure. She looked around for more things to teach him and glancing above her she suddenly remembered the window. She shot out of the hammock with the memory and hastily climbed higher into the tree much to Tiernan's surprise.

"Come on, Tiernan," she called down to him, motioning for him to follow. "Come and see."

Tiernan didn't seem too keen on following her, but he climbed after her anyway. When Alena finally reached the top, she found that she was several feet closer to this window, but it was still out of reach. There was a latch on this window also and she could see it much more clearly. It looked like a pretty complicated mechanism, and Alena wished at that moment that Ian were still here to figure it out for her.

She motioned to the window and the latch as Tiernan came up behind her. She tried to explain her adventure into the top of the tree, the window, the latch, and the concept of freedom. Tiernan became as excited about it as she was. It was Tiernan's idea to let her climb up upon his shoulders, so that she might reach the window. It was precarious and completely terrifying to let go of the tree and trust Tiernan to keep her from falling, but she managed to climb up and sit upon his shoulders. She could almost reach the window, but not quite. Alena was scared to death to kneel upon his shoulders in order to give her the extra inches she needed, but she decided to try anyway. If there was any possibility of getting out of this place, she was going to try.

Tiernan held tight to the tree with one arm, and he used the other to help steady her. Alena managed to make her way up onto shaky knees. Unfortunately, when she reached out to push on the window, it gave her a horrible shock. It was almost like an electric current flowed into her body. It made her twitch and lose her balance, and she found herself pitching forward. Luckily for her, Tiernan was able to reach out and grab her as she fell, although he must have felt the shock too. He had a hard time balancing the two of them at first, and for one ugly moment as she clung to him, Alena thought that they would both plummet to their deaths, But Tiernan was strong and managed to pull them both to safety. Alena was relieved when she could finally stand on a branch on her own two feet. They perched close together breathing heavily. Alena found herself becoming very aware of just how close they were.

"Thank you, Tiernan," she whispered.

She wasn't surprised this time when he answered her with a hearty, "You're welcome."

They made their way down the tree to Tiernan's hammock. When Alena finally lowered herself into the hammock, she couldn't stop shaking. Tiernan insisted on trying to help her stop shaking, by holding her. It was reminiscent of their first episode together when he had held her while she cried. Alena was quite content to be held that way. It was a rare gift; one that she appreciated, but she knew it would come at a cost to the both of them. Alena also sensed that Tiernan was pained by their closeness, even now. She could feel it in every muscle of him.

Alena felt drawn to this tormented man. She both liked and disliked him just as she knew that he both liked and disliked her.

Alena could hear the click-clacking and squeals of the hard-beaked Cephalopods as they observed them. Alena hated them in that moment more than she had hated anything her whole life. She hated that they had electrified the windows, blocking their last hope at escape. She hated that they were placing her together with masculine, fiery-tempered Tiernan. She hated that she felt her resolve slipping. She hated that she felt attracted to him, hated that she could still feel the bruise of his suffocating kiss on her mouth, and she hated that he was holding her now. She pushed away from him.

"I'm sorry...I can't do this," was the strangled cry that escaped from her lips. She tried to slip down from the hammock, but Tiernan caught her by the wrist.

"Stop," he pleaded, trying to calm her, while she struggled. Painstakingly, he searched for words to keep her there. "Stop, Alena—Come."

Something in his voice made her look at him. He seemed so serious in trying to communicate with her that she did stop. His expression was composed and noble even. She found herself wondering in that moment where all his rage had gone. Who was this man that could sit and talk with her now all calm and sincere? He motioned for her to stay with him and that he would give her plenty of space.

"Come," he beckoned for her to sit. Alena sat resolutely in a grumpy heap. Tiernan sat down a short distance from her and motioned to the Cephalopods that observed them in earnest.

"You want to talk about the creepy Cephalopods? The Cephalopods are monsters, Tiernan—horrible, evil monsters!" Alena related passionately.

"Monsters," he repeated in stern agreement with his teeth clenched and the veins standing out at his neck.

Tiernan shared her revulsion for them. She could see it in the fire of his amber-orange eyes. He pointed to Alena and then to himself and then back to her again.

Alena shook her head, "We can't be anything to each other, don't you understand—that's what they want. I'm not bringing children into this hellhole." Alena shook her head in disgust. Tiernan was quiet, trying to understand her outburst. He reached toward her, and she shrank back wagging a finger at him. "No children," she repeated, making a cradling motion with her arms.

It was as though a light went on and Tiernan's expression softened. He shook his head, smirking slightly.

"Alena and Tiernan...," he began to say and then made a fighting motion followed by "...monsters... Alena and Tiernan... free...window..."

"You want to escape from these fat headed Cephalopods too?" Alena tried to translate. "Yeah, I'd love to find a way to fight them but how?"

Tiernan placed both hands on her shoulders and gave her a long look like everything would be okay. Alena felt relief wash over her. Tiernan could be a powerful ally. Perhaps, if they put their heads together, they could come up with something. If only they could communicate with more than just a few words at a time.

"Okay, Tiernan, as long as you keep your hands to yourself, I think we can be friends."

"Friends?"

"Yes, friends...allies!" she answered touching his hand with a slight smile. Sometimes it was positively like talking to a

Neanderthal, but then he smiled back at her, and she felt her heart melt a bit. She was still in a load of trouble; Alena pulled her hand abruptly away.

It was beginning to grow dark in the biome. The wicked Cephalopods didn't intend to leave her in here all night, did they? Alena felt her insides lurch in a panic. They didn't, did they? Alena tried to force the thought out of her mind. Much to her embarrassment, her stomach growled loudly, and she realized that she hadn't eaten all day, but then Tiernan hadn't either. They had been completely absorbed in their odd communication.

"Alena want food?" Tiernan managed to ask with his limited vocabulary, his intense amber-orange eyes boring into her.

"Yes, I guess I'm very hungry. But you must be hungry too. We might as well go and eat if they are going to keep us cooped up here together all night. There is no sense in being completely miserable, right?" Alena found herself rambling off to Tiernan, knowing he probably didn't understand a word of it.

"Yes, we go eat." He slid down the tree motioning for her to follow. Alena sat there for a moment with her mouth hanging open, surprised at Tiernan's unexpected grasp of her language and then followed him to his eating place where the limp kelp leaves lay waiting with the usual assortment of boring sea fruit, vitamin cubes, and gunk. Alena had half-hoped that Tiernan would be given a slightly different diet, since there was never much variety to hers. Eating had long ago stopped being a pleasure. It was just something you did to ease your hunger and fill the empty places. Tiernan stared at her boldly while they ate. The weight of his attention was totally disconcerting.

"It's rude to stare, you know," she finally said.

She tried to explain "rude" to him, but only caused him confusion and consternation, so she gave up. After Alena had eaten her fill, she became aware of another set of eyes watching her. She turned to find Sceria, with her babe in arms, glaring at her fixedly through the glass. Her eyes were filled with the rage that was reminiscent of Tiernan on most days. If Alena would have been on the other side of the glass, she was sure that Sceria would have ripped her to shreds. Alena wondered why she inspired so much emotion with these creatures. What was it about her that motivated so much fury? Was Sceria jealous of her proximity to Tiernan?

"Sceria looks pretty angry, Tiernan. Why is Sceria angry?"

As Tiernan turned his attention to Sceria, Alena watched Tiernan's skin deepen several shades to a flaming crimson bronze. For a moment he looked as heated as Sceria did. They regarded each other with a certain measure of malice before Sceria turned haughtily and walked away. Whatever the reason for their anger, Tiernan was a changed man after seeing her; he was more sober and more reserved for the rest of the evening. Alena attempted conversation about simple things and Tiernan tried to respond, but his heart wasn't in it. When it became almost too dark for Alena to see, Tiernan encouraged Alena to take the hammock.

"Tiernan sleep here," he motioned to the floor below him. "Alena sleep hammock."

With immense relief Alena climbed up into the hammock, leaving Tiernan to stare after her solemnly below. She found herself slightly disappointed that Tiernan hadn't even attempted to share the hammock with her. She wondered what in the world must be going on in his mind. She also wondered at the change in him this afternoon from an enraged monster to a calm, introspective creature. Alena watched as the darkness changed from deep gray to black. She snuggled carefully into the hammock, becoming immediately conscious of her aches and pains. It was amazing how much she was able to ignore while she moved about, but now that she was lying still, she could feel bruises all over. She thought of Kelly and Elizabeth then, hoping that their plan had worked, and that Kelly had been able to collect the darts that the Cephalopods had used on her. Perhaps, it would make the events of today worthwhile.

Alena's thoughts were interrupted by a rich, deep-timbered voice wafting up to her from below. She listened as Tiernan sang a sweet, sad melody. Alena didn't understand the words, but the music was haunting and heartbreaking. She didn't understand the reason, but the sound made her want to weep. Tiernan himself sounded as if he might weep as he finished the tragic tune. Alena knew that the song had been sung for her. She was deeply troubled by it. What did it mean? The music resonated and lingered in her mind and later disturbed her fitful dreams.

Chapter Nine

Alena practically jumped out of the hammock the following morning when Tiernan appeared at her bedside with breakfast. She had forgotten where she was momentarily, and to have his face suddenly appear next to her terrified her. Obviously, she couldn't trust him, not with the raging about that he did with her, but he seemed as calm as a purring cat. She scooted herself over and let him sit nearby.

"Good morning and thank you..." she said as he handed her breakfast.

He answered with the polite, "You're welcome," that he had learned from her, followed by, "Alena sleep well?"

"I slept well enough," she replied, remembering the strange tune that had haunted her dreams.

She glanced at Tiernan and noticed that his eyes were bloodshot and that he didn't look that well.

"You didn't sleep much at all did you?" she questioned.

Tiernan shook his head.

"I'm sorry. I should have insisted that you sleep in your own hammock. It's wretched to sleep on the cold, stone floor."

Alena knew somehow that it wouldn't have made any difference whether he had slept in the hammock or not. The reason that he had not slept had much more to do with Alena and his proximity to her. Something had changed, however, since yesterday. Although Tiernan seemed forever tormented by her presence, he now seemed resigned to it rather than being threatened by it.

"Tell me about the song you sang last night."

Tiernan colored slightly, so Alena could tell that he understood her, at least on some level, but he pretended not to.

"You are a great mystery, Tiernan. I hope that someday you will be able to tell me your story."

"Story? What is story?"

"It's the telling of your life, where you were born, where you grew up, what your family was like, what experiences have made you who you are…?

"Family…? Experiences…? What is experiences?"

"What are experiences," she corrected. There was no use in teaching Tiernan her own language if she couldn't teach him properly.

Alena spent the good part of their breakfast time trying to explain to him the answers to his questions with limited vocabulary. He was a very attentive pupil, perhaps too attentive, although he was careful to keep enough distance between them while he listened to her words. Alena liked his face, she decided. It was a handsome, knowledgeable looking face that was much more approachable and relaxed now that the intense rage had gone out of those amber-orange eyes.

She was so engrossed in answering Tiernan's questions that she did not notice for some time that the door to Tiernan's biome stood wide open with the whirly-eyed Cephalopods waiting just outside the door. How long had they been waiting for her like that, she wondered? After turning back to face Tiernan, she knew it had been for quite a while. She knew from the expression on his face that he had brought her breakfast to keep her here longer and had also kept her talking to keep her from noticing the open door. Alena didn't know whether to be flattered or angry, but she knew she wasn't going to spend any more time with Tiernan than she had to. It was too dangerous for her. She gave him a look of exasperation and slid from the hammock. Tiernan was right behind her.

"I no want you go."

"How about "I don't want you to go.'?" Alena found herself correcting, even as she tried to get away.

Tiernan grabbed her hand, "I'm sorry, Alena, I don't want you to go."

Alena turned back to him for a moment.

"I have to go… If I want to have any self-respect, Tiernan, I have to go. It's all I have left to me."

It was one of those brief moments that seemed to last an eternity. She turned from those enthralling amber-orange eyes only to notice a malicious Sceria studying them fixedly. If ever Alena had seen murderous intent on a woman's face it was now. Was this Tiernan's mate? Was she watching her lover attempt to seduce another, right before her very eyes? Alena didn't know how things were in Tiernan's culture, but she wanted no part in coming between this woman and this man. What other reason could possibly make this woman so malevolent towards her?

"Please stay, Alena."

"No, Tiernan. Goodbye now. It's best that I go."

"Goodbye," he said reluctantly and then finally let go of her hand.

Alena hurried past the waiting Cephalopods and into her cool enclosure. The doors shut behind her and locked. She tried not to look at Tiernan as she headed for her own hammock, but she couldn't help herself. He was waiting for her with a serious expression, his hand pressed up against the glass. She looked away from him as she walked passed him, unconsciously putting her hand to her lips in remembrance of the ill-fated kiss the day before. She pulled her hand away from her mouth as soon as she realized it but not before Tiernan had noticed. His disappointment at being snubbed was tempered by what she had given away with a simple hand motion. She saw him smile slightly as he turned away. It took everything she had not to march over and kick the glass. She stomped off to her hammock instead, glad that Kelly and Elizabeth knew that it was best just to leave her alone at times like these.

Alena swung back and forth furiously for about a half an hour before she was overcome with curiosity and went to find out from Kelly what had gone on while she had been away. Kelly was waiting for her. She seemed amused by Alena's demeanor.

"Relax, Alena, our mission was a success and aside from one monstrosity of a kiss, I think you got off pretty unscathed, didn't you?"

Alena shrugged. She wasn't about to tell Kelly anything of what she was feeling right now.

Kelly examined Alena a little more closely. "I take that back, you are a little bruised, aren't you? That Tiernan was holding you roughly yesterday. If I could have, I would have marched in there and banged him over the head myself just to show him a thing or two. It seems you have been able to set him straight, though. He has been nothing but well-behaved since yesterday morning as far as I could tell?"

"So, were you able to get what you needed for Elizabeth?" Alena asked, trying to change the subject.

"Yes, I think we have plenty, although, it wouldn't hurt to get some more next month if we have the opportunity. That is if you're up to it?"

Alena nodded with a sigh. She was willing to sacrifice some comfort if it made things better for Elizabeth.

"How is Elizabeth doing?"

"She's hanging in there. She's having some early labor pains, but that is not uncommon. She needs to eat more, though. She's as thin as a rod aside from her swollen belly, and she is going to need a lot of strength to get through this delivery. See what you can do to encourage her to eat more, will you? You could use some fattening up yourself, Alena, no sense in you getting sick too. I'm going to need your help with Elizabeth."

"Yes, doctor," Alena answered with a smirk.

Olivia came crawling over and pulled on Alena's leg. Alena bent down and picked her up. Olivia smiled broadly at her and patted her cheek with a soft little hand. She was such a sweet baby. Alena held her close while Kelly kept babbling about food, nutrition, and necessary supplies. It was good for Kelly to have Elizabeth's urgent situation to worry over to keep her mind off more heart-wrenching things.

Chapter Ten

The Cephalopods were behaving strangely. Only a few days had passed since Alena had returned from her rendezvous with Tiernan. The first odd thing that Alena noticed was that there were far fewer of them. There were no visitors, and they seemed to be using only a skeleton crew. Then the waves started. The waves pounded mercilessly against the sides of the biome day and night as the biome shuddered. Alena, Kelly, Olivia, and Elizabeth were all sleeping huddled together on the ground by the following night. The biome was powered down to minimum power on the fifth day, while colder temperatures and lack of light were added to their discomforts. Still the wind howled, and the biome shuddered recklessly as the waves broke over them. Alena could feel momentum building with the oncoming storm, and she felt a new kind of terror come over her. She could see that same panic mirrored in the eyes of her companions, in the eyes of the shy ghost people, and even in the eyes of restless, pacing Tiernan. On the sixth day, the few Cephalopods that were left piled what looked like a week's worth of food in their enclosure and then disappeared—abandoning them to the deafening ferocity of the approaching storm.

"They are leaving us to die," Alena heard herself say, but her voice was drowned out by the noise of the storm. "We need to prepare for an evacuation," she said straight to Kelly's face so that she could hear her. Kelly looked at her strangely but began helping her bundle things together in the extra sets of clothing that were set out for them. They started with Elizabeth's medical supplies, followed by food, and extra sets of clothing. Alena observed that Tiernan had begun doing the same, and she motioned for her albinal neighbors to also begin to prepare. The biome rocked violently in the wind and rain. Alena had never experienced anything like a hurricane before, but she didn't know any other storm that could sustain winds such as these.

Olivia was crying and wouldn't stop. Kelly tried without success to comfort her. A horrible cracking sound could be heard amidst the deafening wind and sheets of rain. They all looked at each other in fear as their biome jolted viciously to the east. The enclosure lost the little power that had sustained it, and they were left helplessly in the dark. The wind and rain continued to pound ceaselessly outside. Alena, Kelly, Elizabeth, and Olivia huddled together in terror. Occasionally they heard other strange shearing noises throughout the center.

As Alena huddled with her companions, the ground began to grow wet, and she realized with consternation that their biome had somehow been breached and water was seeping in. The force of the wind and rain defied all description. She felt the biome shudder once more, and then salt water began to pour in with a roar.

"We've got to get out," Alena yelled to her companions. She sprang for the door in the darkness and discovered after a little fiddling that the doors could be opened since there was nothing powering them. She made sure Elizabeth, Kelly and Olivia, were safely through the door with their bundles before closing it tightly behind them. They stood on the walkway shivering in the darkness. They could all hear the ocean water pouring into the center below. They were all going to drown. For a moment Alena wondered if it would have been better to have stayed in their biome, but they would have drowned in there, unless... Alena had an idea come to her suddenly. If the doors were no longer powered, then perhaps the windows weren't either. They had to get into Tiernan's biome.

Alena pulled Elizabeth behind her down the walkway, and Kelly followed with Olivia. Alena had only gone about twenty steps when she ran straight into something, something much bigger than she was and very alive. She screamed in surprise only to hear that something shouting back at her and grasping her shoulders.

"Alena, is that you?"

"Jim?" Alena would recognize his voice anywhere. "Turn around, Jim. We've got to get into the next biome! Ours has been breached!" She tried to yell over the roar of the water.

"No, I've got to find Elizabeth!"

"Elizabeth? Elizabeth is here right behind me. Turn around."

He did turn around and someone else that was behind him turned around, as well. Whoever was now in front of Jim, found Tiernan's biome door, and wrenched it open, letting them all inside.

They stood together in the grim darkness until Tiernan joined them. It was an odd scene with the seven of them regarding each other with relief. Tiernan, Jim, Kelly, Olivia, Elizabeth, Alena and Ian! It should have been a joyous occasion if it hadn't been such a serious one. Alena had thought that Ian was dead. Well soon, they might all be. Jim stood with an arm protectively around Elizabeth. That was good. They would need someone as strong as Jim to help Elizabeth. Alena looked around. Everyone seemed to be waiting for her to tell them what to do. Tiernan's biome seemed to still be intact, but what about the others? What was the status of her other crew members? Alena knew she would have to go after them.

"Ian, I need you to get up to that window up there and see if you can figure out the latch. You won't be able to reach it unless you're up on someone's shoulders. You'll need some help." She glanced at Tiernan. Tiernan looked wild with fury right now. Wrong choice... Her glance moved to Jim. He seemed overly obsessed with being near Elizabeth right now. "Jim, I need you to help Ian and stay with Elizabeth and Kelly. Kelly, you and Elizabeth gather food and anything else that might prove useful together. If we can make it out of here alive, we are going to need supplies. Be careful of the window, there is a current that runs through it. I think with the power out that perhaps the current is dead."

"Where are you going, Alena?" Kelly shouted worriedly.

"I'm going after Gwen and Miriam. I'm not leaving anyone behind."

"But you can't go alone!" Kelly yelled over the sound of the wind.

"I'll take Tiernan with me!'

"Are you referring to him?" Jim pointed a thumb at Tiernan.

Alena didn't like the look on Jim's face, but she couldn't worry about it. Yes, it was better that she took Tiernan with her. Who knew what would happen if she left Tiernan and Jim together.

"Yes, I'm confident that he can help me."

She grabbed on to Tiernan's hand. He still trembled at her touch even in this situation, but he was determined to help her and followed her, never letting go of her hand. The water was a lot higher now than it had been before. She could hear it pounding beneath the walkway. They would have to hurry, or they wouldn't be able to get back into Tiernan's biome. She and Tiernan felt along the walkway. Alena counted each door carefully as they passed. Gwen and Miriam's would be the fifth one from hers.

At first, they couldn't get the door open. It seemed jammed. Tiernan put his full weight upon it and finally it budged. He pushed it open only to let out a large surge of water. They were about a foot deep in water even with the water rushing through the door.

"Gwen? Miriam?" Alena yelled at the top of her lungs. Miriam was there almost immediately, looking as crazy as she probably was.

"Gwen?" Alena thought she heard a whimper, but she couldn't be sure. "Hold the door, Tiernan. Do you understand? Stay with the door. Alena trudged into the biome, wet now up to her knees. "Gwen?" Miriam followed close behind, too close, holding on to Alena's clothing. Miriam stumbled almost taking Alena down with her. Alena grabbed onto Miriam steadying her. She braced herself against the flow of water and plodded further into the biome. She found Gwen weeping hysterically and holding onto the trunk of the artificial tree in the center of the biome. Alena couldn't get her to come. It was finally Miriam who pried her free.

"Come on, Gwen, its Alena. I'm going to get you out of here."

"Captain?" was Gwen's panic-stricken reply.

"Yes. I'm here."

Gwen now clung to her and Miriam tagged along holding tight to her clothing. Alena thought that they would all drown before they got back to the door. She heard Tiernan calling to her. He was having a hard time holding the door. He let go of it with relief as soon as they passed through. They hurried down the walkway. There were a few other humanoids mulling about in their path now from some of the other biomes. Alena tried to move them in the direction that she and Tiernan were going and incredibly they did. They were anxious to follow someone's lead. She guided them to Tiernan's biome and watched as they filtered through the door: a turquoise colored man, a woman and a child that were a slightly different shade of blue, Alena's ghostly neighbors, and Miriam and Gwen who still clung to her. It was Kelly who finally convinced Gwen to let go, but then she latched onto poor Kelly, who already had her arms full with Olivia.

Alena surveyed them all and they stared back at her with expectation. "How is that latch coming?" she called up to Ian.

"I haven't sprung it yet, but I'll get it, Alena...."

Alena didn't hear the rest, for the storm drowned out his remaining words. The biome let out a sickening shudder, making everyone gasp together in unison, but for now it seemed to remain intact. Tiernan came up behind her.

"Alena, I must go to Sceria."

Of course, how could she have forgotten Sceria? There were probably other humanoids that needed their help as well.

"Try to keep everyone here, Kelly. We are going after one of Tiernan's kind. We'll be right back."

"Hurry, Alena! I'm afraid that you will not be able to make it back."

It took no time at all to get into Sceria's biome. They soon discovered that despite the wind and the shuddering of the biome Sceria was up in her hammock. No matter what Tiernan said, he could not entreat her to come down. It was as though she had given up and had decided simply to die where she was. Tiernan finally climbed up there himself and brought a struggling Sceria and her newborn down with her. They hurried out into the walkway and ran smack into none other than Anthony Pauleni.

Anthony regarded her with contempt. "What are you doing now, Alena? Trying to save the world? We are all going to die here, and there is nothing you can do to stop it!" He laughed coldly. Alena brushed roughly past him with all the self-control she could muster, and her companions followed. "Where are you going to?" Anthony called after them with scorn. Alena knew that Anthony followed them. She was tempted to bar him from entering the biome, but she refrained. Alena noticed that all the women, with the exception of maybe Miriam, shrank from him when he entered.

"Well, what have we here? It looks like an end of the world party. I'm so glad I was invited!" Anthony remarked with sarcasm.

"Shut up, Anthony."

"Shut up, or what? You're not running things anymore, Alena. I'm the king of this castle."

"Shut up or I'll have you thrown out. Do you think I care whether you live or die?" she hissed at him. The water had come up over the walkway now. They could hear it sloshing against the door outside. To go out there now meant certain drowning. Tiernan stood beside Alena and amazingly the turquoise man did too on the opposite side of her.

Anthony looked back and forth between Tiernan and the turquoise man, debating about his chances. "So, you are friends with a bunch of strange breeds, I see. Well, it doesn't matter. WE ARE ALL GOING TO DIE!" he shouted with a distorted grin, "It's just a matter of time."

Jim and Ian had come down out of the tree and now stood behind her.

"Shut him up for me, Jim, and keep him out of the way. Oh, and keep him as far away from the women as you can."

"Yes, Captain. I'm glad to do it." Without warning Jim punched Anthony in the jaw and knocked him out cold.

"That's not quite what I meant..." she started to say, but Jim only grinned at her and wandered over to Elizabeth. The ghost creatures stared after him in shock and huddled closer together.

"I've figured out the latch," Ian said quietly behind her. She turned to him and smiled.

"That's great news. There isn't anyone like you. I'm so glad to see you alive, Ian. You don't know how many times I've wished you were around to help me figure things out." The biome shuddered and lurched again violently. "I just hope we can wait out the worst of this nasty storm."

Ian looked at her with dread, "You're not planning on going out in that storm, are you? You know it's a full-fledged hurricane? By my calculations, it's probably a category 4 storm, Captain."

Alena nodded. "We're not going out there until we have to, Ian, but we may not have a choice."

They could all see the water line rising up the side of the biome. Alena knew that most of the biome lay underwater, and with all the bodies in this confined space, eventually they would run out of oxygen. How many of them were there? Alena began to count... 7 of her crew plus Olivia, 3 of Tiernan's kind, 3 bluish people, 5 ghost people, and herself. All counted, there were twenty of them in Tiernan's biome. Could she get them all out, or would they all die like Anthony insisted? Their best chance was to keep the water out, which had begun to leak around the door, and then to wait until they could go out through the window. But what waited for them out there? Would they be surrounded completely by ocean? What would they do then?

Tiernan was observing her. He placed both hands on her shoulders to reassure her, which she very much appreciated.

Jim piped up, "Hey, you bronze idiot weed, get your hands off of the Captain."

Tiernan dropped his arms and turned towards Jim in anger. Jim stood up to face him. They were both amazingly built, and Alena wasn't sure who would get the worst of it if a fight broke out.

"That's enough, Jim... Tiernan." She stood between them. "Look I need both of you hotshots to mellow out. We are going to be lucky if even one of us gets out of here alive, and I need both of you. In case you haven't noticed, we have a shortage of able-bodied men around here."

"Sorry, Captain, I just didn't think you would want one of these gooks touching you." Jim said glowering at Tiernan.

"Tiernan's okay. He's not bothering me. I can't have you knocking everyone out on my account, Jim," she remarked, looking over at Anthony who was still out cold on the damp floor. "I'll let you know when I need a bodyguard, okay?"

"Fair enough," Jim answered but he still glared like a tough guy at Tiernan before he sat down. Tiernan only glared hatefully back. Alena sighed to herself. She was going to have plenty more to worry about if they did make it out of here alive.

"Sorry, Alena." Tiernan could see she was upset. But then he asked, "What is captain?"

"I was once their leader—before we were captured by the monsters," she said simply. "I haven't been acting as their captain for a long, long time."

Alena moved away from everyone. She needed to think. What was she going to do with Anthony when he awoke? How was she going to get everyone through the window? Most of them could make the climb, but what about Elizabeth and the blue child, and Kelly and Sceria with their babies? There was also the possibility that Gwen would be too afraid to make the journey. What then? Perhaps she worried prematurely. There was a good chance that once they climbed out of the window there would be no place for them to go anyway. Alena paced the enclosure for a long time. Occasionally she felt eyes on her—all of them watching and hoping that she would have enough of a plan to get them out of the prison they had lived in for the last 3 years. Alena wondered then if Tiernan, or the blue people, or even the ghost people had been imprisoned for even longer. Alena also mourned the others—the other humanoids that had never made it into Tiernan's biome and had probably drowned.

Chapter Eleven

The storm had been raging for hours. Alena noticed that the biome shuddered with less frequency, but still the rain came down in sheets and the wind howled with fury. Alena wasn't sure, but she thought that the worst of it was over. Alena couldn't help but observe in the meantime, however, that the air was already getting stuffy. She realized that the lightheadedness she was beginning to feel was caused by lack of oxygen. They had to get the window open or they would suffocate, but by opening the window, they would be subjected to all the elements.

Alena wandered over to Ian who was conversing with Kelly. "It's time," she told him.

He nodded in agreement. "I was going to suggest it if you didn't."

"Kelly, encourage everyone to move away from the center of the biome. It's going to get awfully wet in here."

Alena watched as Jim and Ian climbed the tree toward the window. The wind was still mighty fierce. She told everyone to grab hold of anything loose. It was going to get messy.

As soon as Ian pushed the window open, the wind sheared the thing right off and the rain came pouring in. Ian himself would have been sucked right out the window if Jim hadn't been holding so tightly to him. They were entirely drenched before they had even begun their descent from the tree. Anthony began railing about the rain that had finally brought him around. Tiernan and the turquoise man were doing their best to control him. Alena marched herself over and ordered Anthony to sit down. He was angry, but he complied.

They waited, for what seemed like hours, until the torrential rain turned to just a heavy deluge before they ventured up once more. This time it was Alena and Tiernan's turn to approach the window with Ian following close behind. Alena left Jim to keep track of Anthony and Kelly to keep track of everyone else. Alena climbed onto Tiernan's shoulders and pushed her head and shoulders up through the window frame. She gasped at the tremendous shower of rain that pummeled her head and face. It felt like tiny needles as it fell angrily onto her exposed skin. Alena found that it was impossible to see more than perhaps an eighth of a mile in any direction all around her. All she could see was the downpour and the swirling ocean—salt water everywhere. She felt a pull on her leg. She ducked her head inside and crouched down on Tiernan's shoulders, grateful that he was so strong and steady. It was Ian who had been pulling on her. He motioned to the side of the biome that was just to the left of them. Alena gasped. A massive crack had developed on the side of the biome. If it burst at that level, they were all in mortal danger. The whole ocean would come pouring in. She had to get everyone out, but where could they go?

Alena stood up again and surveyed the sea of water. Hesitantly, she climbed out over the window frame onto the top of the biome. Drenched and cold to the bone, she once again surveyed the scene. Standing on top she could see an immense dark shape bobbing up and down in the water a little way off. Slowly she inched closer. What was it? If she didn't know better, she would think the thing was a boat, but it couldn't be. When she drew close enough, she could see that it really wasn't. It was only a massive upturned piece of a biome that had somehow been sheared off and trapped there by the wind. Could it serve as a boat? Certainly, it was large enough to hold twenty people. She ran back to the window and shoved her head in.

"Come up here, Ian. I need your expert opinion."

Ian climbed up on Tiernan's shoulders and then ventured out next to her. After Ian had surveyed the "boat" he came to the same conclusion that she had. It was worth a try. They were all going to die if they stayed in the biome anyway.

"Alright, Ian, I'm going to leave you up here to supervise. I'm going to start sending up the crew. Are you okay with that?"

Ian nodded.

"Thanks, Ian."

It was harder to climb back down through the window then she could have ever imagined, but Tiernan was there to steady her and help her. She asked Tiernan to stay put and shimmied back down the tree.

"Get them out—Send everyone up and what little supplies we have. Make it fast. We don't have a lot of time. Move—move—move—move—move," she yelled at Kelly and Jim as she hurried toward them.

"What's the rush, Captain?" Jim asked perplexed.

"Well, let's just say that that the biome is compromised, and we are all going to drown unless we get out of here, pronto," she paused. "Women and children first... Let's go!"

She grabbed a hold of the turquoise colored man. "The hammock... We are going to need the hammock." She pointed to it, up in the tree. "Can you get it?"

It took him a moment, but he finally seemed to understand and went to get it for her. Alena was amazed at his speed and agility and made a mental note of it. He was almost ceremonial when he brought it to her.

"Kelly, use this as a sling for Olivia and for hoisting her up and then pass it back. We'll need it for some of the others."

Alena watched Miriam followed by Gwen heading up the tree. They were moving too slow. Kelly went next with Olivia. Alena moved her attention to the ghost women and sent them up next with their children. This was too much for Anthony.

"You're sending those strange breeds up before me?"

"Women and children are first, Anthony, so unless you consider yourself one or the other, you had better get a grip."

Alena motioned to the blue woman and child. Hopefully the child was agile enough to make it on its own. The hammock had filtered back to her, and she handed it to Sceria encouraging her to make a sling. Sceria looked at her hatefully but took the hammock. Alena watched as the blue child climbed up the tree like a monkey. This made Alena smile. Okay, that left Elizabeth. This would take some doing.

"Elizabeth do you think you can climb?"

Elizabeth grimaced, but nodded. She was so over laden with child that Alena hated to think about what she was putting her through.

"Anthony, I need you to go ahead of Elizabeth. You'll need to help her up at the top. Use the hammock that I sent up with the bronze woman, to sling her up through the window. Jim, I need you to follow her, closely. You'll both have to help her through. Anthony grumbled, but did as he was told. Elizabeth's progress was extremely slow, so Alena waited with her two remaining companions, the turquoise man and the ghost man. When Elizabeth and Jim were about two-thirds up, she sent the ghost man. Alena noticed then that the crack in the biome extended almost to the floor now. They had to get out. She sent the blue man up and followed. Elizabeth was up and through the window followed by Jim, and then the ghost. The turquoise man was so agile that he left her in the dust and was out the window in a flash.

Alena climbed as fast as she could. Tiernan waited patiently for her. She could tell he was exhausted. It was upon his back, after all, that everyone had climbed to their freedom. Just as she reached him, the biome gave an ominous groan and she heard it start to give way.

"Hurry, Alena!"

She climbed onto his back, grateful once again for his steady hands, and then she was out the window. Jim was waiting there with the turquoise man. They pulled her up in haste. She turned back for Tiernan, sending the hammock back to him.

"We've got to go, Alena, the biome is not going to hold us," Jim said, with some urgency. "Come on, Alena, its going… Leave him."

"I'm not going without him, Jim. Leave if you must."

Jim tried to drag her off with him, but she kicked at him and actually bit him until he let her go. Ultimately, it was Alena and the turquoise man that pulled Tiernan up through the window. Bless Turquoise. She could not have done it without him. She was forever indebted to him. The three of them raced through the downpour to the upturned biome boat, where Ian helped them aboard.

All were drenched and miserable looking, but all were safely aboard. What now? They all looked at her with questions in their faces. Alena looked around her. They just needed a way to push off from the biome. In the end, it was the collapse of the biome that they had just retreated from that freed them from their predicament and sent them twirling off into the cold and dreary ocean.

They huddled together for warmth while the rain continued to pour. If they didn't die of hypothermia or drowning, Alena still believed that they had a chance. One thing was for sure, they would all be dead now if it weren't for her. Alena knew, however, that they were many besides the twenty of them housed in the biomes who had not been so lucky. How many lives had been lost? She didn't know, but the number was many. The waves turned and tossed them. For hours they endured the elements; the misery seemed to last an eternity. No one spoke; they just bowed their heads in wretchedness against the rain, until at last Ian gave that fateful shout, "Land ho."

Alena was entirely miserable, but she couldn't help smile. She was sure that Ian's outburst had come from one of Ian's cherished books. They were probably about 5 miles out from the land. It was hard to tell with all the rain, but the current was bringing them closer and closer to shore with time. When they were about 100 yards out, Alena asked those that were strong swimmers to bring them to shore. It was Tiernan, Turquoise, and Jim that brought them safely in, swimming until their feet hit bottom, and then they walked the "boat" up onto the beach.

The bedraggled group's worries were far from over. If anything, things were more urgent now. They needed to find shelter and fast. They were all in danger of hypothermia and exposure. Alena sent Tiernan and Turquoise to scout for a place to rest while the remainder of them unloaded supplies. It was obvious that the hurricane had hit hard here. It looked like a war zone. The tropical beach was scarred and littered with seaweed and debris. There were downed palm-like trees everywhere, and still the rain fell, heavily. Alena knew that the hardest part of their survival was just ahead. The next 3 days were critical. Tiernan and Turquoise were not long in returning to them with good news. Alena was relieved to learn that there were a series of caves only a short distance away.

When they reached the caves, they were dark, but comparatively dry. Tiernan led them to a cavern that was large enough to accommodate all of them with a little bit of room to spare. The ceiling of the cavern seemed to vault into the heavens. Alena nodded in satisfaction. Tiernan had chosen well. They were all cold and shivering, and Elizabeth and the ghostly women and children were having the worst time of it. The two most important things to do immediately were to find fresh water and to get them all warmed up again.

"Jim and Anthony, see if you can find anything dry in these caverns that will burn. Ian, I'm putting you in charge of figuring out how to get a fire going, get some of the women to help you make some sort of fire pit. Kelly, see what you can do for Elizabeth and those ghost people if they will let you." The ghostlike souls were already huddled off by themselves in a corner. "Gwen, I need you to organize the supplies." Gwen looked at her wide-eyed and frightened but seemed up to the challenge.

"Tiernan and Turquoise, come with me. We're going to see if we can find some sort of water supply down here." The two men followed her while she tried to explain fresh drinking water or an underground spring to them. Tiernan stopped her mid-sentence turned her around and walked her in the opposite direction. It seemed that Tiernan and Turquoise had already scouted out a water supply. Water gushed out of a crevice in the rock not far from the main cavern and emptied straight down through a large hole into a deeper cavern below. She tasted the water. It was heavy on minerals but seemed safe enough. This was good.

They wandered through some of the nearby passages looking for fuel for the fire, instead. They were able to find a lot of loose brush in the caves that had probably been dragged in by wild animals, but not anything dense enough to burn for any length of time. Anything outside would be too wet to be of any use. They headed back to the cavern with their small armloads.

Ian already had a fire going. The fire cast an eerie dancing light across the cavern. They had only enough fuel to last about a half of an hour, judging by the pile of brush and sticks next to the glowing flames. Alena added her findings to the pile and went to join the others. Most everyone was huddled close around the fire shivering with the exception of the ghost people, who seemed scared to death of the flames and Gwen, who was trying to keep Miriam out of the fire. Ian made room for Alena to sit next to him.

"The fire won't last long, Captain. We do have a good pile of driftwood, but it will be too wet to do anything with for several days."

"Good work, Ian. Hopefully, it will be enough. We can only work with what we have."

Alena looked around the fire. Jim had his arms around Elizabeth, and she was snuggled up to him looking a lot better than she had a half an hour before. What was up with that? A suspicion had started to grow in Alena's mind about who had truly caused Elizabeth's current condition. She would have to have a talk with Jim about it. Anthony sat next to Jim with a glassy, empty look on his face. Kelly was next with Olivia, but she gave Anthony a wide berth. Alena imagined that all the women would be giving Anthony a wide berth. The blue woman and child were next, joined by Turquoise; Sceria was seated next to him, her baby asleep in her arms and then Tiernan, Ian, and herself. *"What an odd group,"* Alena thought to herself. She motioned for Gwen to join them, but Gwen refused, chasing Miriam once more away from the fire. Miriam was making a game of it, and Alena could tell that Gwen was growing tired. Alena left the fire to join her.

"Why don't you go and sit by the fire Gwen. You need to rest and get warm. I can watch Miriam for a while."

"No!" Gwen suddenly looked horrified and started wring her hands.

"What is it?"

"I can't go by the fire." Her voice was shallow, her face pale.

"Sure, you can," she began to say, but then stopped short. There was nowhere for Gwen to go unless she sat next to one of the men, or very close to the worst offender of them all, Anthony.

"No, you can't go by the fire, can you? Well, perhaps you can help me pass out some rations instead?"

Gwen nodded, instantly relieved. Gwen had done a marvelous job getting everything organized. She had laid out their extra clothing to dry, placed the few tools they had together, and organized what little food they had. Unfortunately, there was hardly enough for even two meals when there were twenty of them to feed.

Alena gave Miriam the job of passing out a few kelp leaves to everyone. Gwen and Alena distributed sea fruit. Alena served the men so that Gwen didn't have to. When Miriam had finished her job, she decided to join the ghost people. She plopped herself in the middle of their family group much to the pale people's chagrin. They had just begun to bed down for the night, but thankfully, they made room for her, and she lay down with them as the fire died down. Everyone still looked damp, but at least not drenched. What little light they had was fading fast.

The whole group had to sleep close knit to stay warm. Alena took it upon herself to stick close to Gwen, and thankfully, Kelly flanked Gwen on the other side. She was so busy making sure that Gwen was comfortable, and that Anthony was not anywhere near one of his victims that she forgot to pay too much attention to who was on the other side of her.

"You did good work, today." Tiernan whispered behind her when she had settled herself. Alena felt her skin warm with a blush. This couldn't be happening. She was tempted to ask Tiernan to kindly move somewhere else. She couldn't possibly sleep next to him all night, could she? But everyone was settled now. If she told him to move, she would be calling attention to herself. After all, what harm would it do? It would be okay, wouldn't it? She half-heartedly tried to convince herself that she would be alright. Besides, she was too tired to fight with Tiernan now or any of the others. So, Alena just lay there annoyed in the chilly darkness. She was exhausted, but she couldn't sleep. She was too conscious of Tiernan's proximity to her. It wasn't until she was convinced that he was asleep that she let herself relax. It would be a long night, and she needed her rest.

Chapter Twelve

Alena awoke warm and cozy in the pale light of the morning. Tiernan was watching her, thoughtfully, smoothing the hair out of her face. She tried to sit up, but soon recognized she was held fast by him, and much to her embarrassment, she quickly realized that she had only herself to blame. At some point she had snuggled up to him and laid her head on his chest, and naturally he had placed his arms around her. She was mortified, and he must have recognized it because he released her.

"Tiernan, I'm sorry," she whispered as she pulled away and sat up. She was relieved to see that no one else was awake yet. The morning air was quite chilly, and she was half tempted to lie back down again.

"Don't be sorry, Alena," he whispered, "rest now."

He was right, she should rest, but she was too stubborn to admit it. She pushed herself stiffly to her feet, but then she remembered Gwen. She couldn't leave Gwen right there with Tiernan. She sank back down, sitting herself between them. Tiernan watched carefully her every move.

"Gwen is safe with me." Alena heard him say.

She studied his face. "I know," she finally said, "but Gwen doesn't know. It has been harder for Gwen than for most of us."

"You stay for Gwen?" he asked.

Alena nodded. Tiernan understood more than she gave him credit for. He was one sharp alien.

"You can sleep. I will go," he whispered.

"No Tiernan, stay," she said sighing. "It's early yet and we both need the sleep." She lay next to him and half wished she was brave enough to return to his arms.

"Alena?"

"Yes?"

He struggled for a moment to find words. "I am here."

Alena guessed it was Tiernan's way of saying that she could count on him.

"Thank you. It's good to have a friend."

They both lay there quietly, but neither of them slept. They waited until the others began to stir, and then Tiernan squeezed her hand briefly before pulling himself to his feet. The group all looked disheveled and careworn, but everyone seemed to have survived the night.

The group started out the day by eating the end of their food rations. Food was now the most critical problem for the time being. Alena knew that they would have to move camp again and soon. She wasn't taking any unnecessary chances. The huge headed Cephalopods were out there somewhere and perfectly capable of capturing them once more. Alena divided all of them up into groups. She sent Tiernan and Ian off to scout for a new location. Turquoise and the blue woman and child she sent foraging for any type of food they could find. Alena would take Gwen and Kelly with her to find food sources as well. The white, silver-eyed people weren't too keen on leaving the caves and didn't seem to want to join the rest of the group at all. Alena wasn't sure what she was going to do with them. She couldn't have them just living off the rest of them. Everyone needed to do their part if they were all going to survive. Alena left Jim in charge of the camp and as a lookout for any danger. She asked if he would keep track of Elizabeth and Olivia who were napping and Sceria too since she was attending to a new little one.

"Oh, see if you can get these pale faces to collect fuel for a fire," she added.

"Yes, Captain." Jim seemed happy to just stay near Elizabeth.

"Anthony, I need you and Miriam to do the same, collect as much firewood as you can and anything else that you find that might be useful and Anthony, please keep Miriam out of trouble."

"You want me to babysit?" he spat out hatefully. He stood over her menacingly.

Jim stepped between them. "You'll do as the Captain says and give her no trouble, or you'll spend the morning laid out on the ground, understand?

Anthony looked at them with contempt. "What gives her the right to order us around?"

"Look idiot, you owe the Captain your life. If it weren't for her, you would be buried out there in the ocean. You owe her a little more respect, starting right now."

Anthony called Alena a derogatory word under his breath and walked away. Jim started to go after him, but Alena stopped him.

"Let him, go."

"You shouldn't allow him to talk to you that way."

"Just help me keep an eye on him. He certainly will have to be dealt with, but we have more important things to concern ourselves with right now like survival."

It was still drizzling when Alena, Kelly, and Gwen wandered out onto the beach. Miriam followed after them, and

Alena let her come. The beach was littered with debris, but they gathered seaweed and kelp leaves into piles and lugged them back to the caves. The ghost people agreed to at least wash the food that had been brought in. Alena encountered Turquoise and his group coming back from their journey with an armload of some kind of hairy fruit. She nodded at him. She liked the strange blue-colored people. They were dependable and hard-working; even the child carried an armload of fruit.

The group all gathered back at the caves about midday when a squall came over the top of them. It rained as hard as it had the day before and made foraging impossible. Ian and Tiernan hadn't come back yet, and Alena worried for them out in the pouring weather. She surveyed the piles of food. There was the brown hairy fruit that was green inside when you cut it open, sort of like kiwi, another spiny fruit that was yellow, and the sea weed, of course. They wouldn't starve in the next day or two, but these items weren't going to fill them up either. They needed a source of protein. That was going to be a problem since she hadn't seen a single wild creature, not even a bird, not that it would make any difference. Her people, at least, simply weren't accustomed to eating wild beasts or any flesh for that matter. It was a practice that they had given up centuries ago when scientists had engineered the perfect protein. The Cephalopods had fed them something similar in the form of the protein gunk. Alena sighed. One problem at a time.

Their activities that day had brought to light other serious problems. Everyone's feet were covered with cuts and bruises. Kelly, even now, was busy tending to the removal of slivers and small stones from several sets of feet. They really needed shoes. It was possible to live in the biome without them, but not out here.

Alena wandered over to Jim who was sharpening a long stick near the entrance to the cavern.

"Jim, what are you doing?"

"I'm preparing for the future; we are going to need to defend ourselves from our enemies."

Alena knew that Jim was right to prepare, but she also began to wonder just who Jim thought his enemies were.

"I want to talk to you about something."

"Go ahead, Captain, shoot."

"You know I wouldn't presume to pry into your personal life ordinarily, but this is important to Elizabeth's health."

"Elizabeth?" Jim became alarmed and red-faced.

"Well, I can't help but notice how attentive you've been to Elizabeth, and well, Kelly and I are really concerned about her upcoming delivery. It would be helpful to know who the father of her baby is."

"And you think I'm the father? Isn't Anthony the king of proliferation around here?"

"You tell me, Jim. I'm not here to judge you; it would just be helpful to know."

"Elizabeth's okay, isn't she?"

"Kelly doesn't think that she will be able to deliver, she thinks the baby is too large."

Jim's words came out in a sudden outburst, "What? Does Elizabeth know?"

Alena shook her head.

"What can we do?" Jim looked horrified.

"Kelly says that we might have to cut the baby from her. Evidently, they used to do it pretty regularly in earlier times."

Jim didn't say anything for a long time; he just covered his face with his hands. Alena could see all of the veins standing out on his hands and neck.

"She begged me to do it, Alena," he finally said.

"It's okay, you don't have to explain. Now, that we know what we are dealing with, we can plan better." She got up to leave.

"I'm not like Anthony."

"Of course, you're not."

"Let me explain, Captain, I want you to understand."

"That's up to you, Jim; it's really not my business."

"Please, I want to explain. When they moved you out of her enclosure, she was worried—terrified about Anthony. You know as well as anyone how ruthless Anthony has been. She didn't want that, Alena, and she didn't want any of those strange breeds either. She wanted to make a choice. She wanted to have some control over the situation. When they put us together, she begged me to be with her. I swear to you, I wouldn't have forced myself on her. It was consensual, Captain. Wouldn't you have done the same thing?"

Alena was quiet. She wasn't sure she wanted to know any more of this. She could understand their logic and yes, it was better than the alternative, but no, she wouldn't have done the same thing.

"No, Jim. I wouldn't have," she finally answered.

Jim placed his face in his hands trembling with controlled emotion.

"We were all placed in an impossible situation," Alena continued. "Who am I to say what we should or should not have done? We can't go back and remake our choices; we must go forward and make the best of it. I think I understand why you did what you did even if it's not what I would have done. I want you to know that it meant a lot to me to see you still fighting those monsters a few months back. It kept me going for a while. I didn't feel so alone, Jim, and I want you to know that I appreciated it. And I'll tell you something else. I'm not going back there, I'll die first."

"I'm not like Anthony, I'm not." Jim said miserably in a deep voice. "I care about, Elizabeth, I really do."

"I know, I can tell. Don't be so hard on yourself. It won't do you or her any good, right now."

"But what if Elizabeth doesn't make it because of me? What if she dies?"

"Kelly and I are going to do our best to see that that doesn't happen. I need you to move forward. I need you to help the rest of us survive, no matter what happens."

Alena put a hand on Jim's shoulder. "You can do this. I believe in you."

"Even now that you know the truth?"

"You are not a villain, Jim. I know you have done the best that you can. I'm glad to have you still with me."

Alena left him soberly sharpening his stick. She looked around the room to make sure all were still accounted for. Most were napping or nibbling or talking in small groups. And there was still no Tiernan or Ian. Alena's eyes rested on Turquoise who was watching her with intensity. She made her way over to him.

"You must have a name; I can't keep calling you Turquoise."

He stared at her blankly.

She pointed to herself and said, "Alena." and then pointed to him.

"Obiaponezowani" he said.

"Obiapowhat?" That was a mouthful.

He smiled at her obvious discomfiture. "Turquoise," he said pointing to himself.

"How about Turq?"

"Turq," he repeated. "Cap'n." he said pointing to Alena.

"Okay, fair enough."

He introduced the blue woman as Gennilepeywai and the child as Calabnatai.

"Genni and Calab."

They smiled at her shyly but seemed delighted at the shortened forms of their names. Alena thanked them for their hard work. Alena wasn't sure whether they understood, but they smiled back nodding at her. She headed over to Kelly who was working on one of Miriam's feet.

"We need to start working on some sort of footwear, as soon as possible, don't we?" she mentioned to Kelly with resignation. "We are going to be lucky to even survive out here."

"The way I see it, we were lucky to have made it this far at all. Every day we have from here on out is just a bonus as far as I'm concerned. I know it will be difficult, but I'm grateful for the chance." She motioned to Olivia who was curled up asleep with Elizabeth.

Alena knew what she was thinking. She was glad to have some hope of raising Olivia outside of captivity. Alena watched Elizabeth and Olivia sleeping peacefully.

"Listen, Kelly. I've got something I need to tell you."

"What is it?"

"It was Jim who fathered Elizabeth's child."

Kelly nodded. "Well, that would certainly explain his behavior towards her the last several days. He always treated

Elizabeth like a kid back on the Horizon, but now he can't keep his eyes off her."

"Do you remember what a huge crush Elizabeth had on Jim those first few months of our mission? I was relieved when she finally gave up flirting with him. Jim never gave her the time of day back then, but he seems smitten now."

Kelly bandaged up Miriam's foot with a strip of cloth. Miriam fiddled with it for a moment and then hurried off to join the ghost people.

"Miriam's really taken a liking to them, hasn't she?"

"It's good for them, if you ask me. I've never seen a group so reclusive and fearful in all of my life. They are not very comfortable with us, Alena. And they especially have no liking for Anthony. There is always at least one of them watching him. Have you noticed?"

"No, I hadn't," Alena answered, but Kelly was right. One of them was watching Anthony at that very moment with her mysterious silvery eyes. It made Alena wonder what Anthony had done to gain so much of their attention. Alena shifted her gaze to Anthony, who she caught staring back at her hatefully.

"Anthony spends most of his time watching you, Captain. I think he has it in for you. You'd better be careful."

Alena didn't know how to answer. Anthony was a problem, a big problem, which sooner or later she would have to deal with. Alena pledged to be careful not to put herself in a situation where she was alone with him. She knew she would be safe enough with Jim around or Tiernan or even Turq. She turned her back on Anthony's gaze. He was giving her the creeps.

"You should rest, Captain. I'll keep track of everything for you and wake you when the rain stops or when anything changes. You don't look well, just now."

Kelly was right. She needed some rest. She could feel the exhaustion down to her bones. She hadn't slept nearly enough the night before because of Tiernan. That reminded her. Where were Tiernan and Ian, anyway? They should have come back long before now. Alena caught sight of Sceria cradling her tiny baby. Sceria kept to herself, looking wary and nervous. Every few moments she looked toward the entrance of the cavern, waiting. Alena knew that it was Tiernan she waited for. Alena knew next to nothing of this woman. Sceria was certainly very beautiful with her long golden hair and smooth bronze colored skin. Her eyes flashed angrily when she noticed Alena observing her slender gracefulness. Alena turned away. She didn't want to get into any sort of confrontation with Sceria.

Alena tried to nap, but found it was useless. She felt too many eyes on her. She would have felt better if either Tiernan or Ian were there. Jim came to her a little later, looking anxious and motioning for her to follow him. She followed him out to the entrance of the cave. It was still raining heavily, but Alena could hear a curious hovering sound above the sound of the downpour. That sound could only mean one thing. The Cephalopods were patrolling the area, looking for signs of life. Alena gave Jim a look of fearful anticipation as they crept back into the caves. They were going to have to move camp much sooner than she had anticipated. This wasn't good; this wasn't good at all.

"Jim, we're going to need to keep this between the two of us. Otherwise, we are going to have a huge panic on our hands."

Jim nodded in agreement.

"We must act as normal as possible and get ourselves ready to move out at first daylight tomorrow." Alena whispered.

Thankfully, no one paid much attention to them as they re-entered the caves, with two key exceptions, Sceria and Kelly.

Sceria was obviously disappointed that it was Jim and Alena, not Tiernan and Ian that had come into the cavern, but she continued to stare at them. Sceria sensed immediately that something was wrong. She watched them with narrowed eyes and a shrewd look. Kelly was able to read Alena's expression effortlessly and started bundling things together right away. She even encouraged Gwen and Miriam to help her.

"No sense in living like animals," Alena heard her say to them. "Let's get things tidied up a bit."

Even the ghost people seemed to catch the vision and chipped in to help, although it wasn't until much later that Alena understood why. As the afternoon stretched into the evening it became apparent that Tiernan and Ian would not be returning that night. Alena could tell that many were anxious with worry for them but no one more than herself. What had happened to them? Had they been recaptured? Alena didn't want to think about the possibilities. She found herself missing her amber-orange eyed, biome neighbor tremendously.

Chapter Thirteen

Alena slept fitfully that night. There were several others also shifting restlessly all night long. Alena learned that she should have paid more attention to this restlessness, because in the early hours of the morning she discovered that the ghost people had gone missing, along with half of the food. Not only that, Miriam was missing too. Alena didn't know what to think. In a way she was relieved about the albinal people. They hadn't been contributing much. She was glad not to have to be responsible for them. She wished them well, but she was frantic about Miriam. Had the ghost people taken Miriam with them or had Miriam simply wandered off? Alena organized a quick search for them, but they had left no signs to their whereabouts or which direction they had gone. Alena didn't know what to do. She couldn't leave Miriam here all alone for the Cephalopods to find, but if they didn't leave this morning the Cephalopods would recapture all of them. Alena couldn't let that happen. She shrunk back against the back of the cavern and slunk down to the ground. They had been free for 2 whole days and she had already lost 8 of her companions.

Anthony was watching her with his cold, stone-gray eyes. His mouth upturned into a knowing smile. "We're all going to die, Alena. There isn't anything you can do to stop it."

Alena tried to ignore his odd words and everyone's eyes that were on her. Turning to Jim, she asked him to get everyone ready to move out. Alena jumped when Sceria let out a squeal of joy. She turned to see Sceria launching herself at Tiernan and Ian who had just entered the caverns. Sceria locked herself with Tiernan in a fierce embrace that Tiernan heartily returned. Alena felt her cheeks flush with relief and jealousy all at once. Alena had to restrain herself from eagerly doing the same. She strode over to Ian who was looking very somber. Many of the others followed her. Both Tiernan and Ian were filthy and looked pretty messed up. They had been through some awful ordeal of their own.

"Glad to have you back," Alena told them, not daring to look Tiernan straight in the face. Her emotions were running too high at the moment.

"We're glad to be back." Ian said barely above a whisper.

Alena let out a huge breath, "We've been pretty worried. Are you both alright?"

Ian nodded slowly. "We were delayed several times."

"You didn't happen to cross paths with our albinal companions or Miriam on your way in, did you?"

Ian shifted uncomfortably. "Tiernan and I need to talk to you, Captain, alone."

Alena tried to keep her lips from trembling, "Ian, what is it?"

Ian waited until they were out of earshot, and then his face grew serious, and Tiernan's did the same.

"Miriam's dead, Captain."

"Dead? What do you mean, dead?"

"We came across her body a couple of hours ago. She'd already been dead for a while."

Alena bowed her head with grief and placed a hand over her forehead. Miriam dead, how could that be?

"We didn't have time to bury her, Captain, but we did our best to cover her up, so the Cephalopods will have a hard time finding her, otherwise we would have been back a lot earlier. I had quite a time keeping Tiernan from rushing immediately back to camp to check on the rest of you. We were really worried when we found her, especially since we'd been delayed so long by the...."

"Could you tell what happened to her?" Alena interrupted.

Ian looked at her miserably and nodded.

"Someone must have killed her; she had a big gash wound on her head."

"Couldn't she have just fallen?"

"Yes, but she also had strangling marks, there were huge bruises around her neck along with some other trauma."

"What other kind of trauma?"

Ian shook his head, he didn't want to answer. Alena looked at Tiernan, but he shook his head also. They both looked troubled.

"Did you see the ghost people? Do you think this was their doing?"

Tiernan and Ian looked at each other and shrugged.

"We didn't see them, Alena." Tiernan stepped closer to her.

"A wild animal then—could a wild animal have done this?" Alena started to feel hysterical.

"No, I don't think so." Ian answered quietly.

Tiernan put a hand on Alena's arm. "I'm sorry, Alena, we should talk later. We need to leave."

Tiernan's speaking skills had certainly improved. "Leave?" she asked.

"Evacuate." Ian said.

"Yes," Alena agreed composing herself. "We were in the middle of preparations, just as you returned. We got a little bit sidetracked, looking for Miriam. Did you scout out a good place for us?"

"Yes, but we are going to need to get started if we are going to make it before nightfall." Ian paused looking at Alena earnestly. "The Cephalopods are looking for us, Captain."

"They know we are here." Tiernan added.

"They what? How do they know?"

"Because they saw us." Ian said miserably.

"What do you mean they saw you?"

Ian's face reddened slightly, "It was entirely my fault. One of their craft appeared out of nowhere. I didn't hear it because of the wind. Tiernan tried to warn me, but it was too late. I didn't know what hit me. I was shot down with some kind of stunning instrument. They were turning and coming back for me. Tiernan dragged me off into some undergrowth, and we hid; we covered ourselves in brush. They searched for us for hours, but once the rain started again and the wind got so violent, they had to eventually give up. And Alena there's more…"

Tiernan gave Ian some sort of signal and Ian stopped mid-sentence. "We will talk about that later. There will be more of them coming." Tiernan declared gloomily.

Alena felt sick to her stomach. She had hoped that they would have a little more time to sort things out before the Cephalopods came searching for them, but that was not to be. "We'd better move out," she told them, and then she started giving orders to the rest of her companions. Jim already had everything in order, except for Gwen, who became hysterical when she found that they were leaving.

"We can't leave without Miriam!" she wailed.

It wasn't until Alena threatened to have one of the men carry her out kicking and screaming that Gwen calmed down enough to come willingly. Tiernan and Sceria led out with Alena and Ian bringing up the rear. Elizabeth was immediately a problem; she could hardly walk. After about an hour stumbling along, she could go no further. They had to construct a sort of sling with Tiernan's old hammock and some tree poles they discovered along the way to carry her. This made their journey a little faster, but it was still painfully slow. As they left the ocean behind them, the ground became more earthy and scattered with strange looking jungle plants and exotic trees. Alena was grateful for the cover that these odd groups of trees gave them. Neither Alena nor her companions were used to the great expanse of cerulean sky because of their time in captivity. It made all of them feel safer to be under the cover of the trees.

Ian shuffled wearily along beside Alena. He motioned to a canyon in a mountain pass that was several miles away. "That's where we are headed, Captain. The Cephalopods will have a hard time bringing their craft in there." He grew pale as they neared a grove of sinister looking trees. "This is where we found Miriam," Ian whispered so that only Alena could hear. An odd caw of a bird echoed through the jungle. Tiernan turned the group and skirted a certain section of trees. Only Ian and Alena knew why.

Alena mourned silently to herself. This was the second time she had mourned for Miriam's loss. The first time had been when Miriam had gone insane. Alena's frown deepened. Miriam had not been herself for a very long time, but she deserved a better end than to be murdered out here. Alena looked warily around her. She picked up a long stick to use as a walking stick, but it could also serve as a weapon if need be. She didn't like how ominous it felt to be here, knowing that a great evil had occurred in this odd-looking bunch of low hanging trees just hours before.

The group was nearing a stream ahead. Alena could tell by the sound of the steady flowing water. She welcomed eagerly the refreshment it would bring. They were entirely parched, for they had been unable to carry water with them. The sound of the steady stream was interrupted by angry voices. Anthony was complaining loudly about having to carry Elizabeth, and Jim was telling him to shut-up and make himself useful. Anthony threw up his hands in protest which caused Elizabeth to tumble to the ground. Jim lost it—flinging himself at Anthony in an unrestrained rage, punching him over and over. Soon they were involved in an all-out brawl.

Alena hurried to step in. "That's enough, Jim! Anthony, knock it off!" she ordered as Turq and Tiernan rushed to pull them apart. Both were bloodied, although Anthony had sustained the worst injuries of the two. Kelly came over to help Elizabeth to her feet and survey the damage.

"Anthony is trouble, Captain." Ian said under his breath.

That was obvious. Alena knew it. They all knew it.

"He's dangerous to us," Ian continued. "Mark my words, he'll give us away to the Cephalopods the moment he gets the chance."

Alena was quiet. Was that true? Would he really betray them even now? Alena found herself wondering whether Anthony would prefer to stay in captivity if he were given the opportunity. Anthony was definitely not to be trusted.

"Alright, everyone let's pull it together," she called out. "We'll take a break. Jim and Anthony clean yourselves up and cool off. Everyone be sure and get a good long drink out of the stream. Stay together. I don't want anyone else to go wandering off."

Jim and Anthony glared heatedly at each other but headed toward the stream. Alena was thirsty, but she waited to make sure everyone was taken care of and settled before she took a long drink of the cool refreshing water. Kelly came and put an arm around her. "How are you holding up, Captain? You still look exhausted. It will do us no good if you get yourself so worked up with worry that you make yourself ill. I'm sure our pale faced friends are taking good care of Miriam."

Alena only nodded. "I'm sure you're right, Kelly. Thanks for the concern." Alena hated not telling Kelly about Miriam. Kelly deserved to know the truth. Alena would tell her when the time was right, but she wanted to try and sort out what had actually happened first and talk to Tiernan and Ian at length about the details. The wind started to pick up, and the sound of thunder rumbled majestically off in the distance, making everyone jump.

"Time to get moving. We've got more rain coming in."

They were on their feet and moving again, leaving the sinister trees far behind them. Turq helped Jim carry Elizabeth this time, much to Jim's chagrin. But, thankfully, he accepted the help without incident. Anthony was still simmering and brought up the rear. Alena didn't like having Anthony at her back. She half hoped that Anthony would fall far behind and lose his way.

Chapter Fourteen

There hadn't been any sign of the Cephalopods, but their destination seemed to still loom off in the distance. They were forever moving but seemed to make little progress toward the canyon. The storm was fast approaching with the angry rumble of thunder and lightning streaking dangerously across the sky. The group took shelter a short time later in a grove of trees and watched the rain pour like a waterfall from the sky. The storm was a fast moving one, but it left them soaked to the bone and shivering. They trudged ankle deep in the muck, which stuck to their feet like horrible, black, sucking leeches.

They left easy tracks to follow. It couldn't be helped, even though they kept to the undergrowth as much as they could. Alena found herself studying Tiernan and Sceria together up at the head of the group. They seemed to be made of stronger stuff than the rest of them—more comfortable in their surroundings—more wild. Sceria was becoming irritated at the slowness of their journey. Alena was sure that if it were up to Sceria, she would have left them all far behind. She obviously cared for only Tiernan and her child. Alena found herself wondering why Tiernan didn't just want to leave Alena and the rest of them as well. Tiernan and Sceria definitely had a better chance without them. But Tiernan turned back and made eye contact with her every so often. It seemed reassuring to him for some odd reason.

Alena stopped the group for a meal shortly after midday, more to clean the mud from their feet than anything and to care for the little ones. Eating also helped to lighten their packs a little and restore some energy. The mountain loomed above them now. In another hour, they would probably reach the canyon. She had no idea how much further Tiernan intended to go after that, but he and Ian had said it would be nightfall. She was surprised when Tiernan came and seated himself next to her.

"Can I sit with you?" he asked gently.

Alena nodded, loving the amazingly deep, musical quality of his voice.

"You carry too much, Alena. There are others that can carry the burden."

Alena wasn't sure what he meant at first. Perhaps he felt that she was taking too much upon herself. Perhaps that was true. She had always tended to do that.

"I know," she answered simply. "Thank you, Tiernan, for all you are doing."

"Don't worry, I will stand with you."

His words were odd to her, "Why?" she questioned.

"I will tell you, but now is not the time," his voice was sober.

Alena wondered what he meant, but they were interrupted by Sceria calling to Tiernan in their odd guttural language. Haughtily, Sceria observed the two of them near each other from several paces away. She gave Alena a look of utter contempt before turning her attention to Tiernan. Her face was flushed with resentment as she moved toward them, and it was apparent that she didn't like seeing the two of them together in the least. Alena wished that she could understand what they were saying. Sceria was worried about something, and whatever she said to Tiernan had him worried too. He looked warily around them.

"What is it Tiernan?"

"We need to move."

"Why? What is it?"

Tiernan wouldn't answer which made Alena suddenly angry.

"What aren't you telling me?"

"Alena, you carry too much. Let me carry it this time," was all Tiernan said before he was on his feet and motioning for the others to do the same.

"Alright everyone, on your feet, it's time to move out." Alena ordered crankily. But she didn't like being kept in the dark. She didn't like it at all.

They moved on again with Tiernan leading the way and Anthony in the rear. Tiernan was wary of something out there in the forest, for he kept surveying their surroundings from every angle as they moved through the thick and wild undergrowth. What was it that he was so cautious about? Wouldn't it be better if they all knew what was causing him concern? Tiernan tried to meet her gaze, but she avoided it. She was feeling miffed at him for keeping things hidden from her. It was about the time that they reached the shadow of the canyon that Anthony came running ahead of her and Ian. He was nervous and all in a sweat.

"There's something back there," he said anxiously as he passed them by. "It's hunting us. I'm not going to stay back there and be the first to be eaten."

Alena looked guardedly behind her. It was certainly gallant of Anthony to let her be the first to be picked off. As she glanced around her, she did get the unpleasant sense of being watched or even hunted. What was it that was out there, she wondered? And why was Tiernan keeping it from her? Alena felt little goose bumps travel up and down her neck and a little fury too. She would much rather know what she was facing than be surprised. She was flattered when Ian offered to take her place, but Alena shook her head. If there was something hunting them, she wasn't going to put any of her crew in harm's way.

Gwen became teary as they entered the dark and narrow canyon. She sobbed out loud with fear. The rocky peaks rose up hundreds of feet on both sides. Desperately, Kelly tried to shush her. They were all feeling a bit nervous with Anthony carrying on about whatever it was that was tracking them. Jim kept telling Anthony to shut up, and that didn't help matters any. It also didn't help that the terrain had grown more rock-strewn. The uneven landscape was murder on their already torn feet. When it started to rain again, the rocks grew slippery and unmanageable in places. Thunder echoed between the two peaks creating a hollow rumbling sound. Wet and cold they stood under a stony ledge for a time to let the worst of the storm pass. It was while standing under the ledge that Alena caught her first glimpse of the creature through the trees.

The predator was hard to make out and she would have missed it, if not for the slightest movement in the shadows. Alena felt her skin begin to prickle. Whatever it was, it was large and traveled on all fours. Even from this distance she could tell that it was more immense than any other predator she had witnessed in her lifetime. It was there for a moment and then it was gone, blending with the shadows. Tiernan was suddenly beside her, making her jump.

"We're being hunted." Alena commented crossly in a hushed tone.

"Yes, I know. Sceria will lead us, and I will go behind," he whispered.

Alena frowned but didn't argue. She had to admit that she was out of her league out here. "Do you know what it is that's hunting us?"

"Yes, it is a rothcha."

"What is a rothcha, Tiernan, and how do you know such a thing?"

Tiernan gave her an odd smile. "I have seen one before."

"Where? Was it in the biome?"

Much to Alena's irritation Tiernan wouldn't elaborate any more on the beast. Gruffly, Alena informed everyone that it was time to move ahead. She knew from their groans that they were nearly spent as they slogged back out into the drizzling rain. After being kept cooped up in the biome for several years, this wasn't an activity that any of them were used to, and they hadn't been exposed to the elements for days on end that was for sure. Alena listened to Tiernan's sure-footed steps behind her. What wasn't he telling her? Was it so terrible that he thought that she couldn't handle it? She fumed and bit her lip as she carefully chose her way along the rocky path. They were climbing in elevation. She could feel the air growing a bit thinner as the day wore on. The sky grew darker—more ominous—and was streaked with strange colors. Alena couldn't shake the feeling of being hunted, and she knew that the others felt it too because they were moving at a faster and faster pace all the time. Alena felt irritated at Tiernan, but she had to admit that she was grateful to have him at her back right now.

It was dusk when they arrived at a small cluster of caves that Tiernan and Ian had chosen for their next place of refuge. They had to scramble up the side of the rock face about six feet, but even overly pregnant Elizabeth was somehow able to manage it with help from the others. Eagerly, they filed in one at a time through the four-foot by three-foot opening in the jagged mountainside. They were all hungry and spent. Elizabeth immediately passed out with fatigue. The blue child, Calab, curled up beside Elizabeth. No one said anything. They were too tired. Alena was glad to see that Tiernan and Ian had already stocked the place with firewood. Water wouldn't be a problem with all the rain cascading off of the top of the mountain in long thin streams. But then there was the problem of the creature. Would it come in after them?

Tiernan must have been contemplating the same thing for he began to make a fire outside the opening to the cave. It was hard to get it going with the rain, but the wood was good and dry, and eventually there was a fine roaring fire—the heat of which filtered into the cave and warmed them. Hopefully, it would keep that rothcha at bay, whatever it was. Alena wondered, however, if the fire might attract the Cephalopod monsters. She hoped not. Hopefully, they were far enough out of sight, hidden in the peaks of the mountains.

Many of her crew rummaged through their packs for a bite to eat. There wasn't much left which worried Alena. She hadn't seen a whole lot in the way of edibles on their journey in. Olivia and Gwen were both whimpering on either side of Kelly. Poor Kelly was trying to comfort both. They would be cramped, but at least they would be protected from the rain. Alena surveyed the group. Her eyes settled on Ian. He looked like death warmed over.

"Ian, when was the last time you had any sleep?" Alena asked him, but Ian only shrugged. Alena guessed that it had been several days, which meant Tiernan was in the same condition. She ordered them to take a rest.

"We need to keep watch, Alena." Tiernan argued.

"Jim will keep watch and tend to the fire," Alena answered. "Turq can take the next shift, Anthony the next, and then I will take a turn. I want everyone, except for Jim to get some rest. Jim, you wake Turq in a few hours when you need a break, alright?"

"Yes, Captain." Jim positioned himself near the cave entrance. Alena went to help Kelly with Gwen. She watched Sceria arrange herself near Tiernan and felt another pang of jealousy. She really was going to have to find a way to get Tiernan out of her head. He and Sceria were of the same kind after all. It was natural that they would be together. Sceria's child was most likely Tiernan's progeny. Alena would have to try harder to prevent any deeper attachment to this wild amber-orange eyed man. She grumbled to herself and turned away checking once more on Gwen, who was thankfully now sleeping. Soon everyone was sleeping except for Jim and herself. Alena made her way to him.

"Whatever is out there is evidently deadly, so it is probably a good idea if you keep that fire going."

Jim nodded. "Get some rest, Captain, you look pretty shot. Don't worry, there won't be anything getting past me." He grasped the spear shaped object that he had been working on the day before. Exhausted, Alena didn't have any problem falling into a deep dreamless sleep.

Some hours later Alena was awakened by something fiddling with her clothes. She sat up hastily and found herself face to face with Anthony.

"What are you doing?" Alena demanded.

"I've just come to wake you, Alena. It's your turn to keep watch," he answered with a maniacal grin.

"Yeah, right," she mumbled, not believing him for a second. Having him close to her made her feel creepy all over. "I'm up, Anthony, now back off."

"I thought I would just take your sleeping place, if you don't mind? No use sleeping in a cold spot when you already have one warmed up for me."

"Knock it off, Anthony. Go find your own spot. I'm not having you anywhere near Gwen."

Anthony hesitated, calculating his response. Alena didn't like the look of his eyes, or his demeanor, or his hot breath on her face. She waited, suddenly frightened. Someone rustled off to Alena's left which seemed to make Anthony reconsider whatever evil he had considered.

"Another time, then Alena," he whispered meaningfully and moved off.

Alena was immediately on her feet and heading for the cave opening. Anthony made her sick. She watched as Anthony positioned himself near the opposite wall near Ian. She didn't relax until she was sure that Anthony was asleep, his heavy breathing mingling with the others. She kept herself turned sideways in the cave opening so that she could see both inside the cave and into the darkness without. Not surprisingly, the fire had burned low with Anthony tending it, so Alena built it up again with fury.

Alena paced angrily within the cave opening. She had been wrong to give Anthony a shift. Anthony wasn't going to be of any use to them on this journey. He was a worthless parasite, a dead weight, a freeloader and worst of all, he was an enemy within. If they had been in any sort of civilized situation, Alena would have had him locked up, put away, removed. What could she do now? Someone would have to be watching Anthony every minute of every day. She grew tired of pacing and sat and stoked the glowing fire. It was comforting somehow.

Alena had no idea what the future would hold for them. Would they even last a week out here? Already her stomach gnawed with hunger, her feet were swollen and sore, and she felt more tired than she ever had. Alena knew that some of the others were feeling even worse. Had she brought them all out of the biome just to die? What kind of chance did they have out here with the Cephalopods looking for them, animals hunting them, little in the way of life's necessities, and an evil degenerate in their midst?

Alena looked up to see Tiernan making his way carefully through the sleeping forms toward her. He looked massive in the shadows, definitely all male. Alena felt her color rising. She was glad that he couldn't see her reddened cheeks in the dark, but maybe he could with those brilliant unnatural eyes of his. He sat beside her, which made Alena's insides churn with a nervous heat.

"Are you alright?"

"Well enough," she answered. "Why aren't you sleeping?"

"I don't need the same sleep as your kind."

"Well, I welcome your company then."

"I can see you are tired."

Alena wondered just what she could say to Tiernan about Anthony's behavior or any of her concerns, but Tiernan was perhaps already a bit too perceptive.

"You worry. Do not worry, Alena. We will be alright. Come, rest on my shoulder."

Was he serious? Did he think that she would snuggle up to him and do just that? Apparently, he did because he placed an arm around her. She found herself oddly comfortable, her head resting on his chest. She wanted to push away but felt herself giving in to the comfy warmth of him.

"Quit being nice to me," she managed to say. "I am angry at you right now."

"Why are you angry?"

"You are keeping things from me."

Tiernan only held her tighter. "I look out for you."

Alena squirmed loosening his hold a bit. "I don't need protecting! I need to know what I'm facing, so I can make wise decisions for myself and for everyone else."

"You are not like females of my kind."

Alena wondered what that was supposed to mean. "Are you insulting me?" she asked, growing bristly.

"No Alena. I like your strength."

"Then tell me what happened to Miriam and whatever else you didn't have time for yesterday. Tell me what in the world a rothcha is and why they are such a deadly threat to us? Tell me why you hate me so passionately at times and then other times you...?" Alena stopped. She wasn't sure she should be asking the last question. She was embarrassed. She was sure Tiernan could feel her body tense.

"Alena, it is not you that I hate..." he paused struggling to explain. "That... is all behind us. I will not hurt you. You are safe with me now."

His answer only made Alena more confused. But she also knew that she didn't want to pry anymore. She sighed. "It's okay, you don't have to explain. Just don't keep anything important from me. Tell me what happened while you and Ian were gone."

"You know most of the story, but there is something you must know. When Ian was able to move again, after the monsters had...What is the word?"

"Stunned him?"

"Yes, stunned him. We found a live monster. It was injured and came out from his craft that had gone down in the wind. Ian went…." Tiernan paused searching once again for the right word. "Crazy," he finally said, peering at Alena to make sure he had the word right.

She nodded. "Go on."

"He went crazy. He jumped onto the huge monster and beat it with a large rock until it died. Even when it was dead, he did not stop; He couldn't. I had to stop him. We needed to leave, before they found us." Tiernan paused again, but this time he was deep in thought. "Ian is very intelligent, but he is not well…"

"Yes, living in the biome has been very traumatic for most of us. Ian has suffered a great deal."

Tiernan nodded. "Yes. Ian suffers a great deal, even more than I do."

"I'm sorry. Why do you suffer?"

"I will tell you, in time, when I am ready." He hugged her to him tightly for a moment. "We came as fast as we could to camp, but that is when…"

"That is when you found Miriam. Tell me what you think happened to her."

"Terrible things happened to Miriam."

"Do you think it was the pale faced ones that killed her?"

Tiernan shook his head, he paused significantly before saying. "I think she was killed by someone who is still with us."

"What? How can that be?" Alena shivered.

"Miriam did not go with the pale faced ones. She probably tried to follow them. But someone followed Miriam."

"How do you know that?"

"There were... how do you say it? Tracks... returning to the caves. Large tracks..."

"So, you're saying one of the men?"

"Yes, Alena... Jim, Anthony, or the one you call Turq did terrible things to Miriam and then killed her."

"You mean... " Alena didn't want to say it. She didn't want to even think it. It had to be Anthony. Anthony was certainly capable of murder and rape, Jim was a possibility, but she didn't think so. Turq was the least likely of the three.

"I'm sorry to have to tell you terrible things."

"Thank you for telling me. It's important that I know so that I can protect the others." Alena became quiet, contemplating the disturbing information. Anthony was the horror of all horrors. What should she do? She couldn't just turn him loose. He would probably lead the Cephalopods right to them. There was the possibility of demanding justice be done with some sort of capital punishment, but Alena wasn't sure how she felt about having his blood on her hands. Whatever she decided to do, it wasn't going to be an easy decision, but one thing she did know; Anthony couldn't remain with them, not now, not ever especially not after what he had done. She shuddered, thinking of Anthony hovering over her just a little while ago. She berated herself again for giving Anthony a turn to keep watch. Who knows what he might have done with the opportunity.

"Are you alright?"

"Yes," Alena said while yawning. Being held by Tiernan was warm and cozy, not to mention far more of a temptation than she wanted to admit. She was going to have a hard time staying in control of her emotions snuggled up to him like this. She stretched, trying to move away from him a bit, but Tiernan didn't let her go.

"Let me finish your shift, Alena. You are tired."

"No, I'm okay. I want to know more about the rothcha. Do you think it is still out there?"

"I do not know. It does not like fire, but once it begins hunting it doesn't stop until it eats. We must turn it off our path."

Alena felt confusion wash over her. This was certainly not information that Tiernan would have learned in the biome. "How do you know this?" she asked warily.

Tiernan sighed. "Ian told me that you and your kind have come from the stars. Alena, this is my home, my world, a planet we call Temarria. I fought a rothcha once, and I don't want to do it again."

"This is your home planet?" Alena choked. "You share a planet with the Cephalopods?"

"We call them the Waratna. They have not always lived on my world. The Waratna took over our oceans and multiplied rapidly. They lay eggs, thousands of them at a time. After only a few years they have been able to destroy most of my people, but there are still some that survive."

"You mean you were invaded by them?"

Tiernan nodded. "At first they killed us by the millions. It wasn't until there were a few of us left that we became—how do you say it—experiments for them. They only mock us now. We are not star travelers. Their knowledge is far greater. We cannot fight them. There are too many. All that there is left for us to do is hide."

"You are taking us to your people, aren't you?" Alena suddenly demanded.

Tiernan's face colored. "Don't be angry, our journey will be a long and hard one, but the only hope we have is to make it to the hidden city of Camaranth. We cannot last out here. If the

Waratna do not find us, there are many other terrible creatures that will."

"How far is this city?"

"Many, many days."

Alena thought about what it would mean for them to make such a long journey, "How will my kind be received?"

"I do not know, but I will watch out for you, Alena, I promise.

"And what about the others?"

"I will do what I can for them, but your ways are not our ways."

"What is that supposed to mean?"

"You are tired; we will have much time for talking." Tiernan said with a sudden tenderness. "Please don't be angry, Alena, for we are many days away. Do not worry about what may never come. First we must survive."

Tiernan was right of course. She had plenty to worry about in the present. But while Tiernan's hidden city would provide refuge for Tiernan and Sceria, what did it mean for the rest of them? Alena couldn't help but be wary. They would certainly stand out among Tiernan's people, and it would be even worse for Turq, Genni, and Calab. But what other choice did they have? If what Tiernan said was true, they would be lucky to even survive the journey.

"Okay, Tiernan," she finally said. "I trust that you know what you're doing, but it's probably better that we keep this between us for the time being."

Tiernan agreed, looking relieved. He held Alena close, and they stared into the fire together. This coziness was a temptation that continued to be problematic. Alena was comfortable here, content to be with him. She acknowledged to herself that when she was with him, she didn't want to be anywhere else. But what did any of it mean? There was no denying that there was something between them, something that kept growing, something that Tiernan had become very careful about, but there was also Sceria to consider. Alena knew that at times in Earth's history there had been cultures where individuals had kept more than one committed partner at the same time. Was that Tiernan's way? She hoped not. She felt the weight of it terribly. Alena felt her eyelids growing heavy. Tiernan encouraged her to sleep. He whispered something about keeping watch for her and taking care of her. She rested her head more and more snuggly on his chest.

Chapter Fifteen

Alena awoke to the smell of something cooking. She was embarrassed to see that most everyone was up and moving around. She found that she lay in her old spot next to Gwen, who was also just waking. Whatever was cooking smelled quite interesting. She picked herself up and wandered over to the fire. Ian was there moving something around with a stick. He seemed happier than she had seen him in probably years.

"Look what Tiernan and I found this morning. He pointed to a dozen large eggs that he kept moving about in the coals at the outer edge of the fire. Sceria, Genni, and Calab kept coming in with handfuls of water which they sprinkled over the eggs. Amazed, Alena watched as the water sizzled and turned to steam.

"Where is Tiernan?" she asked, looking around. He was nowhere to be seen on this hazy morning.

"He and Turq are out foraging to find more for us to eat. I'm sure they will be back shortly." Ian studied Alena with speculation.

Anthony pushed past Alena, purposely bumping up against her. "Did you sleep well, Alena? You had sweet dreams, I'll bet." His eyes shone with malice, and he grinned before exiting the cave.

Alena did her best to ignore him. She started counting heads. Jim was rummaging through what remained of their provisions. Elizabeth sat near him, watching. Kelly discreetly nursed Olivia off to one side of the cave. Gwen finally sat up, rubbing her eyes. All were accounted for other than Tiernan and Turq. Relieved she turned back to the fire and helped Ian turn the eggs with another long stick. She caught a glimpse of Tiernan and Turq coming up the mountainside. She found herself delighted by the sight of them, one man bronze, and the other turquoise.

Tiernan and Turq brought berries and nuts with them. The nuts were hard to crack open and the berries were tart, but no one complained, except for Jim who still was rummaging in the packs. The eggs were a little odd tasting, but at least they were filling. Alena was grateful that at least they would not begin their travels hungry today.

The group traveled light and followed a swift winding stream for most of the day. There was no sign of the rothcha, thank goodness. Tiernan and Anthony went on ahead to find camp. Alena felt that was the best way to manage Anthony that day. Alena didn't want him near any of the women. She was concerned when Tiernan returned later in the day bruised and alone. He looked even wilder than the first day she had seen him. Alena found herself running to meet him.

"Are you alright? Where's Anthony?"

"Anthony is at camp."

"What happened?" She asked appraising his unnatural appearance.

Tiernan's amber-orange eyes blazed with fire. "I'm not sorry, Alena. He—deserved it. He said some terrible things."

"Yes, I am sure he did deserve it, but look at you. You're a mess."

"It was worth it."

"Tiernan, I can't have you getting injured. I need you."

"Anthony is worse than a Waratna."

Alena put a hand on his arm. "Are you alright?"

"Yes," he said, finally meeting her gaze. "But Anthony is not. I do not know if he is alive or dead. I did not stop to see whether he lived when I laid him out upon the ground."

Tiernan was still obviously incensed from his tussle with Anthony. Alena wondered what Anthony could have said to make Tiernan so furious. The group took a short break to rest and to give Kelly and Sceria an opportunity to care for their babies. Tiernan seemed to want to be left alone and stood in the woods apart from the group.

"Where's Anthony?" Kelly asked, concerned.

"It seems that Tiernan and Anthony had an all-out scuffle. Tiernan left him lying on the ground. We are not quite sure in what state. Tiernan said he may be dead."

"I for one hope he is dead," Ian said, joining them. "Mark my words it will be either us or him. You watch and see."

"There's something that I need to talk to the two of you about when we can find some time alone," Alena informed them.

"If it's about Anthony and what Tiernan and I found in the woods, I already know, Alena," Ian answered.

"I need some help deciding what to do."

"Hopefully, Tiernan has made that decision for us," Ian said slowly.

"What are you both talking about?" Kelly questioned.

"We'll talk about it at camp tonight," Alena told them brusquely.

Kelly and Ian both nodded in agreement. Alena watched Sceria approaching the reticent Tiernan. Soon Sceria and Tiernan were conversing heatedly. They argued loudly in their complicated language, but none of the rest of the group could understand a word they were saying. Sceria was pleading furiously through tears. Tiernan's voice only boomed at her with anger and betrayal. And then they were silent. The whole group was silent until Alena encouraged them once again to move out. Sceria hung back away from Tiernan walking close to Genni. Alena wondered just what was going on between them, and what if anything it had to do with Anthony.

It was about an hour and a half later that they arrived at camp. Anthony, unfortunately, was sitting to one side looking dazed and beaten, but also scheming and detestable. He glared at Tiernan hatefully but said nothing. Kelly went to look after his wounds, but he only pulled away and cursed her. Anthony was doing his best to isolate himself from everyone else. He obviously didn't have a single sympathizer among their odd group.

The camp consisted of a large rock shelf that towered over them. It was open on all sides except for the rock face behind them and the shelf above. Alena surveyed it warily. It certainly wasn't going to give them the protection that they had had on previous nights, but it would have to do. They would have daylight for a few hours yet.

They speared fish for dinner. Turq was quite good at it, much to everyone's delight, after Jim had finally been convinced to relinquish his spear to him, that is. Alena noticed that Jim wasn't dealing very well with Turq or Tiernan for that matter. He seemed threatened, even jealous. If things continued as they were, she would have to do something about it. Turq was able to spear almost a dozen fish himself before letting someone else have a try. It was then that Alena, Kelly, and Gwen were given their first lesson by Genni and Calab on how to clean fish. Gwen grew immediately squeamish about the whole thing; Alena managed lamely, while Kelly seemed born for the task, but it felt good to work side by side for their survival.

Tiernan and Ian built a fire, while Sceria cared for her baby and Elizabeth cared for Olivia. Elizabeth didn't look so good. Her face was pale and thin, and she looked positively worn out. Alena wondered how much longer it would be before it was Elizabeth's time. It couldn't be long by the sight of her.

They roasted the tasty fish on sticks and nibbled on berries that they had gathered on their travels that day. When Alena had eaten enough to stave off her almost continuous hunger, she went off by herself to wash up in the stream. She was badly in need of a bath. They all were. She could feel several pairs of eyes following her; Tiernan's were definitely among them, but so were Anthony's. She splashed water onto her face and arms. It felt cool and refreshing. She wasn't about to bathe with everyone in proximity, but she decided it wouldn't hurt to give her hair a wash.

Alena struggled to unbraid her thick hair. It was matted and knotted and full of debris. When she had finished, it was cleaner but still a hopeless mess. She finger-combed it the best she could and braided it up again. Having a clean head improved her mood tremendously, but it only seemed to dampen Tiernan's mood, and he stayed sulkily away from her for the whole rest of the evening. Alena wondered what was up with him and decided that whatever it was, it had to do with Anthony. She wondered once again what Anthony had said to Tiernan to put him in such a foul mood? Whatever it had been, she was sure it was filled with half-truths and downright lies. If Tiernan was stupid enough to believe anything Anthony said, then he deserved to be morose. She couldn't think of anything in her own personal behavior that could cause such a shift in Tiernan, so she chose to ignore him also, although it caused her more pain than she wanted to admit.

Alena divided those who were able into shifts to keep watch that night. The one glaring exception was Anthony, and Alena could read from the other's expressions that it had not gone unnoticed. Anthony stared at her knowingly with a calculated expression. He was a loose weapon, ready to go off at any moment. Alena knew it would be one of the hardest things she ever did, but she would have to devise some way to get rid of him. There was no sense in letting all the others be put in harm's way on Anthony's account.

Quietly, Alena sought out Kelly and carefully related what she suspected about Anthony and Miriam. Of course, Kelly was mortified. The news was an additional burden since Anthony was the father of Kelly's child. Alena didn't know how Kelly lived with that horrible fact. She left Kelly to mourn and contemplate all that she had told her.

Although Tiernan was still angry and brooding, Alena was glad when he placed himself between Anthony and the female members of the group that evening when they bedded down for the night. Anthony and Tiernan made no attempt to hide their bitter contempt for each other.

Tiernan didn't speak to her for three days. He had done what she had asked him to do, but he had made no attempt to be close to her or engage in any type of conversation. He had led them for the last three days with hardly a word. Alena knew that Tiernan was depressed, but what about she could not begin to conceive. Alena was only keenly aware of the heartbreak in the depths of those amber-orange eyes. She had tried a few times to console him, but he had rudely pulled away from her on both occasions and turned away. If that's how things were going to be, so be it, but it had also made Alena more wary about following Tiernan to this hidden city of his. Would she simply be trading one type of captivity for another? If she hadn't heard the Cephalopod ships on several occasions, she may have reconsidered following their present course.

After almost a week of traveling, they were all hungry and spent. Walking all day for several days on end without the proper amount of food was taking a terrible toll on all of them. Muscles ached, feet were bloodied and blistered, and skin was burned by the sun and the wind. Today had been the most difficult of all. The winds had been relentless. They swirled about their bodies like angry demons, and the sinister sky had taken on an austere and threatening appearance that didn't look at all like it should. By the end of the day, they could barely walk against the force of the wind, and to make matters worse, Elizabeth's labor pains had started.

It was with relief that they finally reached their destination on the other side of the mountain. At least here they were somewhat protected from the wind inside the large crevasse that opened-up into a sort of smallish series of rooms. Alena couldn't be sure, but the weather was shaping up to be very much like it had been more than a week ago when they had been trapped in the biome with the hellish wind and sheets of rain. Whatever the case, it was going to be a giant of a storm.

Elizabeth's pains were coming more quickly now, and she was as pale as the cerulean sky. Kelly gave Alena a look that could only mean trouble. Alena barked out the orders to set up camp, and they did what they could to make Elizabeth more comfortable. Jim was practically in a rage. Alena knew it was mostly because he was worried about Elizabeth, but his actions were still alarming. When Genni kneeled next to Elizabeth and tried to help soothe her, Jim screamed at Alena, "Get that freak away from her. I don't want her near Elizabeth."

"Calm down, Jim," Kelly snapped at him. "Elizabeth needs all the support she can get right now, and Genni is certainly being much more helpful than you are."

But this only made Jim more agitated, and he tried to physically remove Genni from Elizabeth's side. Although usually calm, Turq grabbed Jim's arms and pinned them behind him before wrestling him to the ground. Jim struggled until he was almost as blue as Turq in the face.

"Get him off—get the turquoise fiend off," he growled.

Elizabeth was sobbing now. Alena helped Genni to her feet all the while encouraging Jim to calm down, but Jim just grew more upset, while Elizabeth sobbed even harder.

"Alright that's enough, Jim," Alena ordered. "Tiernan, will you help Turq take Jim outside where he can cool off?" Alena followed the struggling threesome out of the crevasse into the stiff wind where Turq finally released him. Jim took a swing at Turq but found himself held fast by Tiernan. All three were big powerful men, and Alena felt a bit intimidated standing there among them. She placed her hands on her hips and stood there stubbornly, looking at their angry faces.

"Jim, I'm only going to tell you this once. If you want to have any chance of getting back in there with Elizabeth, then you have to stand down, right now!"

Jim's face gave her an ugly expression, but he finally nodded in agreement.

"Okay, Tiernan, you can let him go," Alena told Tiernan wearily.

Jim wrenched his arms away from Tiernan roughly and spat. "I don't want them in there, Captain. I don't want them touching her," he growled.

"You don't want who touching her? Elizabeth is going to be lucky enough to even survive. Look around, Jim. These conditions aren't exactly sanitary. She needs all the help she can get."

"I don't want any help from them."

"I don't know what your problem is, but Elizabeth needs you to be calm. You're not making things better; you're making things worse, and she needs you."

"I don't want the freaks in there," he growled again.

Turq laid a hand on Alena's shoulder. "It's okay, Cap'n.

Alena gave Turq a weak smile. "You're a good man, Turq," she whispered patting his arm. "You deserve better." Alena turned back to Jim. "We are not finished with this, Jim. I will respect your wishes for Elizabeth's sake, but I want you to know that I don't find your actions or attitude acceptable in the least."

Jim, looking relieved, moved determinedly toward the crevasse. Alena stepped in front of him. "You are not going back in there until I know that you are calm and in control. I'm going to check on Elizabeth. You are going to stay out here with Tiernan until I come for you. Is that understood?"

Jim's face flushed with color, but he said, "Yes, Captain."

Alena motioned to Turq, "Come with me."

They made their way back into the crevasse. Alena noticed that they had moved Elizabeth into the last "room." Kelly and Gwen were the only ones with her.

"How's she doing?" Alena asked soberly.

"She's doing well enough. She keeps asking for Jim," Kelly answered grimly.

"Tell her that Jim will be here soon."

"Alena, I need your help," Kelly's face was all concern.

"I'll be here. I've just got a few things to straighten out first," Alena sighed. It was going to be a very long night.

She went back into the other room, Gwen followed. All eyes were upon her. Sceria's practically brimmed with poison.

"Alright everyone, let's be calm in all of this. Whatever Jim's prejudices, I can assure you that I don't share them, and I find them unacceptable. But for Elizabeth's sake and Elizabeth's sake alone, I would ask that you all respect Jim's wishes at this time." She looked around at the distrustful faces. "Please, just do what you can to set up camp. There is a huge storm coming in. We will need food and supplies probably for several days, at least, by the looks of things."

Everyone seemed bitter and uptight, but Genni soberly nodded in agreement, and the rest followed suit, even Anthony seemed cooperative.

Alena left them and went back out into the fierce wind to face Jim. He was still looking all fired up, but not as fired up as Tiernan. What was going on now, she wondered?

"Alright, what's happened?" Alena questioned.

But neither of them would respond. They both just shifted uncomfortably. This didn't sit well with Alena. She stared down both of them like an angry lioness until neither would look at her.

"Elizabeth needs you, Jim, so you had better go to her, but so help me if I hear any more foul language or insults coming out of your mouth about any member of our party, I will have you back out here so fast that you won't have time to breathe, is that understood?"

"Yes, Captain."

"Go to her, then."

Jim hurried into the crevasse. Tiernan started to follow before Alena stopped him. He seemed to recoil at her touch. Alena didn't know what to think as he glared at her savagely for a moment with those piercing amber-orange eyes. It was almost like she was facing a gravely injured wild animal that was ready to lash out at her, and then he seemed to regain his composure.

"Look Tiernan," she said, "I don't know what I have done to make you so... so..." Alena couldn't think of a word to describe Tiernan at that moment; "enraged," was the word she finally settled on, "but I really need your help right now." She placed her hand on his arm. He trembled like a wild horse, but did not pull away, while the wind swirled about them.

"Tiernan, I need you to take charge of everyone. I'm asking you because I trust you and also because it needs to be someone who is not of my kind. We'll need food and water for several days. Kelly is asking for my help, and it may be a while before I'm available."

Tiernan stared at her crazily like she had asked him to start the forest on fire.

"Will you help me?" Alena pleaded.

He nodded slowly. "Are you sure that you want me to take charge?" he asked, his voice full of uncertainty.

"Of course, I'm sure."

Something in Tiernan's face changed. He seemed to relax all of the sudden. "Alright," he agreed.

"Thanks and one more thing. Please pay close attention to Anthony. I don't trust him. I don't want him near any of the women."

Tiernan gave her an odd look but nodded again in agreement. They entered the crevasse together with Tiernan following close behind. When Alena had everyone's attention, she told them that Tiernan was in charge. "I don't want to hear about anyone giving him any trouble," she said glaring at Anthony in particular. "Whatever Tiernan says until I return, is the law. Is that understood?" Alena didn't wait for an answer from anyone. Sighing, she made her way to Elizabeth, Jim, and Kelly in the back room.

Elizabeth was having a difficult time of it. Her face was covered with huge beads of perspiration, and she was deathly pale. Jim clung to her side. Kelly's faced was all pinched up with concern. Alena pulled Kelly aside.

"How is everything going?"

"Everything is progressing as it should," Kelly answered. "She is starting to dilate and having contractions about every 5 minutes."

"Then what's wrong?"

"She's very weak. Alena, I don't think she can possibly survive this."

"You said that we could do this C-section. We've made all the preparations...."

Kelly cut her off. "She is too weak; we don't have the proper tools to keep her alive. We'll only attempt a C-section to save the babies once all hope of saving Elizabeth is past."

"Babies...?"

"If Jim is indeed the father, then there is definitely more than one child."

"Does Jim know there isn't much hope?"

"I haven't told him, but I think that he knows," Kelly pressed her lips together in a deep frown.

"What can we do?"

"Just hope that by some miracle that she will pull through."

Chapter Sixteen

Elizabeth labored all night and into the morning while the wind howled angrily outside. She screamed with pain as the first child arrived, a healthy sturdy son. His squalling cry pierced through the early morning hours, waking all that slept. Elizabeth smiled with exhaustion and relief. "Please let me hold him," she whispered weakly, but then doubled over in pain, whimpering. The baby went to Alena, instead.

"There's another one coming, Elizabeth," Kelly told her. "I know you are super tired, but you can do this. Push with the contraction—push."

"Another...? I can't; I just can't."

"Yes, you can, honey, come on."

Elizabeth tried to push, but her weakened efforts were fruitless. After a long time trying, there was still no child. Something was wrong—very wrong—and there was way too much blood. Elizabeth grew paler, and she seemed barely conscious.

"We're losing her." Kelly said desperately.

Jim begged Elizabeth to hold on, "Please, please, don't leave me."

Alena was suddenly conscious of Tiernan standing by her side. "Alena," he said, "Genni can help if you will let her."

"Get him out," Jim cried angrily.

Tiernan didn't need any encouragement and sadly turned to leave.

"Wait," Alena said just above a whisper. "Jim, Elizabeth is failing—If Genni can help, we need to let her try."

"No, I don't want them near her."

"Jim, listen to Alena." Kelly encouraged. "I have done all I can—there is nothing more that I can do. Perhaps Genni has some knowledge that I do not, but there is no other hope for Elizabeth."

Jim put his face in his huge hands and wept. "No, I don't want them here."

Alena let out a noise of complete exasperation. "Go get Genni!" she said to Tiernan. "Sorry, Jim, I'm not going to stand here and watch her die if there is anything that I can do to stop it."

Jim let out a cry of betrayal but did no more to protest. He clung to Elizabeth. Genni was waiting at the door. She hurried into the room and quickly assessed the situation. Alena could see from Genni's face that her prognosis was also not very good, but she hurried to Elizabeth's side and placed something under her tongue. Whatever it was immediately helped with Elizabeth's stamina, because she began to perk up. Genni laid her hands on Elizabeth's belly and felt for the baby. Kelly was saying something to her about the baby's position being all wrong. While Genni nodded in agreement. Elizabeth screamed in agony as Genni adeptly reached inside of her and repositioned the baby. Elizabeth nearly passed out from the pain of it, but with the next contraction she was pushing again.

When the baby arrived, it was blue and limp, but both Genni and Kelly worked the little thing into breathing again. This one was much smaller than her brother, and her weak little cry sounded fairly pathetic. Kelly carefully cleaned out the little mouth, while Genni turned back to helping Elizabeth. Elizabeth was not conscious and barely had a pulse. She had lost a lot of blood. Genni placed some more of whatever it was under Elizabeth's tongue and began pressing on her belly.

Kelly encouraged Alena to take the babies out of the room. Alena handed the little boy to Tiernan and reached for the girl. Quietly, she and Tiernan left the room. Alena was exhausted from being up all night and without meaning to she leaned on Tiernan for support. She was grateful that Sceria and Gwen were there to greet them, and she relinquished her little bundle to Sceria while Tiernan handed the boy to Gwen. Alena felt the earth coming up to meet her, but it was Tiernan who caught her and set her down on the ground.

"You are tired, my little wootchka," she heard him say gently and thought it quite strange. Yes, she was tired, but she couldn't sleep until she had news of Elizabeth. Tiernan brought her some kind of herb, and she chewed it eagerly. The herb tasted medicinal and bitter, but she swallowed it anyway. It had been a long time since she had eaten anything. As Alena sat and waited, she suddenly became aware of the storm raging outside. She had blocked out the sound of it in her efforts to focus on Elizabeth. The wind howled eerily through the crevasse, turning little piles of dust into miniature dust devils. The rain sounded like the roar of a great waterfall. At least the immense storm would keep the Cephalopods off their trail for a time.

Alena wearily began taking in her surroundings. Sceria was already trying to get Elizabeth's little tiny girl to nurse from her. Alena smiled to herself. She wondered what Jim would think of Sceria suckling his child. Gwen was simply happy to be cradling the boy and was cooing over him. Ian, Turq, and Calab were found stoking the fire. Ian held Olivia gingerly on one knee away from the smoke. A strange animal roasted above the hot coals which Turq turned every so often. Whatever the thing was, it smelled delicious, and Alena's stomach growled in anticipation. She wondered what her kind would think of eating such a creature. Certainly, Jim would have no part in it. Fish was one thing, but something as large as a boar was quite another. Ian and Gwen didn't seem to be disturbed in the least, but what about Anthony? She glanced around the room. Where was Anthony, anyway? She got to her feet hesitantly.

She was shocked to find Anthony bound and gagged and shoved in a chasm off the main room. He was struggling against his bonds defiantly, and his cold gray eyes shone with malice. Alena felt Tiernan come up behind her.

"I caught him creeping around last night. He was giving Sceria a bad time. You told me to keep him clear of the women. His actions toward her were all wrong. This was all I could do."

Alena nodded removing Anthony's gag. "What do you have to say for yourself, Anthony?"

But Anthony only spewed hatred and insults from his venomous mouth, so Alena was obliged to replace the gag. Anthony struggled and kicked at her with his bound feet. Tiernan stepped between them. Alena shook her head tiredly, wondering how it was possible for someone to become so degenerate and uncivilized.

Sometime later Kelly wearily made her way into the room and sat next to Alena.

"How is Elizabeth?" Alena asked.

"She's lost a lot of blood. Only time will tell."

"Do you think she is going to make it?"

"Perhaps with some rest, but I'm not optimistic, Alena."

"How's Jim?"

"He's exhausted, but finally sleeping. I didn't want to leave Genni in there by herself until I was sure. She'll monitor Elizabeth for the next several hours and wake me if something comes up. How are the babies?"

"They are in good hands," Alena answered motioning to Gwen, who now cradled the baby girl and to Sceria, who was now nursing the boy.

Kelly nodded with a faint smile. "It's time I looked after my own little one and then got some sleep. You should get some sleep too. Thank you for your help, Alena."

"You're welcome," she whispered more to herself as Kelly went to get Olivia from Ian.

Alena watched Tiernan while he held and rocked Sceria's baby. With a pang of jealousy, she wondered once more if the baby was his child. She found herself wondering if she would ever have a child of her own. She pushed the thought from her mind and tried to get comfortable. She closed her eyes and listened to the sound of the rain outside.

Alena did not know how long she had been asleep, but she was aroused by angry voices. Jim was obviously awake and hostile.

"What is she doing with my son?" Jim's voice was cold and threatening.

"Stand away from her or you will be sorry." Tiernan's timbered voice cut the air like a dagger.

Wearily, Alena pulled herself to her feet. Honestly, it was like babysitting a bunch of prison inmates. Sceria's eyes were narrowed and cat-like; she practically hissed at Jim as he ignored Tiernan and stepped menacingly toward her. Alena dived into the middle of the fray with her own temper.

"Jim back off. You may not know it yet, but you owe everyone enormously. I'm not going to let you repay their kindness with bigotry and hostility. Stand down or so help me, I'll have you tied up with Anthony."

Jim regarded her with an ill face. "How could you? I can't believe that you prefer the likes of them over your own kind. You betray us, Captain," Jim spat at the ground with contempt.

"It's not about us and them, Jim. You need to get that through your thick head. We all need each other to survive. Elizabeth would be dead already without help from those you choose to berate and criticize." Alena took Jim's son from Sceria. "Here Jim, take your boy and nurse him yourself. I think that you'll soon find that you're going to have to choose between your prejudice and the survival of your family."

Jim's eyes simmered with anger, but he chose to let the matter end. He took the child with him and went back to Elizabeth. Everyone in the room was staring at her. Alena sighed and turned away from all the glittering eyes. Things were unraveling rapidly with Jim and Anthony's antics. It was going to take a lot to keep them all together. She tried not to show it, but Jim's comments had disturbed her. He should know best of all where her loyalties lay and that was with what remained of her crew, but that didn't mean that she didn't feel responsible for the others. She owed a lot to all of them. Besides, she didn't know if her crew could even survive out here without their alien companions.

Alena still needed more sleep, but she knew that sleep would never come now. She watched with envy the soft rise and fall of Kelly's chest as she peacefully slept. She shifted uncomfortably, still feeling several sets of eyes upon her. It was lonely being a leader. It always had been. She had given up a lot in her personal relationships to become a captain. Her associations with men had especially suffered. She knew her confidence and her drive were intimidating to them, not that it mattered. Her loyalty to her duties and responsibilities had left little time for intimate relationships. There had never been anyone that she was particularly interested in, anyway.

Certainly, there had been men that had sought after her, but none that could see beyond her physical shell. Alena had wanted none of that—at least not then anyway. She found her eyes drifting to Tiernan. Her cheeks flushed warmly at the sight of him, but he purposefully avoided her gaze. Alena sighed inwardly, wondering what she had done to sour Tiernan's attraction to her. She was surprised at how much she missed it. Alena wondered if it had anything to do with her kind. Undeniably, both Jim and Anthony weren't the best representations of her race. Alena felt the horror of it pressing upon her. She had no idea what to do with Anthony, and her indecision was probably causing some to question her leadership ability. She made her way down the long crevasse away from the others so that she could think.

A short time later she was summoned to supper by Tiernan. The large boar-like animal they had been roasting was cooked to perfection. Alena felt her hunger keenly. She also felt her crew's eyes upon her. Jim's eyes glittered intensely. Alena knew that they watched to see what she would do. To her partaking of the animal was merely a choice for survival, but some of the others might not see it that way. The eating of meat had become immoral and uncivilized over time and finally illegal on their home planet. It was an abomination to murder an animal and a crime to use it for food.

Alena thanked Tiernan wearily as he offered the first piece to her. Jim howled with disgust and hailed her a traitor as she ate the first delectable bite. Ignoring Jim's outburst, she encouraged the others to eat.

"It's delicious! Please eat! We all need to gain strength for our journey."

Ian was the first to follow suit and then Kelly. Jim shook his head in revulsion, but even Jim was forced to relent after a few days, especially out of concern for Elizabeth who remained very weak without any improvement. There was simply no other food source aside from the dandelion-like plants that grew in the cracks and an occasional insect that was found scuttling along the floor, not with the storm raging outside. Jim in desperation had finally even consented to let Sceria nurse his son and daughter, although he obviously preferred Kelly to help him with the matter. Elizabeth had been too weak to give much nourishment to the twins, and they floundered without proper sustenance. Kelly simply couldn't nurse three children by herself.

Anthony on the other hand refused to eat. It was after several long days that Alena finally understood his determined lack of interest. On the fourth day after being bound, Anthony disappeared. He had let himself waste away enough to wriggle free from his bonds. He left evidence that he hadn't been able to get too far with the raging storm, because food and supplies began to disappear, but no matter how deeply they searched for him, he was never found.

The storm had given them all time to rest and Turq the opportunity to show off his talent at moccasin making. From the one slain animal Turq had been able to help each of them fashion a pair of shoes made of hide and sinew along with several weapons made of bone. No part of the animal was wasted. Alena had complete admiration for Turq's apparent skills. What type of world had Turq, Genni, and Calab come from? It was nothing like her own modern world of metal, she decided, not with Turq's obvious ability to live off the land. After some awkward attempts at communicating with Turq, she was able to determine that Turq and Genni's planet had been raided much like Tiernan's, and they had been stolen away to live out their lives in the Cephalopod zoo. What a horrible waste of life for Turq's kind.

After another day, the rain and wind had begun to subside, but the sound of the storm had been quickly replaced by the sound of an occasional searching Cephalopod ship and another sound, a piercing feral scream that seemed to echo through the small rooms of the crevasse over and over and over again.

"What is it?" Alena asked Tiernan after Sceria scrambled into a corner and covered her ears.

"A creature that even the Waratna fear." Tiernan answered with an eerie calm. "She is the veratnil, a beast with claws as long as a grown man and a beak as sharp as a Comaranthene sword. Her wings are larger than most of those ships that search for us."

"She?"

"Only the female scream."

A shower of fine rocks and sand began to come down upon all of them from above.

"What is happening?" Alena whispered, aware that the room had gone silent and all eyes in the room were thick with fear.

"She hunts for us. She will claw through the rock to get at us if there are young to feed."

"But how does she know we are here?"

"The veratnil have a keen sense of smell, especially for blood. She searches for Elizabeth."

"What can we do?" Alena tried hard to hide the panic in her voice but was unsuccessful.

Tiernan studied her face for what seemed a long time, finally deciding to just be straightforward with her. "There is nothing we can do. She will break through and take one of us, perhaps two. Those who are left can escape, but those who are slow or too young will not."

"What? You mean…"

He nodded miserably. "I'm sorry, Alena. We should get ready to leave."

Jim had gone pale with the sudden revelation. Obviously, he knew that Elizabeth was the least likely to survive this ordeal.

"Wait, can't we fight this thing?" he demanded.

"No." Tiernan answered.

"What do you mean, no?"

"A veratnil's body is covered with hard scales from nose to tail. It is suicide to fight her. She will cut you in half before you can blink."

Jim's eyes narrowed. "You're just a filthy coward. I intend to stand and fight until the bitter end if I have to."

Tiernan just shook his head sadly and turned away. "I'm sorry, Jim. You choose death for yourself. There can be no…" Tiernan searched for the right word, "heroes here."

Jim still wouldn't let it go. "Why should we listen to this creep? What makes him think he knows so much about this creature anyway?" He kicked at the side of the crevasse while everyone turned away.

The veratnil continued without ceasing to rip and tear at the rock and scream her shrill cry while they made frantic preparations to escape. Elizabeth was still too weak to even stand on her feet and would have to be carried if she was moved at all. They decided to shift her from the furthest room into the main room with everyone else. She hardly seemed aware of what was going on around her as the sand and bits of rock rained down upon them, but in moving Elizabeth, they moved the veratnil as well. The beast was indeed driven by the smell of Elizabeth's blood. She was enraged at the thicker slabs of stone and having a more difficult time of it, but Alena knew that they had only delayed the inevitable.

For an hour the beast dug and clawed while they huddled together at the furthest point of the crevasse from the creature. They were running out of time judging by the amount of rock that lay strewn like a minefield before them.

"Alright everyone, be ready," Alena managed to say as one long, razor-sharp talon breached the crevasse. The creature made shorter work of it now that it had a claw hold. Alena, Tiernan, and Jim carefully slipped Elizabeth into the hammock sling that they had carried her with and lay the baby girl next to her. Jim looked around in desperation for someone to help him with Elizabeth and his tiny daughter. He had alienated almost everyone with his bigotry and hatred. Alena doubted anyone would step forward and help him, but amazingly Turq did just that. Despite all that Jim had done and said, Turq generously took his regular place at the other side of the sling to his own detriment and to the loss of his own bighearted family. Alena studied Genni and Calab, but there was no anger or sense of betrayal in their determined faces. Gwen shivered next to them with fright but sheltered Jim and Elizabeth's baby son.

The veratnil had worked an entire set of raven black talons all the way through the rock and everyone shrank at the sight of them. They were terrible to see. Alena didn't want to see the rest of the creature, based on the deadly dark shiny scales that covered the beast's entire foot. What type of mythical nightmare of a creature were they about to behold? They huddled tighter together. Olivia wailed with fright. Desperately the veratnil raked at the rock and then paused quite suddenly, lifting completely off the crevasse with a dreadful cry. The back draft from her wings swirled the sand and debris about them in a mighty wind, and then they heard another sound, the drone of a ship, close at hand.

It took Alena a moment to understand that Tiernan was yelling for them to go now—to escape—to flee. Frantically they stumbled over rocks to the entryway and raced through the opening with Sceria in the lead. Alena would not leave until all her people were out, which made Tiernan crazy, so he picked her up and practically shoved her through the opening in the crevasse. Tiernan had her by the hand, and they were running for their lives. Alena heard the creature cry with rage far above and behind her and the sickening tear of metal. She turned to see the most horrifying nightmare she had ever witnessed. Whether the veratnil was protecting her young or whether the creature had developed a taste for the Cephalopods she did not know, but the immense creature had hold of an alien ship and was ripping it apart in midair. Alena didn't envy the Cephalopods in that horrific moment. One look at that deadly half-dragon, half-pterodactyl-like creature made her heart stand still and her blood run cold with fear.

The ship obviously no longer had the ability to fly and the creature simply let go of it and let it crash on the rocky cliffs below. Alena watched as the ghastly veratnil descended, settling swiftly upon the ship and scooped out its gooey Cephalopod contents. Alena felt her stomach lurch with horror. What manner of creature was this? She faced forward, never once turning back again, as they stumbled headlong through a jungle of vines and trees. They ran for a long time, until they could hardly breathe and they could hear the cries of the veratnil no longer.

Chapter Seventeen

As Alena panted for breath and waited for everyone to rejoin them, she became aware that Tiernan still had tight hold of her hand. He seemed suddenly aware of it too and pressed her hand to his lips. They regarded each other for a long moment before he let go of her. She read in his face relief and deep affection but also grief and pain.

"What is it that pains you about me?" she started to ask, but then Ian found them and Sceria next, followed by Kelly and Olivia. A few were ahead of them, but most came up from behind and filled in the spaces around them. The last to arrive were Jim and Turq carrying Elizabeth and her baby girl. The narrow escape had been hard on Elizabeth, and her breathing was very shallow. Kelly attended to her immediately, while Ian took charge of Olivia. Alena surveyed all of them, making sure all the others were well and accounted for. She wondered briefly what had become of Anthony but shrugged it off. Anthony was no longer her concern. Their biggest concern was to find food and shelter for the night and not become food for the beasts of this wild and dangerous planet.

It was no wonder that Tiernan and Sceria seemed made of stronger stuff. With all the horrible things that inhabited their planet, how could they not be? Alena was tired and still winded from their mad race through the jungle. But as exhausted as they all were, they couldn't afford to linger, not with Elizabeth's ability for attracting veratnils. Tiernan seemed to come to the same conclusion, and he was up on his feet as soon as Alena glanced in his direction. Alena encouraged him to lead out while she took her usual place somewhere to the rear of the group. She could tell that Tiernan loathed this arrangement, but he went along with it anyway.

They traveled along the fast-moving narrow river. Tiernan kept the group moving at a terrific pace that only seemed to increase with time. Alena was having a hard time keeping up, let alone Kelly and Gwen who carried babies, and Turq and Jim who carried Elizabeth. Tiernan and Sceria were getting too far ahead, and only Ian seemed to be able to keep up with them. Alena called to Ian, asking him to slow the pace. Ian called ahead to Tiernan who immediately complied, but it wasn't long until he returned to the previous furious pace. Why was Tiernan in such a big hurry? It wasn't for their safety, she was certain. Tiernan didn't seem to be bothered by the fact that everyone was falling behind. What was up ahead? She called to Ian to slow the pace, who called to Tiernan once more. They repeated this pattern all afternoon until finally the sound of the river turned into a roar that drowned out their voices.

Alena finally met up with Tiernan at the base of a gigantic waterfall. He sat waiting for the stragglers of the group to arrive, of which Alena had made herself the last. Teasingly, Alena punched him in the shoulder as she came upon him.

"What's your hurry this afternoon?"

Her question was answered as soon as she crossed with the others into a large hollowed out cavern behind the falls. Tiernan's eyes crinkled in the corners into an amused smile as Alena gazed in wonder at what lay before her. The cavern was packed with supplies and not just any supplies: dried and preserved food of many varieties, vessels that held liquids, clothing and blankets of intricate weave and design, tools of all shapes, and weapons of curious metal that gleamed when they were unsheathed. Where had it all come from? All eyes were upon Tiernan as she turned to him with the question that everyone wanted to ask.

"What is this place?"

"We have reached the Falls of Avantioch, the furthest outpost of my people. I helped to stock this position, myself, only twelve moons ago."

This bit of information seemed too much for anyone to absorb, even harder than coming upon a fully stocked cavern. Jim was the first to speak up among the murmur of excited voices.

"What do you mean your people? You mean there are others like you on this planet? This is your planet?"

Alena almost chuckled with the incredulity that shown on Jim's face. She and Tiernan had kept that particular secret successfully between them until now. There were others that seemed almost as incredulous as Jim, but Ian was not one of them. Alena wondered about this but let it go. She had many questions for Tiernan. If he had been here twelve moons ago, then that meant he had been in captivity less than a year. She realized that she knew absolutely nothing of his capture and how he had come to be imprisoned with them in the biome. What had brought him out here into this wilderness? If this was the furthest outpost from Tiernan's civilization, how far were they from the hidden city of Camaranth? Were there weeks still or merely days?

"How far are we from Camaranth?" she questioned aloud.

The question made Jim look at Alena with the same incredulity that he had at Tiernan's remark, and his face reddened noticeably. But Alena noticed that Sceria's did as well.

"You knew that this was his home planet?" Jim asked with exasperation.

Alena chose not to answer Jim but waited calmly for Tiernan's response.

"Almost a moon," was his reply, which meant that they were at least 24 days away.

"Alena," Kelly stepped toward her, "is Tiernan taking us to his people?"

Alena faced everyone's astonishment with complete calm. She would have liked to have revealed these things to all of them in a different way, but there was no turning back now.

"Yes," was all she said, before everyone erupted with questions and concerns at the same moment.

Jim was louder than the rest. "You can't be serious?"

Alena reddened slightly but held her ground.

"I think our best chance at survival is among Tiernan's and Sceria's people. You will have to make that decision for yourself, but that is where I intend to go." She paused rubbing her forehead with weariness. "You'll have some time to think on it for a few weeks yet, but the most important thing to do right now is set up camp and get organized." Alena turned to Tiernan. "Tiernan already knows what supplies are here. I expect you all to follow any instructions that he gives you and be thankful for any of these provisions that he chooses to share with you. That is all I have to say about it."

Alena was relieved when Tiernan took charge and the rest chose to follow him, even Jim. The travelers ate dried venison and fruit, washed down with a tankard of sweet wine. Perhaps it was the spray from the falls, perhaps it was the sweet, tangy wine, or perhaps it was the abundance of a few simple comforts, but soon everyone began to relax. Even Elizabeth, who was now snuggled in a blanket with her twins, seemed improved; at least her dark eyes shone a little brighter from her sweet pale face. Tiernan seemed to notice this and brought forth a packet of strange smelling herbs from one of the many bundles stowed in the cavern. He handed the herbs to Kelly and instructed her on how to make a special tea for Elizabeth.

"It will help her to regain her strength," he said in that wonderful timbered voice of his.

Ian and Jim went to draw water for the camp in large earthenware jugs, while Turq, Genni, and Calab gathered materials to make a small fire. Tiernan gave Gwen the task of sorting through the cookware and dishes to find a cooking pot. Alena shook out blankets and made bed rolls for each of them. Those with children cared for their babies, while Tiernan sorted through some of the other supplies. Alena couldn't help but wonder how all these things had come to be here in this cavern; obviously, Tiernan couldn't have brought them here himself. Some of the items would have been very hard to carry over the wild terrain without many hands or even pack animals. Alena watched Tiernan sorting what appeared to be clothing into piles. He felt her eyes upon him and looked up.

"There's a shortage of women's clothing, I'm afraid, and we'll have to work something out for the little ones, but these will give us more protection than the biome rags we have been wearing."

Alena looked down then at the clothes she was wearing. They were indeed little more than rags. Clothing had been the least of their worries. She helped distribute a set of clothes to everyone. Tiernan was telling everyone about several areas near the falls to wash and to bathe in. He handed Alena her stack of clothing and a lump of something that smelled wonderful.

"What is it?" She wondered aloud.

"It's for washing with. We call it sonanthim."

It was something like the soap she supposed, although it was in a solid form and not a liquid. How long had it been since she bathed with soap and immersed herself in water? Alena knew it had been a lifetime ago.

"Why don't you take Gwen with you and go for a swim? I'll keep track of things up here and make sure no one steps out of line." He placed another item on the top of Alena's stack. It was sheathed in intricate leather, the hilt made of something fine like brass. Even to her untrained eyes Alena could tell that the workmanship was exceptionally fine. Tiernan briefly unsheathed it for her. The blade gleamed dangerously in the cerulean sunlight. "Take this with you just in case you run into trouble."

Thankfully, there were still hours of daylight left to them as she and Gwen made their way through the jungle-like plants to a deep pool of amazing blue. They respected each other's modesty as they slipped out of their clothing and bathed on opposite sides. Alena was delighted at the feel of the sun warmed water on her skin. She soaked for a bit, but then she went to work scrubbing herself with the sonanthim. She was amazed at the amount of grime that sloughed off her skin. She took a lot of joy in cleaning herself from head to toe. She had almost finished washing her hair when she felt a prickle go up her spine to the base of her neck. She swung around, surveying the dense growth of trees that surrounded the pool where she bathed. What was out there? And was it watching her and Gwen? She glanced over to where Gwen was. Gwen was already moving toward her.

"So, you feel it too?" Alena asked her.

Gwen nodded. "Someone's watching us, Captain."

"Someone?"

"There was someone moving through the trees a moment ago." Gwen's eyes were wide with fear.

"You're sure it was a person and not some kind of beast?"

Gwen nodded. "I saw his shadow—It was the shadow of a man." She started to shake.

"Where?"

Gwen motioned to the other side of the pool.

"It's going to be okay," Alena told her as she hurriedly rinsed the sonanthim out of her hair. "Come on, let's get to shore."

They made for the cover of trees and stood back to back while they dressed. Alena awkwardly pulled on a pair of leggings and a sort of tunic over her head. She belted the tunic with a colorful sash. Gwen struggled to do the same. They replaced their moccasins, and with Alena clutching the hilt of the knife in one hand and the sheath with the other, they warily made their way back to camp. Neither she nor Gwen could lose the feeling of being followed, so they started to run. Alena couldn't be sure, but she thought she heard a deep, perverse laugh from behind them.

Their cheeks were flushed, and they were out of breath as they came within sight of the Falls of Avantioch. Ian saw them first and came to meet them. He smiled appreciatively at their fresh-faced appearances before his expression changed.

"Captain, what is it? What's wrong?"

"Are all the men in the camp?"

"Yes?"

"Tiernan, Jim, Turq and yourself have all remained here at the falls the entire time that Gwen and I were gone?"

"Yes, Captain. Tiernan wouldn't let anyone leave." Ian watched Alena's face with some perplexity. "Have you had some trouble?"

"We're not alone in this jungle. I need to talk with Tiernan."

But Tiernan was already coming towards them, looking concerned.

"What's happened?" he questioned, already sensing her agitation.

"There was a man down there by the pools, watching us. Ian has already assured me that it was none of our group. Could there be some more of your people out here?"

Tiernan paused only for a moment. "Not likely. Besides, they would have used the cavern. Things were just as I had left them when we first arrived. I don't think anyone has been here since."

"Then the only other possibility is Anthony. He has followed us here. We best be on our guard."

Alena saw Jim's face darken at the mention of Anthony's name.

"Tiernan, will you take Turq and see if you can flush him out?"

He nodded, although slowly, like it was personal for her to ask it of him. Tiernan's mood was noticeably darker as he and Turq went to look for Anthony with long knives strapped to their belts. They each took a change of clothing with them. They were gone for what seemed like a long time.

Gwen and Alena found a large basin in the cavern and filled it with warm water heated from the fire. They helped bathe the children in it. Even Calab got a good scrubbing from his mother. Elizabeth looked terrific after she was cleaned up and given a new change of clothes; and her little babies after being bathed smelled positively sweet.

When Tiernan and Turq returned, Alena had to take a step back, both were so changed in appearance that she would hardly have known them aside from their bronze and turquoise colored skin. They also wore leggings and tunics; except they looked far better on the men. Each wore weapons belted at their side. Alena blushed at the thoughts that went racing through her head at the sight of Tiernan in this more masculine attire. He seemed to be pleased by his effect on her.

"You both clean up wonderfully," she couldn't help comment. "Let me look at the both of you." She circled the two of them and came to a stop in front of Tiernan. "Any sign of Anthony?" she questioned.

Tiernan frowned. "No, other than a few footprints. He is good at hiding and doesn't want to be found. One thing I know for sure, he is nowhere near the pools at the moment. I think it's safe enough for the rest of our group to wash up."

As the last of the group bathed and donned their new clothing, Alena was pleased by the transformation that had come over them. It was as though they had finally shed the last remnants of their prison by literally casting their dirty rags into the fire. The group gathered together around the campfire after they had tucked Calab and Olivia in bed. Tiernan served them a hot soothing drink of strange herbs, while a sapphire moon rose and the first bright stars began to appear. This was Alena's first real look at a total night's sky on this planet called Temarria. It had rained every night since their escape from the Cephalopods. Her only other view of the night sky had been through her window in the biome.

The sight of this amazing star-filled sky was almost more than Alena could bear. She had dreamed all her life about traveling to other worlds and visiting distant galaxies, becoming one day a captain of one of the big Carillion Starships, but she never in her wildest dreams could have imagined that she would have instead become a simple captive of this tiny planet. At least she had bought back some of her freedom by escaping the biome. She noticed Tiernan watching her.

"The sky is beautiful," she said softly.

"Which star do your people come from?"

Alena sighed, whispering, "I don't know. Your sky is new to us. We are lost."

Some of her crew looked at her sadly as they wandered off to their blankets for the night. Alena knew that they had given up dreams and aspirations too. They all had a different road now.

Everyone filtered off to bed except for Alena and Tiernan. Alena had first watch and Tiernan had the second, but he chose to stay with her at least for the time being. Alena tugged at the tangles in her hair. With her flight from her disturbing bath earlier in the day, she had not had time to braid it, and it had become a tangled mess.

Tiernan broke the silence. "I think I might have something that will help you with that." He left her alone briefly by the fire. Alena heard him rummaging through a pack before he returned and seated himself next to her. He placed a bristly object in her hand. She stared at it in fascination near the campfire. It was a fine brush with an intricately carved handle.

"Here, let me," he said taking the brush back from her.

He started carefully, brushing out the worst of the tangles and then became slightly more forceful, brushing in a sort of rhythm. It was therapeutic for Alena and strangely intimate for him to brush her hair like that. He continued brushing until her hair was exceedingly soft and shone in the moonlight.

"Thank you, Tiernan. That feels much better."

He placed the brush in her hands. "Keep it, Alena. It is a gift for you."

"It's beautiful."

"For a beautiful woman," he said softly.

Alena felt her cheeks flush with the compliment. Why was he speaking to her this way? She turned to him, watching his face in the soft glow of the fire, but he wasn't trying to woo her as she had first supposed; he looked only miserable.

"What makes you so unhappy? Aren't you looking forward to rejoining your people soon?"

Tiernan hesitated. "There are many who I would like to see again, but my life is forever changed now."

Alena nodded. "The Cephalopods have certainly done a number on all of us, but that doesn't help me understand your grief. What troubles you?"

He stared at her for a long moment. "I had hoped to return under better circumstances."

"What do you mean?"

"There were twelve of us that set out more than a year ago. They are all dead or missing now, except for Sceria."

"I'm sorry," Alena laid her hand on Tiernan's shoulder which made him tremble a bit. "What happened to them?"

"The Waratna killed seven of them when we were captured. The other four, including Sceria, were with me in the biome, at least for a time. I don't know where they are now. I haven't seen the other three for at least five moons. Perhaps they perished with the hurricane."

"But your people would be glad to see you despite the loss of your companions, right?"

Tiernan looked down at his hands. "One of them that is now lost is my younger brother, Niomer. Only one of my parent's sons will return to them."

Tiernan's answer was unexpected, but Alena knew little of Tiernan's life at all. "I'm so sorry, Tiernan. Still, the return of one son is better than none at all."

Tiernan made a face, "How can I make you understand? There are many things that happened in the biome that if they were known would be viewed as unacceptable, even worthy of death by my people. Sceria and I return to them shamefully and without honor."

"The things that happened in the biome were beyond your control. Surely, they would understand that?"

"Alena, what I speak of was of my own choosing, although I did not know the whole truth at the time."

"What is it that you speak of?"

Tiernan shook his head and closed his eyes. "It is too much. It is better that you are innocent of the knowledge."

"Don't you trust me? You can't think that I will judge ill of you? I was there in the biome too. I know the atrocities that happened there. We were all under a great deal of stress."

"Please do not ask further of me. I do this for you, Alena— to protect you."

"I don't need protecting, Tiernan."

"The ways of my people are not your ways."

"You've said that before. Please help me to understand."

"I can't, not now. Please give me some time. I promise that I will help you to understand once we have reached the borders of Camaranth."

Alena was angry suddenly, "Are you ashamed of me? Are you ashamed of my people? Is that what this is about?"

Tiernan paused for a moment too long. He tried to deny it, but it was too late.

"That's it isn't it? That's why you have been so aloof around me lately? There is something about me, something about my people that you find completely unacceptable, isn't there?"

"Alena, please."

"Tell me I am wrong! Tell me." Alena was up and standing on her feet, mad as a hornet.

"I don't want to offend you or bring you pain."

"So, I'm right."

Tiernan stared at her, his amber-orange eyes suddenly blazing. "Please don't make me say something I know I will regret. You can't begin to understand!"

"Why? Is it because I'm not like you? Well, let me make it easy for you. In the morning, I'm taking my people with me, and we're leaving. You won't need to feel responsible for us at all, anymore."

"I am responsible for what happens to you, Alena. If you leave, I will only be forced to follow you, which will be to the detriment of everyone. We cannot last out here forever. Surely, you know that after our experience with the veratnil this morning."

"Are you trying to tell me that somehow I am your captive? What makes you responsible for me, Tiernan, what?"

"You wouldn't understand."

"Try me!"

"No, it would only make everything harder for you. This is my burden to carry."

"I don't understand you at all, but I know I don't want to be your burden or your responsibility!" Alena yelled louder than she had intended. She heard some of the others stirring behind her in the cavern. She instantly lowered her voice. "I'm too angry with you to say anything sensible right now. Either you're going to bed or I am."

Tiernan was only silent.

"Fine then—I'm going to bed. When you are finished with your watch, wake Turq." Alena stomped off to her bedroll between Kelly and Sceria and lay down in a huff. The blanket was more comfortable than she wanted to admit, although she tossed and turned with fury.

Kelly's voice came to her in a whisper. "He's in love with you, you know."

"What are you talking about?" Alena whispered back.

"Whatever it is that Tiernan finds distasteful in all of us has not kept him from going head over heels for you."

"That's impossible!"

"Think about it, Alena. This morning when the veratnil came his concern was primarily for you. He wouldn't leave until you did. He's always watching you, keeping track of you, even when he is trying to act like he is not. He's had many opportunities to leave us, and I wouldn't blame him if he did with Jim and Anthony's antics, but he always chooses to stay, not for the rest of us but for you."

Alena listened to Kelly's words, but she didn't know what to think of them. If Tiernan loved her, then why wouldn't he just tell her? Was there really something so shameful about her kind that it created an impenetrable wall between the two of them? She snuggled down into the soft blanket and shifted to her other side. She came face to face with Sceria who hurriedly erased the look of loathing that was apparent on her face. Had Sceria been listening? Alena didn't know how much Sceria understood from her conversation with Kelly, but she had been given the opportunity to eavesdrop.

Sceria never spoke in any language but her own, but Alena knew that Sceria probably understood a lot, if not everything that was said. Tiernan had avoided Sceria for the most part since that day the two of them had argued, just as he had avoided Alena since that time. Alena found herself wondering if Sceria were somehow tied up in Tiernan's grief too. Alena lay awake, simmering in her anger and confusion for a long time.

Chapter Eighteen

The day dawned too soon for Alena. She had not slept well. But she couldn't sleep at all now that the sun was up. Grumpily, she got to her feet. She brushed through her hair and braided it behind her. After carefully stepping over several sleeping bodies, she went to splash a little water on her face. Ian was the only one up since it was his watch. He was adding fuel to the fire and tending to a big pot of water that had been set among the flames.

"How did you sleep, Captain?" Ian asked in a knowing way. "And where are you packing us off to today?"

Alena gave him a berating look. "Alright, Ian, that's enough."

Ian smiled. "Sorry, Cap, I couldn't help myself. I would like to know, however, what your plans are for our crew."

"My plans haven't changed."

"Since before yesterday or since last night?"

Alena couldn't stand it anymore. She balled up her fist and slugged him.

Ian laughed heartily. "Okay, okay, I know I've crossed the line, but Tiernan is a good guy. I know he makes you angry, but I also know he would do anything he could to protect you."

Was Ian giving her advice about Tiernan too? Alena stomped away from the cavern.

"Hey, now wait, Captain, Tiernan won't be very happy if I let you go wandering off by yourself." Ian's remark only made Alena want to hurry her pace. The last thing she wanted to do was to face Tiernan right now. She found a large flat rock next to the stream some distance below the Falls of Avantioch to sit on and reflect. She was still fuming and embarrassed, especially by the fact that she and Tiernan had evidently been overheard by everyone in the camp. Alena was completely unprepared for the filthy hand that came from behind and clamped over her mouth. She felt her head slam against the rock and blood trickling down the side of her face. Anthony—she had forgotten about Anthony.

He dragged her off into the trees, while she kicked and bit and struggled, but she was disoriented and couldn't break free. "I have waited to wipe that smug look from your face for a long time." Anthony laughed a low and sinister laugh. "That day has finally come, you pretentious, stuck-up wench!" Anthony hit her across the face and then threw her to the ground, leaping on top of her, but Alena hadn't lost her wits completely, not yet. She rolled out from under him and half-wriggled, half-crawled into the thick underbrush. He grabbed hold of her leg and pulled her back, trying to pin her down, but she wasn't going down without a fight. He hit her again across the face, knocking the sense out of her, blurring her vision. Blinded, she wriggled free, crawling back into the underbrush, kicking with all of her might. She made contact with something and heard a grunt, and then she was up and running, but with her vision blurred and blood seeping from her head, she could not make sense of her surroundings. It was like running blind.

Alena could hear Anthony running behind her, inching closer. She was swift on her feet for a girl but no match for Anthony's speed. They both went crashing through the undergrowth of the jungle. Alena struggled to keep her feet under her and the many branches above from taking off her head. She was scratched and bruised all over, but that didn't matter. She could almost feel Anthony's hot breath on the back of her neck. He was so close, too close. She turned to dodge him, but he had gotten ahead of her. She screamed as she ran straight into his solid chest. She couldn't understand how he had come to be there. It didn't make sense. She let out a strangled cry as strong arms enveloped her.

"Alena, Alena. It's alright. I've got you now."

It took Alena a moment to understand, as she kicked and fought that it wasn't Anthony's voice that spoke to her, and it wasn't Anthony's arms that held her now. She tried to see through the sweat and blood and tears that drowned her vision.

"Tiernan?" her voice came out like a tiny mew, she recognized only a bronze blur—the color of his skin, and then she blacked out.

Alena was in and out of consciousness. She had the vague sense of being carried. She heard voices at times…Tiernan's and Ian's. She laid her head against Tiernan's chest, and then the darkness swam up to take her. Alena remembered vaguely being rolled into a blanket and shadows dabbing at her wounds along with the sound of many voices.

Alena's head pounded as she awoke. She reached up to touch her head and found that it had been bandaged.

"She's coming around," Kelly's voice practically boomed through her head and seemed as though it was amplified a hundred times. Alena wanted to vomit. She blinked her eyes a few times, trying to clear her vision. Tiernan was kneeling next to her on one side looking anxious and Kelly was on the other.

"How do you feel?"

Alena tried to sit up, but the world spun crazily, and she had to lie back down. "My head hurts, and I'm dizzy," she said closing her eyes again.

"Stay with us." Kelly was saying.

"It's alright, I'm here. It just hurts to open my eyes, and I feel as though I might lose my stomach."

"Bring me some of that strange concoction of yours, Tiernan," Alena heard Kelly say.

Kelly propped up her head and Tiernan pressed something strong and bitter to her mouth. "Here drink some of this. It will help you," he said with a kindness she had never heard in his voice before.

It tasted awful, but Tiernan was right, with each sip she could feel energy seeping back into her body and her stomach starting to settle.

"Thanks," Alena felt for Tiernan's hand as he removed the cup from her swollen lips. "Thank you, Tiernan for finding me," she said quietly.

"No more wandering off, alright?" Tiernan whispered in reply, helping Kelly to lay Alena's head back down.

"No more..." she agreed. "Anthony. Where is Anthony?"

"Don't worry about Anthony, just rest. You are safe."

Tiernan stayed with her until she slept, and when she awoke he was still there, although it was now the middle of the afternoon.

Alena sat up with a start and then grabbed her head. "We should be moving. We're wasting time. Get everyone packed up."

"Sshh, Alena. Lie back and rest. You are in no condition to travel. We cannot carry both you and Elizabeth. It will not hurt to linger another day."

Alena looked around. The camp seemed meticulous and everyone was busy performing a task, even Elizabeth, who was sitting up and folding stacks of material cut into squares... diapers? Tiernan certainly seemed to have things well in hand. Alena stretched. Her limbs felt cramped and achy. She was bruised in many places, especially her face which had taken quite a beating. Her cheekbones felt swollen and on fire, especially on the left side. Her hair was matted with dirt and blood. She looked down and discovered that her tunic was also covered with dirt and dried blood.

"Ugh, I must be quite a sight."

"I'll get you a new tunic and help you clean up a bit."

Alena nodded. A basin of warm water was brought and Tiernan helped her wash the blood and dirt from her hair. His hands were gentle, especially around her head wound. Why was he doing this? He could have Kelly or Gwen help her. He wrapped a blanket around her and turned away so that she could change into the other tunic.

"Why are you doing this?" Alena asked as he bandaged her head with a fresh strip of cloth.

He gave her a long searching look and frowned. "I blame myself for what happened today, Alena. You would not have gone off by yourself if you had not been angry with me."

"This is not your fault. I should have been more careful. I forgot about Anthony and what he is."

"What is he?"

"He is a monster, the worst of what our kind can become," she answered, carefully choosing her words.

"Explain "monster" to me, Alena. You call the Cephalopods monsters and yet you refer to Anthony by the same name.

Anthony is not like most of your kind, then?" His amber-orange eyes blazed with seriousness.

"Anthony has become worse than the Cephalopods. He betrays and murders his own. No, Anthony is not representative of my people." Tiernan eyes relaxed and filled with relief.

"Where is Anthony now?" she asked.

Tiernan faced looked pained again with the question. "We have searched for him, but he cannot be found. Our first concern was for you, Alena, to get you back to camp. When we returned to search for him, he was gone." Tiernan took her hand with a look of worry. "I'm sorry, Alena, for what he has done to you." He touched her swollen lips briefly and then gently kissed her on the forehead. Alena felt him tremble as he did so. Was it still so hard for him to be near her, she wondered? Why did he tremble? Was it distaste that he felt when he touched her? Why did he even bother?

"I'm sure, I will be fine. Thank you, again for helping me. I wouldn't have escaped without you this time."

Tiernan was quiet and deep in thought. Alena wondered what he was thinking. Was he remembering other incidences that he had observed between her and Anthony in the biome? Her suspicions were confirmed when Tiernan continued with, "You're certainly a fighter, Alena." He turned and reached for something nearby and handed it to her. Alena recognized it as the deadly yet beautiful knife that he had given her the day before. "It would make me feel better if you would keep this with you at all times." He reached around her waist and clasped a leather belt around her tunic. "Here, tuck it in here," he said showing her how to carry the knife in her belt.

He was right. The knife would have been useful to her this morning. With Anthony wandering around out there, none of them were safe, especially the women. Alena then noticed the hilt of the weapon that gleamed in Tiernan's own belt. It was larger than the one she carried and far more detailed. He followed her gaze and fingered his own knife.

"I will not hesitate to use it if I come across Anthony again. I hope you understand that."

Alena nodded and turned away. It was not Anthony she worried about, however... it was Jim. Hadn't he also been given one of these masterfully forged blades?

"You must be hungry. Would you like me to bring you something to eat?"

"I am hungry, but I don't need you to wait on me." Alena started to get up on her feet, but found she was still unstable. Tiernan was at her side urging her to sit back down. She tried to wave him away but ended up leaning on him instead.

"Really, Alena, you should rest."

"I don't want to rest!"

Tiernan shook his head. "You sure are stubborn. I wonder what it would take to keep you down." He helped her over to the campfire. Gwen was there with Ian. Ian looked upset. Was Gwen comforting him? That was something new. A few days ago, Gwen wouldn't have gone anywhere near one of the men alone. It was good to see her making some progress. But what was wrong with Ian? As soon as Ian turned toward her, however, Alena knew. His face colored to a dark shade, and he wouldn't look at her.

"You're not blaming yourself for what happened are you?"

"I know you wouldn't have run off like that, Captain, if I hadn't been teasing you," he hung his head miserably.

"You are not responsible for Anthony's actions or mine. Personally, I'm grateful that you went and told Tiernan where I had gone. Otherwise, I wouldn't be sitting here alive."

"You don't understand, Captain. I didn't tell Tiernan you had left. I just let you go. I thought you just needed some time to yourself. I didn't think any harm would come of it. I should have followed you."

Confused Alena turned to Tiernan. "How did you know where to find me then?"

Tiernan's eyes flashed with wildness, ever so briefly, but he didn't answer. He handed her a bowl of what looked like hot stew and a long spoon.

Alena turned back to Ian. "How did he know? Weren't you with him, Ian, after he found me?"

"I don't know, Captain. I followed him. I never suspected that anything was wrong until he bolted out of the cavern about five minutes after you left and went sprinting off in your direction. He yelled at me to follow him." Ian hung his head. "I felt so bad when I saw him carrying you, all beaten up and bloody. I'm sorry that I failed you, Captain."

"You didn't fail me. Please don't blame yourself. No one could have predicted that Anthony was out there waiting for me," she paused trying to find the right words. "I think very highly of you and your judgment. You were right about me just needing time to myself. I don't blame you in the least for what happened."

"You see, Ian," Gwen piped in. "I told you, the Captain wouldn't blame you."

Ian looked relieved. He did turn to Tiernan, however, his interest piqued. "How did you know that the Captain was in trouble?"

Tiernan tried to act as though Ian hadn't said a word. "Alena, would you like something to drink? Some wine perhaps?"

"Some water please."

He turned and left them. Alena, Ian, and Gwen stared after him. Why was he being so evasive at answering the question? He had avoided it twice now. What was he trying to hide?

"He seems so totally aware of you, Captain; it's almost as if..." Ian's voice trailed off.

"As if what?"

Ian shook his head. "I don't know. I don't understand it. He always seems to know what you're in need of even before..."

"Before what?"

"Even sometimes before you do, Captain."

Alena sucked in an uneasy breath. Could that be true? Alena wondered about it the whole rest of the afternoon as she watched Tiernan and the others pack up much of what was stocked in the cavern for tomorrow's journey. They were leaving the heavier items behind and whatever else Tiernan deemed unnecessary. After watching him, Alena determined that he was a natural leader. He seemed comfortable with giving orders. The only one that gave him any trouble was Jim—misguided, prejudiced Jim, but Tiernan seemed to even handle him okay. Alena noticed that Tiernan had indeed given Jim his own dangerous blade to wield.

That night was a chilly one behind the falls. Alena found herself wishing that Tiernan were lying beside her to warm her. Strangely, when he returned from his watch, he settled himself next to her for the first time in many, many days. As he placed an arm around her, she snuggled into him, wondering once again about what Ian had said earlier. Could he read her thoughts, somehow? Did he know what she felt about him? Was he really so aware of her?

"Rest now my little wootchka." he whispered to her in the darkness. "We have a long journey tomorrow."

She felt her heart beat faster. He had called her that once before. She felt him tremble slightly as she snuggled closer, enveloped in the scent of him. It was as though he used every ounce of his energy to remain in control. It reminded her of their earlier days in the biome. He had been so full of fire and anger then. He had held her like this during their first real encounter while she cried, but something had changed since then— something she didn't understand, although it tied him to her in some way. She wondered if she would ever understand this amber-orange eyed, alien man.

Chapter Nineteen

They journeyed for four whole days, following the river, stopping only for small breaks and to sleep for the night. Tiernan stayed with Alena at the rear of the group nearly the entire time while Sceria led them. For the first several days he even carried Alena's portion of the supplies for her. They didn't speak much, but Tiernan was a constant presence beside her, helping her until she felt almost like herself again. He was dependable and considerate, but he was also detached and meditative. Alena wanted to understand the wall that loomed between them, but she couldn't, and Tiernan was not ready to explain it to her. Alena began to wonder if he ever would.

There had been no sign of Anthony or the Cephalopods. Alena hoped that they would see neither of them again, but she knew that her hopes were probably in vain. On the fifth day of their travels, they passed several ruined dwellings scattered here and there along the way. By the early afternoon, however, they were beginning to come across clusters of abandoned buildings or what were likely to have been small towns; all were mangled and in ruin. Alena watched Tiernan's face grow more somber the further they journeyed. How hard it must be for him to see the devastation of his people. They began to follow what appeared to be a wide road, although it was now overgrown and scattered with boulders. Alena could see a great hill ahead of them covered in tiny white objects.

"The Dreaded Hill of Tavonsheigh," she heard Tiernan say under his breath. Alena wondered what made it so dreaded. It looked steep, but manageable. Drawing closer, she discovered that the tiny white objects were actually stone markers, tens of thousands of them. It was then that she understood; it was a graveyard that entirely covered this enormous dreaded hill. Alena could feel her skin prickling like she was walking among the souls of the dead. She felt many horrible things all at once: terror, wretchedness, hopelessness, suffering, pain, and despair. She fell to her knees with grief, tears running down her face. How many lay dead here?

Tiernan knelt by her side. "You feel it too, then?" He seemed surprised by her emotion. He helped her to her feet, wiping her face. "There are more than 300,000 that rest here, most of them women and children. They were slaughtered by the Waratna, after their husbands and fathers were lured away to the battlefields of Havetdoon. Everyone thought that the women and children would be safe here in the stronghold, but it was not to be. Those few that survived the battles returned to find their families massacred." Tiernan was quiet, taking her hand. "Come let me show you the city of my boyhood; let me show you Tavonsheigh."

They climbed to the top of the hill where the others stood waiting. As she reached the pinnacle, Alena was unprepared for the sight of the immense city of white stone that filled the deep valley below. The city spanned ten miles at least and was surrounded by a great stone wall which contained four enormous gates. The gates were made of polished stone and metal; they marked the northern, southern, eastern, and western sections of the city. A colossal castle or citadel of white stone was located in the center of the city surrounded by bands of magnificent inner walls. Everywhere Alena gazed there was one glorious edifice after another. This was not a civilization of simple people but of great master builders. She hardly knew where to look as they descended the Dreaded Hill of Tavonsheigh, which was still scattered with stone markers all the way down to its wide base.

A river ran through the city. She could hear noise of it as they passed through the eastern gate. Despite the sound of the river or an occasional caw of a bird, Tavonsheigh was strangely quiet—a great ghost city of stone. Enormous columns rose to the sky along the faces of the immense structures that lined the great square. There was a colossus of an obelisk in the center of the square and three gigantic fountains that no longer sang with the sound of water, their magnificent statues stood gray and still.

Alena watched the others in her group taking in the city for the first time. She could tell that Ian's mind was full of all kinds of scientific calculations as he observed each column and trajectory and the layout of each wall. Jim seemed impressed by the scale of the fortifications, Gwen by the beauty, but Turq and Genni seemed entirely overwhelmed. Perhaps they didn't have cities of such an enormous magnitude on their planet. Calab, however, seemed practically giddy running in and out of the columns. Alena smiled at his enthusiasm.

Tiernan lead them straight towards the citadel, stopping occasionally to explain a landmark or something of interest. They passed through many passages and sets of walls. These passages seemed to Alena almost like a labyrinth in their complexity, but Tiernan seemed to know the way as they passed through courtyards and a half a dozen gates on the way. The beautiful city seemed untouched by war aside from the dreaded hill behind them and the occasional overgrown appearance of some of the dwellings. Alena could not understand how so many could have died when the city seemed so well protected. What had the Cephalopods done to annihilate the people of Tavonsheigh? She turned back to the hill for a moment to take in its appearance from where they walked.

The Dreaded Hill of Tavensheigh was immense even from this distance and cast a gloomy shadow over the part of the city that they had just traveled through. Alena stopped briefly and squinted to the top of the hill. There appeared to be a lone figure standing there at the top. Alena gasped audibly. She rubbed her eyes and looked again, but the figure was now gone.

"What is it, Alena?" Tiernan asked stopping just ahead of her.

"I saw someone at the top of the hill. I think Anthony has followed us here."

Tiernan didn't seem too concerned. "Anthony will never be able to find his way to us through the inner-city walls."

Alena was sure Tiernan was right. She already felt lost in this goliath of a city. It took them a good deal of time to reach the giant citadel. It was a stunning castle of great beauty with huge spires that rose high into the cerulean sky, but it was also a mighty fortress, a stronghold with massively thick walls. The size of the fortress itself made Alena dizzy. It dwarfed anything of ancient comparison on her home planet even the Colosseum of Rome or the Great Pyramids of Giza. They had to cross a system of elaborate bridges to enter it and once inside, they were once again in a labyrinth of passages.

Tiernan led them into what appeared to be a great banquet hall, down several flights of stairs, through a huge kitchen, down another flight of stairs into a large storeroom. The supplies here dwarfed what they had found in the cavern behind the falls about a hundredfold. Tiernan took them through this room up a short flight of stairs into what looked like servant's living quarters. There was a spacious sitting room surrounded by smaller sleeping rooms complete with what looked like bunk beds.

"This is where we will spend the night," Tiernan announced, dropping his pack off to one side. "You can wash up here," he said motioning to a huge wash basin where water was piped in from the outside river. The water looked discolored for a few minutes, but then ran pure and clear. Sceria seemed displeased with the arrangements and began complaining to Tiernan in their unusual language. Tiernan cut her off with a few short statements, and Sceria went sulking off into one of the smaller rooms. Jim and Elizabeth took the room next to Sceria with their twins, Turq, Genni, and Calab took another, and Kelly took the last single room with Olivia. Only one large room remained for Alena, Gwen, Ian, and Tiernan.

Alena plopped her stuff next to one of the lower bunks and sat down. She removed her moccasins and rubbed her feet. She was sore today, probably because they had walked further today than usual. Tiernan watched her with his customary intenseness. He seemed a little edgy.

"Come with me, Alena. There is something I would like to show you."

Alena was half-tempted to refuse. She was in no mood for anymore traveling that day, but she was curious. She reached for her moccasins.

"Leave them. It's only a short distance within the fortress. You won't need them."

Ian and Gwen were also bursting with curiosity and Tiernan invited them to come along as well. The others napped or tended to their children, so the three of them followed Tiernan on a little explore of the citadel. They backtracked through the storage area and up the stairs and through the kitchen, down several corridors to an immense intricately carved doorway. There was a huge round knocker on the door and Alena, Ian, and Gwen all jumped in surprise when Tiernan rapped the door with it three times, then twice more, and then three times again in a sort of pattern. The sound echoed eerily down the long corridor. They could hear something shuffling behind the door and then a grinding noise as the door was unbolted and pushed wide.

There behind the door stood an aged bronze man with a long reddish gold beard. He walked with a cane and was blind, but he recognized Tiernan immediately, greeting Tiernan with apparent gladness in the language of the Temarrians. Although he seemed rather old, his voice was rich timbered and steady, almost as amazing as Tiernan's voice.

Tiernan talked briefly with the old man, while the three of them looked on in amazement. They had not expected to encounter anyone alive in the city of Tavonsheigh and certainly not some wizardly looking individual. Tiernan introduced them to this wizened old man, and he bowed his head before each of them as they were introduced. Maiser Runcan, as he was called, stopped before Alena when Tiernan introduced them and took her hand. He had no color in his sightless eyes, but Alena felt as though he could see into her soul. He held her hand for a long time while he seemed to consider her, and then Maiser Runcan spoke softly.

"What does he say?" Alena asked Tiernan while still focused on the wise old blind man.

"He says that he has been waiting for you to come."

"Waiting for me? What do you mean?"

"Maiser Runcan has the gift of foresight. He has been waiting for this day."

"You mean he knew that I would come?"

Tiernan hesitated, but finally answered affirmatively, "Yes, he has prophesied that travelers would come from the stars since the time I was a small boy. He often spoke of a pale-skinned woman with dark colored hair that would lead many to save our world."

"You can't possibly believe that I..."

Tiernan stopped her mid-sentence. "I did not tell him anything about you, Alena. I only told him that I had brought some friends for him to meet."

Alena was taken aback. Could this old man really have foreseen her and her companions? And if so, he couldn't possibly believe that she could save them somehow? Besides, if Tiernan had known about this prophecy, why hadn't he said something about it before?

"How long have you thought that I was part of some prophecy?" Alena asked, noticing then that Gwen and Ian were following their conversation with close interest.

"For a while now."

Alena didn't know what to say to this but hoped that there would be more time for an explanation as Maiser Runcan beckoned for them to follow. Alena wondered if the prophecy was the real reason that Tiernan and Sceria had stayed with them and lead them here. It certainly would explain at least some of Tiernan's strange behavior.

Maiser Runcan led them up a long and winding stair into a high tower. Alena guessed that it was one of the tall spires that she had seen outside. The top of the tower contained a circular room filled with many interesting astronomical objects, scrolls and books, and herbs and bottled potions. Maiser Runcan stroked his long gold-red beard and indicated that he wished for them to be seated on the intricately braided blue mats on the floor. Alena became immediately conscious of her blistered and bare feet. Why had Tiernan encouraged her to come to this blind old man without her moccasins? She was grateful that he couldn't see her dirty feet. She tucked her feet self-consciously beneath her legs as she sat cross-legged on the floor. Tiernan, as always, was watching her.

Maiser Runcan brought forth a long wooden box and a small basin filled with water. Alena was mortified when Maiser Runcan knelt before her and indicated he would like to bathe her feet. She was about to decline until she noticed the stern look on Tiernan's bronze face. Would she insult this old man that was obviously of some importance to Tiernan's people if she refused? She relented, allowing this wise old man to kneel before her and bathe her feet. He did so with many fine words that Alena could not understand along with bizarre ritualistic motions. When he had finished, he dried her feet and opened the long wooden box.

Inside the box was a pair of long sky colored wooly stockings, beautifully tooled dark leather boots, and a sword and scabbard of phenomenal splendor. Maiser Runcan placed the wooly stockings upon her feet, rather adroitly and ceremoniously for such an old blind man. The comfy pale blue stockings were followed by the long boots that almost ran to her knee. These intricately tooled boots made of fine leather were oddly a perfect fit as if they had been made specifically for her. Alena felt her face flush with disbelief. This experience was getting stranger and stranger with each passing moment. She glanced at Tiernan and caught a glimpse of the disbelief in his own amber-orange eyes. Ian and Gwen were merely mesmerized by this whole bizarre experience especially when Maiser Runcan placed the sword and scabbard across her lap and bowed his head toward her; she bowed to him in turn, which seemed to be the right thing to do. Maiser Runcan smiled at her in approval and brought forth another box. This one was square and a lot heavier. Inside were a half dozen leather bound volumes; the first of which he gave to Alena, three he gave to Ian and two he gave to Gwen. Ian fingered his volumes lovingly. A light shone in his face that Alena hadn't seen in a long time. Ian had a deep love for books, but Gwen was perhaps just as excited. What did the books contain? Alena turned her attention back to Maiser Runcan who was speaking to them somehow in their own language.

"It is necessary that you gain more knowledge before reaching the hidden city. These volumes will be of help to you in understanding our language and our people." He rose to his full height which was considerable for an old man and stroked his long gold-red beard. "I am honored to have finally witnessed your arrival in Tavonsheigh. Gratefully, I have completed the task that was given to me." Both Tiernan and Maiser Runcan studied Alena for a moment and then Maiser Runcan continued. "My fine young friends, I must bid you farewell, for the time has long passed since the ruin of Tavonsheigh. It is time now to rest my bones with my brothers. I have waited far too long since the sign of your coming." Maiser Runcan bid them all to rise and motioned to their leather-bound volumes. "Share your knowledge with your companions. They will need your leadership and your wisdom."

Maiser Runcan placed a hand upon Tiernan's shoulder and talked to him briefly in the language of the Temarrians. Tiernan soberly bowed his head and glanced in Alena's direction. She saw pain flicker ever so briefly in Tiernan's amber-orange eyes, before he squared his shoulders and resigned himself to whatever Maiser Runcan had asked of him.

Maiser Runcan turned to Gwen and spoke softly to her. "Do not fear, my dear Gwen. You will find your bravery." To Ian he gently said, while laying a hand on both shoulders, "Your scientific prowess will give you the confidence and self-respect that are now lost to you." His words to Alena were affectionately these: "Precious Alena, you will gain the fulfillment and happiness you desire in your service to my people." He touched the sword he had given her. "This is Wrayna. She can only be wielded by one who is pure and generous. Use her wisely." His final words were to all of them, "Be watchful, for there are many trials yet to pass through on your journey to the hidden city of Camaranth. The one who follows carries malice. There are others among you who harbor feelings of treachery and disloyalty. They may execute irreparable harm. It is vital that they are not allowed to succeed. Go now and may the hope of all living and those who have paid with their lives go with you."

They each bowed their heads in turn to Maiser Runcan as they followed Tiernan, single file, from the circular room. Alena was last of the four to begin descending the spiral stairs. Her mind whirled with questions as she held tightly to Wrayna. She could feel the sword fill with energy as she grasped the hilt. This was so strange to her and so unexpected that she almost dropped the sword in fright. Alena turned back to ask Maiser Runcan what it meant but found the circular room to be empty. Maiser Runcan had apparently just disappeared. Alena stood in the doorway for a time completely baffled. Eventually all Alena could think to do about it was to attach the sword to her belt. She was careful not to touch the hilt as she did so. Alena descended the winding stairs; she was well behind her companions now.

Alena had many questions fill her mind. Who or what was this Maiser Runcan? Was he a wizard or some sort of specter? How had he known of their coming? And what did it mean for her and her crew and the others? She shook her head in bewilderment. Had this whole experience been merely a dream? The items she had been given seemed real enough. There was no disputing that her feet were no longer bare and the sword in its scabbard was now belted to her side. She fingered the volume that Maiser Runcan had given her and wondered what it might contain. He had said that she would find happiness and fulfillment on this hopeless planet. Alena didn't know what to believe and obviously she wasn't the only one that felt that way. Ian and Gwen wore dazed expressions as well when she met up with them at the bottom, but Tiernan's face appeared the most disbelieving of all. His amber-orange eyes widened as she appeared before them in her fine boots with the sword belted at her side. He seemed to not want to look at her as he turned away from her searching gaze and headed down the corridor beckoning for them to come along. Lamely Alena, Gwen, and Ian followed with Alena wondering what she had now done to further widen the gulf between them. Whatever it was, she didn't have the patience for Tiernan's detachment. Alena hurried to catch up with him while Gwen and Ian gave knowing looks to each other and purposefully lagged behind.

"Do you want to explain to me what just happened back there?" she asked as she reached his side. Alena grabbed Tiernan's arm to slow his pace, and he practically jumped out of his bronze skin. "Hey, whoa... What is the matter with you, Tiernan? Sometimes you act as though I am poison to you."

Tiernan stared at her with a wild, crazed expression. The veins bulged in his neck, and his hands clenched in anguish. He was quiet…too quiet. Silence hung agonizingly between them until finally Tiernan managed to regain some sort of composure. His rich timbered voice stumbled painfully over his words, "I'm sorry. It is too much. Please give me some time to come to terms with all that has happened here."

"What has happened?"

"Please, Alena."

"Tiernan, I'm confused! Did you bring us here knowing that Maiser Runcan waited for us?"

"I did not know for certain that it was for you and the others that Maiser Runcan waited. I am still not sure what to believe." He stared at her hopelessly as if there were something inherently wrong with her.

So that was it. That fatal flaw that was so abhorrent to Tiernan was getting in the way again. He doubted her, and he doubted her place in the prophecy. Alena felt her cheeks flush with annoyance. Well that was fine. She wanted no part in this prophecy business anyway, but she was sick and tired of Tiernan judging her and her people. She charged on ahead of him and refused to stop when he called desperately for her to wait.

If Alena thought Tiernan's response to her had been bad, it was infinitesimal compared to Sceria's. Sceria practically shrieked with rage when she caught sight of Alena and tried to tear the sword from her belt, but the sword had a power of its own and repelled her touch sending Sceria flying with a shock to the floor. Tiernan had arrived by this time and hurried to stand between them. Sceria began shouting at Tiernan with obvious venom, and he shouted almost as angrily in return. This continued back and forth while everyone gathered around them nervously.

"Come on," Alena finally said to the others, "Let's see if we can rummage up some food for supper."

Everyone else followed with the exception of Elizabeth and the twins who were sleeping, or at least trying to with all of the noise. Alena and the rest of the group were able to find much more than food in the large storage room. Jim was the first to appear before Alena in a pair of long brown leather boots, and the others were soon to follow, but none of the boots were as fine as Alena's or matched their rich dark color. There was clothing for everyone. Alena passed out a fresh tunic for each of them. Alena was able to find a tunic of cerulean blue that matched her stockings which she kept for herself. Ian found jars of spices and was sniffing them, along with Kelly and Gwen. Olivia played on the floor with everything she could get her grubby little hands on. Jim was trying on a sort of chain mail type shirt while Turq and Genni examined some leather pouches, and Calab was jumping off everything he could climb on to. They were having such a good time that only Alena noticed when Tiernan and Sceria joined them.

Tiernan still looked as mad as a wild boar. He was holding Sceria by the arm and pushing her towards Alena. He made Sceria apologize to Alena which she did, although begrudgingly. There was something about Sceria's face that Alena didn't like, but she let it pass. Sceria had never had much of a liking for Alena. She wasn't about to force a friendship now.

Alena watched as Tiernan and Sceria joined the others. They were both sober and introspective, saying little to anyone. The natural light inside the castle was beginning to dim, and Alena watched Tiernan light three lanterns. These were carried back to their sleeping quarters along with their food and supplies.

Jim brought gifts for the twins and Elizabeth much to her delight. Alena was happy to see Elizabeth smile.

Tiernan and Sceria said nothing during the evening meal. Their silence was ominous and overshadowed the conversation. Soon no one was speaking at all. Everyone welcomed sleep that night as much to rest from each other as to rest from the exertion of the day. Alena listened as Tiernan tossed and turned in his bunk for what seemed like hours. He wasn't sleeping and neither was she. Alena wished that she knew how to mend the gulf between them, but she knew that it was not to be. Whatever it was that Tiernan found distasteful about her was evidently not something she could change. A while later she heard him get up and leave the room. She heard muffled voices outside the door. Who was he talking to? She waited and waited for him to return, but to no avail. At some point in the wee hours of the morning she finally slept.

Chapter Twenty

They had waited for Tiernan for three days. Where he had gone off to no one knew, not even Sceria. But now they were forced to go on without him. The Cephalopod ships had been circling above them for about a day and a half. How their group had been detected, Alena didn't know; perhaps Anthony had been sighted or Tiernan, or perhaps the Cephalopods had some other advanced method of detecting them. The members of her party had been unconcerned at Tiernan's absence at first, for he had told Ian that he wouldn't be absent long. But now with the Cephalopods near, they were nervous and anxious about Tiernan's welfare. The group had packed their gear on the two days previous in preparation for the next leg of their journey and hoped he would return. Finally, Alena knew that they could wait no longer. She had to press Sceria to lead them out. Sceria obviously loathed leading them, but whatever she felt, she hated the Cephalopods more.

They left under the cloak of darkness with only the moon to light their way. It took them at least an hour to get to the western gate which gleamed eerily in the moonlight. They had passed many obelisks covered in what looked like ancient hieroglyphics. Alena recognized that many of the glyphs matched the symbols from the volume that Maiser Runcan had given her, but there was no time to stop and decipher them now.

Alena had been given ample time to study her handwritten volume. The beginning pages were rudimentary, beginning with the Temarrian alphabet. She had even begun to learn a few fundamental words and phrases, although it would have been nice to have Tiernan there to help her with the pronunciation. Sceria had been no help at all in that department. Sceria could barely stand to be in the same room with her, let alone talk to her. The book had come easy at first but grew increasingly more difficult the more Alena read. There were many bizarre pictures and diagrams. She recognized the image of the veratnil throughout the volume. There was even a hand drawn picture of her pale cerulean bladed sword. Alena couldn't escape the crazy feeling that the book was somehow written specifically for her. Ian said that he felt the same about his, and Gwen had already grown scared of hers.

There was a paved road leading out of the western gates of the city, but Sceria didn't follow it. She took an overgrown path instead that headed straight into a stand of enormous trees. The way was treacherous and ill lit, but even Elizabeth was able to travel on her own two feet this time, thanks to a few days rest and Genni and Kelly's care. Alena studied Jim's form, making his way just ahead of her. Jim and Elizabeth both owed a lot to Turq and Genni. Alena wondered if Jim would ever realize it. She heard one of the twin babies whimpering, but the little one was quickly hushed as they trudged deeper into the darkness.

The group traveled by moonlight in silence for at least three hours until Sceria came to a stop at the base of a hill. She began searching the hill carefully until she found a well-hidden door that was overgrown with vines and grasses. Cautiously she began uncovering the large round door along the side nearest to her. With some help from Turq and Jim, they were able to pull the door open just wide enough for each of them to step through single file.

The air inside was stale. Sceria lit a lantern and Alena lit hers also. They were in what looked like an underground tunnel of sorts or a perhaps a mine shaft. Alena held up her light. The earth around them was supported by many strong wooden beams. They rested for a few minutes letting some of the fresh air inside, before they closed the door behind them and made their way into the deeper darkness of the tunnel. Something about the closing the door behind them made Alena wary, as if she were suddenly closed in and trapped. Calab cried out in alarm and Turq quickly lit another lantern, bringing up the rear. Alena wished suddenly that Tiernan was there to explain this creepy place to her. What was this tunnel for and where did it lead? Would Tiernan know where they had gone? And what in the world had become of him?

Alena knew that he had left because of her. She was fertile again and she suspected his leaving might have something to do with pheromones, but she couldn't be sure. That, along with whatever else was bothering him about her and her people, seemed to have driven him away. She couldn't understand him, but she knew that she ached inside at his absence from her. *So much for him staying by her side and being there for her—So much for being his responsibility—So much for promises.* The more Alena thought about it the more she fumed. But she didn't know if she were more upset with him or more frightened at his not being there at that moment.

As they traveled down the long underground passage, Alena could sense something evil lurking in the darkness. Turq grew nervous behind her, so Alena knew that he could feel it too. Sceria slowed the pace of the group and made her way very watchfully, whispering the same strange string of words over and over, almost like a chant. Had Alena been wrong to trust Sceria to lead them? What was Sceria up to and why had she brought them here? Alena felt her skin prickle in warning before she heard a shriek behind her.

Alena turned. The noise had come from Calab who pushed hysterically past her. What was behind them she was not sure, but its hypnotic eyes glowed above and behind them fierce and red in the dim light of the lantern. Turq pulled his long knife from his belt, as Genni followed after Calab. Alena reached for her knife but grasped the hilt of Wrayna, the cerulean sword, instead. She felt the sword surge with energy as she pulled it free. Jim was there too, aiming his own long knife towards the evil presence. The three of them stood side by side with Turq in the middle, facing the giant fork-tongued creature together.

Alena heard a gasp from Jim as the enormous black serpent struck out at him, sending him flying against the side of the tunnel. Turq stood protectively over Jim's limp unconscious body, while the serpent's laughter echoed hauntingly inside Alena's head. Could the others hear the mocking laughter or was it just inside her mind? The black serpent struck out again, and Turq was knocked easily from his feet with his own tortured cry, but he was able to give the wicked snake a determined swipe with his long knife before he fell. The creature's blood ran yellow and steamed and boiled as it ran, but still the creature's laughter echoed inside of Alena's head as it turned its glowing red eyes upon her. Alena didn't know how to explain it, but suddenly she felt completely calm.

Alena held Wrayna before her, and as the serpent moved to strike, she felt the sword send a bolt of lightning from its razor-sharp edge. The energy caused her to lose her balance, and she fell but so did the serpent. She watched as the gargantuan snake coiled in agony, writhing and hissing with pain. It turned its red eyes upon her once more before it shrank backwards into the darkness. Alena tried to stand, but she felt weak as if she had been drained of all energy. It was Ian that helped her to her feet. He was looking her up and down with amazement.

"That was remarkable, Captain, how did you do that?"

Alena was still feeling too light headed to stand. Ian helped her seat herself against the side of the tunnel. Alena put her head between her legs to try and get some blood to her brain.

All she could think of was her fallen companions. "Jim and Turq—Ian, you must help Jim and Turq."

"They are being looked after," Ian said quietly while observing her carefully. "It is my job to look after you."

"Says who?" Alena asked holding her head to keep it from spinning.

"Tiernan said that if any harm came to you, he would tear me apart limb from limb."

"Oh, is that so?"

Alena's mind felt like it was swimming around and around inside her head. She let go of Wrayna which seemed to help immediately. She glanced up at Ian's serious face. "I'm okay, Ian, I swear."

Jim was sitting upright with a dazed look on his face, surrounded by Elizabeth, Kelly, and Gwen, who each held a child on one arm and helped Jim with the other. Turq was already up on his feet with the help of Genni and moving towards Alena. Calab arrived before his parents and practically leaped into Alena's lap.

"That was so cool! How'd you do that?" he asked in his little alien voice. Alena smiled to herself. Calab was starting to sound like an Earth child.

Sceria stood off to one side with a look on her face that was unreadable. Alena studied her, but Sceria turned away. Alena didn't know how to explain what had just happened. It definitely wasn't something that she had any real scientific explanation for. Wrayna had somehow used Alena's life force to turn back the gigantic serpent. Alena didn't know what to think of the mystical sword, but she could not deny that something amazing was at work here. She fingered the hilt where it lay on the ground and then slid it back into its scabbard.

"We should get moving again before that humongous, red-eyed thing comes back," Alena said, trying to turn the attention away from herself. "I don't know about the rest of you, but I don't want to spend another minute down here. Can everyone move okay?"

Jim was up on his feet, a little unsteady, but he seemed alright.

"Your turn, Captain," Ian said, helping her up.

Alena felt like she had no equilibrium. She felt her world spinning. She pitched forward shakily. Ian held onto her firmly.

"Uhh, Captain, I don't think you're in any condition to go anywhere right now."

"We need to leave. We can't stay here. I can walk. I'm just going to need a little help."

Ian took one arm and Turq took the other, and they made their way. The journey through the hill was not incredibly long, but it seemed long in the sinister stretch of darkness with only a few lanterns to light their way. Sceria looked more thoughtful than usual which made Alena nervous. What was going on in that head of hers? Was she plotting another mishap? Alena was relieved when they reached the round door on the other side. They had quite a time pushing it open, but they were finally able to squeeze through.

The night air outside felt wonderful and fresh, but Alena collapsed on the ground. She was tired, spent, and she longed for sleep. She stared at the heavens above her. The moon had nearly crossed the entire night's sky, and there were the beginnings of hazy light on the horizon. Turq and Ian bent over her.

"You alright, Cap'n?" Turq asked.

"Yes, but I think it's about time we found a place to rest."

Sceria was motioning for them to follow.

Ian called up to her, "The Captain says it's time we found a place to rest."

Sceria nodded soberly in agreement, gesturing to someplace just ahead. They followed her to the edge of a nearby forest that was so dense it was impossible to make out what lay two feet ahead of them, especially in the dark.

"She doesn't intend to take us in there, does she?" Jim said aloud. Some of the others also grumbled in protest. Alena didn't blame them for their lack of faith, considering what they had just been through, but they chose to follow Sceria anyway. What choice did they have? The group was blind in the dark and exhausted from walking most of the night. Only Sceria knew the way ahead.

There was another broken overgrown path that led through the dense woods. The path led to a ruined village that was overgrown completely with foliage and trees. Judging by what they could see by the dim light of the moon, this village had been abandoned for some time, decades at least. There was a large pale stone building in the center of a group of ruined buildings that stood intact. It looked like some sort of church or temple. Sceria proceeded up several dozen steps to the great doors, and the rest of them followed. Unlike the doors in the hill, these opened easily, revealing a large domed room filled with many columns that lead to some sort of shrine. Moonlight filtered in through large windows and cast an eerie light upon everything about them. The room felt ancient and almost holy to Alena. She wondered at it briefly but encouraged all of them to find a place to rest. Gratefully, she felt nothing of the foreboding here that she had felt in the tunnel. With some luck, they would find safety here while they slept.

After dropping their packs and taking no more than a few minutes to unroll their beds, most of the crew was asleep within moments. Alena, although exhausted, waited until everyone was settled and quiet before drifting off to sleep.

It was midday before Alena awoke. Sunlight streamed through the grand windows above her. All were asleep with the exception of Ian, who sat in one of the beams of light reading his books. Alena went and seated herself next to him with her own book.

"How's your studying coming along? Are you making any progress?" Ian was examining one particular page with some scrutiny. He pointed to the mural that hung on the wall opposite the two of them and then back to the books that lay open on the floor. In two of Ian's volumes there was an image that almost exactly matched the mural on the opposite wall. The mural itself was entirely shocking. Alena just sat there and stared open-mouthed at the thing. The floor to ceiling painting was of three pale skinned people seated on the backs of three hideous veratnil, but if that was not horrifying enough, the three bore a striking resemblance to Ian, Gwen, and herself. The dark-haired woman in the center wore long dark boots exactly like Alena's and wielded a cerulean sword that could be none other than Wrayna.

"Terrifying, isn't it?" Ian said quietly.

"You don't think that..."

"Yes, I do. I believe that this masterful painting is of you, me, and Gwen."

"But how can that be? This mural was probably painted centuries ago?"

"Just wait until Gwen sees it. I don't think she would ever have imagined herself mounted on the back of one of those gruesome creatures." Ian smiled to himself.

"Do you think this is amusing, because I certainly don't."

Ian's face grew serious. "No, Captain, neither do I. Frankly, I'm pretty concerned about where this is all going, and why it is focused on the three of us. I don't even want to entertain what this mural might mean."

"I think I've had just about enough of all of this mystical nonsense. If Tiernan were here I think he'd be extremely sorry right now. I'd have quite a lot to say to him about taking us to his people, especially like this."

"Tiernan's not having an easy time of it either, Captain. I actually think this is harder on him than it is on the rest of us."

"Yeah, and why is that?"

"I don't know. Sure, it's hard for us, but for Tiernan everything seems agonizing."

Alena was quiet. What Ian said was true. Was Tiernan agonizing even now? She picked up her own volume and started thumbing through it. There were dozens of images of veratnil scattered throughout the odd book along with a few other strange creatures. Well, if the Temarrians thought that she was ever going to climb onto the back of one of those things, they were mistaken. She turned back to the beginning of the book and found the place she had been reading.

"How are you coming with the language?" Ian asked.

"Slowly, but I'm making progress and you?"

"The same."

Ian and Alena practiced simple phrases for a bit before the others began to wake. When Gwen rolled out of bed and caught sight of the two of them studying together, she came to join them and positively shrieked when she caught sight of the mural. The rest of the group, with the exception of Sceria, gathered around Gwen to see what the commotion was. They too were shocked by what lay before them.

"It's certainly an alarming likeness," Alena heard Kelly say.

Jim glanced over to where Sceria was lurking behind them. He motioned to her gruffly. "Do you want to explain to us what this is all about?"

Sceria refused to say anything and slunk away. Whatever their differences, Alena could see that Sceria also suffered, but she suffered in bitterness and anger. What could Sceria be so angry about? Alena began to wonder if the Temarrians knew how to share their feelings. It certainly seemed to be a problem for both Sceria and Tiernan.

The group all began their midday meal preparations. Several of her crew asked Alena what she planned to do next. Alena didn't know what to tell them, other than she wanted to wait to see if Tiernan would return. But what if Tiernan never found them? What if some harm had come to him and he could never return? Alena sensed that everyone felt a little lost without Tiernan. They at least trusted Tiernan far more than they trusted

Sceria. Everyone was growing nervous. But Jim seemed the antsiest of them all. Alena found him watching Sceria with a profound look of mistrust upon his malcontent face. She knew that look and didn't like what it meant. Sighing inwardly, Alena hoped that Tiernan would return to them and soon.

After lunch, they divided into groups and scouted the area. Alena was intrigued by the overgrown ruins that lay all around them. What had happened here and why had it been abandoned even years before the Cephalopod invasion? She discovered a long column that lay on its side broken which contained many glyphs. Alena tried to decipher a little of what it said, but a lot had crumbled and worn away. A flock of birds rose suddenly from one of the ruined buildings, and Alena turned with a start. Something had disturbed the birds, but Alena didn't wait to see what it was; she hurried into the shadows and watched mesmerized as what seemed like thousands of birds rose into the sky. A gray-blue wolf-like creature emerged from the building with a bird dangling viciously from its mouth. Alena watched as it sniffed the air a few times and then trotted off to a large hole under a giant overturned slab of stone. The creature looked around warily, sniffing the air once more, before disappearing into the dark hole.

"Great," Alena said to herself, "another predator to avoid." Although this one seemed tame compared to the other three that they had encountered. It was probably just feeding its young. Silently, she crept away from the den, putting as much distance as she could between her and the wolfish creature before it reappeared. What a rugged and wild planet this was. Alena longed sometimes just for safety, but that didn't seem to be something she could be blessed with for very long, even now as the air suddenly filled with a great tumult of noise.

Alena watched as the hundreds of birds circling in the air suddenly swooped back down with warning cries. She glanced skyward, and her heart filled with instant dread. Veratnil. The birds had attracted the hideous veratnil. Alena could see three of the creatures winging their way toward them from the east. She let out her own cry of warning to her crew, as she raced to the safety of the only building that remained standing.

Alena was the furthest from the doors. She watched all the others reach the stone building where they had camped for the night, well ahead of her. She didn't think she would make it up the steps before the veratnil arrived, but she had nowhere else to go. She stumbled up the stairs, feeling the push of air from the first veratnil's wings. Ian was waiting at the door, beckoning for her to hurry. She felt the veratnil's claws just miss her as she flung herself through the door.

The door was banged shut and bolted as the veratnil shrieked in anger. There was a huge splintering sound as the veratnil raked its claws against the door. Another of the veratnil clawed at the roof. Alena tried to remain on her feet while the large stone edifice around them trembled. She wondered if the three creatures would bring the walls crashing in upon them. About the time she was convinced their shelter would not stand, the shaking stopped, and the creatures moved off. Luckily for all of them, something else had drawn the veratnils' attention. Alena thought she heard the sickening sound of crushing metal, a good distance away, but she couldn't be sure. The veratnil had one strong point, at least, and that was taking down the Cephalopod ships that were always searching for them.

They didn't venture out again until late afternoon. If the group hadn't needed to find a source of water to refill their containers, they probably wouldn't have come out at all. Alena,

Kelly, Ian, and Turq left the others and made their way cautiously through the ruined buildings to the edge of the forest. Alena glanced back at the scarred door of the church-like building and shuddered. The door was a splintered mess and wouldn't hold out against another hungry veratnil. Even the building itself looked like it might topple over at any moment. Alena decided they would have to find another camp and soon. Alena didn't know how intelligent the veratnil were, but she was certain that the veratnil would return. Perhaps it was unwise to linger any longer at all.

Turq gave Alena an encouraging signal indicating that they should follow him. Turq had a knack for finding water, and it was not long until they heard the unmistakable sound of water trickling from a small brook. They each eagerly filled several containers and made their way carefully back to camp. Upon entering the shattered doors, Alena was unprepared for what she would find there and almost dropped her water containers in surprise. Tiernan stood before her, looking bedraggled and careworn, his clothes in tatters. He turned towards them as they entered. His eyes found hers, and Alena felt the shock of his amber-orange gaze all the way to her bones. He was relieved to see her and glad about it, but he made no move toward her. She noticed, however, that his rich timbered voice trembled slightly with sentiment as he spoke to her across the room.

"We need to move out. Now would be a good time."

"Now?" Alena looked around the room, noticing that the rest of the group had almost finished packing.

"Yes, it is not safe to stay here any longer."

Alena, Ian, and Kelly hurried to pack up their things. Genni had already packed up for Turq, so he distributed water to the rest of the group. Alena watched Tiernan out of the corner of her eye as she shoved her belongings into her pack. He was standing in front of the mural with a wild expression upon his handsome face. She wished she could read his thoughts at that moment. She examined his roughened appearance. Tiernan was bruised and covered with cuts and one long gash that went from his shoulder down half the length of his side. What had happened to him? Where had he been? She longed to go to him and embrace him. Alena couldn't stop her knees from trembling just at the sight of him standing there.

His gaze returned to her as she straightened up and then went back to the painting and then back to her again. She felt her face coloring. Blast that stupid mural. Alena could see from the expression on Tiernan's face that it was only further dividing them which wasn't what she wanted at all. Alena wanted to be close to him—to mend the breach that was between them, but she found herself lashing out at him instead.

"If your people think I'm going to climb on the back of one of those things, they are going to be extremely disappointed," Alena said a little too forcefully.

"I'm glad to see that you haven't lost any of your spirit, while I've been gone." A slight smile crossed Tiernan's face which only made Alena angry. She had to restrain herself from bashing him over the head with her pack. She found her eyes tearing with emotion, so she marched away from him, turning her attentions to helping the others in their preparations to leave.

Chapter Twenty-one

The group followed Tiernan into the forest at dusk. Alena followed uncomfortably just behind him which was Tiernan's idea and not hers. She didn't know why he wanted her there, especially since he hadn't spoken a word to her since their departure. Tiernan had been different ever since their foray into the city of Tavonsheigh. The whole ritual with Maiser Runcan seemed to have changed even more between them and not for the better. Alena observed Tiernan's muscular form in front of her. She liked how he moved although he seemed to be traveling with more difficulty than normal. He must have been through something awful, and some of his scrapes and bruises needed to be tended to, especially the long gash that ran down his side. How had it happened?

They came across one of the wolf-like creatures dead along the trail, its gut ripped open and entrails spilled out upon the ground. Alena wondered if it were the mate of the one she had seen earlier that day. The sight of it lying there like that made Alena depressingly sad, and it let loose a flood of silent tears that she couldn't hold back which was not characteristic for her. What exactly she was crying about she wasn't sure. She hated to cry, but today the tears came quietly, pouring down her face. After a sniffle or two, which she attempted to muffle, Tiernan turned around and regarded her with curiosity.

"What's wrong, Alena? Are you alright?"

Alena nodded but couldn't speak. She was afraid the tears might turn into something like sobbing. She motioned for him to continue their journey, which he did, but he turned back more often to check her progress. Eventually, it became too dark for him to see her face which made Alena feel a lot more comfortable.

The group traveled for perhaps an hour before the terrain became quite rocky. They began to climb over rocks and boulders in the dark. Occasionally, someone behind her would slip, and she would hear a short curse in the dark, but other than the occasional grunt and loose rock, the group travelled in silence. They came to a point in the long, rocky climb where it seemed impossible to move forward. The boulder ahead was too large to climb over, especially in the dark. This didn't seem to deter Tiernan, however, he turned back and took hold of Alena, hoisting her onto his shoulders. The physical proximity was almost shocking to them, and Alena hastily climbed onto the top of the boulder.

Alena found that it wasn't actually a boulder but a long rocky shelf that ran into a cave. She waited until all but Tiernan were hoisted up. Tiernan scrambled up some other way, and Alena jumped as he appeared suddenly behind her. He moved swiftly past her, lighting a lantern and holding it up to the entrance. The cave was full of provisions like the other outpost and although it was smaller, it would house all of them, even if a bit snuggly. It was late, and many of those with children began unrolling their beds and setting up for the night, but Alena couldn't even entertain the thought of sleep. She was too wound up. She noticed that Tiernan hung back as well. Perhaps he waited to see where she would settle for the night so that he could place himself far away from her. She sighed, finding a comfortable sitting position with her back against the rock outside the cave entrance. She leaned back and looked up at the stars. She was surprised when Tiernan seated himself next to her. They sat there in ominous quiet, only inches apart in the darkness. After a while, curiosity got the best of Alena, and she could stand the silence no longer.

"What happened to you Tiernan? Where have you been?" she asked, tenderly examining his long gash. He pulled away from her abruptly.

"I had to leave, but I've been close by."

"Why did you have to leave?" she questioned, while feeling the color in her face rising.

"For your safety."

"What do you mean for my safety, Tiernan?" she snorted. "What you are saying is simply absurd." Alena struggled to keep her temper in check, but she couldn't help but continue. "Yeah, I felt safe with the Cephalopods circling us for days while we waited for you and when that huge black snake thing came after us in the tunnel. I think I felt the safest when that veratnil tried to pick me off earlier today. I know I've found myself feeling extremely grateful that you left, so that I could feel a lot safer."

"Alena, don't…."

"Don't what?"

"I can't be around you when you're…" Tiernan stopped.

"When I'm what…ovulating? Grow up, Tiernan. What is it you're afraid might happen? I don't see you running off for days when it happens to the rest of the women here. Besides, you've been around me during ovulation several times before."

"It's different now." Tiernan's voice was strained.

"Why is it different? Is it different since we talked to that Maiser Runcan? Does it have something to do with the prophecy?"

"No, I mean—Yes. "Tiernan was clearly reeling from her directness. "You wouldn't understand."

"Try me."

"No, I can't. It isn't fair to you."

"Is it not fair, like it's not safe?" Alena protested bitterly. She wasn't about to put up with this. Why wouldn't he just come clean with her? She got up to leave. If she didn't get away from him now, things were going to get ugly. Alena tried to step over him, but only ended up stumbling over him in the darkness. She landed squarely in his lap. His arms reached out to steady her, and she could feel him tremble slightly. He seemed shocked... frozen...with his arms snuggly around her. It was a moment that seemed to go on forever. Tiernan took in the scent of her and then held her tighter and tighter.

"Alena, I..." she heard him say and then his lips were on hers, and he was kissing her, desperately at first as she struggled against him and then softly, passionately as she returned his advances. There was no denying the fervor between them as the kisses grew deeper and hotter. But Tiernan was shaking terribly.

"Alena, I can't," she heard him say as he kissed her with anxious longing. With herculean effort he broke free from her, pushed her away, and disappeared into the darkness. Alena was left sitting in confusion on the cold slab of stone, cursing the day that she had ever let herself get so wound up in this wild, bronze man with amber-orange eyes.

She stood up unsteadily and turned, feeling a pair of eyes on her. Alena could barely make out the form of Sceria standing there in the darkness. Had she seen what had just transpired?

Alena hurried to move past her, to find solitude in the bitter darkness. But Sceria stopped her, holding out a small bowl to her.

"Eat these," she said, "they will help you sleep." It was the first time Alena had heard her speak in Alena's own tongue. She took the bowl from Sceria and thanked her, wondering at her kindness. The bowl was filled with tiny berries that looked almost gray in the darkness. She set the bowl beside her bed, but she didn't eat them. It wasn't until much later, after tossing and turning for many hours, that she decided to give them a try. They tasted tart and delicious, so she ate almost the entire bowl. It wasn't long, however, until she began to feel incredibly strange, almost as if she were floating. Alena lost the use of her limbs first, and then she broke out into a terrible sweat. She tried to scream, but nothing seemed to come from her lips. She felt herself floating into nothingness and then darkness.

Alena lived in a nightmare from which she couldn't break free. It was as though she were screaming from every cell in her body and then being burned alive. She was aware of being surrounded by the others, but she couldn't see anything except outlines and blurry shadows. Someone tried to hold her, but it hurt too badly. She squirmed until she was free. Still she burned. She screamed again and again, but no sound came. Her eyes stung and dripped with tears, but it did not clear her vision. She shook uncontrollably until her teeth rattled, and she felt she would go completely mad from the pain. It became too much, and she passed out once again.

When she became cognizant again, she found that she was on her feet flailing. Hands grabbed out to hold her, but she shook them free. She was aware of being in the daylight, the wind whipping in her face and something very large flapping it's wings above her. She reached out to it in her delirium, calling to the creature. The veratnil came closer, hovering directly over her, before she was knocked rudely to the ground by an unknown force and consciousness was lost to her once more.

It was a melody that called her awake the third time—a strange beautiful song that she had heard once before. But she couldn't remember where she had heard it, she couldn't remember anything. Who was she and why was she here? Who was singing and why was she hot and burning still? The song was sad and the voice rich and deep, which triggered something in her mind. Tiernan—Tiernan was singing. He had sung this song to her before. Intrigued she sat up, but her vision was still blurred.

"Shhhh," she heard him say. "Lay still, the worst of it has passed now."

What had passed? What had happened to her? Why was she in this state? Alena tried to remember. She grew conscious of others moving around her. Someone placed a cool wet cloth on her forehead. She lay back and sighed. The cloth felt good. She could feel the pain lessening, yet still she burned from the inside out. She tried to speak—to ask questions, but the only sound that came out was a strange dry croak.

"Don't try to talk just now, there will be plenty of time for that," another voice said, another voice she recognized—Kelly. Water was pressed to her grateful lips. Alena swallowed, feeling the liquid go all the way down her parched throat. She voiced her gratitude with a moan and found herself drifting once more. She was in and out of consciousness for several more long hours before the pain finally left her. Everything was still a blur, and it was evening now. Alena tried to make sense of the shapes in the darkness but recognized little. She was frightened then. Was her vision ruined? She sat up, feeling the blood rush out of her head.

"Hey there, easy now," Tiernan was there at her side, placing an arm protectively around her.

"Tiernan, I can't see. I can't see," her voice sounded gravelly and full of panic.

"It's okay my little wootchka," he whispered. "Your sight will return."

Alena found herself clinging to him in fear. "Are you sure?"

"Yes, and your sense of smell."

"My sense of smell?" Now that she thought about it, she didn't smell anything, which probably meant she couldn't taste anything either. What had happened to her? She tried to remember.

"It will all return. Don't worry, Alena. Here, lay your head on my shoulder."

"What happened to me?" Her mind was in a fog. Tiernan seemed different. Tiernan had left her, hadn't he? And then he returned—It all came back suddenly, and she tensed against him. He had kissed her and then abandoned her, and Sceria had given her some berries. She tried to push him away. This was his fault.

"Alena, it's okay, I'm here."

"Don't, I don't want to be close to you," she struggled, but she was weak. How long had it been since she had eaten?

"Stop, you'll wear yourself out."

"Leave me alone, Tiernan, I don't trust you."

"Alena, I'm sorry, I have been wrong about a lot of things. Please let me help you now."

"What if I don't want your help? Sceria tried to kill me. I don't want anything to do with either of you! How long have I been like this?" It all came out in a dry rush of words.

"It's been three days, but you've come through it, better than anyone I have ever known. You've passed the Washeenah. I'm sorry my little wootchka that I left you, I didn't know."

"You didn't know what? What are you talking about, and why do you keep calling me that?"

"I didn't know that Sceria would do this. I never would have predicted that you would pass this test so easily."

"What test? Is eating poisonous berries some kind of test to your people? Do you think being burned alive for three days is easy?"

"I'm sorry, Alena. No, of course it was difficult. I wish I could have helped you prepare. And Sceria shouldn't have given you so many berries. That was totally uncalled for and reckless." Tiernan's voice sounded angry and bitter. "But this is not the time to worry you about such weighty things. You should rest now. We will have time to talk about this when you have your strength back."

"No, you don't, Tiernan. You are not going to avoid me this time. You sit here and talk to me right now, or I swear I will never speak to you again."

Tiernan sighed, wearily, "Okay, Alena."

"What is this washee… or whatever it is you called it?"

"The Washeenah is a test of purity. Only an important few are ever asked to go through such a ritual, generally only when an individual is called upon to do something critical for the good of our entire people or sometimes to be eligible for a significant bonding. Successfully passing through the Washeenah proves that they are without fault."

"Bonding? What is bonding? And didn't you just say that you didn't expect me to pass this test? Am I somehow impure to your race? What is this fault that you speak of?"

"Slow down, Alena. One question at a time," he said laying a gentling hand on her arm. "My race is not like your race. We are loyal to one partner. We don't do as your race does and move from partner to partner." Alena started to object to Tiernan's opinion of her race, but he stopped her, putting a hand to her lips.

"Please, Alena, let me explain. There is a prophecy that has been passed down through the ages of my people that speaks of a beautiful imposing woman of dark hair and pale skin that has the power to wield the sword of Wrayna, who would save my people from destruction. It was foretold that this powerful woman was to be as pure as the waters of Felusia. Maiser Runcan believed this woman to be you. But I couldn't believe it, not knowing what I did. I doubted. Sceria doubted. We witnessed daily what happened in the biome and well, when Anthony said that he had...."

"That he had what?" Alena interrupted angrily.

"That he had been with you..."

"Been with him? You mean he said that we were intimate? That's ridiculous. How could you believe that? Not when you witnessed what you did."

"I was wrong to believe him. I know that now. But given the circumstances, how could I have believed any different? Anthony bragged about being with every single woman in our group. And when I discovered that he had fathered Sceria's child, I couldn't help but believe it. The evidence was all around me."

Nothing that Tiernan said could have shocked Alena more, "Anthony is the father of Sceria's baby? Are you certain?" she repeated with dismay.

"Didn't you know? Sceria has confirmed it herself."

"No, I didn't. To tell you the truth, I thought that you had fathered her child."

"You thought that I had?" Tiernan almost choked. "Alena, there is something that you must know. Sceria was the wife of my brother. Such a thing would be an abomination."

"Why didn't you tell me all of this before?"

"It's complicated..."

"So, tell me. Keeping it to yourself has obviously done neither of us any good."

"I know that now, and I will tell you once you are stronger. It's really too complicated to get into just now."

Alena gave him a look of exasperation.

"I will tell you, I promise, before we reach the hidden city."

"I'm holding you to that, Tiernan," Alena said, placing a hand firmly on Tiernan's chest. She was growing so tired, and her voice was barely audible now. "Sceria hoped to kill me. Neither of you expected me to survive."

"Yes, that is unfortunately true. But Sceria is grieved by her actions. She will pay dearly for what she has done. I am sorry that we both believed Anthony's lies."

"Where is Sceria, now?" she asked sleepily.

"She is kept under guard. Jim has taken it upon himself to see that she hardly blinks." Alena could hear the trouble in his voice.

"So, things are on edge between my kind and yours," she whispered.

"You could say that but don't worry, things have been better since Kelly assured them you would survive."

Alena yawned. It hurt something terrible to yawn. Tiernan seemed to sense this.

"You should give your voice a rest now," he said gently. "You don't want any lasting effects from your ordeal. It really is better that you sleep." He shifted his weight and encouraged her to lie down.

"Are you going to stay here with me?" she half-muttered, already starting to drift, not certain whether she wanted him nearby or not.

"Yes," she heard him whisper, "I will stay and watch over you."

Chapter Twenty-two

Alena awoke to the hustle of life around her. She blinked hard, then blinked again, trying to clear her vision. Her vision was still clouded, but a tiny bit improved. She sat up, listening to the babble of sounds around her. At least the whole ordeal had done nothing to damage her hearing. She tried to clear her vision once more and sighed. The blurry patches of light and color were going to take some getting used to. Kelly brought her a steaming cup of something, but Alena could neither tell what it was nor taste it; she could only recognize that it was an odd shade of brown. Ian came and plopped himself on the other side of her.

"It's good to see you up, Captain, how are you?"

"I can't see anything or taste anything, but all the heat seems to have left my body," she answered hoarsely.

"I'm glad you're improving. We thought we were going to lose you a couple of times, especially when you called down that veratnil from the sky.

"I did what?" Alena sat up straighter.

"Don't you remember?" Ian asked her oddly. "Well, I guess you were pretty out of your mind. Maybe you don't remember."

"Tell me." Alena had a vague remembrance of what Ian was talking about, but she had imagined it was only a dream.

"You'd been burning with fever for a long time. You hadn't moved, hardly at all, and then suddenly it was like you had gone crazy. You were kicking and thrashing. No one could hold you. You ran out onto the shelf. The wind was blowing terribly, and we were afraid that you would blow right off, but no one could keep hold of you. It was like you had the strength of ten men. You reached your arms to the heavens and emitted the strangest most bone-chilling cry that I have ever heard, and then that veratnil swooped out of the sky. It hovered above you and you practically sang to the creature. We all didn't know what to do. It was Tiernan that finally knocked you to the ground and dragged you back inside, and that didn't make the veratnil very happy. I'll show you the claw marks that it left in the shelf when you're feeling strong enough."

"What did the veratnil do after Tiernan brought me inside?"

"That's the strangest part of this whole thing. It didn't try to harm any of us. It just gave a strange cry of its own and settled into the gully below us. Everyone has been afraid to leave for fear that the thing will eat them. Occasionally, when the creature ventures off to hunt, we're able to resupply ourselves with water and other necessities. We've thought about making an escape, but it's been too risky to move you."

"It's still out there?"

"Yes, sometimes it even comes close to the cave and claws at the shelf and tries to get a look inside. Tiernan says it's a male and it's the biggest one he has ever seen."

Alena didn't want to talk about the veratnil anymore. She didn't want to think about what any of it might mean for her. It frightened her. She definitely didn't want to see the thing. Perhaps it was a good thing that her vision was so clouded right now.

"How are the others doing?" Alena asked, trying to change the subject. She could hear some of them mulling around her and listening to their conversation.

"Better now that you are starting to recuperate. Things were super tense for a while, but I don't want you to worry. We just want you to get better."

"What has happened? Ian, please tell me."

"Well, Tiernan and Jim got into a huge scrap. Maybe it's good that you can't see the both of them. It was pretty ugly, but it happened because they both care about you. Jim's been pretty much fighting everybody in your defense, and I think Tiernan is pretty deep into his feelings for you."

"What are you talking about?"

"Tiernan has been more distressed about you than anyone, and that's saying something because we've all been so anxious about you, Captain. Tiernan's practically banished Sceria from the rest of the group and doesn't care how nasty Jim gets with her. He has hardly left your side in three days even when we all tried to keep him away from you. Kelly had to step in and demand that he give you some space so you could recover. Kelly's been a champion in all of this trying to keep everyone from killing each other."

Alena heard Kelly come up and sit on the other side of her.

"I think Ian is exaggerating a bit—and filling my patient's head with way too much information right now. Off with you, Ian. Alena still has a lot of recovering to do, and I don't want you filling her head with all of this right now. Her job is to recover and not worry about the rest of us."

"Where is Tiernan?" Alena asked as Ian got up to leave. Kelly shooed him away and answered Alena for him.

"Tiernan is out with Turq, Genni, and Gwen, trying to scout out a way to get us out of here. We've all been a little confined the last few days. Even the children are feeling it. I don't think

Elizabeth has had any sleep between the care of her twins and Jim's escapades. How are you feeling?"

"Okay, I think. My throat feels amazingly dry. Actually all of me feels extremely dry."

"We need to get more liquids down you. Even your eyes have a dehydrated look about them. Hey Jim," Kelly chirped, making Alena jump, "bring the Captain some water, will you?"

Alena heard Jim's grunt of agreement from across the cave. She was grateful when he brought her a pouch sloshing with the water. She drank it eagerly, while Kelly encouraged her to slow down. "Too much at once will make you sick, Alena," she warned, taking the pouch from her.

Kelly was right of course. Giving a dying man too much water would only kill him. Had she been that close to death? Alena had experienced too many brushes with death lately.

"Would you like to get up and walk around a little?"

"Sure, "Alena agreed, although she didn't feel so certain with her sight the way it was and all.

"Don't worry, I'm here to lean on," Kelly reassured her.

Alena hadn't taken more than a short half turn around the cave before Tiernan, Gwen, Turq and Genni came scrambling in. With them came a gust of fierce wind and the horrible sound of something—claws, grating against the side of the cave.

"Get her down," Tiernan yelled. "Don't let it see her."

Alena stumbled to the ground, while someone hurriedly threw a blanket over her. The clawing continued along with the steady beat of huge wings and a disconcerting cry that made Alena want to get up and run to the creature, but strong hands held her down, pinning her to the ground. "Hold her, keep her down," Tiernan was saying. Alena struggled, found it hard to breathe, and fought desperately against her human captors. This continued until the clawing stopped and all became quiet as the veratnil finally left them.

"Let me breathe," she screamed with rage. The blanket was pulled from her, but a hand was clamped firmly over her mouth.

"Shhhh, Alena," Tiernan whispered, "Please don't do this. You don't want it to come back, do you?"

Alena didn't know what she wanted. Reason told her that she shouldn't want to go near the creature, but somehow, she wanted very much to be with it. She was drawn to it in a strange and compelling way. What was happening to her? She found that it was easy for her to break free from her captors without the blanket over her. She was mostly blind still and angry and confused. They were her enemies. They were keeping her from what she most desired. She moved in the direction of the cave opening where the light in her vision was the most brilliant.

"Stop, Alena. Please stop." It was Tiernan's desperate, terrified, sorrowful voice that stopped her and made her turn. What was she doing now? She struggled to understand what was happening to her and what had become of the self that she was accustomed to. Alena began to shake, feeling trapped somehow between two worlds and drawn at the same time to both.

"Alena, Alena, please."

It was Tiernan's voice that won in the end. It was with caution that he approached her, speaking to her with all the calm and reassurance he could muster, while she shook from head to toe like a scared wild animal. She collapsed into darkness as he reached her, frightened and completely spent.

"We've got to get her out of here and away from it, as soon as we can—before it drives her mad," were the words being spoken as she regained consciousness. She lifted her head making out the shapes of the people that surrounded her. "I thought you said that she was not going to have any ill-effects from this Washeenah ritual or whatever you call it?" Jim's angry voice bounced back and forth in her head. "What do you call what just happened?"

"It's alright, I'm okay," Alena said in a gravelly voice. All attention was suddenly turned in the direction of her voice.

"She's coming around," she heard Kelly say, "Everyone give her some space."

Alena started to sit up, but she felt dizzy. Tiernan reached out to steady her. "Get away from her," Jim said, pushing Tiernan's arm away from her. "Haven't you done enough damage already?"

"Are you crazy?" Turq retorted with anger. "It's because of him that she is still with us at all."

"I would appreciate it if you would all stop talking like I am not here," Alena grumbled. She reached toward Tiernan herself and let him steady her. "Look, I don't know what's happening to me, but I think I would like some time with Tiernan and Kelly to sort it out. You can all go back to doing something useful until I have something to report."

"That sounds like the old Captain to me," Ian said to the others. "Why don't we make up something for supper while they talk? I'm starved."

Alena waited until she was left alone with Tiernan and Kelly. Kelly handed her the water pouch and encouraged her to drink while Tiernan helped steady her shaking hands. She leaned on him, feeling suddenly relieved by his presence. It was Tiernan's voice that had saved her from...saved her from what?

"The veratnil calls to me, Tiernan, and compels me to..." Alena tried to sort through the confusion in her mind. "If it were not for your voice calling me back, I would have gone. What is happening? What does it mean?" She could feel him tense slightly as she spoke.

"So, you feel compelled to go to the creature? What I have feared must have happened then, but my voice was able to call you back? That is quite interesting—yes, very interesting." Tiernan seemed to be half-talking to himself.

"Just what do you fear has happened?" Kelly demanded.

"Yes, what has happened to me?"

"Alena, I believe the veratnil has become bonded to you and you to him. The prophecy foretold that this would occur as it will also one day for Ian and Gwen. A bonding between one of our kind and the veratnil has not happened for millennia. My people have not experienced such a bonding since the days of Malucia. We no longer have the knowledge of exactly how it occurs. I had thought that the bonding would have to be total and complete, but it appears not to be so; otherwise, there is no way I could have called you back."

"I felt like I was being torn in two when you called for me, when you both called for me..." Alena said with a frightened whisper. She was frightened at the thought of being tied somehow to the creature, but when it called for her there was nowhere else she wanted to be except—except for with Tiernan, and somehow the pull to be with him had been stronger, at least this time. She turned towards him wishing she could see his face. She knew he was studying her.

"I am here for you, Alena. I don't have the answers that you seek right now, but I will be here to help you work them out. For now, I think it's best to just get you feeling better. Do you think you can lay low for a while and not draw attention from that giant creature out there, at least until I can figure out what's best to do?"

Alena nodded, but didn't feel reassured. There was too much at work here, too much she didn't understand, and Tiernan only made it more complicated for her. A part of her wanted to scream and run away, and the other part wanted only to be right where she was. Kelly gave her a looking over and said that she looked a bit less dehydrated. They both helped her drink some more, and Alena was grateful when Gwen brought her dinner, good, quiet, and sweet Gwen. It was hard to imagine Gwen having to go through any of what she had just been through.

It was growing late in the day. The blotches of color that Alena could see lost their brightness and faded into gray. She ate the last bites of her stew carefully. It hurt a bit still to swallow, but it felt good to have something solid in her stomach. Alena didn't know whether to be angry or flattered when they placed her bed furthest from the cave opening against the cave wall and then placed their bedrolls between her and the door. Was she a prisoner or were they protecting her? Tiernan lay closest to her but was quiet and thoughtful; he seemed almost sad. Alena wanted to ask him why but sensed that he didn't want to talk about it tonight. Alena was still exhausted anyway and eagerly sought the relief of sleep from her worries.

When Alena awoke, she could feel the tension in Tiernan's whole body. He was holding her tightly which seemed to be driving him completely crazy. He seemed to want her and abhor her at the same time. Carefully he pushed her away from him, slipping out of his bedroll and wandering away to join the others, who were getting their breakfast. It made Alena angry and sad all at once. Why was he like this? She didn't understand it, especially now that he knew the truth about her. Was she unacceptable to him even now?

Alena sat up and looked around the room. Her eyesight was much improved today. Her eyes were still blurry like she needed correctional measures, but she was able to identify the objects around her. This improved her spirits quite a bit. Ian brought her a steaming cup, which actually seemed to have a bland taste to it, although Ian informed her that it was extremely spicy.

"Tiernan said that this would help you."

Alena scowled at the mention of his name. "It's a shame he couldn't bring it himself, and he decided to make you his whipping boy instead. I'm glad that you're here, though, have a seat."

"Don't be too hard on him, Captain. I know he cares about you. I actually have a theory why he acts the way he does, and I wanted to talk to you about it." Ian was trying carefully not to be overheard.

Alena lowered her voice, "What do you mean?"

"Well, you know the books that were given to me by Maiser Runcan?"

"Yes?"

"Well, while you have been recovering, I have been studying them, and I came across something really interesting."

"What is it?"

"Well, I was trying to figure out what had happened to you with this Washeenah and this veratnil that you seem to go all crazy over, and I came across this section about bonding."

"Tiernan says the same thing is going to happen to you," Alena told Ian.

"Yes, I know, that was another reason I wanted to understand it so badly, but let me finish. I came across this section about bonding between the Temarrians. Alena, listen to this," he pulled his book out of his tunic. "The Temarrians choose a mate not by sexual attraction, or common interests, or by family alliances as our people have done but by a complete compelling magnetism that only occurs once in their lifetime. The Temarrians don't mate by choice, it just happens to them. Someone comes along, and something happens that binds them to that person for life. Any sexual deviance from this bond-mate is punishable by death."

"Are you telling me that Tiernan's people mate for life like eagles or wolves? And they have some compelling bond that draws them to their mate? Why are you telling me this?"

"Think about it. Tiernan stays with you like he is compelled to do so, and yet he is conflicted about it. I think something happened to him beyond his control that bonded him permanently to you. Something that he doesn't believe was supposed to happen, but it did, and he is uncertain what to do about it."

"That's crazy!"

"It makes perfect sense, Alena. Everyone in our group can see that he's crazy about you and angry at the same time."

It did make sense, but Alena didn't want to believe it, not when she knew for herself that Tiernan was attracted to her, cared for her, but somehow loathed her all the same. It would be a tragedy to be bonded for life to something that you loathed, and she didn't want to be that something, not if it made Tiernan miserable. She cared about him too much. If she could admit it to herself, she even loved him. No, this bonding thing simply couldn't be true.

Kelly and Gwen came over to them. "Time to go and get the rest of your things packed up, Ian. Tiernan wants us to leave right away. We've come to help you, Alena."

They made short work of rolling up her bed and stuffing her pack. "Why do we need to leave, now?" Alena asked.

"Because that creature of yours has moved off for a bit, and Tiernan wants to get out while we still have a chance at it," Kelly paused, unrolling a long white cloth. "We need to wrap your eyes, Alena. Tiernan says the sunlight will be too bright for them."

"But I don't want to wrap them. I'm just beginning to see again."

"I happen to agree with Tiernan. Let's give them more time to heal, doctor's orders."

Alena sighed, but allowed Kelly and Gwen to wrap the long cloth around and around her head, covering her eyes. She was totally blind now. Quietly, she heard her crewmates filter from the cave with their belongings until only she and Tiernan were left. She felt him tremble as he took hold of her, guiding her to the cave opening. Cautiously, he lifted her down to waiting hands. When Tiernan was once again behind her, they all stopped to listen before moving off again.

Chapter Twenty-three

Sometimes Alena walked and sometimes Tiernan carried her. He wanted to care for her himself and refused help from the others, even though they could have moved faster by sharing the load. Always he would tense or tremble when touching her, even for something as simple as holding her arm to guide her. Alena began to seriously consider what Ian had said to her that very morning. There was something extremely complicated going on between Tiernan and herself.

Only an hour later Alena suddenly felt a pain penetrating through the very heart of her, and her mind rang with horrible piercing cries of outrage and sorrow. She doubled over and would have fallen if Tiernan hadn't been there to catch her. She grabbed her head in agony.

"What is it, Alena? Are you alright?"

"The veratnil…" she managed to say, "has discovered my absence. I can't get its cries out of my head."

Soon she was whimpering with anguish and Tiernan whistled for the others to stop. Something was pressed to her lips which made her feel sleepy, and she was grateful at last to lose consciousness.

When she awoke her eyes were no longer bandaged, and she could see a great deal more than before. They were in a large room that didn't seem to have any windows and only one door.

The room was circular in shape with a flat roof. Candles were lit on sconces attached about every five feet to the circular wall. It looked like a training room of sorts for some kind of sport. She sat up feeling the cool air that filtered down to her through vents in the ceiling. Most of her crewmates were sitting together talking quietly, while their babies napped and Calab skipped in a circle around and around the room. Tiernan sat off to one side by himself. Alena's vision was not clear enough yet to see his expression, but his slumped shoulders told her of his sullen mood. Sceria sat crumpled on the opposite side of the room from Alena looking positively bedraggled. Alena gasped at her haggard appearance. She got to her feet to approach and see more clearly the fallen creature, but Jim suddenly stood in her way.

"Stay away from her, Captain; she's a wicked one and will only do you harm if she can get her dirty hands on you."

"What have you done to her? Has she even eaten?"

"Why does it matter? She tried to murder you. She gets what she deserves."

All eyes were upon Alena now. "This is inhumane. You can't let her suffer like this. Where is her baby?"

Jim looked around. "Who last had her brat?"

Gwen brought Alena Sceria's baby. He made a piteous weak noise as Alena took the baby in her arms. The poor thing was totally emaciated. "Hasn't he eaten either?"

"We've tried to feed him, Alena, but he won't take milk from me or Elizabeth," Kelly offered.

"Surely, you haven't denied Sceria her own child?"

All eyes were on Jim now, and he shifted uncomfortably.

"Move aside, Jim, this baby needs his mother."

Alena placed the child in Sceria's shaking arms. "Genni, will you help her? Turq get her some broth or something to eat." Alena looked around at all of them. "No one under my command is to be stripped of their basic comforts, especially food, is that clear? We've all suffered enough."

"But she tried to kill you, Captain," Elizabeth muttered.

"We don't know all of the complexities of why she did what she did. I think Sceria should be given a chance to explain her actions, but in the meantime, I will not tolerate Sceria or her child being mistreated. Is that understood?"

They were all looking at her strangely. "Welcome back, Captain. It's good to see you behaving like yourself again," Ian said. His comment eased the tension somewhat. Jim looked perplexed and angry, but he allowed Turq and Genni to attend to Sceria's needs.

Tiernan crossed the room from his lone position and stood with Alena. "We need to be ready to leave again as soon as everyone has been cared for." Tiernan then took Alena's arm saying, "That includes you. Let's get you something to eat."

"That was a generous thing you did for Sceria," he commented to her quietly as he led her away.

"Tiernan, how could you allow that to happen?"

"If she were among my people, Sceria would already have been executed. I think Sceria would have taken her own life herself if it were not for the child."

"Does the boy even have a name?" she asked, feeling suddenly ashamed for not knowing that bit of information before now.

"She calls the boy, little Niomer, after my brother."

Alena tried not to look shocked, but Tiernan knew her facial expressions too well by now not to notice her discomfiture.

Tiernan looked as though he were peering at something far away before he spoke. "When she named the boy, I assumed he was my brother's child. If I had only known the truth in the beginning, everything would have turned out quite differently." He turned back to Alena, staring at her with his familiar intensity.

"What would have turned out differently?" Alena asked him softly.

But Tiernan avoided the question. He handed her some dried fruit and jerky with a flask of water. "Here, eat up. We need to get to the Pool of Mirimithia before sunset."

When Alena had finished eating, her eyes were wrapped again just as a precaution. She stumbled quite often along the journey, but Tiernan steadied her visionless awkwardness. Alena continued to think about what Ian had spoken to her about earlier. Was Tiernan really bound to her and was she bound to the veratnil? And what would it all mean for her, for Tiernan, and for the rest of them?

The air was hot and dry; the mid-afternoon sun beat mercilessly down on them. Wrayna hung at Alena's side, useless in her blind state. It thumped again and again against her left thigh as she stumbled along. Alena yearned for the use of her eyes but tried to rely on her other heightened senses. She could hear the others walking steadily behind her and Sceria being dragged roughly along. Sceria was far too weak for the journey and stumbled and fell often. It was happening with more regularity as time went on, and Alena cringed at the hateful words that were cursed bitterly towards the poor woman each time Sceria was dragged back to her feet. Finally, Alena could bear the sound of Jim's cursing no more, and she halted in her tracks.

"I need to rest. I'm a little dizzy," she half lied to Tiernan.

"Are you alright?" He asked seating her on a large rock and pressing cold water to her lips.

"Yes, Tiernan, I just need to stop for a while. I'm sure there are others that could use the rest too. Would you make sure that everyone gets a good long drink?"

"You're a good soul, Alena," Tiernan said quietly, instantly understanding her intentions.

"Hey what's up? Why are we stopping?" Ian asked as he came up to them.

"Alena needs to rest."

"Oh right…" Ian whistled back to the others to halt.

Alena sat patiently listening to the others mingle, trying to give Sceria as much time as she needed to recover until even Tiernan became restless to move on.

"Are you ready now to continue?" he finally asked with fervor.

The pattern continued several times before they reached the Pool of Mirimithia with Sceria being dragged behind and abused, while Alena made excuses to stop and rest so that Sceria could do the same. When they reached the Pool of Mirimithia, the sun had just set and there was still a bit of light in the sky, much to Alena's delight, as Tiernan helped to remove the bandages from her eyes. Her vision was clearer, but still she blinked at the silver light of the evening. She could see the dark outline of the jagged mountain peaks to the west and a magnificent round body of water about the size of a Carillion Starship which reflected the sapphire moon in its full splendor. The scene was breathtaking, haunting, and mysterious all at the same time.

"Tiernan," she whispered. "Tell me about this place."

"Beautiful isn't it? It's an ancient pool of myth and song. There have been many words written about its beauty. Some say that it possesses amazing healing powers, while others are convinced that if you gaze into it long enough, it will tell you hidden secrets about your past, present, and future."

"It feels, almost alive," Alena said with a shiver.

Far away an odd shape flew across the moon and cast a shadow momentarily upon them. Alena felt a sudden pain in her heart, and the cries of the agonizing veratnil filled her head. Tiernan took hold of her then, almost desperately. He ordered the others hurriedly into the moss-covered, columned, stone structure on the Mirimithian shore and dragged Alena behind him in a dead run.

Alena wanted to scream at him then and tell him how wrong he was to tear her away from the creature that was searching so earnestly for her. She wanted to claw him and rip out his eyes and beat him over the head, and yet another part of her loved him completely with an intensity she had only begun to recognize. Tears streamed down her face, and she sobbed in agony as she was pulled inside the mysterious shrine-like edifice. She couldn't control her sobbing as Tiernan knelt beside her.

"It's okay, Alena. Sshhh. It's going to be alright," he tried to reassure her, but this time Tiernan was wrong. It wasn't going to be alright. She was being torn entirely in two, and he was at least partly the cause of it. Another hand reached out to her, and Alena saw through tears that it was none other than Sceria that had reached out to comfort her along with two whispered broken words: "I'm sorry," before Sceria was pushed rudely away. The words gave Alena pause, and she ceased weeping.

Tiernan was giving orders to set up camp, while Alena tried to pull herself together, all the while Tiernan kept a firm grip on her, not allowing her to move in any direction. Alena resented his hands upon her and struggled against them. She found she had enormous strength suddenly and pulled free of him. Wild-eyed she turned upon him, striking out, her eyes flashing, reveling in her freedom. She felt the pull of the veratnil keenly and started to run, but Tiernan continued after her and wrestled her to the ground outside.

"Alena, stop. Please don't go, not yet."

Not yet? The words registered somewhere in her brain and stopped her cold. What did he mean? Did he know then that she must go?

"If you know that I must go, then why are you keeping me here with you?" she growled.

"Please Alena, just give me a little more time." The anguish in his voice was audible to everyone. Alena became aware then that all the others were crowding the door, staring at the two of them with their mouths hanging open. She tried to calm herself, make sense of what she felt compelled to do along with what she felt in her heart. She stood once again on the precipice between two opposing worlds. Would she have to choose between them? Her eyes met Tiernan's tortured amber-orange ones, and she realized in that moment that he was far more distressed than she was.

"Please Alena, stay." He let go of her, knowing there was nothing he could do to hold her if she decided to go.

The veratnil called for her, a sad heart-wrenching sound from far away, which tugged at her heart and made it impossible to stay even one moment longer.

"Please!" he whispered as she rose to leave, reaching out to her as he got to his feet.

If she hadn't turned back to him just then, there would have been no stopping her, but his face looked so incredibly sad and wretched with grief that her impulse to leave turned into wanting to comfort him instead. She found herself taking his outstretched hand and returning with him through the crowded door that was immediately shut behind them.

A strange disquiet settled over the group. All eyes remained on Alena and Tiernan. Feet were shuffled and shifted, but otherwise there was no movement. Alena's eyes met each one of the group's in turn. She read in them unease, dismay, and fear. And in each face there was a question, a question only she could answer.

"I must follow a different road soon," she heard her voice say, sadly. "You must follow Tiernan, now. I trust that he will take you to safety and look after you. Turn to Kelly if you have any doubts. She must be your voice of reason. Turq is another that does well to look after the needs of everyone. They both know as I know that it is best for all to follow Tiernan to the hidden city. It is important that you all stand together in this," Alena said glancing at Jim. "The road ahead will not be easy for any of us." Alena turned her attention briefly to Ian and Gwen wondering how soon they would follow her into the strange unknown veratnil world. She could tell that they were wondering the same thing.

Alena found that she was still holding Tiernan's hand in a tight grip. She looked up into his piercing amber-orange eyes which were calmer now but still filled with grief. He wouldn't look at her but encouraged their group to move forward with their preparations for making camp for the night. Tiernan finally released Alena's tightly held hand and gently encouraged her to set up her own camp. After rolling out their beds and eating a simple meal of flat bread and dried fruit and jerky, most sought solitude to think about the events of the day and their uncertain futures but not Tiernan. He led Alena away from the others to a secluded spot behind a heavily gilded altar of sorts. They sat together face to face holding both hands.

"Thank you for staying," he whispered and tried to smile. He was outwardly as calm as a quiet morning, but his eyes raged with grief, anger, and pain, like in the earlier days when she had first felt his eyes upon her in the biome.

"Tell me why you suffer, Tiernan. Tell me why you have always suffered being near me. Don't lie and tell me that you don't. I have always known that you do."

"I don't want to burden you, Alena. You already have so much to bear."

"Please, Tiernan, I need to know. It would help me to understand why I feel so torn apart inside."

Tiernan shook his head sorrowfully. "It wouldn't be fair to you."

Alena stroked his hands and made him look at her. "Ian told me something, just recently. He said that when your kind finds a mate, they are somehow bound to them for life, and it is not always someone of their choosing. It just happens. Is that true?"

"Yes," Tiernan answered miserably.

"Are you bound to me then? Is that what this is all about?"

"Alena... I...," he shook his head.

"Answer me," she said gently. "Tiernan, are you bound to me?"

"Yes," he finally answered, the agony in his voice made Alena's chin tremble with heartache.

"Why didn't you tell me?"

"Maiser Runcan said it would be unwise. I didn't mean for it to happen. It wasn't supposed to happen. It's not a part of the prophecy that was foretold." He drew away from her, placing his head in his hands. "Oh, Alena I have made such a mess of things. I can hardly bear to live. If only I had known who you were. I would have taken my life instead of letting anything like this bonding happen."

"Don't talk that way, Tiernan. Surely it can't be that awful?"

He looked at her with miserable longing. "I don't know how it could be any darker for me than it is now. Even now out of pure selfishness, I hold you back from what I know you must eventually do."

"I thought I was the one making that choice. Whether you know it or not, I have deep feelings for you."

"But that is what is so terrible. I have used your feelings for me to my advantage, to overcome the bond between you and the veratnil. Alena, forgive me, I just can't bear to be parted from you."

"But you've been parted from me before, when you abandoned me, remember?"

"I was always within a short distance, usually within sight of you until the last couple of days." His voice sounded far away, and he fingered the long gash that had only begun to heal with Kelly's tending.

"What happened to you?"

"I had a run in with an old enemy of ours."

"You don't mean Anthony?"

"Yeah, I became quite distracted being away from you. Unfortunately, I think he got the best of me this time. I passed out from the want of blood, because when I awoke, he was gone. He must have thought I was dead because I can't imagine him knowingly leaving me alive. Anyway, it took me a good while to recover enough to follow you, and I can't tell you how agonizing it was being parted from you for even that long."

"Why did you have to leave at all?"

"Because," he said with exasperation, "I can hardly control myself, even now, but when you are fertile, it's absolute torture."

"But Tiernan, I would love to be with you." It came out boldly and made Alena feel suddenly frightened.

Tiernan trembled, leaning towards her, gazing at her intently with those amber-orange eyes. "There lies the tragedy. Even if you were not bonded to the veratnil, we could never be together in that way, Alena."

"Never...Why not?"

"The prophecy reveals that you must remain pure in order to wield Wrayna."

"But does it really matter whether I wield Wrayna?"

"It matters to me, and it matters a great deal to my people. I will not put the whole survival of my race on the line for my own needs and desires."

"I don't understand. What do I and Wrayna have to do with the survival of your race?"

"That is what you must learn from the veratnil you are bonded to."

"But how can you live like this, tortured? How can I?"

"I'm so sorry, my little wootchka. I blame myself. My only comfort is that you do not have to carry the burden of this bond, as I do."

"But I love you, Tiernan, is that too different?"

He colored noticeably and found it hard to speak. When he did it was quietly and with much feeling. "Alena, being bonded goes much deeper than love."

"Does it? Are you so certain?" she asked with such intensity, that Tiernan didn't look so sure. "Explain to me how it feels to you," she pleaded with him. "Tell me what happened when you bonded with me."

"Are you sure you want me to tell you this? Haven't I already said too much?"

"Please, I want to know. This might be our only opportunity to talk."

"Here, come closer." Alena snuggled up to the side of him and gratefully he put his arm carefully around her. She loved it here in the crook of his arm. It was like coming home.

"Comfortable?"

"Yes," she told him.

"I waited a long time to find a bond mate, Alena. Nearly all of my childhood friends had found their mates years before. Even my younger brother who was five years my junior had found his bond mate a year before we were taken by the Waratna. I had begun to think that I would be never be bound to anyone."

"Does that happen?"

"Yes, it does to an unlucky few."

"Go on."

"Are you sure you want to get into this? It's getting rather late, and I think everyone has gone to bed."

"I really want to know."

He held her closer. "When I first saw you through the biome, I was immediately drawn to you. I thought that you were the most beautiful woman that I had ever seen. You so closely fit the description of the woman revealed in the prophecy that I was intrigued by you, but watching you soon turned into an obsession. I couldn't get you out of my head. It bothered me a great deal. I had a deep hatred for the coarseness of your race. After watching your violence toward Anthony and witnessing Anthony's bad behavior, I hated being drawn to you, but there was something in me that gloried in your victories over him."

"You were watching me then, even during those times?"

Tiernan smiled. "When the Waratna gave me access to you that first day, I didn't know what to do. For a long time, I stood outside the door. When I entered the room, your scent was completely intoxicating to me. I knew immediately that I was in trouble. I wanted you and didn't want you all at the same time. I sought to do away with you then. I knew that you were my bond mate like I knew the sun would rise, but I rebelled against it. I didn't understand how it could be. After all, you were of a different race and that race was violent and abominable."

"You're calling my race violent and abominable and you were standing over me trying to decide whether to kill me or not?"

Tiernan's bronze face reddened. "I know. It seems a little self-serving. I thought I could handle just leaving you be, until you found your way into my biome. Then everything changed. Your tears tore into my heart. When I held you, I found myself wanting to protect you and devote myself to you. It was so difficult not to give myself to you even then. Holding you that day was the hardest moment of my life."

"I'm sorry. I hope you know how grateful I was."

"Don't be sorry. I am glad I was there for you, but each time after that only heightened my desire to make you my bond mate. It didn't help that you were amazingly attractive to me, and you smelled absolutely wonderful."

"But all the while you loathed me too."

"Yes, Alena. That is true. You weren't exactly my idea of a perfect companion, and when you started sharpening sticks, I thought that you meant to bring harm to me, like you had to Anthony, and by then I had practically gone insane with every waking thought of you. I was filled with anger. I honestly did not know how to handle it."

"You were pretty enraged the last time the Cephalopods dumped me into your biome. You were pretty rough, and I really thought that you wanted to murder me."

"I did, Alena, especially when you laughed at my discomfiture. You have no idea how close you came to death."

"I didn't laugh at your pain, Tiernan. I was laughing at the idea that you thought I had any chance of protecting myself against you." Alena smiled. "But you kissed me then, instead, and that is the moment when you were bound to me... isn't it?"

"Yes, you passed out and I thought I really had killed you. I was so relieved when you came to."

"The kiss of death."

"What?"

"Nevermind...."

"It was a huge relief afterwards, although I realized immediately that it was not to be a normal bonding."

"What do you mean?"

"Well, usually both parties are bound to each other and this was obviously a one-sided thing. As I remember, you didn't want to have a whole lot to do with me, afterwards."

"You're not quite right about that."

"No?"

"I was really attracted to you, Tier. I was doing everything I could to not to get close to you. If I let myself fall in love with you then it meant that the Cephalopods had won. I didn't want to bring a child into the world under those conditions."

Tiernan looked relieved, somehow, and played with the loose tendrils of her hair. "I admire your strength. If it weren't for you, none of us would have survived."

"Are you glad you survived? Even with the torment that you live every day because of me?"

"Alena…sweet Alena. I value my bond to you above all else. I wouldn't trade a day being bonded to you. Although it is hard to go forward at times, I would give up being your bond mate only to make things easier for you. I swear to you if I had only known who you were, I would have taken my life before letting you go through any of this. And now I would live 10,000 days so tortured only to be near you." He hung his head misery.

She touched his face in sympathy. "Can you give up being my bond mate?"

"No, only death will release me."

"So, this is how it is to be until one of us dies? I can't believe that, Tiernan."

"You have to, Alena!"

"No, I won't."

"Please Alena, I can't be responsible for the destruction of what is left of my race. Already, I cannot fathom having to face the fury of the sovereign of my people."

"Why must you face him at all?"

Tiernan paused sadly before telling her the awful truth, "Because, I am his first-born son."

"What?"

"I am all that is left of a long line of royals dating back to the beginning of time. It is a careful ancestry of only the purest blood."

"What are you saying?"

"Alena, my blood has never been mixed with a foreigner, especially one of a different race. You must understand that when I bonded with you, I thought that Sceria's child was my brother's. I thought that the bloodline would continue through him and now… now I have entirely doomed the line of kings going back for three thousand years. I have also condemned Sceria to a horrible death. She might have been able to hide that the child was Anthony's, but I cannot let an imposter ascend to the throne. Sceria knows this, and she knows she returns to die."

"But that wasn't her fault. You can't let her die. You know what Anthony is."

"Alena, she also tried to interfere with your life, the consequences if you had perished would have been devastating."

"She knows you are bonded to me?"

"She does."

"Can you bond again if I die?"

Tiernan sighed. "It is rare, but yes."

"And she doubted that I was the woman of the prophecy?"

"You know that she did. What are you getting at?"

"Well, the way I see it, Sceria was doing what she could to fix things. She understands perfectly the predicament that you are both in."

Tiernan was thoughtful. "Perhaps, you are right. Maybe her penalty may be lessened if explained in that way."

"And there is hope for you as well."

"No, don't think that way. Already I must let you go. I would not want to live at all if you died." His amber-orange eyes blazed with fervor.

"Even for your people?"

"I don't know." He held her tightly, almost desperately. "I don't know how to let you part from me, Alena. But I know I must."

"There is an old saying in my world, 'If you love something, set it free. If it comes back to you, it's yours. If it doesn't, it never was,'" she said quietly.

Tiernan hung on her every word, "It is a wise saying."

"Tiernan, trust in my love for you. Know that my heart is torn. Some day when all of this is done, you must believe that we can be together."

He kissed her then, sweetly and carefully, holding her in a tender embrace for a long time. "I will wait impatiently for the possibility of that day," he whispered brushing his cheek against her. "Oh, Alena, if only it could be."

They didn't talk anymore, but just sat in silence reveling in the quiet closeness. They talked half the night, and Alena couldn't escape the feeling as she snuggled closer to him that this was perhaps the last time she would be so near him, probably ever. It made her wretchedly unhappy to think of leaving him, but even now she felt the tremendous pull of longing from the veratnil searching for her outside.

At some point Tiernan and Alena finally slept, for when they awoke, they found that the rest of the group had let them sleep well into the morning.

Chapter Twenty-four

Ian nudged them with the side of his boot. "Wake up, sleepy heads, breakfast is about done, and everyone is packed up and awaiting your orders."

Tiernan looked alarmed then grumpy as he untangled himself from Alena. They moved ever so slowly as they moved apart from each other. Perhaps they both knew that today would be the last—the last time they packed up together, the last time they breakfasted together, and the last time they journeyed together.

After packing up her things, Alena wandered to the edge of the pool of Mirimithia, trying to clear her depressing thoughts. The water was an electric blue this morning almost the color of sapphire and it shimmered in welcome. She heard a strange whispering as she neared its calm border. Was the pool of Mirimithia speaking? She leaned forward trying to make out what it said. She felt Wrayna warm at her side and wondered about it. The water definitely spoke but in Tiernan's tongue. She tried to understand the words, but they were hard to make out other than just a few: "Following her heart… leading home…two paths becoming one." What did it all mean? Alena shivered. She heard Tiernan calling to her. It was time to go.

After heading out, they followed a well-worn path through a forest of trees. Alena stayed close beside Tiernan. He was somber this morning and didn't say much. She placed her hand in his. He looked down at her and smiled sadly but returned the pressure of her hand with his own.

"How far are we from the hidden city?" she asked him.

"From Camaranth? Only seven day's journey at most."

"Tiernan, will you look after my crewmates and Turq and his family?"

"Of course."

"Thank you."

"Anything for you."

The pale blue sun was quite warm in the lateness of the morning. The leaves of the forest rustled in the breeze and seemed to be telling tales of their own to Alena's listening ears, but perhaps she was just imagining things. She did feel a sense of foreboding, however, a sense that the order of the universe seemed off today. Alena's apprehension grew with each step and yet nothing happened. Hours passed this way. They came to an open field. Alena glanced behind at her companions strewn back about a quarter of a mile. Sceria was the last of the group and moving thankfully of her own free will, a little cast off from the group, but all seemed in order. They crossed the wide-open field into another stand of trees. Tiernan and Alena had only taken a few steps into the protection of the trees when Alena heard Sceria scream.

Alena glanced back just in time to see Anthony dragging Sceria off into the trees. Gwen, who was the one closest to them but still a good distance away, stood frozen in terror. No one else moved. Not a single one of the others went to Sceria's aid. Perhaps they all thought that Sceria's life was worthless and that she deserved to die, but what about her child? Of course, it was Anthony's child too.

Alena took off into a run, pulling Wrayna from her sheath. She was not going to stand there and watch Anthony inflict any more pain on someone of her gender, not even Sceria. The sword warmed to her touch. Tiernan followed her, his arms enveloping her from behind. He tried to hold her back, but the Washeenah and the bond had made her stronger than several men. She wrenched free of him. The whole group was yelling at her, ordering her frantically to stop, trying to grab at her and pull her with them as they now ran past her in the opposite direction. What was wrong with everyone? She found herself alone with Anthony and Sceria with the wind whipping around her in the grove of trees. Anthony's evil grin of glee turned almost immediately to dismay. Too late Alena became aware of another menacing presence.

It landed behind her with a sickening thud, making the earth quake all about her. Anthony let go of Sceria now and was scrambling with horror on his hands and knees further into the trees. Alena turned and found herself face to face with the ghastly veratnil. She stifled a gasp, for without question it was not the one that she was bound to. It looked at her hungrily with its keen predator sharp eyes and made a strange warbling noise within its throat. But Alena stood firm, feeling a strange calm radiate through her body. She raised Wrayna before her, pointing it towards the monster's deadly beak. The sword filled with power and sent a bolt of lightning crackling toward the veratnil.

The veratnil shrank from her in pain and anger, taking several steps back. Alena, feeling all too drained of energy already, took several steps back herself until she was standing protectively over Sceria and her crying baby. The wind gusted around her, and while she kept the veratnil before her at bay, another landed, crushing the trees to splinters in the forest behind her, and then another landed close by.

Anthony, who was now cut off, was hollering with terror and struggling through the undergrowth back towards her. The poor howling excuse for a man practically oozed with cowardice. But the ruckus he was causing only attracted the other two veratnil's unwanted attention. With a swift stab of one of the veratnil's beaks and a flick of its deadly claws, Anthony met his fateful end. Alena cringed as Anthony's body was wrenched apart by the pair of them with a sickening crunch. The largest veratnil of the two gulped Anthony down, leaving only scraps for its companion, and then the monster, still dripping with blood, turned a sharp eye upon her.

Alena swung Wrayna straight at the monster, while lightning shot from its razor-sharp edge. The veratnil reared in fury, upsetting the balance of its companion who trampled several stately trees in trying to regain its footing. Alena circled Wrayna in a half circle back and forth between the three of them until they had stepped sufficiently away from her. She felt her life force waning more and more with each passing moment as Wrayna drained her energy.

Alena practically jumped out of her skin when the first veratnil tossed back its head and emitted a horrible scream that echoed all around them. Alena pulled Sceria to her feet next to her, instructing her to stay close, while slowly they backed away from all three creatures until they had the veratnil on only one side of them. Alena placed herself between the veratnil and Sceria. "Keep going towards the others," she whispered to the trembling Sceria, "but slowly, now.

The veratnil watched Alena's and Sceria's every move with their keen killer eyes, but they didn't follow. They just stood watching and waiting—waiting for what? Alena didn't have to wait long to realize that the horrible sound the first veratnil had screamed was a call, bringing even more veratnil to them, but the call also brought her bonded.

Alena knew of his arrival before she could see him. She could feel her heart and his swelling with anticipation and joy, as he came ever nearer. There was a burst of huge wings all around her as another then another veratnil alighted on the shaking ground. Then at last he came, the deadliest and the most magnificent of them all, the one called Megolath. Alena could hardly contain herself. As soon as he was on the ground, she found herself running to him, even through the other veratnil that stood like ghastly sentinels. Veratnil and humankind watched as she vaulted up his shiny, black, scaled back; with her heart bursting with inexplicable joy, she arose with him into the air.

Alena glanced back only once as they shot into the sky. Ian and Gwen were standing among the veratnil in the open field and Tiernan was kneeling on the ground with his face buried in his hands. She felt a sharp twinge of bitter regret seeing him like that in her intense moment of elation.

"I'm sorry for your sorrow amid your delight, my bonded. Do not worry, no harm will befall your companions," Megolath thoughts touched softly on her mind. It was strange. No words were spoken, but Megolath's thoughts filled her mind and gave her peace. Alena lay down then upon his smooth dark scales and let the wind wash over her, enjoying the deep contentment that filled her soul. She knew that Megolath, who felt to her as ancient as time, was filled with the same euphoria.

"I have lived for four thousand years… long before the age of humankind. When I was yet a youngling my kind were bonded

with those akin to you. I am privileged to be your bonded. I never expected that this honor should come to me."

Alena's mind was immediately bursting with questions. *"Why did you not expect it? And why was I chosen? You must forgive my ignorance, as you must know that this is not my home world...There are so many things that I just don't understand."*

"You chose me, Alena. You called me to you. Many years have my kind waited to have such a chance as this."

"I chose you? I don't understand...and besides your kind eats my kind." Alena couldn't help but think of Anthony at that moment.

"It has not always been so. When your kind first came to this planet we lived and died together. It is only since the time of the Temarrian Kings that the relationship between the humans and the veratnil was forever changed. But you are not grieving for this one you call Anthony. You are relieved by his death."

*"It is true. I don't mourn him. His life brought me and many others only pain. "*Alena buried her face further into the veratnil's neck. *"So veratnil and humankind lived together? What happened to change all that?"*

She knew immediately that the question she had asked was an uncomfortable one for him. A thousand thoughts raced through his mind, too quickly for her to make sense of any one of them. She caught only a few words here and there... *"bondage... betrayal... agony..."*

"We were enslaved by your kind as were those who were bonded to us," he finally communicated. *"We became merely beasts of burden to do the bidding of the Kings."*

"But how did that happen?"

"The Kings were jealous, especially when they couldn't bond themselves. They were hungry for power and glory and there was no threat from the outside to make them humble."

"What do you mean?"

"When the humans first came, they were pursued here by a horrible race, much like the Waratna, who had driven them from their planet, except these creatures dwelt on the land and were hard shelled instead. We needed each other to survive, much like we need each other to survive today."

"Why have I not heard this before?"

"The humans have forgotten."

"But how could they forget, especially if they owe your kind for their lives?"

"There were some dark times between your kind and mine. We murdered each other until the land was divided. That is what they remember."

"Well, I hope you won't mind me saying this, but your kind seems quite a bit more adept at killing than mine. How did this race of humans have a chance against you?"

"There were powerful wizards among them, Alena. But even then, your kind would have been obliterated if not for our long memory and the sweetness... of the bond... There was a hope among my kind that we would be reunited again. My strength and your will combined is not something to be trifled with. We...You and I are something to be feared, especially combined with the gift you carry."

"You mean Wrayna? I'm afraid you will be disappointed. The sword weakens me terribly. Even now I can hardly hold myself upon your back."

"You can draw from my life force to wield Wrayna now. That is why we are so powerful together. It was my grandfather and his bonded that carried Wrayna before us.

Alena yawned. She had many more questions. But she was tired… too tired. Wrayna had drained her life force. The motion of flight made her sleepy. She tried unsuccessfully to keep her eyes open as they soared. Megolath sensed this, of course. It would be difficult, if not impossible to keep anything from this wonderful creature.

"Sleep now, my bonded. I will watch over you. You must gain strength for what is ahead."

Alena wondered just what was ahead, but before Megolath could answer, she was fast asleep. She slept long and deep at least until she dreamt about Tiernan.

She was in the courtyard of a mighty palace. Guards dressed in green and silver lined the courtyard on both sides. She could see him standing at the end of the courtyard, a stern expression etched on his strong, sober face. He summoned her to him but stood still, waiting stoically for her to come to him. Anxiously, Alena looked around at her surroundings. Something was wrong here… very wrong. Something was wrong about him, something more than the strange look of his amber-orange eyes. She took an uneasy step toward him and then another. She noticed then that he didn't really look at her but seemed to stare through her instead. What had happened to him since their last parting and why did she want to turn from him and run?

Alena awoke with a start, glad to find that it had only been a dream. Megolath's eyes were upon her, watching her closely…

"Tiernan, the heir to the throne of Kings is bound to you then?" Alena could only nod. Megolath had obviously been

listening to her dreams. She could feel the veratnil's pain as she confirmed his question.

"I'm sorry," she told the creature, "*I'm sorry it causes you pain.*"

"*But you are not bound to him?*"

"*No.*"

"*But you feel very strongly about him?*"

"*Yes.*"

Megolath made a hissing noise which only added to Alena's wretchedness. Her bonded had some deep-seated anger towards Tiernan… at least toward Tiernan's ancestry. What was she to do? She was bound to one and loved the other. She shuddered, once again feeling torn in two.

"*I am sorry for the misery I cause you now. It is unfortunate that you love him. It is a complication that could mean the downfall of us all.*"

Megolath paced back and forth in the veratnil sized cavern that was open on one end to the cerulean sky.

"*He was the one who kept you from me, was he not? What misery and anger he must experience now. Let us hope that his torment does not turn to bitterness as it did in former times.*"

"*What do you speak of?*"

"*The dark days when my kind was made to suffer because of the selfishness of humankind. We were harnessed like pack animals, chained, our children torn from us.*"

"*But how?*"

"*My bonded, only death can separate us now, and so it was in those days. A veratnil once bonded is loyal only to the one he is bonded with, but the humans are also loyal to their king. Therefore, the human king, Malucia, was able to control us all.*"

"*But why would my kind let that happen? I would never let any harm come to you, Megolath. I would die first.*"

"*There is a way to numb the bond, Alena... A drug... You have already seen what this drug can do...*" Alena started to protest, but then she remembered her dream and Tiernan... the strange look in his eyes. Would Tiernan take this drug to numb the pain of his bond with her? Somehow, she didn't think so.

"*Perhaps it will not be something of his choosing.*" Megolath spoke to her mind. Now it was Alena's turn to pace. "I can't let this happen," she said aloud.

"*Alena, you cannot have us both.*"

"*Why not?*"

"*You must choose.*"

"*I can't. I know that no matter what I choose I will always regret that choice.*"

"*Is it our bond that is stronger or your love for this human?*"

"*I do not know. When you are near, the bond is much stronger. When he is near, my love seems to overcome the bond,*" she answered truthfully.

Megolath tried to hide the thought that came to him, but he couldn't. "*He would do his best to keep Alena away from Tiernan, then... I'm sorry,*" he added with simple sincerity. "*The blood of the Temarrian Kings cannot be trusted.*"

Alena was dumbfounded. Surely, this didn't include the Tiernan that she knew? Tiernan wouldn't let what had happened in the days of Malucia happen again, would he? Megolath had to be wrong about the bronze-colored man that she had leaned upon, suffered with, and loved, didn't he? But even Alena had to admit to herself that she didn't know for sure.

"*Only time will tell,*" was the thought that wafted into her mind from her veratnil bonded. Alena nodded to herself and felt a pang of deep sorrow. Was she always going to feel so torn? Somehow, she had to find a way to make it all come together.

"Megolath, you said that the Temarrian people came from another world…and that they have forgotten? Is there some written record of this?

"My kind do not keep records like your kind. Our lives and memories are long… But I can take you to the place where the Temarrians first arrived if you like? It will give us some practice flying together, as the distance is not short?"

"Yes, I would like that very much. But could we have something to eat first? I'm afraid I am really rather hungry."

"Of course, I had forgotten how quickly humans empty their stomachs. Veratnil only feed about four times per moon and are not accustomed to daily feeding. Do you have what you require already, or shall I hunt something for you?"

Alena grabbed her pack and rummaged through it, coming up with a few pieces of jerky, a dry biscuit, and a flask of wine to drink it down. Megolath eyed her with a great deal of interest as she munched but wasn't pleased apparently with what she had selected for breakfast, for he leapt off the ledge suddenly with a huge air rattling swoop and soon returned with a giant fish still wriggling within his beak which he proudly deposited in her lap. This was alarming to Alena, and she couldn't help but leap to her feet in fright, but she did her best not to offend her companion, who was so eager to please. It was going to take her a while to get used to being with such a grand and terrifying creature.

"I'm sorry to disturb you, my bonded…Perhaps it is a little fresher than you are used to."

Alena unsheathed the knife that Tiernan had given her and proceeded to clean the fish, tossing the unwanted sections to Megolath who was content to eat the things she had no stomach for. She ate about a fourth of the salmon-like fish before, casting the rest to Megolath, who paced back and forth. She could sense that he was growing impatient to be off on their journey even before it came to the forefront of his thoughts. Veratnil weren't the most patient creatures evidently. They were both going to have some adjusting to do.

"*Thank you for breakfast. I will be ready in just a moment.*

Alena tried to find a place out of Megolath's watchful eye to relieve her poor bladder and smiled to herself when Megolath finally caught on to her wish for privacy. Veratnil evidently weren't so personal about such things, but this was something she was not going to share with this creature whether she was bound to him or not.

Chapter Twenty-five

Megolath was much more content when they were finally flying again. He had flown gently with her before, but now he seemed intent on getting to their destination as fast as he could, and in the process, "teaching" her, from first-hand experience, how to be his rider. Alena was agitated at first as she attempted to cling to his slippery scales, which scraped up her hands and knees and forearms, that he would behave so inconsiderately. She did not refrain from letting him have the full force of her disdain. But he would only chuckle, tell her it was for her own good, and inform her that he would not let her fall.

Amazingly, Alena found that after about three quarters of an hour she had a good feel for flying with him and knowing where to hold on, where to place her feet and hind end, and which scales to avoid. After fifteen minutes more, she had learned to balance with only the use of her feet and inner thighs until Megolath decided to dive and do loops and all types of maneuvers that seemed bent on throwing her off. Alena adapted to each of these until she was pretty good at flying, for a beginner anyway, by the time they landed on a jagged ridge above a huge river gorge. She was sore and had a hard time standing on her feet when she finally dismounted.

"That wasn't so bad was it?"

"No… you were right…that's the best way to learn… quickly anyway…" she rubbed her glutes. *"Wow, where are we?"*

"Only a small distance from the wreckage. Careful now, it's a long fall if you slip," he warned, keenly aware of her wobbliness from the long ride.

"Wreckage? There's still a wreckage? After thousands of years?"

"It's overgrown and hidden there on the upper ridge. I'm afraid I am too large to take you there, at least not without taking out several dozen trees. Besides, I don't know if the cliff is stable enough to hold me and what's left of the ship. You'll have to climb up…It's not too far. There's an enormous tree that lies sideways. It was thrown over as a sapling at the edge of impact and just to the left of it you will find the ship, although the bulk of it is imbedded in the ridge."

It was a steep climb, but not too far like Megolath had said. The ship itself would have been easy to miss as overgrown as it was if she hadn't looked to the left of the great sideways tree that was now white with age. The ship had become part of the ridge. There was no other way to explain it. Giant trees grew through its broken shell and over it, while the earth had filled in all around it and covered its giant metal hull with thick vegetation. But the scars from its impact remained, even thousands of years later, in the crumpled, haphazard look of the ridge. Alena tried to guess the size of the ship by walking the perimeter but was unable to get too far, only far enough to determine that the ship was much larger than the Horizon had been but not quite the size of a Carillion Starship.

The race that had flown this ship was more advanced than her own world, however, judging by the strength of the non-corrosive hull and the length of the drives, although most of it was imbedded deep in the ridge. She wondered what had caused Tiernan's race to abandon or "forget" this technology. Alena wished that Ian were there with her or even Gwen. Either of them could tell her a lot more about what lay in front of her. A shift in color on a section of the hull made her step closer. Carefully, she pulled back the vegetation that surrounded it and brushed the earth away. There were symbols there. The first symbol she uncovered was familiar and curved at the top like a giant Egyptian ankh, and the second near as she could tell was of a falcon with a large slanted eye—the eye of Horus? She held her breath. Were these Egyptian symbols or was this just some strange coincidence? The other symbols were too deeply embedded in the earth to get to without some serious digging.

Alena felt the air stir violently above her. Megolath had grown impatient waiting for her, she supposed. She sighed not wanting to leave but feeling the pull of the bond drawing her back to her kingly veratnil; she headed back down the ridge.

"You are a curious one to spend so much time exploring."

"And you grow impatient waiting for me, Megolath."

"There is no need to spend time discovering when you only need a moment to confirm what I have already made known to you."

"Seeing the wreckage has only further intrigued me."

"Yes, your mind is full of questions…Which question shall I answer first?" he asked as she climbed upon his back.

"You said that The Temarrians were fleeing from another race. Did they come here on purpose or were they forced here? The way that ship is imbedded in the ridge, it is obvious that they crashed."

"Yes, they came like a meteor out of the sky. They were fleeing their home world, the last of their race to leave their

embattled world. They were at the beginning of a long journey to meet up with the others of their kind who had managed to escape, and who had taken up residence on a planet far out of the range of the hard-shelled ones."

"Where was this planet that you speak of?"

"That I do not know. Their ship was damaged beyond repair. They were marooned here..."

Alena would have asked many more questions, but she was interrupted by the drone of a Cephalopod ship not too far distant.

"It is coming toward us..." Megolath's anxious thoughts flooded into her mind. *"If it does not shift course, it will overtake us."*

"Why does that worry you? I have seen several of these ships taken down by veratnil and torn apart. Surely, it is no match for you?"

"Their ships have been recently outfitted with weapons that burn through flesh. Several of my kind have had their wings burned entirely through and have plummeted helplessly to their deaths. Besides, usually it takes several of us to take one down. We don't engage in battle by ourselves unless we absolutely must, or they threaten our young. The Waratna have learned to put shields on these smaller ships as of late because of our earlier successes. They hunt us now with only one purpose in mind, and that is to be rid of us."

"So, what shall we do? You are too large to hide and obviously these ships are faster than you are?"

"We wait and hope that we are not discovered."

"And if we are?"

"Then we must do our best to stay alive."

"That's not especially comforting."

The ship had begun to turn, much to Alena's relief, but her relief was short lived as the Cephalopod ship began to circle back. The ship must have picked Megolath up on its scanners. Without warning, Megolath flung her from his back and vaulted into the air.

"Run, Alena! Hide!"

Alena scrambled into the underbrush and watched in horror as the ship turned in Megolath's direction firing as it went. Megolath did his best to stay out of the range of the weapons, but it soon became a sort of battle dance between ship and veratnil as they engaged each other in fiery combat. Megolath did well enough to stay unharmed if he stayed above the ship, but he was making no headway against penetrating it with his powerful beak. It was as if he bounced off the thing every time it came within his deadly grasp, and there seemed to be no end to the flood of fire that poured from the horrible ship.

This dreadful dance went on above her for what seemed an eternity, and Alena could see that Megolath was beginning to grow tired. The ship was shielded somehow, and to make matters worse, Alena had picked up the unmistakable drone of another ship coming their way. She had to do something or Megolath would be dead in a matter of minutes—but what? What could she do? Her hand went automatically to the hilt of the sword. She unsheathed Wrayna from her side, feeling it warm to her touch and stepping out into the open she pointed the sword at the Cephalopod's hull. Lightning crackled and flew from the end of her sword and enveloped the ship, which caused it to shudder momentarily and lose power. Alena could see the ghastly large-eyed Cephalopod struggling to regain control, but it was too late; as Alena turned the sword away, Megolath was finally able to penetrate the metal hull and send the ship hurtling to the bottom of the gorge. Now that Alena knew what to do, the second ship met a similar fate and her deadly dark companion lost no time in devouring the contents of both Cephalopod ships much to Alena's discomfiture and satisfaction.

By the time Megolath returned to her side, he was so full that he could hardly fly or was it that his wings were too singed? She couldn't tell. She watched him swerve recklessly back and forth as he flew from the bottom of the gorge.

"Perhaps you shouldn't eat so much," she teased with relief as he arrived.

"Maybe you should be a little more careful where you point that sword." he grumbled back at her.

"Oh, did I do that? Well, maybe you shouldn't toss me off next time. We are supposed to be a team, aren't we?"

"I was trying to protect you."

Alena cringed at his words. *Oh, no not this one too.* Alena tried hard not to throw a fit. "Let me get something straight with you, Megolath. I don't need protecting!" she growled at him aloud.

He stared at her strangely and tried to muffle a veratnil laugh. She had never heard a veratnil laugh, but the sound was unmistakable, like the long mocking warble of a huge bird.

"What are you laughing at?"

"Oh, my bonded, you have a fearless heart. Forgive my laughter. Courage is an admirable quality in a race as frail as yours."

"Well, frail or not, I was good enough to save your hide."

Megolath continued to warble, which made Alena angry. She would have marched away if he hadn't wrapped a huge black talon around her and drawn her to him.

"Stop now, don't be angry, my bonded. You are right, of course. You did save my hide today. There are far too many of my kind that have not been so fortunate."

She pouted a little, not certain whether she was ready to forgive him and tried unsuccessfully to wiggle out of his talon. *"How many have not been so fortunate?"* she finally asked, remembering the Dreaded Hill of Tavonsheigh.

"Hundreds perhaps a thousand."

"A thousand?"

"Veratnil are not as prolific as humans, my bonded. They are rare comparatively. If things continue as they have, then we face extinction far sooner than humankind."

"How many veratnil remain then?

"Eighty-three if all have survived since yesterday."

"That's all?"

"That is all. Come… climb upon my back. We are not far from the Valley of Formation. You have seen the Temarrian peoples' beginnings. Let me show you the place of my hatching."

"Are you sure you can fly?"

"Yes, Alena, although a bit more slowly perhaps. We are not safe to remain here much longer, anyway. The Waratna, or the Cephalopods as you call them, will be missing their scouts and will soon come looking for them.

A short slightly wobbly flight took them to the wide valley of Megolath's birth. The Valley of Formation was at the base of a horseshoe shaped canyon of creamy-blue cliffs that were littered with caves. Immediately, Alena was struck by the solemnity of the place for the valley floor was scattered with both giant and tiny sun-bleached veratnil bones; the sight of which made Alena want to weep. She knew only too well from Megolath's thoughts what had happened here. The Waratna ships had come in mass and executed them all. There were a few torn ships strewn among the bones, but this had been a slaughter for the veratnil—the tragic massacre of mothers and their young.

"I'm so sorry," was all that she managed to communicate through blurry tears.

The sound of more approaching ships forced them to take shelter out of sight in one of the many caves dotting the cliff side. The cliffs were large and perfectly suited for a veratnil mother and her hatchlings. Alena grimaced at the number of eggs that remained in untended nests. What a tragedy it was that the Cephalopods had come to this planet. She could hear their ships circling the valley for quite a while, but eventually they moved off to search elsewhere.

"Will any of them hatch?" she asked Megolath, already knowing the answer.

"No. They have gone too long without tending from their mothers."

Alena stroked Megolath's shiny scales and then lay down upon his back.

"You are tired little one. The shadows grow long. We shall camp here for the night."

Alena nodded, too tired to argue, but wishing she would not have to spend the night above this valley of bones. Gently, Megolath urged her off his back and went to find her some dinner, but she was already asleep by the time he returned, curled up in her bedroll.

When she awoke, she was starving and didn't care how fresh the food was this bright cerulean morning, although she had to admit that she was missing having human companions, at least at meal time.

Chapter Twenty-six

They spent the morning flying, diving, and twirling until Alena's cheeks were flushed with exhilaration. She absolutely relished the experience. Piloting a veratnil with the wind in your face was much more of a sensory experience than flying a ship. She laughed out loud as Megolath left the forest of trees and glided barely an inch above the shimmering silver lake, splashing her all the while with his wingtips.

"Okay, that's enough, I'm positively soaked. Besides, aren't you afraid that we'll be seen out here?"

"The Waratna stay away from fresh water. They are afraid of it, even when they are secure in their ships. I've seen a few Waratna shrivel up and die in fresh water. It's not a pretty sight. They will go far out of their way to completely avoid it. Without the salt, they do not survive…"

This was undoubtedly an interesting piece of knowledge and perhaps another way of fighting the nasty creatures as well. Perhaps if they were able to change the salinity of the water in the areas that the creatures inhabited, they could be rid of them or at least put them on the defensive. Right now the slimy Cephalopods definitely had enormous advantages over both the veratnil and humankind. Alena wondered how her human companions were fairing. They were probably only a few days from the hidden city of Camaranth.

"Your companions are safe, although perhaps a little uneasy in their travels." Megolath started to warble over what he found immensely amusing. *"They are followed by several of my kind who are only watching over them, but they don't seem to like the honor I have bestowed upon them, and they are frightened out of their skins."*

"Well, that should be understandable after the experiences we've had with your kind. It's not comfortable to watch one of your own consumed by huge, deadly creatures, whether that certain someone deserved it or not." Alena shuddered, just thinking about it.

"There are two among your companions that are especially tormented. Is it because they know they are worthy of the bond, Alena?"

Megolath was referring to Ian and Gwen, she supposed. *"It is quite terrifying to think of being bonded to such a creature as you. Your size along with your razor-sharp beak and enormous talons make you absolutely petrifying. It took me a long time to wrap my mind around it and even consider it. It may never have happened if Sceria hadn't poisoned me with those berries."*

"The Washeenah only makes the bond stronger. Sceria has done us both a marvelous favor. Generally, only a few berries are eaten by a human. Our bond is extraordinarily strong."

"Yes, I feel it too."

"I hope it is enough to keep you happy." Megolath thought earnestly, although also a bit sadly. *"I feel the pull of the other one at times."*

"The other one?" she questioned, knowing full well it was Tiernan that Megolath was referring to.

"Yes, be careful my bonded. Your feelings could mean the defeat of both of our races."

"*Don't worry, I won't let any harm come to either you or Tiernan if I have anything to say about it.*" Alena paused, trying to collect her thoughts and trying not worry about the two very different beings that mattered more to her than life itself. "*Tell me, my giant companion, how you know that my friends are safe at such an enormous distance?*"

"*Veratnil are fairly solitary, unless we are raising young. We must communicate over long distances using the rays of the sun, the flight of the wind, the shifting of the earth, and even the flow of water. Veratnil have keener senses than humans do, but I will teach you to hear the babble of voices in the world all around us. Even now I can hear the flood of voices of my kind that are impatient to see you and eagerly await our return.*"

"*Our return?*"

"*Yes, they wait for us to lead them against the evil that has come upon us, as my grandfather did in those former dark days with his bonded. But they must wait a while longer; this is our time to become strong together both in body and in mind.*"

"*Tell me about your grandfather and his bonded. What happened to them?*"

"*Alena, it is a story I will tell you, someday, but now is not the time for its telling. We really must prepare for what is ahead. We have so little time.*"

Megolath and Alena spent the next several days practicing together in flight. Alena learned to anticipate Megolath's every move merely by the twitch of his tail or the flick of a wing or the shift of his shiny black scales. It was at this point that they began practicing with Wrayna. Alena was amazed at how absorbed she became with becoming one with both the veratnil and the sword. Her life force seemed endless with Megolath's strength to draw from, and she was learning to cast the lightning that shot forth from Wrayna wherever she willed it. The wildness and rawness of it thrilled Alena in a way that left her breathless and hungry for more. At times, Alena felt that she became the lightning that shot forth violently from the razor-sharp edge of the sword. At the end of their sixth exhausting day of practice together, Megolath's mind filled to boasting with what a powerful force they had become in so short a time.

"You have a strong mind little one, and you and I together are now a terrible power to be reckoned with. Tomorrow we shall honor my kind with our presence if you are willing."

The thought of being among the veratnil frightened Alena a bit, not because they were so deadly, but because she didn't want to disappoint Megolath or his kind. She and Megolath had become powerful together, it was true, but what hope did one veratnil and his bonded have against a whole race of Cephalopods seeking the genocide of both Megolath's and her kind?

"Do not worry, Alena, there is infinitely more hope for both of our races, now that you and I have come together."

Megolath brought her a wriggling fish for dinner, once more, which she ate ravenously. He watched her with genuine interest devour the whole of it, aside from the scales and bones. Alena supposed she was growing quite uncultured after just a week with the beast, but she just didn't care, although she might have cared if any of her human companions had been around. Her heart felt wild and free, and after so many years in captivity, she welcomed heartily the liberation she felt. Megolath began to warble.

"If you are not careful, Alena, you will become more veratnil than human."

Megolath's comment gave her pause and made her consider all over again what it meant to be human. Was she losing something of her humanity or was she gaining a new-found perspective instead?

Alena didn't sleep as soundly as she had on all the previous nights that she'd spent with Megolath. Perhaps it was her nervousness at meeting the rest of Megolath's kind, or perhaps it was her shadowy disturbing dreams that she failed to remember the next morning when she awoke. Crankily, she pulled on her long dark leather boots which had conformed so closely to her calves and feet that they seemed almost a part of her now, much like Megolath and Wrayna and… She didn't want to think of him. It hurt too much if she did. Hopefully, Tiernan, Ian, and Kelly and all the others had all made it to the hidden city by now. She couldn't help wondering how they had all been received.

"They reached the hidden city yesterday; my kind are no longer with your friends. Where your companions have gone, the veratnil will not follow."

"Why not?"

"We are not welcome, at least as visitors."

"What is that supposed to mean?"

"The Temarrians shoot us down and eat us when they can; they take our scales and beaks and talons and use them for weapons."

"Well, that would seem fair, considering that you eat them as well, but now I am curious. What can they possibly shoot you down with?"

"A single well-aimed arrow combined with their wizardry."

"Really?"

"It's happened more times than I care to remember. The Temarrians are skillful archers and brilliant wizards. The Waratna wouldn't have a chance against them if the arrows could only pierce the armor of their ships, and that is why humankind seeks our beaks and talons."

"So, you stay away from them?"

"They are easier to hide from than the Waratna."

"Do they know how few of your kind remain on this planet?"

"If they do, they do not care. All they are concerned with is their own survival."

"Is that any different than the veratnil?"

"The veratnil know that they cannot survive without human help, but neither can the Temarrians survive without us, not for long anyway. The city of Camaranth will not remain hidden forever. Perhaps they will think better of the veratnil now that you and I are bonded, but let us talk of more hopeful things. I am eager to introduce you to my magnificent race today. We should be getting on with our breakfast. The time grows short; they will be expecting us."

Alena vaulted free of Megolath as they landed among the waiting veratnil. She should have felt intimidated among the dozens of enormous dark creatures, but she felt strangely bold as all the hawk-like eyes were trained on her and Megolath. She leaned on one of his deadly talons and stared bravely back at the scaly mob as they pressed in around them. She stepped forward as she was introduced as Megolath's bonded and drew Wrayna, which sent the veratnil on edge and made them step back from her. A rumble of approval went through the host of them. Megolath practically beamed with pride.

"Am I making a good impression?"

"You are indeed." Megolath answered as he began to address his fellow veratnil in the veratnil way.

Alena could only interpret a fraction of what was being communicated. Megolath's thoughts were too fast for her to follow. Eventually, she found a place in his shadow to shelter herself from the hot sun and waited for his oration to end. There was quite a deal of excited chatter at one point which made Alena too curious to wait for an explanation.

"What is happening?"

"We are discussing the details of our attack on the Waratna. My kind are excited that we have found a way to disable the Waratna shields with the use of Wrayna. It will make all of the difference."

"We are going to attack the Waratna?"

"Yes, we have discovered their nearest base submerged in a salt lake not very far from here. They are picking off too many of our numbers now that there is an outpost close by. We must act now while we still are a formidable foe and while we still have you."

"While you still have me? Where do you think I am going to go? Are you trying to be rid of me, already?"

Megolath didn't answer but went back to conversing with his fellow veratnil. She caught glimpses of the layout of the base in Megolath's mind but not much else. She listened to their unintelligible babble for a while before saying to Megolath, *"It should come as a surprise."*

"What should come as a surprise?"

"The attack should be a surprise. We will be more successful if they don't know we are coming. We can catch them in their hive so to speak."

Megolath was quiet. Alena could tell that he was considering her point of view, although it was not the veratnil way.

"How can we fight them if they are safe in their outpost?"

"We will not fight them underwater but take them in more manageable numbers. We'll get them as they launch. I don't know if I can take down all of their shields all at once."

There was what sounded like outrage when Megolath communicated her thoughts to them. They were certainly a brawny bunch that faced opposition with beaks and claws and no mystery, just a straightforward fight to the death. It must be hard to be secretive, being as large and deadly as they were. But after much grumbling they agreed that her thinking was wise, and they would let her lead them, especially since their numbers were continuing to dwindle against the Waratna. They had lost another two of their kind just this morning when they had been overcome by a squadron of Waratna ships. Megolath became very sober when he heard the news. Alena could feel his grief immensely right to the center of her heart. She gasped at the depth of his feeling for his lost brothers.

Alena and Megolath and two of the other veratnil went out on a scouting mission to get a layout of the base. It was an hour before they reached the salt lake, and Alena could smell the decaying brine of the salt water before she saw it. It wasn't at all pleasant like the ocean but strong, pungent, and distasteful. She resisted the urge to cover her nose. She urged Megolath lower, instead, so she could get a better view.

They stuck to the shadows and kept their distance, alighting on a rise above the shore. It would ruin everything if they were sighted now. The base was circular in shape with launch tubes radiating like spokes from eight sides like a huge octopus. It looked like a giant pinwheel from their angle. Carefully, Alena began to consider their options, but a strange high-pitched siren like sound screamed from one of the launch tubes. Immediately, they shrank back, but there was nowhere to go. The long afternoon shadows were all the cover they had. Either the Cephalopods were too arrogant to think that the veratnil were bright enough to be any sort of threat or the Waratna pilot simply didn't notice them. He simply sped right over the top of them, followed by a second Cephalopod ship a moment later. Luckily for Alena and her dark companions, they were obviously in a hurry to get somewhere.

"We should move along before they notice us and decide to do something about our curiosity." Alena told Megolath nervously.

Megolath agreed wholeheartedly, making the journey back to the other veratnil quiet and without incident.

They decided to attack the outpost at dusk which seemed far too soon for Alena. Supposedly, that was the time when all he ships were in. How many Waratna were stationed there, she wondered... a hundred... maybe two? She hoped she was ready to handle the thirty or forty ships that were housed there, but, for now, they could only rest and wait and plan. The afternoon stretched on and on. Alena wished they could just get it over with. She grew more and more agitated as time went by and began pacing back and forth.

"Relax, little one. You're making us all edgy."

"I just want to get it over with...It's so hard to face them. It dredges up all sorts of unpleasant memories."

"I know, I see your dreams, Alena... I know what you've been through."

The first group would leave in about an hour. Their mission would be to act as decoys and draw a few of the ships out. The second group would follow a few minutes behind the first. Megolath and Alena would direct that group and disable the shields. The third group would contain the bulk of the veratnil fighters and would position themselves at the end of the launch tubes, taking on the remaining ships as they launched. They would take out as many Waratna as they could. It was a simple plan and with a little luck it would work. Alena hoped that it wasn't merely suicide for Megolath's race, but she also knew that they couldn't just sit and wait for the Waratna to pick them off a few at a time either. They had to do something, and this was as good a plan as any.

The flight to the Waratna base was almost as agonizing as the battle itself. Alena's nervousness grew exponentially as time passed. She was glad for Megolath's reassuring thoughts and strength in flight. He was a commanding leader, and the veratnil that flew with him treated him with complete respect.

The first group of veratnil were already in some trouble when they arrived. One of Megolath's kind was already down and nursing a burnt wing and there were three Waratna ships on the tail of the other two. Quickly, Alena unsheathed Wrayna and lit up the sky with crackling, fiery lightning.

The Waratna ships lurched in midair and one even hurled crazily toward the ground and erupted into a huge fireball upon impact. The remaining two were immediately dealt with by the arriving veratnil. The sickening sound of tearing metal filled the air. But their little victory was short lived. Alena could hear the unmistakable high-pitched, siren-like sound already screaming from the launch tubes. She was amazed at the speed at which another eight ships were launched. She sent lightning hurtling toward each of them. It crackled and sizzled and burned, disabling controls, shields, and weapons. But just as soon as

Alena was able to disable the first set of eight ships another eight were launched. She was quickly beyond her ability to handle the number of launching ships. She couldn't possibly prevent the disaster that threatened to overwhelm them all. She began to panic, but she was not doing this alone.

"Focus, Alena. You and I together can do this. Easy now, draw on my strength."

Carefully, she disabled the second set of eight only to hear the launch tubes begin to scream again. The air was filled with horrific sounds, burning fuel and metal, and the horrible cries of the veratnil who were ripping open their prey like birthday packages. Their elation soon turned to dismay, however, as the third set of Waratna ships were able to take flight with their shields intact and the scream of the tubes began again.

What could she possibly do to keep this from escalating into disaster? There were too many of them for her to disable, especially with another set launching. Desperately, she sent a trail of lightning streaking towards the three closest to her which caused one of them to go careening into the salt lake, silencing the launch tubes closest to her and Megolath. Then it came to her; Alena was dealing with this the wrong way. In one deft motion, she turned the lightning upon the water and the results were immediate and terrible. All the launch tubes became eerily silent, the water was alive with lightning, but the base grew immediately dark as she electrocuted hundreds of slimy horrible Cephalopods right inside their base.

Only five ships remained now. There would be no more coming to their aid, but she and Megolath had now become the object of their seething rage. The five came at them from all sides, spewing their weapons. Megolath did his best to outmaneuver them, but the weapons were too much for one veratnil and his bonded to take on alone. A painful scream emanating from Megolath made her body come alive with anger and adrenaline. She was not going to allow the Cephalopods to hurt her anymore, especially by injuring what was most important to her. She struck out at the one closest with a strange vengeance. The violence coming from the end of her sword took out not only the ship she was aiming for but the one behind it as well, making them easy prey for the dozens of veratnil that circled around them.

Her violent outburst lasted until she finally faced down the last, which came just within a breadth of them before finally being immobilized. Although in a final act of desperation, the monster was able to send his useless ship barreling toward them. Megolath barely swerved out of the way in time. Alena could see the terror mixed with fury in the face of the Cephalopod as it hurtled passed them. The ship shattered horribly upon impact, and then it was over.

Alena watched dazed as the veratnil celebrated by feasting upon their victims. Megolath was elated at their success and complimented Alena on her amazing power, but she didn't want to listen. She could only hear the cries of the injured veratnil and feel the silence of the few that were dead. Alena surveyed the scene of battle, forcing herself to look upon the horror of it all. They had slaughtered the Waratna, so Alena should have been happy, but she only felt sick and numb instead. How often would she be called upon to do this? How many battles would there be before they were done? Alena knew there would be far more than she wished to endure.

They had lost two veratnil in the battle and that was two too many, for now the number of veratnil had dipped to 79. There were many others with burns of various degrees that would need to be tended to, including Megolath. She tended to one of the burns with a cool wet cloth while he ate. He offered to share his bounty with her, but there was no way that Alena would ever be able to stomach a Cephalopod. It was far too barbaric for her to partake of the creatures that she hated with so much loathing. Alena waited while Megolath ate his fill along with his deadly companions, but it wasn't long before she was encouraging Megolath to turn them all towards home. It wasn't safe to stay here any longer.

Alena relished the feeling of the cool night air rushing past her on their flight home, but no matter how fast or hard they flew, she still couldn't get the smell of lightning and burning Waratna flesh and metal out of her mouth, hair, and clothes. She tried frantically to block out the horror of it all, but it was no use. Revulsion clung to her like a frightened child. There would be no running from it, for there was nothing would that could erase the awfulness of the night's battle out of her mind.

What had she done? Why was she doing this anyway? Surely the Waratna would come after her and Megolath with a vengeance now. She was sure that she would never be safe again as long as there was even one Cephalopod left alive. They were cold and soulless creatures, who wouldn't stand for their rebellion against them. Was there really any point in trying to turn back the tide that had already destroyed so many lives?

Alena knew that the answer to the question had to be yes if it meant freedom for her and for what remained of her crew. It was all worth it if it meant that Kelly's, Turq and Genni's, Jim and Elizabeth's, and even Sceria's children could grow up in a world without captivity, violence, and death. It had to be worth it if each Waratna that was eliminated brought her that much closer to being with Tiernan again. She had to believe that. And, oh how she wanted to be with him right now. If only he were here to hold her. Hastily, she pushed the thought out of her mind. This was all worth it if the veratnil and her beloved Megolath would survive and go on to thrive in this world that had first belonged only to them.

Chapter Twenty-seven

Alena slept for two days straight. When she awoke, she found Megolath and a few of his kind in the midst of planning another attack on one of the outlying bases of Cephalopods. The bulk of the veratnil had dispersed, not wanting to make an easy target of themselves by all staying in the same location at once. Besides, they had learned from their last battle that numbers weren't nearly as important as getting to the bases before the ships were able to launch, electrocuting the lot of the Waratna while they remained beneath the water. All that was really necessary were maybe five or six veratnil to clean up any stray ships that might already be on patrol.

It was relatively easy to take down the bases. The hardest part was generally just trying to get enough sleep, nourishment, and rest between the slaughters of the Waratna. Even though Megolath was quite a power to be able to draw upon in the use of Wrayna, each "battle" left Alena feeling utterly exhausted; the resulting nightmares weren't helping her much either. Alena not only witnessed the electrocution deaths of the Cephalopods in her waking hours but constantly in her sleep as well. She couldn't get away from the horror, the ghastly large–eyed bodies, and the smell of salt and brine, burning metal, and singed flesh.

They were able to take out three additional bases before the Cephalopods finally got smart and set up patrols of twelve or sixteen to watch for them. They had quite a scare on the last attempt and barely escaped with their lives for the Waratna were ready and waiting for them this time. They lost another of their companions in that raid. So, now they had to be content with picking off ships one at a time, at least for the time being. Taking down one lone unfortunate ship after another was all that they were able to manage in the weeks following the horrific slaughter of the four Waratna' bases.

It was after a run in with an unexpected ship that almost unseated her and sent her tumbling that Alena decided that she was in desperate need of a break. She was just plain weary of the whole thing. One look at herself in the clear lake as she bent down to clean the blasted taste of lightning out of her mouth and throat was all she needed to know that she didn't even look human anymore, at least not like anything civilized. She was in need of a bath, clean clothes, and a decent meal. After scrubbing herself and her clothing clean and laying them out to dry, she paraded half-naked through the veratnil camp much to the shock of Megolath and his two other companions, who were resting lazily in the afternoon sun, probably because she looked like nothing more to them than a pale, hairless goat, and they had never seen her this way before. But Alena didn't care at all at the moment. Besides, why should she? She hadn't seen another human soul for at least five or was it six weeks now, aside from the group of riders on some horse-like creatures she had observed from far away several weeks back. She realized with some disdain that it was probably more like seven or eight weeks since she had been among the society of her friends now that she thought about it.

Alena was hungry for human companionship and a good meal with something—anything other than wild fruit and fresh meat. A nice loaf of bread would taste so wonderful. This got her wondering about her companions. How were Elizabeth and Jim holding up with their twins? How were Kelly, Olivia, Ian, and Gwen fairing? How did her crew like the people of Camaranth? Were they being treated well? And what about Turq and his family? Had they been accepted into the Temarrian culture? What had happened with Sceria and her child? And Tiernan— her heart warmed at the thought of him. She had so many questions about Tiernan. Was he well?

"Your companions are fine…" Megolath's thoughts filtered into her own, *"and if you like I will take you near the hidden city so that you may have a glimpse of the city of water for yourself. I could use a change of scenery myself for a few days."*

Alena's clothes were still a bit damp when she put them back on, but she knew the wind would soon dry them. Eagerly, she vaulted onto Megolath's back, seating herself high upon the ridges of his scales. Megolath flew off in a northerly direction into the big wide sky. The view as they traveled northward became breathtakingly lush. She didn't know whether there was more land or water beneath them as they flew over lakes and rivers, streams and rivulets until finally the world below was awash in shades of blue and white. Megolath turned over an enormous expanse of clear water and headed east toward an area that was thick with mist and rising foam. Alena knew from Megolath's thoughts that they had arrived at their destination, but all she could see was a mighty waterfall.

The enormous almost circular falls made the Horseshoe Falls of the Niagara look like a tiny trickle in comparison. The sound of it was absolutely deafening. Alena reveled in the experience of flying in the mist that rose up from the depths of the mighty falls. She laughed as the spray hit her face and covered her. Megolath swept in a little closer and the roar of the water became all encompassing, but that is also when Camaranth suddenly began to take shape. The hidden city was part of a fabulous world of water more than anything else. Alena guessed that most of it lay hidden beneath, behind, and around the gigantic falls. It would be almost impossible to notice the city at all, unless you knew it was here; that is why it had remained hidden for so long.

Alena could see the outline of a white cliff almost unseen among the great billowing haze of the falls. There were a group of beautiful bronze people down there watching them, waiting for them. As Megolath drew ever closer, she knew unmistakably that Tiernan was among them. She stiffened in her seat, unprepared for the flood of fervent emotion that suddenly rushed over her.

He stood waiting for her with a dozen armed archers with their arrows already pointed heavenward. What a handsome sight he was there among his people. She could almost see his face now. Tiernan must have known she was coming, felt the nearness of her long before they arrived, for he stepped eagerly forward, and Alena felt her heart beating crazily with longing for him. But Megolath felt it too. She cursed when Megolath changed direction abruptly, soaring back into the air.

"It was wrong of me to bring you here, forgive me."

"Take me down," she growled. "Let me down."

"No, Alena, that is something I cannot do. I know that you want to be with him more than anything else in the world right now, but it would mean the end of my kind if you were to go to him. You would no longer be free, little one, and neither would we. You must believe me. I will do everything in my power to keep you from falling into his hands, even though you will definitely hate me for it."

"But he loves me, I know he does. He wouldn't let any harm come to me, nor to you when I explain things to him. Please…please Megolath, take me back." Alena felt herself growing more and more hysterical as they flew further and further away.

She heard Tiernan's voice upon the wind calling to her, pleading for her return, and the sound of it pierced her to the center. She wanted to fling herself from this beast that held her captive and run to her amber-orange eyed man, but her captor knew that too and climbed speedily into the heavens. Alena grew anxious with desperation at being torn from what she wanted most, but jumping from Megolath's back would only mean suicide now. She pounded on his shiny scales and cried and raged, but it was no use. There would be no going back to Tiernan if Megolath had a say in it, not now, not ever.

Alena didn't talk to Megolath for two days, neither did she eat or sleep much either, thanks to her Cephalopod nightmares mixed with images of being torn from Tiernan. She was in a terrible mood and completely unhappy. The bond between Alena and Megolath was powerful and should have been enough for her, but somehow it wasn't. Something that she needed was missing. What was it? What would make her feel whole? It was a different sort of comfort and companionship, she decided, the kind she wouldn't find in a world of black shiny scales, and lightning swords, and Waratna blood.

Alena was craving Tiernan's companionship like no other—the steadiness of his hand, the smell of his skin, the touch of his lips. This was madness. Megolath had to be wrong about Tiernan. Alena had to know for herself. If that brief glimpse of him hadn't been enough to drive her completely crazy, the sound of his commanding voice carried by the wind had been enough to leave her terribly wanting—hungry—desperate to see him, to talk to him, and to be held by him once more.

Megolath was observing her sadly. *"How long do you intend to go on like this?"*

"Until you promise to let me see him."

"You know that I won't do that."

"I won't be your prisoner, Megolath."

Alena marched away from the suffering beast. She couldn't bear to see what she was doing to the creature, but she couldn't help it either. She was so completely torn between the two of them that she was entirely miserable. Another day went by and another with little communication. Megolath pleaded with her, but she refused to take flight with him. She was not going to be coaxed by the joy of their bond to give in to Megolath now. Alena was almost glad when he left with the other two veratnil to feed. She knew he would be gone for a few hours, and even though she knew she was a least a day's journey away on foot, she struck out heading for the hidden city of Camaranth. Alena knew that Megolath would be missing her soon; there would be no hiding from him, their bond being what it was. He would find her, but she had to do this; she had to find out the truth on her own.

Megolath swooped down on her just two hours later. She had to lay herself flat on the ground to avoid being picked up in his sharp talons.

"Where are you going?"

"You know perfectly well where I am going."

"Little one, be reasonable. You are putting us all at risk."

"I have to go. I must see him. I must know for myself that what you say is true."

Megolath alighted before her making the ground tremble. He barred the way with his gigantic leathery wings.

"You won't succeed in stopping me, forcing me to stay will only make me despise you, you know."

"Yes, I know…"

"You said that the Temarrians and the veratnil were going to have to work together to be rid of the Waratna. Tell me, Megolath, how is that going to happen if you refuse to even let me see my friends."

"Your friends and the common people of Camaranth are not who I am worried about."

Alena paced in front of Megolath angrily.

"Without Tiernan I would be dead by now, and I would never have become your bonded. You know that, don't you?"

"Yes, that is something that I am keenly aware of."

"Megolath you are just going to have to trust me, I will not let any harm come to you or your kind."

"You don't understand. There are methods… wizardry… potions… that can make you powerless to protect us."

Alena sighed. Stomping back and forth in front of Megolath was making her feel even more agitated.

"You can't keep me from him."

"No, perhaps not. Perhaps it is necessary that you judge for yourself. Perhaps I have been wrong all along." Megolath straightened his wings taking down several trees in agitation, sending up dust and leaves and making Alena sneeze. He glared at her with his monstrous glowing eyes before finally saying, *"Promise me that you will be guarded when you meet with him. It would be better if you did not drink or eat anything given to you unless you know for certain that it has not been tampered with… and remember, my little one, that I will be close by should you need anything at all."*

"You mean you're letting me go?"

"Yes, climb upon my back. I will take you to the gates of the city. I cannot bear the wedge that has come between us for even one more day."

Megolath was quiet during the rest of their journey to the hidden city. Alena knew how pained the creature was, but she didn't know what else to say or do. Upon arrival, they dived straight down into the gigantic, cloudy mist of the falls.

"This is where I must leave you," Megolath said sadly, skidding to a stop on the slippery wet rock surface just before a massive set of gates hewn straight out of the cliff. There were twelve Camaranthian archers standing watch at the gates, much to Alena's chagrin, with their arrows pointed directly toward them. Megolath was in very serious danger if any of them decided that they were a threat, but they seemed only curious at best. Tiernan must have known she was coming, but instead of being there to receive her, he had sent Kelly and Ian instead.

"Thank you, Megolath. You must know what this means to me," she said all in one breath as she leapt down from Megolath's back and ran toward Kelly and Ian. *"I will not be far away... Please remember..."* was the sad thought that wafted into her mind as Megolath took flight and disappeared. Alena hated the pang of regret she felt for Megolath as Ian reached her first and enveloped her in a huge bear hug, followed shortly thereafter by Kelly.

"Wow, you both look great," she said, standing back a little to look at them. "It seems that the people of Camaranth are feeding you well. You're both the perfect picture of health." Ian and Kelly had both lost the gaunt look of their captivity and subsequent journey and had filled out in all the right places.

"Well, you look positively wild," Kelly responded, "like you've been living in a veratnil cave." She smiled at Alena with amusement. "What have you been up to, Captain? Rumor has it that you've grown completely savage living with the veratnil and combating the Cephalopods."

"Is it true that you've been able to bring down a base?" Ian interrupted with some impatience. Obviously, they were as eager to get intelligence from her as she was from them.

"We've brought down four, Ian, but the Cephalopods are onto us now."

"Four? But how? That is several hundred Cephalopod ships." Ian whistled. "Tiernan will be ecstatic to hear of your success. Perhaps there is reason to hope after all."

"Where is Tiernan, anyway?"

Kelly and Ian looked at each other uncomfortably before Kelly answered. "Let's just say that Tiernan has had it pretty rough since he got a glimpse of you several days ago. He just couldn't handle having you disappear on him again. He wanted to make sure that you were coming to stay this time. You have come to stay with us, haven't you?"

Alena wasn't sure how to answer, so she avoided the question. "How is Olivia? I bet she has grown quite a lot—and the twins? Are they both well?"

"Yes, they are all happily thriving. You probably won't even recognize the twins. They grow so much in those first few months, you know."

"Jim and Elizabeth and Gwen are well?"

"Yes, you'll see them all soon enough." Kelly seemed to be growing a little uneasy with her questions.

"And Turq, Genni, and Calab?"

"Tiernan, is waiting to see you," Ian interrupted. "He won't be too happy if we keep him waiting much longer." He tried to sound light hearted, but Alena could hear the strain in his voice. "Shall we go inside the city?" Ian held out his arm for her.

"Yes," Kelly breathed with what seemed like relief. "We'll have lots of time for catching up later. But we really should be seeing you inside."

"Hey, what's wrong with you both? Is everything alright?"

"Well, of course, it's just that Tiernan really is incredibly eager to see you."

Alena took Ian's arm and went with them past the line of archers to the city gates. The amazing pale gates were opened slowly revealing a smaller set of gates and another group of armed guards.

"I'm afraid that you will have to leave your weapons here before entering the city," Kelly whispered, motioning to Wrayna that hung at her side.

"I will not do anything of the sort," Alena responded with agitation. Ian patted her arm firmly. "It's okay, Captain, your weapons will be safe here. You won't have any trouble retrieving them after Tiernan has met with you. It's just a policy of the hidden city. No one can enter Camaranth armed without the consent of King Tiranus."

"Well, get permission then. I'm not leaving Wrayna with these men."

Kelly looked alarmed, while Ian only tried to reassure Alena. "Perhaps they will make an exception in your case. There isn't a soul in this city that doesn't know who you are and that Tiernan is bonded to you."

Ian approached the guards and was soon in a heated discussion with them. Kelly looked a little too relieved when the second set of gates were finally opened, and they were ushered through. What was everyone so tense about? Alena was immediately suspicious. Just what was going on? Her hand unconsciously went to the hilt of her sword. Megolath had warned her to be careful. She owed that to him and to his kind.

Alena gasped at the grandeur of the hidden city of Camaranth as they passed through the shimmering gates. Everything blended with the water. It was a city of varying shades of blue and violet and pale shades of green. The city streets were a grand system of well mapped canals, even the boats and bridges were the same pale shades of blue, green, and white. A sleek elongated boat stood waiting for her, docked at the end of the nearest passage. She was swiftly ushered in, and too late, she discovered that Ian and Kelly were not coming along.

"Wait, aren't you both coming too?" The words slipped uneasily from Alena's mouth.

"The palace isn't far...We'll see you this evening," Kelly called a bit too cheerfully as the craft was immediately shoved off. Both Kelly and Ian waved to her.

Alena hardly knew what to think before she was whisked hurriedly down the deep canal and around a wide bend by a handful or brutish looking guards. She pulled away from the one that held her arm, trying to think of something which she could say in Tiernan's language, but nothing came to mind. He seemed reluctant to let go of her and tried once again to take her arm. Alena began to protest, but it was then that the shimmering palace came into her line of sight. It was like something out of a fairy tale and sparkled like crystal. Alena leaned forward forgetting everything for a moment in the shadow of the majestic castle. She had never seen such a structure. It was made of some polished stone that reflected the brilliant cerulean blue of the sky. It loomed larger and larger above her until before she knew it, they had arrived.

Alena stepped from the long elegant boat into the courtyard of the sparkling palace that stood surrounded on all sides by streams and fountains of fresh flowing water. Guards dressed in green and silver lined the courtyard on both sides. And there standing at the end of the courtyard she could see her handsome Tiernan with a sober expression etched on his strong, attractive face. Oh, how she missed and loved him. Tiernan summoned her to him, but stood still, waiting almost stoically for her to come to him. Alena felt her skin prickle. Anxiously, she looked around at her watery surroundings. Something was amiss here. Something felt wrong about him—very wrong—something more than the strange look of his amber-orange eyes. Why didn't he come to greet her? She took an uneasy step toward him and then another. She noticed then that he didn't really look at her but seemed to stare through her instead.

What had happened to him since their last parting, and why did her anxious heart tell her to turn from him and run? She remembered her dream suddenly. The one that she had dreamed on her first night with Megolath, and it became instantly apparent to her that what Megolath had told her was heartbreakingly true. Everything began to unravel for Alena, and she stifled a sob. If Tiernan would partake of that drug to numb his bond with her, then he was capable of drugging her to numb her bond with Megolath too. Then, what Megolath and the whole race of veratnil feared would come true. The veratnil and the Temarrians would both be doomed, and Alena could never ever let that happen.

Alena stopped all too suddenly, which made all the guards anxious with nervousness. She knew with swift clarity in that moment that they were all just waiting to seize her. She could see it in their tense stiffness and suspicious eyes. A simple hand signal from Tiernan was all they needed to rush toward her.

"Stand back," Alena warned angrily, cursing under her breath at the trouble she had brought upon herself and her bonded, all because she had put so much faith in Tiernan's feelings for her. Perhaps he didn't love her. Perhaps he was simply bound to her and that was all?

She pulled Wrayna from her sheath and held it before her, willing streaks of lightning to crackle and spark before all of them, only making the guards gasp and step back in terror. "What's become of you?" she yelled sorrowfully at Tiernan as she began to back away. "How could you let this happen?"

For a moment the dead expression left his face and was replaced with a look of both anger and yearning that immediately reminded her of the first time they had faced each other in the biome; his eyes burned a fiery, furious orange. He looked for a moment as if he might come after her, but it was too late. Megolath was already there, waiting for her. How Megolath had managed it, she didn't know, but she was glad, for he had been dead right about Tiernan.

With tears streaming down her face, she turned and ran back to Megolath—back to her beloved bonded—back to her wild world of flight, lightning, and war.

Megolath's scales were slippery and dripping with water. Alena struggled to climb into her slick seat; her own wet tears weren't helping. Several arrows bounced off his thick hide as they took flight. Somehow her brain registered that Megolath must have come through the falls, and it was back through the falls that they must return. She clung to him, cried, and struggled to keep her hold through the onslaught of water that pounded her mercilessly on their way through. They soared quietly away, letting the wind beat and dry them and make them miserably cold. Alena shivered, reading in Megolath's thoughts only his own heartache for her being as devastated and torn as she was between two opposing worlds.

Alena cried for a good hour before becoming strangely quiet, resigning herself from that time forward to her only possible future which was one of blood, violence, and war. That was her entire life now and that is all it would ever be. She had a mission to complete, and she would continue eradicating the Waratna until not a single one remained or she or Megolath were dead, whichever came first. She steeled herself against her feelings for Tiernan and for her crew. They had betrayed her, but she wasn't bitter. She was their captain, and it was her job to make this stinking planet right for their survival.

Chapter Twenty-eight

The Waratna became complacent after there were no more attacks on their bases, and Alena and her veratnil warriors were able to take down a fifth base a few weeks later. There was no more smugness on the part of the Cephalopods after that, however, and the veratnil had to immediately retreat into hiding as they were categorically hunted down and killed. Their number had already dipped to seventy-five. The Cephalopods patrolled together in greater numbers, so it became harder to pick off an occasional ship. Alena and Megolath dug in and waited, first one week and then another. It gave Alena an opportunity to study the book that Maiser Runcan had given her. She hadn't picked it up in ages. Some of the diagrams made much more sense to her now, but what was most intriguing was that there were half a dozen pictures of three swords together shown in different configurations towards the end of the book. She wondered what they meant. She speculated on just how well Ian understood his own books by now. Would he have understood what the unusual configurations intended? She really missed just having another human to talk things over with. She put the book away, staring up at the sky.

She noticed a large patrol of Cephalopod ships far away to the south. They looked like birds from this far away, but Alena knew better. She would recognize them anywhere now. The

Cephalopods kept coming in greater numbers than ever before. Where were they coming from? Alena and the veratnil had taken out all the bases within at least a thousand kilometers. Alena was sure of that, and yet, they had to be coming from somewhere.

It occurred to her one morning that there must be something more than just the veratnil that was attracting the attention of the Cephalopods. They seemed to be coming and going from all directions, as if they were systematically criss-crossing the planet in search of what? Was it humans that they searched for—or others like her? She couldn't stand the thought of being taken captive again nor could she bear it if any of the other people on the planet were captured and made to suffer what they had all suffered. Whatever the Waratna were up to, she had to stop it and soon but how? She paced back and forth under the cover of the forest.

Alena was alerted to a few unexpected visitors a few hours later. Megolath warned her lazily of their arrival.

"There are five Temarrians and one of your friends coming in our direction. Shall I have a few of my companions get rid of them for you?"

Alena sat up with a start.

"No, not if they mean us no harm. What do you think their purpose is in coming, and how did they find us?"

"They seek you, Alena, and they are well-armed."

"Well, I would hope that they would be well-armed out here with all of the deadly wild animals, not to mention with veratnil like you entertaining the idea of eating them," Alena teased, listening to Megolath's hungry thoughts, but she was curious. Just what did they want with her?

"Have the one of my kind brought to me. Keep the others at bay."

Alena wished she could have seen the Temarrians faces when the veratnil swooped down on them, but nothing was as comical as the sheer look of terror that was on Jim's face when he was deposited in front of her by the veratnil Megolath called Maya. Jim picked himself up off the ground and tried to dust himself off while swearing up a storm.

"I am glad to see you haven't changed much since I saw you last." Alena grinned.

"Geesh, Alena, isn't there a better way to treat your friends than to have them plucked up by a deadly beast straight out of the sky? I honestly thought the thing was taking me off to feed her young."

"You've come uninvited to their camp. You are lucky to even be alive. Just why have you come?"

Jim swore again and rubbed his biceps. "You certainly are a frightening force to be reckoned with; no wonder you have the Cephalopods buzzing and all of Camaranth in an uproar."

"Yeah, just what are they saying about me in Camaranth?"

"That you are lawless, wild, reckless, and dangerous!"

"Dangerous? Who exactly am I supposed to be dangerous to?" Alena asked angrily.

Jim reddened noticeably. "Look, Captain, I didn't come to argue with you."

"Why did you come?"

"Tiernan asked me to come."

"Since when do you do Tiernan's bidding?"

Jim narrowed his eyes at her, "Maybe you didn't know it, but Tiernan is next in line to be the king."

"I know it, but what difference does that make?" Alena leaned forward expectantly.

Jim sighed. "If it weren't for Elizabeth and our twins, maybe it wouldn't make any difference, but strict allegiance to the King Tiranus is all that is keeping my family alive right now."

"So, you are all hostages in the city?"

"No, Alena, not exactly, but we are required to follow their laws, and they give us shelter, food, and safety from the Cephalopods in return."

"There is no safety from the Cephalopods. You are just lying to yourself if you think it is worth it to give up your freedom for a roof over your head and a loaf of bread."

Jim was quiet. "You don't know how it is," he muttered finally.

"How is it, then? Enlighten me."

"I can't bear to lose Elizabeth. She is still not strong. I don't think she and the twins would last out here in the wild and Turq... Well, Turq and his family haven't been treated well at all. I do what I can to keep them alive."

"I see. So, the Temarrians sent you to come out here after me because they know you will return to your little family. Tell me, how does Tiernan feel about all of this?"

"Tiernan is out of his mind with grief, Alena, and believe me, they are using him to get to you as well. Tiernan's father is not too keen on having you make war with the Cephalopods. He thinks that you are drawing too much attention to this region."

"And he thinks that he can hide indefinitely somehow?"

"Well, they have been able to so far with an exceptionally strict set of rules."

"And I am a danger to these rules, a threat to their way of life, because I choose to fight these monsters? The real danger is that he has no real control over me or what happens, is it not?"

Jim eyed her warily, "There has been a lot of unrest in the city since we came, and people are starting to question. They don't know what to make of you, Alena. They see your distance from Tiernan as a betrayal of his bond with you, and yet, there are rumors that you have taken down entire Cephalopod bases."

"The rumors are true. We've taken down five now." Alena let the truth sink in. She could tell Jim was impressed, but also cautious. "And Tiernan, what does he say about all of this?"

Jim ran his fingers through his hair and frowned, "Tiernan is pretty wretched. He has tried to stand up to his father and reason with him, but Tiranus is steeped in tradition and doesn't take well to new ideas. Tiranus is anxious to quiet the confusion that has filtered into the hidden city. He uses us to keep Tiernan in line. Let's just say that he is not too happy that his son is bonded to you, especially since you have such an unusual deadly army at your fingertips. It doesn't help that there is that ancient prophesy about your arrival to this planet. Tiranus is trying to use Tiernan's bond with you to his own egocentric advantage; that is how we knew where to find you."

"What do you mean?"

"Tiernan knows where you are as long as you are within a few hundred kilometers. It's part of the bond, I guess."

"And Tiernan told him where to find me?"

"Tiernan is not himself. He wants so terribly to see you that he is practically as desperate as his father to get his hands on you, but he doesn't want any harm to come to you. He was so shaken up after this last episode with you that he has refused to take the numbing drug they have been administering to him. And that is not a good thing, Alena. He has not been well since you left him. I am afraid he's going completely out of his mind. I've never seen a man so conflicted in my entire life. I think his father is trying to flatter him in to believing he has a chance with you."

"So, why have you come?"

"King Tiranus wants a meeting with you. He said it would be most unwise to refuse."

"And if I do refuse?"

"Turq, Genni, and Calab will die."

"So, it is to be blackmail then. He intends to force me to choose between one of my own and the veratnil. But that choice has already been made has it not? I will not return to the city."

"Alena, please reconsider. You don't know what it's been like for them. I can't see Turq suffer because I have failed, I owe Elizabeth and the twins' life to him. Don't any of us matter to you anymore?" Jim swore again under his breath.

"I am glad to know that you and Turq have let go of your differences. It's about time you treated him like a person," she paused, turning away from Jim slightly so that he couldn't see her face. "You go back and tell Tiranus that if he so much as touches a hair on anyone's head that I will swoop down on the city with my army and pick it apart piece by piece."

"He'll never believe it. I've never met a more arrogant man. Please, Alena, you know I'm not the begging kind. Are you willing to risk Turq, Genni, and Calab's lives just to see? I can't believe you are so willing to betray your own people for a bunch of enormous, grisly creatures."

Jim would never be able to understand. "Without these grisly creatures, as you call them, the Temarrians will not survive. None of us will, Jim. Tell me, have you seen the people of Camaranth take down a single Cephalopod or ship?"

"Yes, actually I have."

"Oh really?"

Jim looked a little sheepish but thrust his chin forward. "It was a damaged ship, but they did take it down."

"Yeah, with what?"

"A water hose," Jim told her with a little laugh.

"You've got to be kidding?"

"They are easy to kill once you get them on the ground."

"Okay, go ahead and ask how many ships the veratnil have taken down," Alena demanded with her hands on her hips.

"What's the point in this discussion, Captain? I've heard rumors that it has been in the hundreds, thanks to you."

"In case you haven't noticed, Jim, both the veratnil and the Temarrians are on the defensive. All that is left of the civilization of the entire planet is in the hidden city. Do you think that the Cephalopods are going to let you just go on living once they find you? Do you think they would let the Temarrians get powerful enough to become a fighting force to defeat them? We are just play things to them—just a morbid science project. They might keep a few of us around to put in their little cosmic zoo, but the rest of us are dead once they find us."

Alena paced back and forth. "Tell me, do you want your little girl and little boy growing up in the hellhole we've been in for the past several years?"

"No, of course not," Jim grumbled angrily back at her.

Megolath sauntered over a little closer.

"Everything alright over here?"

"Yeah, it's fine," Alena answered as Megolath stood protectively over her. Jim looked warily up at the creature.

"Jim, I'm not going to put myself under the control of some idiot king who is so arrogant about being in charge that he puts the entire population of Temarria in danger. I am not just fighting for myself and the veratnil. I'm fighting for you and your children;

I'm fighting for freedom from oppression and captivity. I will not trade one form of imprisonment for another, Jim, not while I have breath in my body. I will not take orders from Tiernan's father or anyone else unless I find that it is in the best interest of our survival. The Cephalopods will find Camaranth and when they do, you and this idiot king don't have a chance."

"I understand where you are coming from, Alena, but that doesn't help Turq and his family."

"Sometimes you have to make sacrifices to ensure the survival of the rest."

"Not when it's Turq, you don't. I cannot accept that." Jim's eyes flashed, and he stood up to her, even with Megolath standing over her. She had to admit that Jim was being really brave, just now. There had to be something Alena could do to save Turq, Genni, and their son.

"Where are they?" Alena asked, an idea suddenly taking shape in her mind.

"What?"

"Where are Turq, Genni, and Calab? Do you know where they are being held?" Alena smiled broadly. She would show this calculating King Tiranus a thing or two.

Jim nodded and after watching the scheming look on Alena's face, he couldn't help breaking into a grin too.

They went at dusk when the light was poor. Jim rode behind Alena on Megolath, and the other Temarrians had the privilege of being carried in the talons of five other veratnil much to their discomfiture, especially through the pounding waterfall. The veratnil were as silent as bats, creeping into the city. They had to be quick. Tiernan would know they were there. Jim stealthily pointed the way to the prison and to the section where Turq and his family were kept. Silently, Megolath landed in the shadows letting Jim jump to the ground. Alena counted on the fact that Tiranus would be too complacent to have moved his prisoners. Did he really think that he and his army were any match for the veratnil? But, of course, he most certainly did.

On Megolath's command, the half dozen taloned veratnil raked the prison walls with their claws, digging carefully. The noise brought the whole city awake and a rush of armed guards, but by that time, Turq and Genni were already being winged away by a pair of veratnil, and Calab was with Alena on Megolath.

"Be sure to give Tiranus my message," Alena called to Jim as they disappeared into the night. She saw a lone figure standing out in the open as they flew away and knew with a surety that it was Tiernan. He saluted her as they took to the sky. Alena felt sad seeing him there, watching her fly away from him once more. She wondered what he must be feeling just now and if he hated her even more. She also wondered what his father would say about this evening's adventure. Hopefully, Tiranus would realize his ridiculousness in trying to control her and his son. Alena hoped Tiernan wouldn't suffer needlessly because of her. But all that mattered right now was that Turq and his family were no longer in danger and were no longer being used as pawns.

Turq was waiting for her when she arrived, looking a little harried but also grateful. Alena handed Calab down to him. Calab was overly animated about the whole evening and words were already spilling from his mouth nonstop. Alena smiled, "It's good to see you Turq. I'm sorry about all the stress you've experienced while breaking you all out tonight. It can't feel very comfortable to be clawed out of prison by a half dozen veratnil."

"We did much better once we saw you. Thank you for coming in after us, Alena. We owe our lives to you, once again.

Genni has been sick and well, things haven't been so good for us since we arrived in Camaranth."

"Where is Genni?"

"She's lying down, away from the veratnil, over there," he pointed to a sheltered location among the trees. "I'm afraid that this adventure has given her quite a shock. She'll be feeling better now that Calab has arrived safely. I should get back to her, though."

"Go on, Turq. Don't worry; I'll be there soon. I'll see what I can rummage up to make your stay here with us a little more comfortable."

Alena went through the packs that had been unwillingly left behind by the Temarrians who had accompanied Jim. After choosing the finest of the three packs, Alena carried them over to the waiting family.

"I'm afraid that this is the best I can do; there is mostly just bedding and food."

"Thank you, Cap'n," Turq whispered gratefully. Calab was already diving into the packs. "Hey, look at this," he exclaimed pulling out a beautiful metal bow that sparkled in the moonlight.

"Would you like me to get a fire going? I haven't had a fire in a good long while, but I'm sure I could manage it if you would like a warm cup of tea?" Alena asked gently.

"No, Alena, that's alright. We are tired and just trying to take in the events of the evening," Turq seemed ill at ease, his brow furrowing with concern.

"It's all going to be okay. The veratnil and I will watch over you and your family."

This didn't seem to make Turq feel any better, however, for his brow furrowed even deeper.

"What is it? Why are you so distressed?"

"There has been much said about you, Alena, and the veratnil in the last several weeks—a lot of things that don't put you and the veratnil in a very good light. Don't get me wrong, I appreciate what you have done for me and my family, putting yourself at risk to free us, but we've been through a great deal, and I just don't know who I can trust anymore."

"I understand…"

"I'm sorry."

"It's alright, Turq. I am not expecting anything from you or your family. You are free to come and go as it pleases you. I just didn't want you to be used any more as a bargaining piece by King Tiranus and neither did Jim."

"Jim? You've talked to Jim?"

"Yes, he was here earlier today. Tiranus tried to convince me to turn myself in to him, so he sent Jim to tell me that if I didn't meet with him, then your lives would be forfeit. We couldn't let that happen."

"Where is Jim now?"

"He returned to the city with me. He wanted to protect his family."

"That is not good, Alena."

"No? And why is that?"

"Tiranus is swollen with pride. I've never seen a man so arrogant. He will do something horrible to punish you for what you have done and perhaps Jim too."

Unfortunately for both Camaranth and Alena, it wasn't long before Turq's prediction came true.

Chapter Twenty-nine

The news came from Megolath three days later. Tiranus' army had marched out to meet them. Whether they meant to seize her or kill her, she didn't know, but Tiranus' stupid, self-important act of supremacy also inadvertently caught the attention of the Cephalopods. Tiranus must have realized his horrible mistake too late as the sky filled with dozens of Cephalopod ships.

Alena had very little time to decide whether to fly to their aid or leave them to die. She had every reason to let them die and to save herself and her veratnil army, but she couldn't live with herself if she left them all to be slaughtered, or worse, captured, no matter what their intentions were toward her. She had a hard time explaining this to Megolath, but he and the other veratnil were willing to do as she wished, give their lives for her, as it were, especially if it meant bringing down the Waralna as well.

When Alena and her army of veratnil arrived, there were at least 30 ships already bent on the annihilation of the Temarrian force. The only thing that the soldiers of Camaranth had going for them was that they were comparatively small and there were a lot of places for them to hide. Their arrows were no match for this fleet of ships. Already dozens of scorched soldier's bodies littered the ground.

As the veratnil army came into view of the horrid panorama, Alena sat high upon Megolath's haunches and filled the sky with ghastly blood red streaks of lightning, already knowing full well that there were too many ships and there would be great cost of life on the part of them all. She was able to disable eight or nine ships before the full force of the battle turned squarely upon her and Megolath. The Cephalopods wanted her good and dead. That was obvious by their attention to her and Megolath alone.

Grimly she faced each ship, sometimes several at a time, with full knowledge that any slip up would mean her and her bonded's doom. Once she accepted the fact that this was the end, she relaxed, expertly guiding the sparking sizzling streaks towards each enemy.

At every turn Alena expected to die, and when she didn't after several long moments, she began counting each ship as it was disabled and torn apart: five… eight… twelve… thirteen…. eighteen…. twenty-one… twenty-five… thirty. Her brain told her that there shouldn't be any left; they should all be gone now. She quickly surveyed the skies which were still filled with at least twenty more ships. Just where were they coming from? A ship shot directly over her, firing down upon them. Alena sent the lightning screaming above her, and that is when she noticed a dark foreboding shape deep in the heavens above her—a gigantic ship hidden in the clouds.

"Climb!" she screamed aloud to Megolath, "Climb!" But he was already climbing before the words could even escape her tongue. They were connected. They were one, she and her bonded, in mind, in spirit, and in purpose. Their purpose together was to take down that mother of a ship. The smaller ships zoomed around them desperately. Alena took out four or five of them as she and Megolath positioned themselves directly beneath the mile-wide mother lode. The spectacular size of it would have made anyone shrink from it, but Alena summoned her will and combined it with Megolath's power in a huge blast of energy that sent a bolt of terrible snow-white lightning arcing toward the center of the humongous ship.

Alena was unprepared for the explosion that followed. The heavens seemed to be breaking apart, and the force of it knocked her from Megolath's back and sent her rocketing towards the planet, along with the other Cephalopod ships that were in their immediate vicinity. She rammed into one dark object and then another on her descent to the ground, and it took her quite a few bumps before she realized the veratnil were trying their best to break her fall. Megolath's grief at being unable to reach her went screaming through her mind as talons raked at her body, but ultimately, they were not able to grasp her as she fell through the trees to the ground below.

Alena knew her body was broken and that she would die now. She felt herself fast losing consciousness, as she tried to make sense of the pain that washed over her. She was not able to move, except for her elbow, forearm, and right hand which she found still grasped the hilt of Wrayna. In one last act of defiance she turned the point of the sword heavenward with the hilt resting upon the ground and sent lightning streaking above her in every direction. She thought she saw several ships fall and hoped amid the pain that it was enough, while the words, *"Hold on… hold on… hold on, my little one,"* repeated themselves over and over in her mind. Megolath was coming for her. He would find her crumpled body.

"Goodbye, my bonded, goodbye," Alena whispered in agony and waited for her last shaky, shallow breath.

There were Temarrian voices in the forest and hurried footfalls coming in her direction. The shadow of Megolath fell over her; her bonded had finally come but so had the Temarrians and Tiernan. Alena tried to speak—to tell the Temarrians not to harm Megolath, and to tell Megolath not to harm the Temarrians, but her words came out in choking gurgles.

"Hold on little one…Hold on," Megolath knew the words she couldn't say.

"Shhh, Alena, don't try to talk. I'm going to help you, but you need to lie still," Tiernan spoke calmly, but she could hear the alarm in his voice.

"Don't worry," she wanted to say, for she would die now, and he would be free—free to bond again, and she was glad for him. He kissed her on the forehead, and she tried to smile, but the pain was too much, and she passed out instead.

Some time later, Alena had a vague recollection of being moved onto a stiff board and then being bound to it. Where was her bonded; where was Megolath?

"I'm here."

"Don't let them take me, don't let them take me. I want to die here with you."

"Rest now, little one… It is the only way."

"It is the only way to what?"

But Megolath didn't answer. They lifted her up slowly and began to carry her… away from Megolath, away from her bonded. She wanted to scream, but the pain was too much, and she lost consciousness once more.

Alena awoke in a darkened room. At first, she didn't have any inclination of where she might be, but the pain soon reminded her of her fateful fall. She closed her eyes again and opened them trying to make them focus, but she felt foggy. There were curtains around her bed and someone slept in a chair on the other side of it. She lay in the quiet dark and listened to the rhythm of the other person's breathing. She knew it was Tiernan that slept there. She had listened to him breathe while he slept countless times. She tried to adjust her position but found that she could only move her right arm. Warily, she felt the bandages around her head and left shoulder and ribs. Her left forearm was elevated in a sling of sorts and she could see that her left leg was elevated too. She seemed to be wrapped from head to toe in slings and bandages.

Alena wanted to scream at the injustice of it all, for here she was bound and helpless. Why hadn't she just died? Her survival put her whole bonded's race at risk to Tiranus' foolishness. She tried to clear her head to think. Had they already drugged her? Where was Megolath? She could still feel a connection to him which meant he was alive, but she could not hear his thoughts. What had they done to her? Was Megolath simply too far from her to hear him? She tried to choke down an angry sob but ended up crying out in pain instead. Any deep intake of air was excruciating. She tried to calm herself with small shallow breaths, but she had awakened Tiernan, and he pulled back the curtain and leaned over her. Carefully, he took her hand.

His touch felt like a bolt of lightning going through her. It warmed her whole body. Alena loved and hated him all at once. She wanted desperately to pull away from him, and at the same time she wanted to hold on to him and never let go. The tears came steadily, and Tiernan did his best to mop them up.

"Are you in terrible pain, my little wootchka?" His words were gentle. "Do you need something more for the pain?"

"No," she managed in a strangled whisper. "I'm just so very angry at you."

Tiernan looked sad. "Yes, I know, and for that I will be forever sorry. I will never stop hating myself for what I have put you through." He brushed the hair out of her face. "Perhaps you will forgive me someday."

"I should have died. It would have been much better that way."

"No, Alena, please don't talk like that. It was hard enough being away from you. I couldn't stand it if you died, especially if you died angry with me."

Alena's heart surged with feeling, "But you would be free to bond again, and the veratnil would also be free and…"

"Sshhh," he said putting his strong fingers to her lips. "It would have been better for no one. You must rest and build up your strength."

"How can I rest when I know what your father plans for me and my bonded? I would rather die than let that happen."

Tiernan looked downcast, "Alena, you don't have to worry about that anymore. Nothing is going to happen to your bonded or the rest of the veratnil either; I promise you that."

Alena sobbed and then moaned in pain. "I don't believe you," she whispered. "How can you promise that? Surely, you are not blind to the faults of your father? He will not rest until he has me under his control and all of the veratnil too."

Tiernan was quiet for a moment. "My father is dead… He was one of the first to die in the battle with the Waratna thanks to his own stupid folly." There was pain and bitterness in Tiernan's deep-timbered voice.

"Oh, I'm sorry…" Alena told him. Tiernan looked so sad. She wanted to reach out to him, but she held back.

"We lost many, but it would have been so much worse if you hadn't arrived with your army. You were absolutely terrifying to watch. All Camaranth is singing your praises. You have saved us all, my little wootchka."

Alena felt her cheeks flush. She tried not to whimper as she turned her face a little more towards Tiernan. "How many casualties?"

"Several hundred."

"And the veratnil?"

"I think only five."

Alena cringed. Oh, if only Tiernan understood just how great the number five was. "What about the Cephalopods? Did we get them all?"

"Yes, at least all of those that you and the veratnil engaged in battle. I still can't believe the power you can wield. He shook his head. Alena, do you know that you took down at least fifty ships and that doesn't count that huge monstrosity of a ship that is now strewn over the entire region. The beauty of what you have done is so incredible. I think I finally understand."

"Understand what?" she asked, studying his handsome face.

"Why it is you have to do what you do..."

"And there have been no other ships?"

"We have seen a few other scout ships in the last several days, but they haven't managed to locate the city, at least not yet."

"Where is Megolath?" Alena demanded suddenly.

"Megolath?"

"My bonded—my veratnil." Her voice came out dry and raspy.

"He's near, Alena." Tiernan smiled. "He gives the people of Camaranth quite a shock every time he swoops in here to check on you, but he is safe. I've ordered the archers to let him be, as long as he doesn't hurt or damage anything."

"Thank you." Alena's heart skipped.

"It's nothing."

"Not to me," Alena said in a croaky whisper.

"Let me get you something for your throat. Its sounds awfully dry. You're in need of nourishment too; I'll be right back."

Tiernan talked to someone at length just outside the door which made Alena wary. Was she being guarded or maybe held prisoner? She tried to push the thought away. What could she do about it anyway if it were true? Alena hoped with all her heart that Tiernan was being truthful and that she didn't need to worry. She began to wonder just how broken she was. She couldn't even feel her legs which caused her great concern. Would she fly again? And where was Wrayna? At least with her sword Alena could protect herself. She still had one good arm.

Tiernan came back after some time with a warm cup of something steamy, which he fed to her one small spoonful at a time, once he had propped her up a little bit. Even that small amount of repositioning was agony and made sweat pop up in beads on Alena's forehead.

"Just how broken am I?" she asked painfully between bites of salty broth.

Tiernan tried to sound optimistic, "You've broken a few bones, but you'll be as good as new, soon enough."

But Alena could hear in his voice a deep underlying concern. Her condition must be incredibly bad then. Perhaps that explained the lack of feeling in the lower half of her body.

"Why can't I feel my legs?"

It was a long moment before Tiernan spoke. "You have a lot of swelling right now. It's putting a lot of pressure on your spine. Once the swelling goes down, everything will be alright. Don't worry."

"But there is a chance that I won't ever have any feeling, isn't there?" she demanded.

"Alena, you need to rest now and concentrate on getting better."

"Answer me, Tiernan, so help me. If there is anything I need from you right now, it is total honesty."

He examined her face warily for a long time before answering just as she feared. "Yes, there is a chance."

Alena closed her eyes. So, she could live the rest of her life crippled and broken. Her outsides would then match her insides. How pathetic.

"I think I just want to sleep now," she muttered wretchedly.

Tiernan nodded. "I'm sorry, Alena." He placed his hand in her good one. "I am here if you need anything, anything at all."

Alena wanted to believe him, but she couldn't. She was still tremendously angry. She turned away from him, but sleep wouldn't come for her.

"Why did you do it, Tiernan?" she finally whispered into the silence.

It was some time before he spoke in that deep-timbered voice she had come to love. "I was wrong. I know that now. I was trying to numb the pain, but that is no excuse. It was difficult returning to the home I once knew—I am a different person than I was when I left. It was hard to be once again in the society of my parents, my family, and my childhood friends."

Tiernan continued after a slight pause, "No one will ever understand what we went through in captivity unless they have experienced it for themselves. The things that mattered in my life before just didn't matter anymore. My father couldn't accept that.

He couldn't accept my altered way of thinking and the things that had happened to me. He thought I meant to purposely defy him. He made things impossible for me, for Sceria, for all the rest of us that lived in the biome, most especially for Turq. I couldn't stand the pain—feeling it every waking moment of every day. I wanted relief. I thought it would help. I realized how wrong I was the moment you screamed at me in the courtyard, and then when I saw you fighting, doing everything you could to fight the Waratna against all odds, I realized how completely I had failed you. I will never fail you again, Alena."

Tiernan hung his head miserably, his strong shoulders slumped. Alena had never seen him look so vulnerable or broken. Not even she could question his sincerity.

"Thank you for explaining it to me," she whispered, trying to keep the emotion from her voice.

Tiernan's amber-orange eyes softened as he leaned over her. "Oh, how I have missed you," he whispered just inches from her face.

"I've missed you too."

He kissed her on the forehead, and Alena felt herself warm to his touch. "Sleep now, my little wootchka. I have exhausted you with so much talking." Tiernan began to sing to her then in his deep, rich, musical voice. It was the same tune he had sung in the biome. The sound of it brought her deep contentment as she drifted off to sleep.

Chapter Thirty

When Alena awoke again, she heard hushed voices in deep conversation. Kelly was there talking to Tiernan. Alena wasn't sure how to feel about Kelly, After all, hadn't she and Ian pretty much betrayed her? Perhaps they too had felt that they had no choice in the matter. Alena tried to hear what Kelly and Tiernan were saying, but she could only get bits and pieces.

"She knows then…?"

"Yes."

"How did she take it?"

Alena couldn't quite catch Tiernan's answer other than the word—okay—followed by a few garbled words and another word—veratnil.

"They are such ghastly beasts—perhaps it is a blessing for all of us."

"Any sign of Ian and Gwen?"

"No, the last I…" Kelly's voice trailed off and Alena was hard pressed to hear any more. Alena did hear their footsteps, however, as Tiernan walked Kelly to the door. Just one set of footsteps returned, and they were not Tiernan's. Alena felt her cheeks flush with disappointment. Kelly pushed back the curtain quietly so as not to wake her. She jumped when she saw Alena's eyes staring back at her.

"Oh, you're awake. Why didn't you say something? Tiernan will be so put out that he missed talking to you, since he'll be away for a few days. He's been here watching over you for the last eight hours straight." Kelly adjusted Alena's pillows and propped her up a little. "I was just about to give you another round of medicine."

"I don't want any medicine."

"Of course you do. How else can you manage the pain?"

"I'll manage."

"Well, I can see that you are back to your typical, feisty self."

"What's that supposed to mean?"

"Look, I know you're upset with me, Alena, and I know you have reason to be, but you don't know how it's been."

"I think I have a good idea. You've all been squabbling amongst yourselves about what you think I should be doing while I've been out there busting myself up to keep the Cephalopods from annihilating everything on the planet."

"Alena, I am your friend. I love you like a sister, but when are you going to figure out that we just can't win? It's so much better to just lay low and not draw attention to ourselves. Then we have a chance at some sort of life out here."

So, this is how it still was? It was almost like Alena was back in the biome, fighting against the Cephalopods with everything she had, while all around her everyone around her was too afraid to take a stand.

"Just look where it's got you, Captain," Kelly continued. "Look at yourself." She took the sling from off Alena's left arm and seated her up a bit. "Is that comfortable? You probably won't need to elevate that arm anymore. The swelling has gone down quite a bit."

"Yeah, I am pretty banged up, but to me it is all worth it if Olivia can grow up in a world free of captivity. I guess you would have rather stayed in the biome." Alena didn't hide the irritation in her voice.

Kelly was silent. Deep down she had to know that Alena was right. They were both quiet for a long, long time.

"I'm sorry for what's happened to you, Alena. Of course, I want freedom for Olivia. It's been hard here in the city, but things should be better now with Tiranus gone, at least until the Cephalopods find us, which is now more likely than ever with Ian and Gwen out there behaving like they were you."

"What do you mean they are behaving like me?"

"Oh, they've gone off and bonded with those horrible pterodactyl-like creatures."

"When?"

"Right after you were brought here."

Alena wished she could have asked more questions, but they were interrupted by someone being ushered ceremoniously into the room. Kelly bowed her head toward the handsomely-dressed bronze woman who was accompanied by a thin, harrowed-looking Sceria, who Alena hardly recognized. Life had been hard on Sceria. Kelly said a few short words and practically fled from the grand woman's presence. One look into the intense amber-orange eyes of the attractive woman and Alena knew she was in the presence of none other than Tiernan's queen mother. Sceria looked positively petrified to be near her, but stepped forward to greet, Alena.

"I've been asked to act as your interpreter. I'm sorry that I was the only choice," she said in a barely audible voice full of melancholy.

"It's wonderful to see you, Sceria. I hope that everything has been well for you." Alena meant it sincerely and watched Sceria relax a bit. At least she spoke a bit louder when she introduced Alena to the formidable woman known as Queen Valoria.

"It's good to finally meet you," Alena tried to say in her best Temarrian.

"So, you are the distasteful, uncultivated woman of alien race who is bond mate to my son?" Valoria challenged with apparent disapproval. "I had to see you for myself."

Alena hardly knew how to respond to such a declaration and looked to Sceria to see if she had interpreted it, correctly. Sceria warily repeated it to her in English. Alena's eyes flashed; she wasn't going to be subdued by this woman's attitude or her conduct, no matter who she was.

"If you would like to address me in a more civil manner, I will consider speaking with you; otherwise, your interview with me is quite over."

She watched Sceria's deep bronze face empty of all color as she interpreted Alena's response to the queen.

Valoria's expression was one of shock followed by a twitch of amusement. "Well, you definitely have nerve. Sceria has told me much of you and your disagreeable people. But I also must acknowledge that I owe the life of my son to your unrestrained strength of will. You will need that if you are to become queen."

"Queen, I don't intend to become queen."

"Certainly, you do not want to cause my son further embarrassment by returning to live among the veratnil like some wild animal, especially now that you are unable to ride."

Her words were painfully direct, and it was Alena's turn to be shocked. How could this woman be so cruel, or was she merely testing her?

Valoria continued. "My son has already polluted the blood of kings by bonding himself to you. The people will not stand by him without a proper bond mate who remains at his side. There will be no other option other than to pass the throne to Tiernan's cousin, who is an imbecile. I'm told that you are passionate about fighting those creatures that have overrun the planet. My bond mate didn't have the backbone for it. You must consider the power that you can wield as queen of Temarria. Becoming a proper bond mate to my son is the only thing that could possibly make you at all acceptable to me." Valoria turned to Sceria. "I have said all that I have come to say." They left the room as ceremoniously as they had entered with only a brief look of apology from poor Sceria.

Alena was still reeling from what had transpired over the last several minutes and would have screamed aloud in anger if Megolath's arrival hadn't interrupted her thoughts.

"You are finally awake I see."

"Oh Megolath. I'm so glad you are near…Why in the world did you let them take me?"

"It was the only way you could have survived."

"You should have just let me die. All is at risk now… and I may never fly again, and they want me to be queen. I don't trust them… any of them… How are we going to fight the Waratna now? What if…"

"My little one, what will be, will be… but one thing I am certain of is that Tiernan means no harm to you. I saw how he cared for you. It was several days before you arrived at the city. If he had wanted to control us, he would have done so by now."

"How do you know he hasn't drugged me? They've had me on all sorts of things."

"All for pain and sleep, thank goodness. I can hardly stand to feel your pain and have welcomed relief from it. I would know if he had used the other."

"Oh…" Tiernan so far had been truthful with her then and had stood by and watched over her. *"Megolath, what if I can never fly again… What will happen to all of us?"*

"You will fly again… perhaps a simple harness can be fashioned if you do not regain feeling, but you are strong, and we need you now more than ever."

Yes, she had to believe that. How else were they going to fight the Cephalopods? After all, who else could wield Wrayna? She would have to leave Tiernan's care once she felt well enough. That was the best choice for everyone, except perhaps for Tiernan and maybe herself. The longing she felt for Tiernan washed over her like a ceaseless rain. Alena pushed the emotion down and tried to find her courage. How could she do anything else besides return and fight, especially when she was the only one standing between the annihilation of two races? That is what she would have to do even if it meant that the kingdom would go to Tiernan's imbecile cousin, but how could she do that to him? How would he ever forgive her?

"You wish to return to me then, when you are well?"

"Yes," she answered with earnestness, although it would be entirely heartbreaking to wrench herself from Tiernan once more. She would have to do it while they were apart, or she just wouldn't be able to bear it. If only there was some other way…

"I am glad to know that you would have returned with me if given the choice."

"What do you mean would have?"

"Alena, my little one, you do not have to choose between us."

Alena wondered if she was going crazy. Had she heard Megolath correctly? *"I don't understand? I cannot wield Wrayna if I stay here with Tiernan; for there is no way that I could possibly remain celibate being near him all of the time."* Even the thought of Tiernan's arms around made her warm with yearning.

"You have only been led to believe that it is necessary. The Temarrians believe that you must be celibate, but that is a false tradition. It is something that they simply do not understand because they are not like you."

"Not like me? What are you saying?"

"Even the veratnil who are bonded with riders mate with other veratnil. How else could we survive? The Temarrians are different than you in that they can either choose a mate or become a rider, but you can have both, Alena, because you are not bound to Tiernan. The ability to wield Wrayna comes from having only one bond, Alena, not from celibacy as they suppose."

"But you told me I had to choose."

"Yes, and I believed it, but I am not sure anymore. I was only trying to protect myself and my kind from certain extinction. I believed Tiernan to be a threat to our survival."

"You've always been pretty straightforward about that. But what has changed your mind?"

"Watching him with you. His bond with you is as keen as mine. Without his father influencing him, he seems trustworthy. Besides, I don't want you to die unhappy, my little one. I almost lost you. I know how much this has torn you up inside. I don't want to be the one to keep you from being complete."

"So, are you telling me that I can be Tiernan's queen and live here in Camaranth and fly and do battle with you as well?"

"If that is what you like."

Alena was speechless. To be able to have a life with both Megolath and Tiernan was more than she could hope for, and it made fighting off the Cephalopods that much more important to her. She pushed herself more upright with her good hand, which made her toes tingle. Her toes were tingling… that was a good sign. Yes, a very good sign.

"Careful, you'll toss yourself out of bed at this rate."

"Megolath, have you seen Ian and Gwen?"

"Yes, my bonded, and they seem entirely happy with the veratnil they have chosen."

Alena smiled. She was certain that all Camaranth was in an uproar about it, telling wild tales about the crazy aliens that had bonded with their veratnil. She was glad for Ian and Gwen and envied that they were out flying.

"You will be flying again soon enough." Alena could almost hear him warbling at her. She lay back into the pillows and sighed.

It was three days before Tiernan returned, and that was torture for Alena. No one seemed to know where he had gone and for what purpose. But Alena had continued to improve in his absence and was certain that she was regaining the feeling in her legs as the swelling diminished. By the third day she could wiggle the toes on both feet, and Kelly had removed the bandages from her head and had helped her to wash her hair and clean up enough so that she was starting to resemble herself. When Tiernan finally came into the room looking worn and exhausted, Alena was trying to brush through her hair.

"Wow, you are looking so much better. Here let me do that for you." He took the brush from her and began brushing her hair in long, soft, rhythmic strokes.

"When did you get back? You look positively exhausted."

"I've only just arrived."

"You should have stopped to rest. I wouldn't have known the difference."

"I would have. I've already been away from you for long enough. I couldn't wait any longer to be near you." Alena adored the deep timber of his voice.

"Where on Temarria have you been?"

"I've been out searching for Gwen and Ian."

"You have? But why?"

"Because I had hoped to make it easier for you to stay, but I suppose that is impossible now." Tiernan sounded old and tired. "Kelly tells me that you are regaining feeling in your legs."

"Yes, I can wiggle my toes," she demonstrated for him.

Tiernan nodded. "I am glad for you, Alena."

"You don't seem to be."

"Of course, I am. I just thought I had a better chance of keeping you with me if…"

"If I couldn't fly?"

"Yes…" he said with honest uncertainty.

"What does that have to do with Ian and Gwen?"

"Well, it is kind of a long story. There are other swords much like Wrayna, not as powerful, mind you, but powerful enough. They have been kept in my family for many generations with the hopes that one day one of my bloodline would wield them. We have all tried from one generation to the next, without success. I thought perhaps that if Gwen and Ian could wield one of them, you wouldn't feel so guilty about not being able to wield Wrayna if you chose to…"

"…be with you, instead," she finished for him.

Tiernan sighed and his bronze color deepened. "Yes, Alena, but I know there's no hope for that now. I know that your only choice right now is to fight. I want you to know that I understand it. I've seen what you can do. I just can't keep myself from hoping. The bond is strong; that's all."

"I know." Alena took the fine brush from Tiernan and encouraged him to sit next to her on the bed. "So, what happened with the swords? Can either Ian or Gwen wield one?"

"They both can, which is amazing. It has been a very long time since there were three swords that could be wielded at once. There is an old tradition that if the swords are combined together, they have unimaginable power."

Alena couldn't hide the eagerness and amazement in her face, wondering about the possibilities, but Tiernan's handsome face was downcast.

His deep-timbered voice softened. "You'll be going then, when you are well." It was a statement rather than a question and he breathed out slowly. Wearily, he reached beneath her bed and pulled out her carefully wrapped sword. "We had quite a time trying to return it to its sheath. We had to place it in your hand to do it."

"Thank you." She lovingly handled the hilt and felt it warm to her touch. "I've been missing it, and it's been here all along." She fingered the sword's strange intricacies before asking, "You didn't happen to come across Turq and his family while you were out searching for Ian and Gwen, did you?"

Tiernan nodded. "They took quite a lot of convincing, but we actually brought them back with us. Jim was the one that convinced them to return. I don't blame them for not trusting me. I know that my father put them through a lot of inexcusable misery."

"Jim went with you? Things must be improved between the two of you then?"

"I think we've learned to respect each other. Jim has been the most level-headed of anyone. You should have seen him stand up against my father when he first tried to take Turq and his family away. Both he and Turq have agreed to be my head advisors if I become king."

Alena frowned, "That reminds me, your mother came to see me a few days ago."

"She didn't." Tiernan's amber-orange eyes burned boldly.

"Your mother is quite a woman. She has no love for me, that is definite, but she is convinced that you cannot become king without me beside you. Is that true?"

"Don't let that worry you, Alena, I just want to enjoy the time that we have left together." He brushed a strand of hair from her face.

"That might be a good long while," Alena teased.

"I really hope so. Of course, I want you to get better eventually, Alena, but honestly, I hope that it's weeks and weeks away. It was almost impossible for me to leave you for three days, but I had to, just in case you might reconsider."

"Tiernan, you know that I would love more than anything to be with you, don't you and to be your queen?"

"It's okay. I'm not trying to change your mind. I know it's not meant to be."

"Well, that depends…"

Tiernan tried to control the emotion in his voice, but his voice deepened noticeably, "I don't understand? It depends on what? You are obviously regaining the strength and feeling in your limbs."

Alena pulled Tiernan closer until he was just inches from her face, "It depends on if you are willing to allow your queen to go off into battle, or on any other whim she chooses on the back of her deadly veratnil?"

"I still don't understand. You know I would do anything for you, but Alena, you can't be both queen and wielder of Wrayna."

"And if I could?"

"Then I would be the happiest man on the planet, but we both know that isn't possible." He trembled at the closeness of their proximity, his amber-orange eyes blazing.

Alena turned her face to him and kissed him on the tip of his nose and then gently on his bottom lip before saying. "I have learned that it is possible, Tiernan, so if you are willing to give me my freedom and are willing to do everything in your power to make me trust you again, I hope to stay with you for a very, very long time."

Tiernan looked earnestly into her face, trying hard to believe the words that she had just spoken. When he found that she was completely serious, he kissed her long and deep trying ever so carefully to be gentle with her but ended up only clumsily grinning at her because he didn't know where to place his hands on her broken body.

"I'm sorry, my little wootchka. I don't mean to hurt you," he grinned again giving her the tiniest kiss imaginable. "Tell me just how it is possible?" His amber-orange eyes burned into her, making her warm with pleasure. She was only too glad to relate what Megolath had told her about Wrayna and the bond, whereupon Tiernan tried without success to envelope her once more.

"You can touch here and here." Alena told him, laughing. She guided his hands to the few unbroken places.

Tiernan kissed her then in such a loving and tender way that Alena wanted it to go on forever. When he finally stopped, he laughed with joy. It was a magnificent thing to see Tiernan so happy. His warm, amber-orange eyes pierced into her soul with longing, "I've changed my mind. You need to hurry up and get better. If you were recovered right now it wouldn't be soon enough, for I am enormously impatient to finally become one with you, my beautiful, spirited, bond mate."

Afterward

The strange light was growing ever larger and brighter on the horizon. The few months that Alena had been given to heal had been scarcely enough to be ready for this moment. Gwen and Ian had been managing well enough, but they truly needed her now. Tiernan helped boost Alena onto Megolath's sprawling back.

"Be careful."

"You be careful too," Alena gave Tiernan a brief, nervous smile.

"Are you ready, my bonded?"

"As ready as I can be."

Megolath rose steadily in the air giving Alena time to find her balance. She'd had to take it slowly over the last little while. At least she'd been given the last couple of weeks to practice with her barely healed body and limbs, but her muscles were soft and not prepared for what she knew must come. Alena grasped Wrayna's hilt as she rose to meet Ian and Gwen, who were mounted on their magnificent pair of deadly, black veratnil. Determinedly, the three of them raised their swords together in unison as one giant ship after another appeared over the horizon. Their swords sang together in a giant burst of power as they pointed the streams of multi-colored lightning toward their oncoming enemy. There would be no turning back for any of them now; the hidden city of Camaranth was hidden no more.